THE
WOMAN
AT THE
GATES

BOOKS BY CHRYSTYNA LUCYK-BERGER

SECOND WORLD WAR
The Girl from the Mountains
Souvenirs from Kiev: Ukraine and Ukrainians in WWII – A Collection of
Short Stories

THE RESCHEN VALLEY SERIES
No Man's Land: A Reschen Valley Novel Part 1
The Breach: A Reschen Valley Novel Part 2
Bolzano: A Reschen Valley Novel Part 3
Two Fatherlands: A Reschen Valley Novel Part 4
The Smuggler of Reschen Pass: A Reschen Valley Novella – the Prequel

THE
WOMAN
AT THE
GATES

Chrystyna Lucyk-Berger

Bookouture

Published by Bookouture in 2021

An imprint of Storyfire Ltd.
Carmelite House
50 Victoria Embankment
London EC4Y 0DZ

www.bookouture.com

ISBN: 978-1-80019-163-1
eBook ISBN: 978-1-80019-162-4

For the family, especially Julia, Kaitlin, Alex, Sam, Anya and Olyanna,
and all of you who were raised in a free country.
Knowledge is power, but it is also the key to understanding,
and to empathy.

PROLOGUE

Summer 1945

Castle Neubeuern, Bavaria

It was Konstantin who evoked the memory of apricots, a memory so strong the air suddenly bloomed with the golden, sun-warmed scent. Antonia pulled her nephew closer to her, like a cushion against the impact, and dropped the children's picture book flat onto her lap. She remembered the carelessness of that sweet, perfumed juice running down her chin. The feel of her lover's finger catching that drop and putting it to her lips. And she remembered the apricots that had sustained her sister's family on a horrible journey into darkness.

Antonia impatiently rubbed at the sting of tears. With all that she had endured, with all that they had survived, she was going to cry over apricots? The memory of apricots?

No, the memory of that apricot orchard. Her home. Her life. *Him.*

Antonia's nephew pushed himself away, the metal bed frame squeaking as he shifted. "And cherries," he added. "I miss apricots and I miss cherries."

On Antonia's other side, Nestor yawned. He was still too young to remember apricots from Ukraine, or the tart summer cherries for that matter. Nestor was too young to read, but his finger moved along the pages of the German picture book titled *Unser Bauernhof*—Our Farm. Except it wasn't *their* farm. *Their* farm was in the Carpathian lowlands, in the village of Sadovyi Hai. Here, beyond the lead-pane windows of the castle attic, it was the Bavarian hillsides that Antonia looked upon.

Nestor pointed to the word for cherry tree in German.

"*Kirschbaum*," Konstantin read.

"*Kirschbaum*," Nestor repeated, then went back to the small orange circles on the initial illustration. "*Marillenbaum*."

To prevent herself from succumbing to a second gut punch, Antonia pressed Nestor to her. "And you? What is it that you miss?"

As soon as it was out of her mouth, she covered his ears and kissed his head. Nestor's only memories would be the scratchy, dark and noisy ones of war. He'd known nothing else.

Outside the dormitory rooms, the wooden floorboards creaked from the staircase to the corridor as if they were on a ship. The others—displaced persons, as the Allied forces designated them—were heading up from the dining room. Some had spent the evening playing cards, or the old guitar from the music room. Others had sat in the castle gardens and listened to the crickets, thanking God they had survived. Or, more likely, wondering why they had. The children were being children. Instead of parents covering their mouths to hush them against discovery, or to prevent a beating, or capture by Nazis or Soviets, these children and their parents now loudly negotiated the brushing of teeth. Tomorrow, they would live to see another day, and that was why they pursued the frivolity with such passion.

As the boys fought to turn the next page of the picture book, Antonia tuned into the symphony of Eastern European languages. Polish, Latvian, Lithuanian, Czech, Russian and Ukrainian all intermixed in this old castle in Bavaria—just a short drive to Berchtesgaden; a short drive to Hitler's bunker—now secured by American troops.

Antonia coughed and the boys gave her room, but the irritation quickly passed. Out of habit, she ran a finger beneath the thin, cream-colored scarf wrapped around her neck, and half-consciously checked the size of the growth at the base of her throat. Before she could assess it further, someone knocked on the door and Lena appeared.

"Mama," Nestor called to his mother. "Aunt Antonia is reading to us."

Lena did not seem to hear. She raised her hand, revealing an envelope. But it was the expression on Lena's face that made Antonia close the book in her lap.

As her sister's gaze locked with hers, Antonia was again whisked back to Sadovyi Hai. They were back in their village orchards, back to the first days in the secret underground organization. Lena's and her first fight but not their last battle. In the time it took Lena to close the space between the doorway and the bed, Antonia relived the torture in the Soviet secret police interrogation room and the terror of being captured by the SS. Lena's eyes reflected the value of unconditional love. Forgiveness. And freedom's heavy toll. Antonia's heart clenched at the fear of breaking again.

Lena knelt by the side of the bed, as she did when she said her prayers, then extended the envelope, but Antonia had already seen the Red Cross emblem. She already understood that one of their men had finally been found.

PART ONE

1941

Lviv, Ukraine

BORDERS
AUGUST 1939

0 50 100 150 KM

UKRAINE 1939

STATE BOUNDARIES
UKR. ETHNIC TERRITORY

CHAPTER 1

March 1941

Lviv, Western Ukraine

She yanked the sheet out of the typewriter and considered the final lines of her article. Words mattered. And these words could get her killed.

Behind the Soviet-issued textbooks, in the hidden wall compartment, was the metal box containing the remaining articles, the photographs sent from the west, and the files on students who might be potential recruits for the clandestine Organization of Ukrainian Nationalists. Antonia retrieved and unlocked the box, removed the prepared folder, and added her article. She slipped the envelope into the secret compartment of her briefcase, which otherwise carried her students' German literature essays.

Outside her office window, aside from the spray of water in the courtyard's fountain, everything was still. When she stepped into the foyer, the halls were empty. The aroma of floor cleaner and the sour smell of cabbage from the café battled one another. Antonia glanced at the large clock above the entrance. It read ten after eleven. To the left hung the Soviet Carpatho-Ukrainian flag, which had replaced the Polish colors two years earlier. To the right, the lion-imprinted crest of Lviv. Regardless of the regime, that flag never changed.

Antonia tucked the briefcase beneath her arm and was heading for the exit when she heard brisk footsteps behind her.

"Professor Kozak?"

Arranging her expression first, Antonia turned to face Dr. Bodnar. The dean's shock of white hair and long, white mustache were his trademarks at the university. That, and his two well-tailored suits: a brown one for fall and winter, and a gray one for spring and summer.

"You're leaving rather late," he remarked.

She indicated the briefcase with a tired smile. "The freshmen's last essays of the term."

Dr. Bodnar's gaze shifted to the floor between them. "I received word that the Soviet secret police chief has been relocated. I wondered whether you'd heard anything to that effect? Or about his successor?"

"I had no idea. His wife said nothing to me the last time I saw her. But I am usually the last to hear anything."

If what Dr. Bodnar said was true, it was a tragedy. Antonia had cultivated a good working relationship with the chief and his wife. The university had used that to their advantage. More precisely, Dr. Bodnar had used it to his advantage.

"If our students would only stop getting arrested," the dean grumbled, "we would not need to deal with them at all."

"Youth fights for its ideals compulsively. They are spurred by the rash belief that justice and freedom are won by making noise and exhibiting passions." *And who could blame them?* Antonia's sympathies were with the students. The need for freedom was as natural as the need for air and water, necessary for survival.

Dr. Bodnar held up his hands. "Whoever takes charge of the commissariat may not be as, well, understanding with our students."

Antonia glanced at the double doors before her, eager to be on her way. She should have been at the art studio twenty minutes ago. And she really did need to mark those essays at some point. "I suppose we'll learn who the new chief is soon enough. After all, this isn't the first time Moscow has restructured the department."

As she bade Dr. Bodnar goodnight, she absorbed the news, wishing she knew more. Her light tone had belied the pang of anxiety she felt. It had taken years to build a cautious relationship with the chief and his wife. The authorities in Moscow—or maybe even as close as Kyiv—must have been displeased about or suspected something to have simply "disappeared" them.

Antonia crossed the university's courtyard, her heels clicking on the pavement. A spring shower earlier that day had left the air heavy, and the pathway through Kościuszki Park glowed beneath the weak street lamps. Just before reaching the statue in the center, she heard footsteps scurrying. Shadows disappeared into the shrubbery of the side gardens. Antonia steeled herself; there was only one reason anyone would be about at this hour.

Sure enough, Kościuszki's pedestal had been daubed with anti-fascist and anti-Soviet slogans, the paint still wet. A moment later came the inevitable response: headlights lit up the park, and the Soviet secret police emerged from their hiding places.

Antonia froze but kept the briefcase loose at her side. A flashlight caught her and she squinted against the glare. A plainclothes policeman appeared from behind it and lowered the lamp.

"*Shanovna* Kozak?"

"Yes." Behind her, students were struggling to break free of their captors.

"Sorry, Professor Kozak," the policeman said. "This has nothing to do with you."

But it did. Secret police would never reveal themselves—call her by name—unless they intended to warn her, to let her know that they knew exactly who she was, where she was, and when.

He told her to go on her way, leaving Antonia in a quandary. Should she go to Viktor's apartment first? Pretend to go to bed and then slip out to the art studio later? Her acquaintance with the chief had been public, or rather her friendship with his wife, a woman whose strong influence over her husband's policing affairs had maybe led to their quiet and unannounced removal.

Behind Antonia, doors slammed and vehicles accelerated away. The park fell quiet again. She estimated that half a dozen students had been arrested. They had been reckless. They needed leadership. They needed discipline and training. They needed her, because when Antonia Kozak broke the law, she did everything in her power to make sure she did not get caught. She now zigzagged through the city, checking that no dark cars followed her, no hatted man or stern-faced woman tailed her. *Your enemies are everywhere*, Stalin warned. *Trust no one.* That warning now applied to everyone in the Soviet Ukraine.

Despite her frustration, she understood why those students insisted on making their voices heard. She herself had been impelled to join the Organization of Ukrainian Nationalists to help free Ukraine from foreign rulers. Initially, she too had been prepared to fight those who repressed her country's language, traditions and cultures; a Ukrainian's very right to exist. The Habsburgs, the Hungarians, the Poles had all taken their turn, beating her homeland into submission, choking its citizens' hopes, and suffocating the country's very soul. For as long as Antonia could remember, there had been sliding panels and secret doors to be discovered in her Carpathian village, and the music of their defiance had sustained her.

The Polish regime had shown little tolerance for the nationalists' clandestine activities. One by one, Ukraine's professors, authors and revolutionaries were purged, imprisoned, and executed. That was when Antonia realized that martyrdom would achieve nothing. The country needed leadership and it needed a strong voice to rally support and give the people strength. Her tactic now was to raise her voice, but to do that she had to outwit the enemy and survive.

She was very late now but at least, if anyone had been following her, she had shaken them off. Only when she was alone in the rear courtyard of the art studio did she use her key. Above her, lights glowed from a pair of neighboring apartments, but she did not see anyone looking down, no curtains suddenly dropping into place. Tightening her hold on the briefcase, she pushed the door open and took the stairs to the cellar. In the furthest storage room, tonight's team was already at work.

Ivan Kovalenko was setting up the mimeograph to produce the illicit copies of *Our Nation's Voice*. His sister, Oksana, looked up from the typewriter they used to create the stencils. Meanwhile, Viktor—his back to Antonia—was writing furiously at a makeshift table propped between two workhorses. She threw the Kovalenko siblings a knowing glance and indicated that Ivan should come to her.

In the corner, he bent down and pecked her cheek in greeting. "What took you so long?"

"I wanted to make some changes to my article."

He was always concerned about her. Ever since she'd first appeared in the marshes outside their village, insisting that she fill her brother's place in the Organization, Ivan had kept an eye on her.

She took in Viktor's profile. A lock of dark hair hung over his brow, nodding in agreement with the words flowing onto the pages. She loved watching him work. He was like a deep-sea diver. On occasion he would come up for air, absently reach across the writing table they shared at his apartment and kiss her hand before going back under.

"How long has Dr. Gruber been going at it?" she asked.

Ivan waved a hand. "Since he walked in."

"The manifesto?"

"Appears to be so. He said the two of you were working very late last night as well." Ivan's eyes flashed with a spark of envy, but then that slow smile spread across his face.

He was not one to be easily impressed and that smile was something he seemed to reserve for her. In all other respects he appeared to be a rough and tough Cossack, with his reddish-blond mustache, which he'd recently trimmed, and the long hair, which he had not. In his suede boots, he stood a whole head taller than her and reminded Antonia of the long-ago warriors her sister wrote about in her novels.

Ivan now reached for the edge of the spring-green scarf around her neck. "Did you have that growth checked?"

"I did." Her fingers fluttered upwards and she threw a look at Viktor's profile again. She ought to tell him about the diagnosis first, but Ivan was like a brother. A meddlesome one—as she imagined Oleh might have been had he not been shot dead by Bolsheviks.

"Will the doctor remove it?" Ivan asked.

Antonia folded her arms and leaned against the wall. "I don't have time for vanity projects."

"Don't take it too lightly." He sounded disapproving.

"I'm not. The clinic prescribed home remedies. It's my thyroid, as expected. It explains why I've not been able to sleep."

He started to say something, but she cut him off.

"Have you heard from Pavlo?"

"He's on duty tonight. Why?"

Antonia propped her briefcase on a shelf of paints and brushes and other paraphernalia before turning back to him. "I ran into Dr. Bodnar, the dean. He says the People's Commissariat for Internal Affairs has a new chief. Just like that. No announcement, nothing. And the police picked up some more students in the park this evening. The agents made themselves known to me."

Ivan shook his head. "I suppose this is not a good time to tell you that Division One deployed our new agent to Kyiv."

Antonia frowned. "You mean 1309? The one who claims he can flip the Soviet secretary?"

The Cossack winced.

Antonia sighed and threw Viktor a look. If anyone had cared to ask her, Agent 1309 was not ready for the field, but Viktor had caught her at a weak moment and cornered her into recruiting the political science graduate against her better judgment. She rubbed her forehead. If it went awry, she would be the only one responsible, and all because she had not stood up to Viktor. Was there a connection between 1309 and the chief's removal?

Ivan's mouth was set in a grim line. He shook his head as if to dispel her thoughts. "Anyway," he said. "I'll put the post office to work and alert the cell, see if we can find something about the new man in charge."

The "post office" was the Golden Lion tavern near the castle, which the Organization had purchased and Ivan now ran. It was where their couriers met, how they planned missions, and where they took deliveries of everything from printing ink to small weapons. They also received information about possible "windows" along the borders, where their people might escape into the west.

"I had three new recruits," Antonia said.

"Have," Ivan said. "You have three. Don't second-guess yourself. We still need the numbers."

Stilling her doubts, she retrieved the briefcase and flipped it open, unsealing the false bottom. She removed the folder and took the articles and announcements to Oksana for stenciling before showing Ivan the files.

"All of them are clean," she said quietly. "The families aren't listed anywhere."

"Have you decided what roles you want them in?"

Antonia pointed out the young woman and her boyfriend. "Couriers within the university grounds. Both are excellent writers—I've brought articles from both of them. The third one, Pavlo should meet. The young man's family owns a hotel in the Carpathians, near the Slovakian border. Could be a potential safe house. And they have automobiles. Three of them."

Ivan grunted with approval. "I trust your judgment. If you say they are trustworthy, then take them on." He squeezed her shoulder. "Now, let's get this newspaper out."

Antonia presented Oksana with the few black-and-white photos she'd received from their headquarters in Berlin via courier. They wouldn't have time to prepare stencils for them now. She examined a picture of their commander, Andrij Melnyk.

"The exile seems to have aged him," she said, handing it over.

"He and Viktor could almost be related," Oksana remarked.

She held the photo of Melnyk a little higher and Antonia compared it to Viktor. Both had similar noses, keen eyes, and strong features. The two men had met during Melnyk's first exile from Ukraine, when he took refuge with Viktor's family in Salzburg. Years later, when Viktor's outspoken defense of Jewish academics made him a target for the SS, Melnyk returned the favor, securing him a position teaching political science and history at the university in Lviv, which now fell within the Soviet bloc. Dr. Gruber was not the first Austrian national to escape fascist Germany, but he was the first Austrian-Ukrainian member of Antonia's secret cell.

Viktor's first task within the Organization had been to punch a hole into the west, to create those windows on the borders. An alpinist and veteran of the Great War, he accomplished this with ease. Antonia had come to idolize him almost as much as she did Melnyk. He was currently engaged in drawing up a manifesto that would set out a new framework for the Organization, based on less autocratic, more democratic principles. The challenge was finding a way to reach out to every section of Ukraine's multi-ethnic population, including Polish and Jewish citizens, at a time when the country resembled a tinder box with sparks flying all around it.

"This is good," said Oksana, looking up from typing Antonia's article.

Curious, Ivan peered over his sister's shoulder, his expression quizzical.

"I'm appealing to émigrés in the United States, Canada, Great Britain, France," she explained. "We need them to understand our situation under the Soviet regime and align with our—"

Suddenly Viktor cleared his throat and raised his pen in the air, his brow furrowed—a sure sign that they were disturbing his process.

Ivan, who clearly had something he wanted to say, waved for her to come closer.

"Hitler and Stalin have fallen out," he said, keeping his voice low. "There are some within the Organization who feel we ought to plead our case to the Germans."

"What? Why?" Antonia demanded.

"To offer ourselves up as an ally against the Soviets," Ivan said.

Viktor's pen slowed down, as if he were straining to listen in.

"If diplomatic relations fail," she said, turning her attention back to Ivan, "Germany will likely break its pact with Russia and declare war. But uniting with the Nazis? Have you forgotten Kristallnacht?"

"With Germany, not the Nazis," he stressed.

"Ivan, Germany is Nazi." She saw Viktor raise his head slightly. "The Aryans call Slavs *Untermenschen*. You're saying the Organization of Ukrainian Nationalists should associate with that? I don't believe it! That's exactly the kind of rhetoric that has poisoned us. We're here, in this cellar, to rectify it."

"The Organization is already split in two," Ivan argued. "The hard-liners won't like being ignored."

Antonia stared at him. "You mean Stepan Bandera and his radical mob? He never, ever accepted Melnyk's election as commander." She slapped her thigh, then pointed to Viktor. "Bandera says Ukrainians for Ukraine. Dr. Gruber here is Austrian and I've never met a man who has fought harder for our country."

At the sight of Ivan's expression, Antonia deflated. "Viktor is one of those outsiders Stepan Bandera wants to see expelled! How can anyone take him seriously?"

Oksana's attention had also gravitated to their conversation. Ivan's sister had separate compartments in that head of hers, Antonia thought. She worked as if she were three different people, which was why she could join the discussion while typing the final lines on the stencil.

"There's real momentum building behind Bandera's more radical ideas," she warned. "I wouldn't dismiss him or his followers so easily. The same thing happened in Germany with Hitler, and look what happened there."

With a flourish, she extended Antonia's finished page to Ivan.

He scanned it and Antonia caught a glimpse of something in his eye, something that was torturing him.

"It's very, very good," he said. "But what if those allies you are looking to align with decide, strategically, they need Russia on their side?"

Even Viktor looked up at this, his eyes darkening as he examined the Cossack. Antonia stiffened. She saw something she'd never have expected to see: Viktor was seriously considering Ivan's theory, and it scared him.

"This is a joke, right?" Antonia turned back to Ivan. "Ukraine on the side of the Axis?"

Ivan folded his arms across his chest. "The Nazis are the ruling and controlling party, sure."

"Emphasis on *controlling*," Oksana interjected, the typewriter clacking away again.

Viktor's gaze returned to his manifesto, but Antonia could tell he'd lost focus.

"Power comes and goes. It shifts," Ivan continued. "And when it does, we want Germany on our side."

Antonia raised her eyebrows. "Truly?"

Oksana stopped typing this time. "France and England waffled far too long over Poland, even the Sudetenland. They blow a whole lot of hot air and let Hitler do what he wants. It's like tying up a wolf on a five-meter leash, then forgetting to fasten the other end to a post. Now he's running amok in the woods and there's no calling him back."

Ivan placed a gentle hand on Antonia's arm. "I'm not saying we shouldn't try, but we need to be realistic and keep our options open. If Germany recognizes us as an independent country—"

"They'll play you for a fool," Viktor said angrily. He whipped off his glasses and Antonia saw his blue-gray eyes were glazed over with worry.

She went to him as he began arranging the sheets, tapping them together and then laying the pile aside as if all his efforts were for naught.

"What is it?" she asked softly.

Slowly, Viktor focused on her. He covered the top page with his hand, scowling. "I had one idea I wanted to add to what you'd written last night."

"One idea," she teased gently. "Are you going to show me?"

"I'm almost ready to start printing," Ivan warned.

Viktor ignored him. "You're not going to be pleased. You'll say I'm trying too hard to placate the Banderites."

Antonia lifted his hand and he offered no resistance as she picked up the top sheet. It was in German.

Oksana cocked an eyebrow as she handed the next stencil to Ivan. "See? Banderites. Bandera's followers already have a label. I'll say it again: I don't think we should brush Bandera or his followers off. We ignore them, they'll take hold and run a javelin right through us Melnykites."

Ivan tipped his head and scratched the back of his neck. "Melnykites?"

Oksana shrugged, but Antonia could see she had a point. The Organization was splitting and if nothing was done to prevent it, they would soon be pitted against one another. Melnykites. Banderites. Those who followed their elected leader. Those who followed the radical rebel. What hope was there if even the four of them could not agree on what to do if Germany invaded Soviet Ukraine? How were they to withstand anything that came their way?

Returning to Viktor's work, Antonia sought comfort in a task with which she was more familiar. Identifying three troublesome lines, she made amendments in Ukrainian and handed the text back to him. "This is more moderate. You're disenfranchising Melnyk's supporters if you say it the way you had it."

"Melnykites," Viktor muttered, squinting at her handwriting. He gave the slightest shake of his head.

"It has to be in the language of those fighting for the cause," Antonia added. "The German culture and your values are too different to ours, Viktor. Our readership here will understand this better if I translate it. We have to ensure there's as little room for misinterpretation as possible. If we're to prevent this split—"

"It's already here," Ivan grumbled.

Antonia pressed on: "Then we must formulate this so that our vision calls to everyone."

Viktor swept his glasses off again, clamping one end between his teeth, but he looked chastised rather than angry. "If you think this is right… Fine."

She sighed. *Fine*. In private, he would have made her work harder for it, made her be more precise with her meaning. He never challenged her when others were in the room.

"You're the political expert," Ivan called to him. "But she is the wordsmith."

Viktor made as if to protest but something suddenly banged above them. A door. Everyone gazed up at the ceiling. Footsteps crossed the parquet floor of the sculpture hall above. Antonia exchanged a wary look with Oksana as the floor creaked. Someone rolled something heavy across the room. Oksana reached behind her and flicked the light switch. They waited in the dark now. Antonia laid a hand on Viktor's shoulder.

She could feel Viktor's anger simmering as he leaned into her. "Ivan doesn't even read what I wrote and he defends your changes," he muttered. "What does he—"

Ivan shushed them.

Antonia stepped away and waited. The party above did not lock up and leave for a good half hour. It was almost one in the morning when Oksana turned on the light and the four of them wordlessly went back to work. They finished the copies of *Our Nation's Voice* just before dawn fanned across the cityscape.

At Viktor's apartment Antonia put on a pot of coffee and pulled out a chair at the kitchen table. She glanced out the window at a view dominated by the domed roof of the opera house, then turned her attention to Viktor, who sat opposite her, cleaning his glasses. When he was tired, the rims of his eyes turned bright pink. Today, they were almost red. She'd raised her concerns about Agent 1309 on the way home and he had defended himself. She had not intended to apportion blame, but he'd reacted as if she had.

"Oksana and Ivan will get the latest issue to the couriers today," she said to lighten the mood.

Viktor slipped his glasses back on and blinked. "He loves you."

Antonia scoffed. "Of course he does. He feels he must replace my older brother."

"You think he's interested in playing your big brother? That's where you're mistaken."

"Stop it, will you?" Her laugh was terse. "Jealousy is very unbecoming of you."

The coffee began boiling. She rose and waited a moment. "He and Pavlo have been in my life for as long as I can remember."

"Yes, yes, your brother's friends."

"They are also my friends. We all grew up together. Oksana is like everyone's baby sister."

The four of them had shared more than a few tragedies together. Oleh's death, however, had wedged something rock-solid and impenetrable between Ivan and herself. She wished they could get around it.

She turned to Viktor and examined his expression, but he was already lost in thought. Despite her exhaustion, her mind tortured her with the image of Oleh running through the orchard, then flying forward, arms spread out in that awful dive as the shot sent him tumbling into the tall grass. A cello case. He'd been carrying a cello in that case, not guns.

Antonia poured Viktor a cup of coffee and sat down across from him. "I think he feels it's necessary to protect me, for whatever reason, and never expected that I would soften the way I have with you. You are as much a surprise to me as I am to you. But I believe that Melnyk may have been the only one who could have foreseen how well suited we are when he assigned us to work together."

Viktor laughed softly and reached across the table for her hand. "From the first day I met Melnyk, he spoke of you. He's terribly proud of you. And so am I."

"He saw your drive, your commitment," she said. "If Ivan is correct and our only chance to rid ourselves of the Soviets is by collaborating with the Third Reich, it could strengthen the position of Bandera and his radicals. Their dream is to run our country the way Mussolini runs Italy. Melnyk is counting on us to help him prevent that. And we can start by delivering a template for a free and independent Ukraine, ruled by the people."

"Be honest," Viktor said. "You want a seat on Melnyk's first government."

She smiled and winked. "Right next to yours."

He slipped an arm around her waist and pulled her onto his lap. She was about to tell him of her visit to the doctor, but Viktor's hand began to stroke her breasts, then fluttered to the scarf around her throat and undid the knot. He kissed the nape of her neck, his breathing changing.

"I'm not like a brother," Viktor said into her ear. "You cannot mistake that."

Antonia leaned into him, willing the image of Oleh—and Ivan—to disappear. She turned to kiss his face. "No, you are not."

More than any man she had ever known, Viktor was her equal. Together, they were formidable. Together they would bring real change to Ukraine. Together, they would stand at the forefront when Melnyk—when the Organization of Ukrainian Nationalists—finally freed the country from foreign and tyrannical rule.

Antonia paced before the chalkboard, hands behind her back. In her hurried scrawl, she'd written Erich Maria Remarque, *All Quiet on the Western Front.*

"When Paul Bäumer is released from the front and returns home for the first time," she said, "Remarque places him in his childhood bedroom, looking through his collection of books. What does this scene—as he is seeking comfort in those old words—tell us about the character?"

Several of her students raised their hands, but Miloš Kaminski, in the sixth row above her, looked about to burst. She called on him.

"Frau Professorin, Remarque sent Bäumer back home to face the loss of innocence. Paul Bäumer's experiences in the war had stripped him of his childhood and his optimism for the future."

"But what of his ethics?" Antonia asked. "Think of the boots they stole from their dying comrade. What is the entire theme of the novel? What of—"

At the top of the auditorium, the door opened and Dr. Bodnar's head of white hair appeared. The dean threw her a cautionary glance and took a seat in the uppermost row. She wondered whether his visit had something to do with the two students who had failed to come to the lecture. She would not be surprised if they had been among the group who'd been arrested in the park the other night.

"Herr Kaminski," she said. "You were saying?"

The young man's eyes widened and he darted a glance at the dean.

Antonia tried again. "On the influences of military propaganda, what was Remarque's stance on the ethics?"

"On the ethics, Frau Professorin?"

Antonia lowered her chin. "Yes. Is it ethical to encourage youth to join the military? Is it patriotic? Is violence for glory ethical?"

"Yes, Frau Professorin."

Antonia rocked back on her heels. "I am not interested in your personal opinion." Her eyes flicked to the dean. "I am asking what Remarque's message was in his novel. What did his characters convey through their story?"

"I'm sorry, Frau Professorin, I've lost my train of thought."

Antonia pretended to look at the clock. "Fine, you may all thank your comrade here for the new assignment. Two pages maximum on the ethics that Remarque was arguing and how it compares to our patriotic duty to the Soviet Ukraine. Due next Tuesday."

She did not care if they ever wrote those papers. Sixty students and one hundred twenty sheets all repeating the same thing. As original as the bleating of sheep. She stuffed her papers into her briefcase as her students shuffled off, wondering what it would be like to teach in a country where free speech was written into the constitution.

The dean was already making his way down to her lectern.

"Dr. Bodnar." She extended her hand to him. "How can I help you today?"

"The head of the People's Commissariat for Internal Affairs is in my office."

The secret police chief. Antonia's mind began clicking. So, the new one was not wasting any time. He was going to check on her before she checked on him. "About my students, I assume."

"Maybe. He specifically requested you. His name is Major Kiril Vasiliev."

"Then shall we go see what it is Major Vasiliev is looking for?"

Dr. Bodnar rubbed a hand over his bright white mustache before yanking the door open for her and leading her to his wing of the building. Just before they reached his office, he stopped her.

"Whatever this is about," he said, "be careful. I've learned he has a reputation for being… thorough."

"Thank you." Antonia pulled herself together and walked in.

When Major Kiril Vasiliev rose from his seat, it was his height and his physique that Antonia noticed first. Beneath the blue and red uniform, he had an athletic build—long, lean torso and long legs. His thinning blond hair, swept back, revealed a high forehead but youthful face, his skin bright and smooth save for a dark mole to the right of his upper lip. He was perhaps in his late thirties, maybe early forties. But it was his eyes darting everywhere that lent her the impression of an eagle. With his height, she imagined he was looking down on her—hovering, searching for the next prey. He was a handsome man but Antonia immediately sensed that he was a cold man, a calculating man. And dangerously so.

Behind her, Dr. Bodnar said, "Professor Kozak, as you requested."

"*Shanovna* Kozak, a pleasure." Kiril Vasiliev's voice was deep and smooth. It reminded Antonia of butterscotch. He reached for her hand—his fingers perfectly manicured—and she gave it to him. He kissed her knuckles and then held her hand lightly. "It is a great pleasure to meet you. I read your article on Remarque in the *Literary Journal.*"

She was unable to keep the astonishment from her voice. "You read my work?"

"Yes," he said humbly. "I am most interested in your take on his novels."

Antonia shook her head.

"And I have also learned from Dr. Bodnar that you are Lena Rem's sister. Truly? I have read all of her novels, and our Kyivan State Theater recently put on her play *Don Cossacks.*" He turned to Dr. Bodnar, his eyes raised in exaggerated delight. "And the dean has informed me that her husband—your brother-in-law—is Roman Mazur, the painter? That he runs an art studio here in Lviv?"

Antonia nodded stiffly, dreading that her sister and her family were already known to this man. That the art studio, where she'd secretly printed *Our Nation's Voice* just the other night, was of interest to him now. Kiril Vasiliev was taking inventory, she reminded herself, and very likely because he had something on her. And he was in need of collaborators.

She steeled herself with that knowledge, realizing that he was doing the same thing she did for the Organization. He was vetting her.

"You've landed in a hotbed of culture," she said lightly.

"I am delighted to be in Lviv," he said, "where so many of Soviet Ukraine's remaining talents are now under one banner, one collective…" he spread his arms as if to envelop Dr. Bodnar and her together "… Union. I am going to take great pleasure in getting to know you all very, very well."

Those eagle eyes zeroed in on her, dove from above, and she could imagine the piercing, warning cry as he swooped in for her hand once more.

"Now, Dr. Bodnar, if I may use your office to speak to Professor Kozak here?" Kiril Vasiliev said. He gradually released her hand but his eyes stayed on hers. "We have incarcerated two of her students, and I'm here to fill in the details."

Antonia held the major's inquiring gaze and she caught one more thing in those eyes of his: Desire.

With this knowledge, her entire stance shifted. She now knew how she could get the upper hand when she would need to. She carefully chose her next words.

CHAPTER 2

May 1941

Lviv, Western Ukraine

Either you were already dead, or you were a Soviet collaborator. So went the saying. Which was why Ivan Kovalenko suspected everyone of collaborating on some level. Everyone, except for two people in the room. He waited for the group of select members—ten in all—to take their seats among the stacks of canned goods, *horilka*, beer barrels and disinfectant. He hated big assemblies, and compared to meeting with two or three members of his cell at any one time, this was a big assembly.

The Golden Lion was located on the first floor of the old press club, and down the road from the secret police headquarters. Ivan did his best to ensure such meetings were a rarity. Nobody from the underground cell came for long. They decided things over a quick *kvass*, careful to avoid behavior that would tip off the secret police. The tavern was a post office for the underground. And a depot. They exchanged messages, assigned missions, delivered papers and pamphlets, and stored their equipment and arsenal in the cellar.

As a tram rumbled by and the foundations shuddered, Ivan paced in front of the group, his instructions clear. It was time for a number of their Organization's high-profile members to escape out of the country and into the waiting arms of the Ukrainian diaspora in the west. Before they were twisted into becoming

Soviet collaborators. Before they were dead. Because Major Kiril Vasiliev had deployed undercover agents to infiltrate and root out the Organization throughout the territories.

"We have no miniature cameras. No magic pills or potions." Ivan pointed to his skull. "You are to use your brains, your eyes, your ears, your noses, your damned instincts. We've trained you to see and recall everything. We've trained you in reconnaissance and sabotage, in espionage and withstanding torture. The reason you're here now is because you're the ones who've managed to outsmart the secret police thus far, and you're going to have to continue to do so as we start evacuating our most valuable assets."

Ivan tapped the easel at the front of the room, a paint-stained sheet hanging over their intelligence. Pavlo Derkach, one of the three people Ivan trusted, took that as his cue and moved up front.

Shorter and blockier than Ivan, Pavlo wore a matching mustache and suede boots, earning them the nickname One and a Half Cossacks. But whereas Ivan was a pure descendent of the warriors, Pavlo had to go back three generations. He had light-brown hair and bright blue eyes, while Ivan was blond with brown eyes. And whereas Ivan had a thick head of hair, Pavlo would likely go bald, just like his father.

"Most of you know me here," Pavlo said. "I am a police officer, but within the Organization I lead a team of border guards who are loyal to our cause."

The Half Cossack acknowledged the four sentinels among them before whisking the sheet away, revealing a map of western Ukraine. The borders of Slovakia and Poland undulated along the Carpathian Mountains. He used the tip of his pointer to circle where the borders met, then indicated the large swath of wilderness around that. Ivan moved to the back of the room and stood behind the group.

"As most of you are aware, our window on the Polish border has closed," Pavlo said. "The Germans are trigger-happy, anticipating anything and anyone that resemble Poland's Home Army partisans. Our new route is over the Slovakian border." The Half Cossack indicated Viktor. "Dr. Gruber here has positioned our friendlies on the other side, established safe houses and transport."

He paused and scanned the group. "We have safe houses set up in an eighty-kilometer radius on both sides, the locations of which will be shared on a need-to-know basis. All of you here will take turns helping our people across the border."

It was a complex network of forgers who falsified documents, couriers who delivered messages, and agents who organized and carried out their covert operations. Ivan's rule was to have at least three degrees of separation between individuals. Today's meeting breached that rule. That was what was making him nervous.

Besides Pavlo, with whom Ivan had helped organize the underground movement back in their home village of Sadovyi Hai, the one other person Ivan trusted implicitly was Antonia. She was not only courageous, she was sharp and collected. He had watched her grow into one of the most notable women at the university, rubbing shoulders with dignitaries and powerful enemies, but she could hold her own in any setting. It was rumored that she had once drunk an entire Russian delegation under the table.

Though their family orchards had bordered one another and they had practically grown up in each other's laps, Antonia was untouchable. Especially now. She was a far cry from that young girl who'd shown up in the marshes, insisting she take part in the underground's tactical training. Ivan could picture her now, standing there in her embroidered blouse, her waist-long cinnamon hair woven into a crown of braids, driven by a thirst for liberty and the need to avenge Oleh's death. On that day, Ivan had been wracked with guilt and wholly conflicted. He'd expected Oleh's little sister, now grown into a young woman he desired more than anything, to accuse him of being responsible for her brother's death. But she never had.

She could go anywhere and be anyone. Anyone but his. Once—and only once—Ivan had managed a taste of what that might have been like. Instead of satiating him, her kisses had made him hungry for more, but Antonia had made it clear to everyone that she was passionate only about one man: Melnyk. Melnyk and the cause. Ivan had learned to live with his hunger, to suppress it as one does during Lent. The day she appeared on Dr. Viktor Gruber's arm, however, the pangs returned with a vengeance.

She looked at him now, his most trusted partisan, and gave him the slightest nod. As always, it cheered him. *I'm like a feral dog, happy to snatch up any scraps I can.*

Pavlo set the pointer down and stood, legs apart, arms behind his back. "We have three problems facing us now. One, Stepan Bandera has made it clear that he would rather tear apart the Organization than acknowledge Melnyk as our true commander. Two, German counterintelligence exploited this by recruiting first Melnyk, and then Bandera. Instead of supporting our struggle, the Nazis are testing us, pitting us against one another."

To the consternation of his audience, Pavlo then stepped away from the easel and returned to his seat.

"You said three problems," said a voice at the back.

"That's correct," Antonia said. "Three, the Soviet secret police. They know that the German Abwehr have recruited Melnyk and Bandera, and they are using that against us."

She went to the front, her navy-blue blazer and skirt authoritative, like a military captain. She wore a soft gold-colored scarf tucked into the collar of her white blouse, concealing the growth on her neck. But Ivan knew it was there.

Antonia pinned up a portrait of a blond man with a straight, long nose and deep-set eyes. He wore the Soviet uniform and insignia of a major and the disdainful countenance of a lord.

Ivan bristled. His sister had passed along her concerns that Kiril Vasiliev had acted on his lust for Antonia. Though Oksana assured him that Antonia could hold her own, and had thus far managed to thwart the major's advances without offending him, Ivan wondered how long the tactic would work.

"This," Antonia said, "is Major Kiril Vasiliev, head of Internal Affairs for the district of Lviv. In the past two months, he has planted several moles in an effort to root out our administrative groups around the Galician region. We've lost some of our key members. Some of you are too young to remember how it was when the Polish regime purged our *intelligentsia*. Those of us who lived through it will never forget what it was like to wake up to police raids in the middle of the night and have our parents taken, our clergy go missing, our sisters, brothers, uncles and aunts persecuted. Those who fled to the east, thinking they could continue our political activities at the heart of Soviet Ukraine, were gravely mistaken. In Stalin's view, a dissident who defies one regime will likely find ways to defy the other. Activists fell under suspicion of being collaborators, their activities monitored by the secret police. And those same secret police are here now, in Lviv, and they are hunting us."

Antonia locked eyes with each individual before continuing. "Here's what we have on Kiril Vasiliev. He pretends to be a genial host, putting on parties to lull people into a false sense of security, encouraging them to drink until they lose control. He, meanwhile, remains fully in control of his faculties, observing, listening. He is disciplined, precise, and he trusts no one. And I mean, no one."

"It's a sad way to live," Viktor said.

Antonia acknowledged him. "It is. But highly effective. And dangerous for us."

"Has he no weakness?" one young woman asked. One of Antonia's students, now a courier. "He certainly has at least one?"

"Beautiful women?" one of Pavlo's border guards suggested. The room chuckled nervously, the suggestion clear that Antonia and the student were perhaps those beautiful women.

Antonia smiled patiently and pointed to Viktor. "Sword fighting. When he discovered that Dr. Gruber was a champion fencer, he challenged him to a match."

"Who won?" came the question.

"Viktor did," Antonia said matter-of-factly.

Ivan looked away from the secretive glance they exchanged.

"His weakness," Viktor said, twisting to face the group, "is that he cannot tolerate any challenge to his masculinity. He was quite sour after our match. Not a gracious loser at all."

Heads nodded and Ivan brushed a hand over his mustache.

"Kiril Vasiliev then challenged Dr. Gruber to another match," Antonia went on. "On that occasion, he won. Since then, we have managed to establish a delicate relationship with him."

She returned to the easel with its map of the Ukrainian border. "There are two people we need to get out immediately, before Vasiliev disappears them. I will meet with you in teams. Let's get this mission going."

As the members of the group began talking to each other in low voices, Viktor approached Antonia and whispered something in her ear. She turned to answer him, their noses nearly touching, and this intimacy stoked Ivan's contempt for the man. Of all the people in the room, Viktor was one Ivan trusted the least. It was irrational, he understood that. The man had helped set up a first-rate escape route and was Melnyk's most valued outsider. But Ivan could not trust him because Viktor Gruber had managed to do the one thing nobody else in the group had: break through Antonia's carefully constructed shell and win her love and loyalty.

Multiple degrees of separation and staying on the move to avoid being tailed were essential. Three weeks after the meeting, Ivan got off the train in Drohobych and hitched the satchel over his shoulder. A single Volga was parked outside the station, sputtering fumes. Swirling from the driver's window was a thin trail of cigarette smoke. Two Soviet soldiers were grinning in the driver's direction. That was definitely his ride.

Ivan yanked open the handle and climbed into the passenger side. "Let's go."

Oksana stamped out her cigarette and shook her hair out of her eyes before turning the vehicle around. The two soldiers lifted their hands, but she ignored them. She took the southwest road out of town.

Ivan loved his sister's upturned nose, the spatter of freckles across the bridge of it, and her carefree energy, but he pointed to the butt in the ashtray. "When did you start this filthy habit?"

Oksana shrugged. "About the same time as you put me in charge of the safe houses. You know, not all of us Ukrainian women go around wearing *vinky* and ribbons in our hair, embroidered blouses, and—" She glanced at him askance. "We can't all be like Antonia."

"Have you got something against Antonia?"

"Not at all. Why would I? But she really needs to learn to have a little more fun."

"Like you?"

She smirked and blew him a kiss.

"Ivan, if it was up to you, Cossacks would still be riding across the steppes and kidnapping dark-eyed Natalias and Katias."

"Where did you get the Volga?"

"That kid Antonia recruited—Lesek. The one whose family has a hotel."

He glanced back at the empty road behind them. "I'm not happy about the vehicle," he said. "It's too obvious."

"You mean, I'm too obvious, right? You want me to hitch up Maya for you next time? You can ride her all the way to Truskavets."

Ivan rolled his eyes.

"Besides," she snorted, "how else do you want to transport so many bodies up the mountain?"

Ivan settled back to watch the countryside. "How's school?"

She smiled, looking out at the road again. "Graduating at the end of the spring, as planned. I've just been assigned to a grade school near Truskavets."

"My sister, the teacher. I'm surrounded by smart women."

"Smart and beautiful." She grinned and drove on.

The sky was overcast and fog clung to the low hills on the horizon. In Truskavets, Ivan had Oksana stop at a newsstand and he purchased a paper, then took a few minutes to make sure that the people watching for him saw him. When the church bell rang midday, he pulled out an apple from his bag, bit into it and linked his arm through Oksana's, pulling his coat collar up. That was when he saw Viktor walk by. The Austrian touched his cap and headed for the sanatorium's park. Oksana and Ivan followed at a distance. If Viktor stopped at the fountain, Oksana could drive Ivan back to Drohobych because the mission was called off. If Viktor passed the fountain, Ivan and Oksana would circle back to the vehicle and pick him and Pavlo up. Viktor moved on and veered off onto the boulevard leading to the mineral baths. The migration was on.

After they were back in the vehicle, Oksana steered it to the rear of the sanatorium. Viktor appeared with Pavlo, and both climbed in before she drove off again.

"Excellent," Viktor said. He patted Ivan's shoulder. "Most excellent."

"Our birds are set," Pavlo announced.

Their candidates were Slavko and Daria Holub, two of the Organization's higher-ups in Galicia. He was a judge, she was an attorney and, in the past four months, the secret police had questioned them both.

The safe house was located on a high plateau some kilometers outside of their home village of Sadovyi Hai, high enough to transmit and receive radio signals and far enough from the eye of any guards or patrols. The hut was used by a family Ivan and Pavlo knew, but only when the sheep were at pasture, which would not happen for another couple of weeks.

Oksana parked the Volga about a half kilometer away and they camouflaged it.

"We have to walk," Ivan told the others. "It's a rough and steep slope from here and there's still some snow on the ground."

When they reached the safe house, Pavlo introduced the Holubs to Ivan. They gathered around the table where Viktor took over the maps. With his index finger, he traced the backroads to the southwest and tapped the border of Slovakia, ten kilometers from Sadovyi Hai.

"That's all mountains," Viktor said, sweeping a hand over dark green and brown swaths. He looked at the Holubs. "And thick wilderness. It's a steep climb."

"Viktor will escort you over the border here," Ivan said, showing them the Ulychka River.

"Our friendlies," Viktor continued, "will connect you to our allies here in Ulič, then here in the Tatra Mountains."

Pavlo leaned on the table and smiled charmingly at the wife. She was biting her bottom lip. "The terrain there is much like it is in Sadovyi Hai. In other words, it's pleasant."

She pursed her lips, revealing fine, thin lines around her mouth where her lipstick had run a little.

"When it's safe," Viktor said, "our people in Slovakia will take you to the train station in Košice. You will receive tickets to Vienna where our outside ops will meet you, and then you will await instructions."

Slavko Holub sighed and rubbed his forehead. He was a heavyset man, and had already voiced his concerns about the climb. "Will we be resettled in Munich, then?" he asked.

"We asked that we get to Munich," his wife said. "I have family there."

Ivan shrugged his shoulders. "That information comes when it comes."

Viktor glanced at the clock and strode over to a cabinet. From deep inside, he removed a shortwave radio and got it working. The Slovakian language crackled through and everyone tilted their heads toward the device. If the code over the radio came in the form of a weather report for "blue skies"—the sign that it was safe to cross—they would be on the move tonight. But at 16:55 the announcer predicted rain, and Viktor nodded as if he had expected it.

"Everyone relax," he said to the lawyer and his wife. "Today is not the day."

Ivan cracked his neck and rubbed it. He was tense. This would be the first time they'd used this new window.

"I'm going outside," he told Pavlo.

"All right. I'll go over the new identity papers with them," he replied.

Outside, Ivan gazed at the tops of the western ridges and breathed in. At the sound of someone moving behind him, he turned and faced Viktor. The professor removed his glasses and wiped them with his coat sleeve before putting them back on. He peered at Ivan.

"I'm going to ask Antonia to marry me."

Ivan flinched. Antonia had once mentioned that Viktor had sworn never to marry. It was how Ivan had explained her easy attraction to the Austrian. Viktor abhorred any institution or government whose purpose was to manipulate and control an individual's right to freedom. Viktor was safe. Antonia would never feel as if she were betraying the cause. Obviously, something had changed for Viktor, but had it changed for her as well?

"I thought you were an atheist."

Viktor chuckled. "A civil ceremony, of course."

"Congratulations, I suppose. I mean, if she says yes." Ivan extended his hand.

Viktor shook it, his palm astonishingly soft against Ivan's callused one. He suddenly had the sensation that he was giving Antonia away with this gesture and withdrew. He stepped off the porch and propped himself against the corner of the house. The air vibrated from the din of the waterfall pouring into a nearby gully.

A moment later, Viktor moved his way once more. "What is the story with Oleh?"

"I thought she'd have told you by now."

"I'm asking you."

"It's really—" *None of your business*, Ivan wanted to say. He wanted to protect at least that one thing between Antonia and himself. The murder of her brother—his best friend. The event that had led her to him. And also distanced her from him.

But Viktor pressed on. "Oleh was part of the Organization. I know that. And their mother hated it."

"It's not that simple," Ivan said. "He was a phenomenal musician, a cellist. Their mother saw to it that he got into the music academy in Lviv. He came home for the summer break, to help in the orchards, but then she forbade him to do that as well. It was his hands, his fingers she wanted to protect. He got bored. After all, Oleh loved music, but before he got serious about his studies, he was forever wrestling Pavlo and me, and causing all sorts of trouble."

"Trouble that led to his death?"

Ivan scratched the back of his neck. "Something like that."

"You were running weapons?"

"On a very small scale," Ivan defended. "We were raiding the Bolshevik bunkers. Everyone did it; we were still kids back then. It was…" Exciting. Fighting for their freedom was exciting.

"Then?"

"Then Pavlo and I saw the local cadre moving in and setting up a camp. We decided to get the real stuff. We borrowed Oleh's cello case. Oksana was our decoy."

Viktor's forehead rumpled and Ivan looked away.

"Anyway, the cello case. It was the easiest thing to hide the weapons in. I carried it out. We got stopped by patrols, but they didn't check the case. Word got out the base had been robbed." He shrugged.

"So the Bolsheviks came looking for you," Viktor guessed.

"Oleh and I were similar in build. Blond hair, too."

"A case of mistaken identity?"

"The description included a cello case. By that time the weapons were safely hidden on Pavlo's property and the cello was back in the case." Ivan sighed. "Oleh knew nothing about it. Pavlo and I... well, at that point..."

Viktor tipped his head. "You were no longer friends with Oleh?"

"It wasn't like that. We just... I don't know. You grow apart, right? Pavlo and I were the same... class. The Kozaks were more intellectual—especially the mother. She came from Lviv originally."

"Antonia said that Oleh liked to play his music outside in the orchards," Viktor said.

"There's a creek and a nice spot. It appealed to his poetic nature. I guess he too, was starting to see that our interests were different. He tried to be like us—like Pavlo and me, but his mother really kept a tight rein on him."

"Antonia was with him that day. The day the patrols showed up as he was coming back from the orchard."

"Yeah."

"Oleh ran. He thought they'd found out he was a Nationalist."

"Yeah."

Viktor shook his head. "You blame yourself, don't you?"

Ivan scuffed the ground with the heel of his boot and looked off toward the gully.

"It's the one thing that's prevented you from telling her how you really feel about her."

"Look," Ivan said gruffly. "You and I need to work together. I think it's best if we lay this aside. I'm happy for the two of you. But, Viktor…?"

The professor looked up at him expectantly.

"Don't ask her before she gets what she needs out of Kiril Vasiliev. You'll jeopardize all she's trying to do. You and I both know the major is infatuated with her. That could prove to be useful. But only if he thinks she's… free."

Viktor sniffed and narrowed his eyes. "I hear you, Ivan. I hear you."

Ivan paused and peered at the man. Kiril Vasiliev's interest in Antonia was the very reason Viktor was going to ask her in the first place. "Dr. Gruber," he now warned. "That's an order."

The professor cleared his throat.

Pavlo stepped out as Viktor went back inside the hut. The Half Cossack, as usual, was perceptive. He clicked his tongue and signaled that Ivan should follow him. They walked over to the gully, the waterfall dropping a good six meters to the river below. Pavlo said nothing but he was waiting. Ivan finally broke Viktor's news to him.

"Ever since we were children," Pavlo said afterwards, "we all thought you and Antonia… Do you remember how we used to tease you? Mr. and Mrs. Kovalenko?"

"She hated that," Ivan said. And that had always stung. "You're the only one with the fantasy."

"Really? You aren't in love with her any longer?"

Ivan breathed in deeply, clenching his hands. After a moment he said, "Antonia's made her choice. She wants someone who is her equal."

"Damn it, Kovalenko, you put that woman on a pedestal then dug a two-meter-deep trench around it to stand in."

Ivan turned away but Pavlo grabbed his arm, his mouth set and his expression earnest. "You underestimate yourself completely. You *are* her equal."

"Shut up, you runt." Ivan jabbed the Half Cossack in the chest, but the scrub stood his ground. "If you think Antonia has any interest in a man who'd rather wield a sword than a university degree, you're more of an idiot than—"

But Pavlo did not let him finish. He spun back and stalked through the meadow, leaving Ivan to stand alone. When he'd disappeared back inside, Ivan faced the rushing water, again. Forget it. He'd stick to what he did well, and that was get their people safely over the border.

Their "weather man" predicted "blue skies" three days later, and barely in time. Pavlo had to return to work. Viktor was also to return to Lviv by the end of the week though he was determined to make this first run with them. When it was time, Oksana got the Volga ready to go. It was nearly eight and the dusk was gathering when she delivered them to the trailhead.

"Five after ten," Ivan reminded her. "Just in case."

She nodded and drove off. Ivan offered Daria Holub his hand as they stepped into the dark forest. The trail quickly turned into a steep climb. A screech owl sounded, and further up, the call of roe deer, like banshees. Daria Holub halted. Ivan soothed her and they continued onward. Behind them, Judge Holub was not doing much better, so Ivan waited.

Catching up to them, Viktor muttered, "This one's going to take longer than planned."

"It's a half-hour climb," Ivan told the big man.

The judge looked over his shoulder. "So you've told me. A few times."

"These are thick woods," Ivan assured. "I doubt even the Soviets know about this trail."

In the darkness, Ivan heard the man mutter, "The Soviets know everything. It's their job."

Ivan took up the rear with Daria Holub. Sweat rolled down his back beneath his shirt. The lawyer, however, proved to be a real trooper, as if to compensate for her husband's grumbling and extra strain. Several meters before they reached the top, Viktor halted and crouched. They all followed.

"We're just about there," he said.

After crawling over to Viktor, Ivan took the offered binoculars from him. Across the Ulychka River was a barbed wire barricade. Several Soviet border guards were standing and smoking cigarettes.

"Are those ours?" Ivan asked.

"Them and the two on the other side."

Two Slovakian sentinels were walking with a flashlight some meters further down the river.

"You're sure about that," he said.

"The taller one's got an arm patch on his coat."

"Is that not normal?"

Viktor nodded. "Yes, but it's turned upside down."

Ivan squinted into the binoculars and then the light hit correctly. As the man passed beneath a lamp post, he caught sight of the patch. The cross was indeed upside down. Ivan handed the binoculars back to Viktor.

"Now what?"

Viktor pointed ahead. "We need to get down there and then wait until it gets properly dark. You'll monitor from here. I'm going to make sure these two get across and then I'll meet you at this spot."

When they backed up, Ivan said his goodbyes to the Holubs.

"May God keep you," Daria Holub said.

"Glory to Ukraine," Slavko Holub added.

Ivan hid in the brush where he could watch the crossing. He shrugged into his coat, his teeth grinding more from adrenaline than cold.

A few moments later, he spotted shadows moving along the riverbank. From the maps, he knew there was a pipeline bridge and then a break in the chain-link fence on the Slovakian side. He wondered whether the judge would make it across. On the other side, their friendlies were waiting to bring the Holubs to their safe house in Ulič.

At 22:05 sharp, Ivan saw the Volga pull up alongside the road near the checkpoint. He saw Oksana's slender arm waving at the border guards. All of this was necessary, as Pavlo's border guards had sent word that their shifts were being regularly and unpredictably changed since Vasiliev had installed new security measures.

Ivan watched the flirtatious salutes and dips at Oksana's side of the car. She stepped out then and threw open the hood to expose the engine. The decoy was on. Ivan switched back to the riverbank. The shapes were difficult to see but then he saw them disappear behind a treeline. Only a single shadow reappeared. Viktor was returning. The Holubs were over the border.

Ivan smiled to himself, but it was too early to celebrate. Only when he got the message that they had landed in the hands of their ops on the other side would he call this a success.

A week later, one of his couriers delivered a package of Bavarian pretzels and mustard. Inside, a small cowbell that said "Munich." The enclosed postcard read, *Wish you were here.*

CHAPTER 3

June 1941

Lviv, Western Ukraine

By June, Viktor had helped get eight people over the border, but Antonia was nervous that their mysterious disappearances did not seem to cause a stir among the secret police. The Cossacks and Viktor all rationalized that a more recent rumor was perhaps troubling the Soviet security forces. News trickled over the border that hundreds of Ukrainian men of military age, who had earlier migrated to work in Germany as Ostarbeiter, had been recruited into the Wehrmacht over recent months. Word from the Organization's council included the names of two divisions: Roland and Nachtigall.

The troops were rumored to mostly be supporters of the rebel, Stepan Bandera. What Antonia could not understand was the lack of response on her side of the border. The Soviets gave no mobilization orders, nor had they called for any fortifications within Ukraine. Before Ivan or Pavlo could get any further information, Pentecost arrived, and Antonia and Viktor were overloaded with end-of-term examinations. Despite the stillness—or likely, because of it—Antonia sensed Major Vasiliev lurking in Lviv's every nook and cranny.

That weekend, as the church bells rang all around the city, Antonia crossed Kościuszki Park with Viktor. The air was scented with the last of the lilacs, but the garden's tulips and daisies were already replaced with foxglove and begonias. There were plenty of people out for a stroll or hurrying—as Antonia and Viktor were—to their extended weekend celebrations. It was Lena who had suggested they come over for *nalysnyky*, Viktor's favorite. Antonia's sister usually made a selection of the crepes with both savory and sweet fillings.

A man with a little brown dog on a red leash passed them, followed by a woman with a pram and two fair-haired girls in tow, their braids bouncing over their shoulders. On the other side of the park, a group burst into peals of laughter. To the left, another group was singing. The atmosphere was cheerful. Antonia hooked her arm into Viktor's and smiled.

When they reached the art studio in the Sofiyivka district, Antonia noticed the boxes of frames and supplies stacked outside the door.

"Roman's exhibition starts next month," she said. "It will feature a selection of his Galician and Hutsul paintings."

"Including the portrait you sat for?"

"Yes. And he's going to ask the artist's union for permission to travel abroad. But you know Lena. She's anxious about being left alone, especially with the baby due in a couple of months."

Viktor gave her a reassuring squeeze. "Maybe she can go to Sadovyi Hai for the summer."

At the apartment building, Antonia removed the spare key her sister had given her to avoid climbing up and down three flights of stairs in her condition. Before she pushed open the door, Antonia halted at the sight of a brown dog coming around the corner. It was the same one that had passed them in the park. The same red leash. And the man with the hat, short-legged and round like the dog, he was the same, too. He did not look at them but hunched into his coat as he passed the apartment building.

Antonia put a hand on Viktor's arm.

"The dog," he said in a low whisper.

"Do you think Major Vasiliev is having us watched?"

His eyes narrowed, but Antonia stepped back onto the walk, pretending she'd dropped something. When she turned her head, the man and the dog were disappearing through an apartment door further down the block. A coincidence then, but she could not shake the foreboding. As they climbed the stairs in silence, Agent 1309 popped into Antonia's head. Where was he? And what had he managed to accomplish in the past three months?

She had no chance to mull it over as Lena opened the door before they could even knock. Behind Antonia's sister, Konstantin zipped across the hallway, dark hair bouncing. The five-year-old threw her a woeful look before yanking the sitting-room door open so hard that the translucent window rattled in its frame.

Roman called from the kitchen. "The least you could do is greet our guests, Konstantin. Where are your manners?"

"Someone's not happy," Antonia remarked when her brother-in-law appeared.

Lena smiled apologetically and invited them in. Everyone embraced and kissed each other's cheeks before Roman gently pulled Antonia aside and pressed something cool into her hand.

"Is it finished?" She opened her palm to the gold locket. The piece had cost her a small fortune, but it was what was inside that made it valuable. She released the catch and it popped open. Antonia stifled her pleasure. Roman had finished the miniature of her portrait. She had sat for it several times, and it had taken him many painstaking hours to complete it, but here was its tiny copy, and it was beautiful. She held it up close, her back to Lena and Viktor. The tiniest strokes of the brush depicted the red highlights of her hair. He'd put in the brown and gold flecks of her hazel green eyes—tiny, tiny strokes but masterfully done. The background was lapis blue. Roman had also managed to depict the top part of the orchid pin she'd worn on her dress.

She pecked Roman's cheek. "Viktor will love it, I'm certain. I'm going to give it to him tonight."

Antonia shrugged out of her spring cloak. In the sitting room, Konstantin was lining up his tin soldiers along the coffee table, quietly humming to himself.

"What's gotten into my nephew?" she asked Lena. Usually he threw himself at her.

Lena and Roman exchanged a look before Lena hung up their coats.

"He wanted a puppy, and we said no." But Lena's grin was mischievous and she tugged at her earlobe. Antonia bent down to be eye level with her. Her sister was terrible at keeping secrets.

"What is it?"

"We're going to get him one, but only after the baby comes. And we'll do it when we're back in Sadovyi Hai for the summer."

Antonia watched the men drift into the sitting room, then steered her sister into the kitchen. Lena rubbed the sides of her belly.

"Are you well?"

Lena said she was, her eyes on Antonia's flowered scarf. "And you? It hasn't gone away, has it? Will you have it removed?"

"I don't have the time."

Ignoring Lena's exasperation, Antonia leaned over a bowl of fresh berries and plucked one.

Lena playfully smacked her hand. "We pray first."

"I have a little happy news myself," Antonia said, snatching a piece of cheese off the platter. She turned her back on the kitchen door and whispered, "I just happened to be cleaning out Viktor's suit coat pockets…"

"You did not!" Lena admonished. "Antonia, you know I don't approve of you behaving as if the two of you are married. And even if you were married, what are you doing going through his pockets?"

"I was only getting his suits ready for cleaning. Some I need to mend."

"And?"

Antonia could hardly keep a straight face but looked meaningfully at her sister. "I found a box…"

Lena gasped.

"Inside, a beautiful, simple diamond—"

"Goodness." Lena gripped her by the forearm. "But he left the Church. And you… well, I can't remember the last time you've been."

"Don't start."

Lena let go of her. A strained smile. "When do you think he'll ask you? Will you say yes?"

"I've decided I will. You know, we met on Pentecost weekend three years ago. This morning, he referred to you as his sister-in-law. 'I can hardly wait for the sister-in-law's *nalysnyky*,' he said this morning."

"I thought he swore never to marry."

"I swore I would never marry," Antonia reminded her. "It's romantic, him hiding the ring. I thought you would be delighted." The most romantic thing Viktor had ever done for her prior to this was put a bouquet of forget-me-nots into an Easter basket.

Lena tugged her deeper into the kitchen. "You challenge one another in so many ways, but that competition could very well be bad for a marriage."

Antonia pulled away from her, but Lena went on, "Viktor is a good man, and you make a strong couple, both headstrong, ambitious, intelligent…"

"And? What's wrong with that?" Antonia said sourly. "We're not romantic enough for you? I'm the big sister here, remember? Not once did I share my reservations about Roman and you."

"I worry that your egos and not your hearts attract you to one another, that's all." Lena placed a cool hand on Antonia's cheek. "I wonder whether you will both vie for power and end up resenting the other when one of you must step back."

"Honestly, sister," Antonia huffed quietly, "you make it sound like the political intrigues in your Kyivan Rus dramas."

Lena looked disappointed and Antonia felt the history between them. She knew her sister inside and out, but Lena had long ago lost access to all that Antonia was. And it had been Lena's choice. Lena had abandoned the Organization. Lena had married the Polish artist despite their parents' protests, and Antonia had supported her. And it was Lena who had made Antonia swear to never talk about her activities with the underground. Lena did not even know that Roman allowed them to use the basement of his studio. One more detail to add to Antonia's layers of secrets and guilt, assuaged only by the knowledge that she was trying to protect her sister.

Picking up a platter of cheese-filled *nalysnyky*, Lena said, "Perhaps you're right. I'm letting my fantasy get the better of me. Help me with the food?"

Antonia put an arm around her sister before she could leave and said, "You're the clairvoyant one—tell me who is the right man for me."

But Lena's frown deepened. "You already know that."

Slipping from her grasp, Lena carried the food into the next room, as if to let Antonia figure it out. And when Antonia did, she almost laughed out loud.

"We were just children," she whispered when Lena returned. "We were hardly ever romantic. For heaven's sake, we used to spit cherry pits at each other to see who could make the most red marks on our white tunics. Do you remember how angry Mama was?"

"Everyone in the village believed you two... Well. You didn't stop talking to me about that kiss for months."

"So?" Antonia shrugged. She'd been innocent then.

"You might never have said a word to him about it, but you told me everything you felt then."

When Lena took the next platter out, Antonia followed her into the corridor but kept her voice low so the men could not overhear her. "You're an incurable romantic. You and your wild Cossack romances! Honestly!"

Back in the kitchen again, Lena smiled wistfully. "Ivan makes a wonderful Cossack."

Later, at the table, they remained standing to pray, and Antonia took in her family. Roman was a handsome man, with dark and gentle eyes, but he had a melodramatic and tragic air. The cliché of the Parisian artist. Her sister, however, was a classical beauty in every sense of the word. She had a rounder face to Antonia's heart-shaped one, more prominent cheekbones, and a shy countenance. Lena spent an awful lot of time observing people, just as she was gazing at Antonia now. Her sister was fascinated by the past, writing her stories, poems, and plays. Meanwhile, Roman's paintings were filled with the depictions of a world they'd never quite known but dreamed of: pastoral scenes that mingled Polish and Ukrainian accents the way one mixes blue and yellow to create green—so that one could no longer separate them. Whereas Lena and Roman saw a world filled with traditions and heritages worth preserving, Antonia and Viktor used their skills in rhetoric to design Ukraine's future. Yes, they were loud. They were brazen. And, yes, Antonia thought as she made the sign of the cross, perhaps she and Viktor were inspired by one another's ambitions, and maybe, just maybe, they were subconsciously trying to outdo one another. But they loved one another. About this she was certain.

Just before Roman poured Crimean champagne, Antonia presented Viktor with the locket containing the miniature portrait. He seemed delighted and kissed her cheek warmly in front of the rest of the family. But when he did not produce the ring or make any indication of proposing marriage, either that day or by the time they returned to work, Antonia wondered whether she had been terribly mistaken about his intentions.

Sixty-eight pencils scratching in the auditorium. Antonia paced around her podium. "You have twenty minutes," she called to the room. A few heads looked up, other students turned their pages, and still others bent deeper over their notebooks. The final exams were always nerve-racking for the students. For her, they were the most mundane part of the job.

At the sound of the door opening, where she'd explicitly hung a sign warning against disturbance, Antonia scowled. Her blood chilled as Major Kiril Vasiliev swept in, removed his cap, and nodded curtly to her. Not a single student looked up. But when she recognized the short-legged, round man behind him—the one who had resembled his dog—Antonia's heart dropped to her knees.

Both took a seat, and she saw the Dog Man place a briefcase on the floor. Kiril Vasiliev crossed his long legs and balanced his cap on a thigh.

The minutes ticked by slower and slower. Keeping her eyes on her students, Antonia continued her pacing. Twenty minutes to consider why Kiril Vasiliev was here. What the Dog Man had on her. Twenty minutes to go over her every step, her every word with Viktor through that park on the way to the Mazurs. And what about Viktor? She'd left him at the apartment that morning to grade papers. He wasn't due on campus until after midday. She had twenty minutes to identify the hundred types of traps Kiril Vasiliev had set. The sliding panel in her bookcase. Had she locked her office? Would it have made a difference? The metal box. She tried to remember all its contents.

She looked at the clock. Sixteen minutes. Kiril Vasiliev set his cap off to the side and folded his hands. His companion whispered something, but the major's eagle eyes remained on her.

Marika, one of Antonia's underground recruits, rose, stone-faced. She placed her notebook on the lectern, gave Antonia a nod and walked out of the room through the lower doors. Antonia watched her go. Had Marika or one of the students turned her in? Or was it agent 1309? She'd forgotten to ask for news of him.

The next student got up, then two others. Each of them was curt, silent. This was not unusual. They were concerned. They never smiled after an exam. They never showed their fear, their anxieties. Not to her, anyway. Antonia glanced up at Vasiliev then stepped behind her lectern. She reviewed the first pages of the notebooks, but the words swam together. She checked the clock again. Twelve minutes.

"You have ten minutes," she called.

Kiril Vasiliev moved again and leaned forward. The other man kept his arms crossed over his chest, his knee bouncing. She canvassed the remaining students, hurrying to finish their exams. None of those present were working with the Underground, neither as couriers, nor for *Our Nation's Voice*.

Relieved to see the last students were finishing up and leaving their exams on her lectern, she called the exam to end. It was four minutes early, but the last two strays did not complain. They stood up, handed in their booklets, and by the time the last one left, Kiril Vasiliev was already coming down the stairs.

"Major," Antonia extended her hand. He kissed her knuckles. Surely, if he was here to arrest her, he would not go through the motions.

With raised eyebrows, he indicated the pile of books on the desk behind the lectern. "May I?"

"Certainly."

The second man, wearing a tan blazer, much too warm for the weather, lingered near the first row.

"I wonder if you would indulge me," Vasiliev said in that butterscotch-coated voice. "There's a game I really enjoy playing. Take any book from the pile."

He turned his back on her. Antonia removed one of the books. "And now?"

"Open to page twenty-two and read the second paragraph or verse aloud, and I will tell you whose book you have there."

Antonia's first thought was that he was showing off, but she opened the page and read the middle lines of *May Song*.

"Goethe," Vasiliev called before she completed the fourth line. His back was still to her. "Another one. That was easy."

The next book was *Mephisto*. "Page?"

"Same page. Second paragraph," Vasiliev confirmed.

She read.

"Klaus Mann."

"That's astonishing," she said, meaning it. The companion's expression had not changed.

"It's a little hobby of mine. I study sentence length, structure, variation and position. The use of details. Details are very important, don't you think? Sound devices, say alliteration, onomatopoeia, repetition." Vasiliev had walked to her side of the desk, and picked up another tome by Goethe. He stroked the spine. "Especially repetition. Then there is tone. Use of local color. So many, many things. I have a whole list."

He looked up and stacked the books back together, straightening them. "It's like a fingerprint. Every author has one. Non-fiction is much easier to work with, but I like a challenge. In my line of work, it's my job to dissect the fiction. Discovering the truth beneath the mask of characters."

Vasiliev's eyes narrowed. "It's like rooting out any of the lies my suspects might be hiding. But I'm getting ahead of myself."

He was so close, she could smell him. Mahogany. Steel. Antonia tried to keep her breathing normal, but her heart was racing and colliding against her breastbone. "Am I suspect, then?"

Vasiliev smiled indulgently. "Would you mind? Please collect the students' notebooks. Agent Nikolaev and I would like a word in your office."

Her steps were heavy as she led the two men down the hall. Antonia's mind raced. Agent 1309. Her students. Was Vasiliev here for her? Or for them? Had the major and this Nikolaev already been in her office? But when she unlocked it, everything appeared in order. Nothing unusual, nothing out of place. Outside the window, Marika and the other Organization recruits were lingering around the fountain. One of them must have caught sight of movement behind Antonia's window, because he straightened and turned his back on her, shielding the others from view. Beneath the arcade, she heard laughter, but the air in her office was thick. She went around to her desk, the bookshelf behind her, that hiding spot burning a hole into her back. The policemen lowered themselves into the chairs before her.

Vasiliev indicated the pile of exam notebooks. "We're here to confiscate those. Three of them, that is. For now."

He then named the three students involved in writing *Our Nation's Voice*. Holding her breath, Antonia searched through them and handed over the notebooks. She could not even warn them, those students at the fountain. Vasiliev opened them up and gestured to Nikolaev, who then produced three files from his briefcase.

The major nodded over the exam books, then took his time turning all three back in her direction—opened—and pushing them across the desk to her. Meanwhile, Nikolaev placed the other files before her.

"I'd like you to compare the articles in these folders," Vasiliev said smoothly, "with the essays these three students have written."

Antonia opened the first file and recognized newspaper clippings from recent issues of their paper. She peered at Marika's articles, pretending to read them, but she knew them. She'd edited them. The next two folders also contained clippings. Though there were never any bylines, no names anywhere, Antonia knew which article belonged to which student. And she also knew that Vasiliev and the Dog Man were not only here for them.

The major suddenly rose, took the three examination books and placed them, one at a time, onto the matching folders. Each exam matched the file of that particular student.

Antonia steepled her hands and gazed at him. "I don't understand, Major Vasiliev. What am I looking for here?"

But his benevolent smile indicated he was not fooled. He drummed his fingers on the tabletop as if he were mimicking the keys of a typewriter. "The author's fingerprint."

Antonia leaned back and narrowed her eyes.

"You are a literature professor," Vasiliev said, sitting back down. "You are also fluent in at least four languages that I know of. Would you say that when one writes in Ukrainian, proceeded by something in German that one might still maintain the same tone, the same style of writing? Does Goethe sound like Goethe in German and in Russian? In Yiddish and in German?"

"I could argue very much the opposite," Antonia said. "Languages are intricately woven together with the nuances of culture, of vocabulary. I find my students—whether they be Polish or Ukrainian, or Russian—are never as authentic in the voice of their foreign language—in German, in my students' cases—as they are in their native language. A foreign language is like wearing a"—she glanced at Nikolaev's blazer—"an ill-fitting suit. You're never quite comfortable in it. A foreign language is a costume. At least, that's what my experience has been."

Kiril Vasiliev turned his head to Nikolaev. "Exactly why we're here today. To unmask."

"That would be difficult to do," Antonia tried.

"So one loses their authenticity when working in a second language?" the major challenged.

"Likely," she said cautiously. "Though professional translators are trained to remain authentic to the original meaning."

He wagged a finger at her. "There you are. Professional translators. A person who is fluent in both languages because one parent is a German speaker and the other is Ukrainian?"

Antonia froze. Viktor.

She barely noticed as Kiril Vasiliev indicated the briefcase, as Nikolaev handed the major two more files. Kiril Vasiliev withdrew another clipping from one of them.

"I have been studying the messages and styles from several newspapers and journals," he said. "Please. Take a moment. Read them. What is your assessment? Are they the same author?"

Saliva was building up in Antonia's mouth and she took as normal a swallow as she could. It was impossible to concentrate on the words with him watching her. It was Viktor's article. The one she had helped him write. Kiril withdrew another few sheets, placed them before her. Her work. Viktor's work. Her work again. Viktor's work again. In both German and Ukrainian.

Throughout history, our enemies have set out to conquer us as a people. We must act to liberate. "I'd need more time with this," Antonia said.

"I don't believe you do."

One finger. One smooth gesture. Nikolaev rose and Antonia with him. The agent came around the desk and gripped her arm. Kiril Vasiliev went around the other side, removed the three Soviet-issue textbooks, slid the panel and removed the metal box, his long fingers clutching the top handle.

"I think we'll continue this questioning at headquarters," he said.

He shoved her before the office windows, handing Nikolaev the metal box. Four men moved from the arcade and swarmed the fountain. Antonia saw Marika's eyes go wide with fear, saw the boys struggle in the grips of those Soviet vultures. Those students who had been in the arcade melted into the shadows beneath. How was Ukraine to win her independence with so many cowards?

Vasiliev's voice, so smooth it was like he was caressing her. She shivered.

"You can either come with us quietly—"

"I'm coming quietly," she said.

His eyes flashed. "Good. I think Viktor would like to see you. At least one last time."

CHAPTER 4

June 20, 1941

Lviv, Western Ukraine

Outside the Golden Lion tavern, sparrows and finches hopped from one table and chair to the next, pecking at yesterday's crumbs. The three churches nearby rang their bells. Half past seven in the morning. Ivan unlocked the door. Inside, the tavern was cool thanks to the exposed brick walls. The floor plan was made up of cubbies and niches that created the privacy ideal for his meetings with the cadre's members. But on sunny days, Ivan rolled out the blue-and-white-striped awning. Those visiting the old market would come for their first drinks or late coffees when he opened at nine. There was a view of the castle, and the sidewalk was bathed in warmth at least until early afternoon.

He began wiping down the tables. Behind him, he heard the click and whirr of a bicycle and turned just as a young boy pulled up, slid off, and handed Ivan a stack of the morning edition. Ivan paid him with money from his pocket and tucked the bundle beneath his arm. Each issue would be stuffed with the latest copy of *Our Nation's Voice* for later pick up and distribution. But the boy had a wary look in his eye as he removed his cap and lifted the seam inside.

"This, too."

He passed over a sheet of paper, which Ivan rolled out and read: *September 13, cancelled.* Agent 1309 had been compromised.

Ivan looked at the boy, reached into his pocket and withdrew a couple of coins. "Go on now."

He then kicked over one of the chairs but pulled up. Down the street, Oksana, followed by Pavlo, were heading over with grim expressions. They wouldn't be bringing him the issues they'd made the night before in broad daylight. No, it was trouble they were bringing, not *Our Nation's Voice*.

He shoveled the two of them inside. Pavlo yanked off his beret and stalked to the bar, his dimples deeply creased. The Half Cossack looked into the kitchen in the back then checked the inside of the tavern. Ivan cast Oksana a questioning look, but she pulled a face just before Pavlo returned.

"The place is clear," Ivan said.

"Viktor and Antonia did not show up," Pavlo hissed.

"What? Where are they?" Ivan asked.

"If we knew," Oksana snapped, "we wouldn't be here."

Ivan rubbed a hand over his mouth and handed Pavlo the slip of paper about Agent 1309. "Start at the beginning. You were supposed to go to the art studio. Meet. Do the paper. What about Roman? Has he heard anything from either of them?"

Pavlo shook his head. "We intercepted him on his way in this morning. He hasn't heard anything from them or about them."

"Three degrees—" Ivan began.

"It's too late for that," Pavlo cried.

"Then Vasiliev's found something," Ivan groaned.

"They were always so careful," Oksana said. "That's impossible."

Ivan and Pavlo looked at one another. Ivan tapped the bar with his knuckles and jerked his head to the door. "Let's go. Let's see if they show up."

Ivan was relieved to see that Oksana had borrowed an old, black GAZ. Viktor's apartment was located on the other side of the opera house on a quiet residential street. Oksana slowed, her eyes straight ahead as Ivan examined the landscape. The building was surrounded by high wrought-iron railings, but Ivan winced when he noticed that the gate stood ajar. As Oksana drove slowly by, Ivan studied the upper-story window just above the white lilac bush. The muslin curtains were pulled shut.

He reached over to Pavlo in the passenger seat. "Was the gate locked when you came?"

"No. It was like this when we arrived."

Viktor and Antonia always locked that gate behind them, but that did not mean the other residents did.

"It's time you play police detective," Ivan said.

Oksana drove around the corner, stopped the car and they watched Pavlo leave. Ivan fidgeted with a small tear in the seat next to him, Oksana occasionally looking at him through the rear-view mirror. Suddenly, she started the motor.

"Here he comes."

Ivan waited until Pavlo was in the car, but he could tell the news was bad. "And?"

"Trashed. The compartment you'd fashioned in the desk? Gone. The fake identification papers for our people? Gone. Kiril Vasiliev definitely has them."

"We need to get to the Mazurs," Ivan said. "At least get Lena to Sadovyi Hai."

"Lena's due soon," Oksana reminded him. "I'd check and see whether Roman is being watched or followed. He should decide whether Lena is in danger."

Ivan gritted his teeth, but a glance from Pavlo told him his sister was right.

Oksana parked near the art studio and the men got out. Pavlo, still dressed in his police uniform, walked ahead of Ivan on the opposite side of the street. He reached into his pocket and stopped. Ivan approached the studio. He went inside. Pavlo would stand guard and only intervene if necessary.

Inside, there was the smell of clay and the sound of hammering. In the sculpture hall, someone was sanding a half-foot wooden carving. The exhibit hall was to the left and to Ivan's relief, Roman was inside, working with two other men, supervising as they hung one of the paintings. Ivan had to take in a deep breath as the workers moved aside and revealed the painting.

Antonia was depicted on a dark blue background. Her signature crown of braids with those red highlights glowed beneath filtered sunlight. The hazel eyes were alight, bringing her to life. She wore a light green dress and was posed on a settee, one arm resting across her lap, the other draped over the chair. The lightest pink orchid was pinned to her dress. A side table to her left, all the etched details included, carried a stack of books in four languages. But it was the eyes that Ivan kept coming back to.

Catching sight of him, Roman left the men to their work and came to join him. He indicated the portrait: "She had me make a miniature. For Viktor. Did she show it to you?"

Ivan shook his head.

"For a locket. A beautiful one. Gold. It was difficult to do but…" Roman looked at him meaningfully. *What was he doing here?*

"Sorry," Ivan started, and raised his voice. "I didn't mean to disturb you. I was wondering whether you had a pamphlet or a flyer for your upcoming exhibit?"

Roman checked his expression. "Certainly," he said, playing the game. "Please, follow me. How many copies do you need?"

In the small administrative office, Roman shut the door. Ivan knew his presence was creating alarm.

"Antonia?" Roman asked. "Viktor? The others were here asking about them. What's happened?"

"They've been picked up," Ivan said, and told him about the apartment.

Leaning on the desk, Roman took in a deep breath. "How much do you think Internal Affairs knows?"

"I don't. But we should get Lena to Sadovyi Hai. And yourself. If they even suspect the studio's been involved, you're going to be picked up—if they aren't already coming for you."

Down the hall, he heard Pavlo's voice. "Inspection! Who here is responsible for the building? We had a complaint about the noise from one of the neighbors."

"Jesus," Ivan breathed. "That's it. We're being followed."

He maneuvered to look out the door and saw Pavlo standing outside the sculpture hall. Two men in hats stepped past him to enter the studio. Pavlo turned to them. "Are you gentlemen responsible here?"

Ivan softly shut the door behind him. "They're here."

"Who?" Roman asked, his eyes wild.

"Vasiliev's men. Listen to me. How do I get out of here?"

Roman indicated a room off to the side. Ivan looked in. It was a kitchenette with a window facing the back courtyard. Across from it and between the narrow passage, he recognized the black GAZ parked in the street.

"Listen to me," he said to Roman. "We've practiced this. You know nothing. Absolutely nothing. I need you to go out there and present yourself. They might only take you in for questioning, all right? In the meantime, we'll get Lena and Konstantin out of the city. Now."

"No," Roman whispered, his panic barely hidden. "Leave Lena out of this. She'll know something is wrong."

"There is something wrong," Ivan hurried.

"Leave her," the artist said vehemently. He rubbed his face as if that would pull him together. "I'll be sure to do what you've prepared me for."

Ivan clasped the man's hands quickly, his last glimpse being Roman walking out of the office. He heard voices, someone asking whether he was the principal artist at the studio. They wanted to see the premises. Pavlo's voice then, "All right, but then I want to talk to Mr. Mazur about the complaint."

Ivan could not make out the rest as the Half Cossack's voice and those of the others faded.

If Ivan was right, Roman would only be questioned, but they had done everything to make sure not to leave a trace of their work in the cellar. The only thing that might have led Vasiliev's goons to the art studio in the first place could be the familial connection, a suspicion. A simple guess. Ivan prayed for the best and escaped through the window.

Back at the tavern, Oksana rested in the office. She'd been up with Pavlo the entire night. Ivan hung a sign on the door that claimed a family funeral as the reason for being closed. When the telephone rang, he snatched it up, relieved to hear Pavlo's voice on the other end.

"I'll be by in an hour."

Ivan replaced the receiver. If Pavlo had said half an hour, it would have meant Vasiliev had his claws in Roman. But one hour was what they had agreed upon if Antonia's brother-in-law was released. Then the secret police had found nothing. Except they had. A lot, if they had arrested Viktor and Antonia. It would only be a matter of time before the major would track the rest of them down.

Pavlo arrived not more than twenty minutes later. Sleepy-eyed, Oksana came out and they took a table at the back, a few Russian eggs and some *horilka* between them. They toasted, downed the shots, and Ivan leaned back. Some weeks ago, they had managed to flip a senior guard inside Prison Number One. This was Pavlo's source of information. Ivan waited as the Half Cossack downed a second shot and another egg.

"Roman's fine," Pavlo finally said. "For now. They asked very general questions. He's begged me not to say a word to Lena about it. She should not know what happened."

Ivan nodded. "All right. And Viktor? Antonia?"

"They're both there. And some of the students. Vasiliev found their articles and ordered their arrest after comparing their works."

Oksana scoffed. "Comparing their works?"

"Yeah, style of writing, something like that." Pavlo looked at them both knowingly. "I doubt that's it, though. I think September thirteenth had something to do with all this."

"Christ," Ivan said, remembering Antonia's distrust of Agent 1309. "How are they?"

Pavlo shrugged. "My mole hasn't seen either one of them. He's going to keep an eye out for me."

"Poor Viktor," Oksana said. "Kiril Vasiliev has got it in for our professor. That's what I think."

"What makes you say that?" Ivan asked.

She put a hand on his arm. "Antonia told me that he's cornered her a few times. She asked me not to tell, but you know already, don't you? It's why you told Viktor not to propose to her yet."

"And you think Vasiliev will spare her?" he asked angrily.

Oksana cocked an eyebrow. "I think he's going to use her to get to Viktor. That's what I think."

Ivan wrapped his arms around himself and hung his head. Antonia or Viktor. Tortured. They would both endure it. Even if it killed them. He sprang up and paced the floor before clapping Pavlo's shoulder. "Tell your guy in there to get to her. Let her know we're trying to find a way to get in. And then we need uniforms. We'll disguise ourselves."

Pavlo shook his head, his eyes flashing as he leapt to his feet. "Break them out right from under Kiril Vasiliev's nose?"

Oksana rose, a smile spreading across her face. "You're mad. Both of you."

"Let's do it," Pavlo said, his dimples deepening.

Ivan reached out and clasped his friend's arm to the elbow before pulling him in.

"I'm ready to die trying," Ivan said.

"Let's do it in a way so we don't have to," Pavlo said.

After Pavlo left to go back on duty, Ivan and Oksana checked themselves into a hotel on the other side of the city, just in case Vasiliev was on their trail. They had a late dinner in their room, and though his sister was asleep before her head touched the pillow, Ivan lay awake for a long time. His mind was what tossed and turned, however, tortured by images of Antonia in Kiril Vasiliev's prison cell. In Kiril Vasiliev's hands.

CHAPTER 5

June 20–30, 1941

Lviv, Western Ukraine

Three days in confinement and Antonia was doing a fine job of punishing herself. The major had practically warned her the moment they'd met. He had probably known about 1309 before he'd even arrived in Lviv. And there was nobody to blame but her weak self. The blank walls and small space within her cell at Prison Number One added to the recriminations she inflicted on her conscience.

She did not see him, but Kiril Vasiliev was there at Łącki Street. His men questioned her, and from what Antonia could put together, the focus of the investigation was Viktor and her, along with the poor students who had contributed to the paper. But Ivan's name did not come up. Nor Oksana's or Pavlo's. Nor Roman's.

On the third day, Kiril Vasiliev was nowhere to be seen when she was brought into the interrogation room, but she recognized his handiwork when she saw the photos displayed on the table. Viktor's. Two of their couriers, the forger and the four border guards who had been at the Ukrainian-Slovakian checkpoint. And her students. But still no Ivan. No Pavlo. No Oksana. Three degrees, that's what Ivan had always said. Except that each one of the people in these photos knew the rest of the group from

Sadovyi Hai. Inside, she quailed but she willed herself to sit tall, to arrange her features into a blank expression as the lock turned.

Kiril Vasiliev strode in. Hardly looking at her, he sat down, folded his finely manicured hands and pointed to Viktor's photo.

"Let's begin with his story."

Antonia did not react. She would die today. His questions rolled over her as if they were distant echoes. Kiril Vasiliev maintained control over himself. He did not get angry. He did not move. He continued asking. Over and over. She did not respond. Not one single muscle moved. Eventually, he turned to the photos of her students and replaced their university shots with new ones. She forced herself not to react to the swollen faces. The bloodied mouths. The terror in their wide eyes. She reminded herself that they had known what they were giving up by joining the Organization. She'd made sure they'd understood. Even the forger had been trained to withstand it. The couriers were old veterans of the underground trade. The four border guards. Those were Pavlo's men.

Had Pavlo ever doubted his choice of recruits?

But when Kiril Vasiliev threw down photos of Lena, Roman, even Konstantin before her, Antonia flinched. She had to fight down the scream building in her, the rage that threatened to take over.

"Your sister," the major said in that thick, rich voice. "She's due in what? Six weeks? That's what your brother-in-law told us. What we did not get from him was a satisfactory answer. How is he involved? How is your sister involved?"

Antonia gazed at him as if he were a blank page.

Vasiliev sighed and waved a finger between them. "You know, I have not hidden my… admiration from you. Ever. This could have all been very different."

The night he cornered her at a party. Another attempt, at a ballet, with Viktor sitting on one side of her and, on the other side, Vasiliev's knee and shoulder pressed against hers. Viktor had seen that. But not even the promise of giving herself to him could save her now.

"I can bring Lena in," he said. "If you prefer."

She saw a flicker of something behind his gaze, a slight change of melody at the end of his sentence. Regret? If so, she still had the power to write her own ending. He would have to feed off her first. She lifted her head, and delivered a gaze of sheer contempt.

The major shot out of his chair, unbalancing it, but the front legs landed in place with a thud. "Fine. You're heartless, I can see that. But Viktor? If there's one thing I've uncovered, it is that he is not. Not when it comes to you."

Antonia wavered but before she could collect herself, the door opened once more and Vasiliev's men descended upon her.

That night, they did not let her sleep. They knocked her senseless, doused cold water over her, used electricity. When she still did not talk, two men held her as a third ripped out one toenail after another. Antonia's throat was raw from screaming. Tears streamed down her face. She howled for God's mercy. But she did not talk. Once, she laughed, seeing herself from above, and astonished that this was what her fate was.

Her only words then were, "Let go. Let go. It's okay to die. It's okay."

Each blow they landed meant she was closer to the end.

The scent of apricots. Viktor's lock of hair that refused to stay in place. Ivan's warnings. The sound of hoofbeats, and the murmuring of women as Antonia lay on a cold hard floor. The smell of iron. Of blood. Her blood.

The dreams. The non-dreams. Muscle and sinew welded together so strongly that every movement—especially breathing—created sharp waves of pain. Time blended together. She dreamed of Lena. Then of Roman. Antonia heard Lena screaming and awoke to her own voice and raw throat. The burning pain of her toes wrenched another howl from her. She was in a cell with several other women. She felt hands on her face. Someone was putting pressure on her toes, something cool, but when the pressure was released, the darkness took Antonia again.

Something scraped against the cement floor and Antonia imagined the steel knife cutting her head clean away from her neck. She blinked awake. It was the metal door. Outside, dawn was breaking and weak light filtered through the bars of the cellar window. Two pairs of dark boots and Kiril Vasiliev's butterscotch tone ordering his men to drag her up.

Antonia whimpered. *Not again. Not again. Please no more.* But her lips were too swollen. Her throat too raw. The noise that she produced was that of a wounded animal.

She was in an interrogation room again. The guards slammed her into the chair so hard, the table shook. She blinked against the glare of the lamps, searing her raw and battered face. Her vision blurred but she recognized Kiril Vasiliev's shape standing before her. He made a satisfied noise before retreating behind the door.

A glass of water was on the table, beads gathered along the sides. Hands shaking, she reached for it and drank and groaned when she emptied it, thirstier than before. The door opened again and she turned her head. A guard walked in and set a plate of fried potatoes and sausages in front of her. She flinched as he bent and whispered into her ear.

"Hold on, *shanovna* Kozak. I'm an ally. The Cossacks know that you are here."

Antonia gasped but before she could lift her head, he was gone, the door clicking with finality. It was a hallucination. A trick. Or the secret police now knew about Ivan and Pavlo.

With a trembling hold, she took a bite of potato and imme-diately wanted to vomit. She pushed the plate away just as the door opened once more and this time she struggled to stand up. The dark hair. Eyeglasses. The beard, just a tad longer, as if to mark the passage of the days. Viktor.

They took away the glaring lamps. As they had done with her, they slammed Viktor into the chair. She saw his eyes were glassy and when a tear rolled down, she nodded stiffly.

"Good." Her voice gurgled. Her own tears in her mouth nearly choked her. "Now I know how bad it is."

Viktor bowed his head and reached across the table to grasp her hands. They were both handcuffed but hung on to one another as if the table were a life raft. Besides being affected by her appearance, Antonia could find no marks of torture.

"What's he done to you?" she asked.

Viktor lifted her hands toward her. "This. This is what he's done to me. Seeing you like this. This is the pain he wants to inflict on me."

"You can't let him. We knew going into this what it could mean for us."

Now he was crying openly. She'd never seen Viktor cry. Never.

Antonia closed her eyes. The darkness behind her lids pulled her down but Viktor's hands were gripping her, and she struggled to remain steady. She looked at him again, tried to show that she was brave, but her heart was sluggish in her chest, heavy with grief.

"I made a mistake. I shouldn't have doubted your instincts," Viktor pleaded. "You said he wasn't trustworthy and I insisted…"

He was referring to Agent 1309. Either Viktor suspected or—more likely—he'd been questioned about him, confirming that they had been betrayed.

But before she could summon the energy to take the responsibility onto her shoulders, Viktor grasped her upper arms. "They're handing me over to the Germans. Exchanging me for Soviet agents in Nazi custody."

That was why the major hadn't harmed him.

"The Germans will send you to a concentration camp, Viktor."

"Or they will have me executed."

"Then…" She hung her head. "He's letting you say goodbye to me."

From Viktor, a single sob.

They said nothing for a moment and Antonia suddenly felt there was no time left for leaving things unspoken. She chuckled softly, realizing how ridiculous it was to want to know now. What difference would it make?

"I found a ring, Viktor. Were you going to…?"

"Would you have said yes?" he asked quietly. She squeezed his hand. "Well, at least now I will not be able to make you a widow."

"Or I a widower of you," she said. "I'm going to pray for you. I know you don't believe, Viktor, but I do. I will pray that you live."

He released her and removed his glasses before rubbing his eyes. Then his hands dropped beneath the table.

"I'm taking you with me," he whispered.

Antonia held her breath. Maybe Viktor had negotiated for her. But in return for what?

Viktor shifted in his seat, looked at her meaningfully. "You never fixed the seams of my trousers."

She peered at him through swollen eyes but then remembered the tear in the waistband. When she checked beneath the table, she recognized those very same trousers. His fingers splayed across the top of them and he had a weak but conspiratorial smile.

"It cost you a fortune," he said. "That's what you said."

The locket. He was telling her he had the locket, likely hidden between the lining and the fabric. Antonia's lip quivered, her hope gone. He had no rescue plan. And the guard's whispers had truly been only a dream. She took Viktor's hands in hers again and kissed them.

The rattling of keys. That heavy door. Kiril Vasiliev swooped in with two guards.

"Frankly, Dr. Gruber," the major placed his hands heavily upon Antonia's shoulders and she winced, "I'd prefer to settle this with an old-fashioned sword fight. You lose, you die. I lose, I die. End of story. But that is no longer an option. Let's go."

No longer? What did Vasiliev mean?

One of the guards was already leading Viktor out the door. "Where are you taking him?" she cried. "Viktor! Wait!"

The other guard—was this the ally?—had her in his hold, but Kiril Vasiliev stopped him, took Antonia's chin in his fingers and turned her face.

"It's a shame," Vasiliev said. "Nobody will recognize you now."

He strode out. The guard pushed her forward but whereas Kiril Vasiliev was following the man with Viktor in one direction, the one who gripped her led her down the stairs to the holding cells. On the first landing, the guard pulled her aside and she nearly doubled over as pain wracked her body.

"The Germans have invaded," the guard whispered urgently. "Kiril Vasiliev's been called to handle security in the city."

Antonia stared at the man. "Invaded?"

The Nazis were over their borders then. If the information they'd been given was right, there would be two Ukrainian divisions fighting alongside them. It was as Ivan had foretold: Germany was about to change everything.

The news rattled her to her marrow. "When? What is happening out there?"

"I don't have the details," the guard said. "I'm taking you to your cell, and you must hold on until tonight. We'll be here tonight."

"Who are you?" she asked.

"I'm just Krit."

Krit. A mole.

There was a banging above and Viktor's voice, urgent and begging, but she could not make out his words. She whirled to face the stairwell above. All she saw were the doors to the prison yard falling closed.

"Viktor," she screamed. She tried to wrest herself away from the guard. "Viktor!"

"Stop," Krit said. "If they're going to kill him, there's nothing more you can do."

She stared at him, prepared to fight past him, but he shoved Antonia so hard she stumbled, painfully landing on her knees on the stair below. There was a brief look of compassion as Krit lifted her up, and she realized she had no choice but to trust him.

"Where are they taking him?" she pleaded.

Suddenly, a muffled popping sound outside the stairwell window. Was that gunfire?

Antonia fell against Krit, her knees buckling. "Viktor!" She sobbed and pleaded for Krit to let her go, but he dragged her down the stairs and into the corridor. Antonia was shocked into silence by the scene before her. Vasiliev's idea of handling security was to eliminate the Soviet Ukraine's enemies. Guards swarmed the corridors, gates clanged open, and keys jangled as they shouted orders over the prisoners' fearful cries. A woman howled as she was dragged out of her cell. Above, the report of gunfire again.

Krit pushed her through the chaos, as if intent to escape the scene. Before he reached the last cell, a guard called out the names of Antonia's three students. Antonia watched as Marika—bloodied and broken—was lined up against the wall with several others. But Krit shoved Antonia inside her cell before she could react to the frightened girl's face.

Throwing herself at the door as it clicked shut, Antonia shouted through the crack. "I forgot to tell him I loved him! I forgot to tell him! Please! Tell him I loved him!"

Nobody was listening. Not even the women in her cell. They were all gathered beneath the high window. Antonia slid against the door and crumpled to the ground. When she took in the other imprisoned women, they were as battered and bruised as she. More gunshots popped outside. All heads turned back to the window above them. Antonia hobbled over to the group.

"The Germans have invaded," she said desperately. But this gunfire was coming from men following Kiril Vasiliev's orders.

The women asked her what she knew. What it meant. And one replied, "It means they will kill us all. The Soviet police are making sure they will not meet any of us on the battlefield later."

Antonia faced the woman who spoke. That was exactly what Kiril Vasiliev was doing. She did not know the woman, but they gazed at one another and Antonia reached out to grip her left hand; the woman's right arm was suspended in a sling fashioned from stockings.

"I'm Kira," the stranger said. "Kira Laskava."

"Antonia," she said and stopped there.

"I know who you are."

More gunshots. When it was quiet again, another woman stepped over to Antonia and embraced her.

"How are your toes?"

Antonia looked down at the blood-soaked cloth wrapped around her feet. She had to make it until tonight. That was what the mole had said to her. "I'll be fine."

Kira began to pray and one woman after another joined her. Each one praying for her husband or loved ones.

"Please God," Antonia whispered into her folded hands. "Let him live. Let him live."

No matter how long they prayed the rosary, the executions did not stop. All day long. First, the guards called out names, and when Antonia pressed her ear up against the door once more, she could hear people shuffling up the cement stairwell. This was always followed by the report of gunfire. Then the minutes passed slowly as they waited for the next round.

When darkness fell, there was a different sound. The tinny banging of food bowls. Pressed up against the far wall, the women huddled in fear, but Antonia stood before them and tried to console them.

"They're bringing food. It's dark outside. They must be finished for the day." She bit her lip. *For the day.* And Krit had said that, tonight, they would come for her.

A moment later, a dish of bread and a bowl of water slid through the opening. The mass of women behind Antonia swelled and pushed forward, but Antonia ran to the slit, peered through it. Nobody was there except the guards she'd seen before. No Krit. No Pavlo. No Ivan. It had been a trick, then. Vasiliev was torturing her now in another way. That night was long and painful, and nobody could console her.

The next morning, Vasiliev's men continued decimating prisoners. But now there were no single shots, just bursts of semi-automatic gunfire. Antonia and Kira listened at the door together with two other women, but her hope of rescue had died. The Germans had not invaded. A Ukrainian army was not coming. Antonia's body would be piled into a mass grave along with the other prisoners.

Kira suddenly pushed away from the door, her eyes wide. "They're working along this side of the corridor."

Soon enough, names in this room would be called.

The sun had changed position by the time the guards appeared. "Nataliya Sheptovska, Domka Gora, Lara Mistetska."

Antonia realized she was digging her fingernails into her clutched hands. The three women stepped forward, heads hung. There was whimpering from the others. The one called Domka was an older woman, and she shuffled towards the door, her jaw working, but no noise came from her. Lara was a beautiful, yellow-haired woman. She could not be more than twenty years old. And Nataliya, dressed in a mulberry-colored dress that had been torn at the shoulder, cast a look toward Antonia and Kira.

"Doesn't look like the Germans are coming fast enough," she said bitterly. Antonia could not answer her.

The remaining women gathered beneath the window. Many minutes dragged by before they heard the hail of gunfire.

Vasiliev's vultures came twice more that day. But not Krit, which could only mean that he had been one of Kiril's men, planted to feed her false information. Ten women from their cell were called up. Most likely ten people from every cell had been taken. Over one hundred people in a day. There were only eight women left in Antonia's cell. And this time, no bread. No water. Kira led them into prayer again.

On the third day, it was the other side of the corridor once more. It was a cruel game. But at midday an eerie silence fell. No more footsteps, no more names called, no more gunfire. Antonia and the others became restless. It was worse than the racket that led up to the murders. Two of the women suggested they get onto each other's shoulders to look out the window.

Antonia was too broken to assist. One managed to get near the window well but all she could report seeing was the gravel of the courtyard and the brick wall across the yard. No matter which way she craned her neck, she could see nothing else.

"Hello?" Antonia called near the door. She shouted it again and again.

Then a man's voice, "Who's there?" He was in the next cell.

"Antonia Kozak," she called. "How many are there of you?"

"Two," the man said. "That's all. The other cells are empty."

That left ten of them down here. A nice round number. It had to be their day. But where were the police? Where were the guards?

"The Germans must be here," one woman surmised.

But Antonia shook her head and muttered, "There is no invasion."

"Shh," one of the women hissed.

And then the sound of crunching footsteps through the courtyard, muffled but unmistakably there. Men were coming down the stairwell, faint but real.

"They'll rape us before they release us," the woman next to Kira said.

From the cell next door, they heard the exclamations of the two men. No. They were next. Ten. Eight women plus the two men. The final round of executions.

Antonia slid against the wall, the last of her strength evaporating from her body. She curled up just as the keys slid into the lock of their cell. But Kira was trying to lift her up.

"They will not find you on your knees," she hissed.

Wincing, Antonia struggled to get up.

"Antonia," came a gruff voice. No last name. Not an order. It was a call.

Leaning between Kira and the woman next to her, Antonia straightened. At the door, a tall man and a short man. In Soviet uniform. A laugh bubbled up and then a cry of relief.

The One and a Half Cossacks had come for her.

She careened forward and into Ivan's outstretched arms.

"Is this all of you?" he asked over her head.

"Yes," Kira said behind her.

Antonia turned to the women, and with the last of her strength, gave an order: "Go. Go, now! Hurry!"

Pavlo and Ivan gripped her arms on either side and led her toward the stairwell. Krit was ahead of them with two men, likely those who'd been in the next cell.

"We haven't found Viktor," Ivan said to her.

Because he was one of the first to be executed. But she could not find her voice.

As they led her out she caught sight of an empty prison room, the walls smeared with blood. They burst out the back door and into the courtyard, heading for the gate beyond. Black smoke rose against the sky. Somewhere a fire was burning. There were gunshots ringing throughout the city. Antonia twisted and saw the stone walls along the perimeter splattered with bullet holes and blood. A pile of bodies, one on top of the other. *Viktor!* When Antonia tried to break out of Ivan's grip, he shielded her.

"We have to go, now," he urged. "If we're caught dressed like this, the Germans—or the Ukrainians—will shoot us on sight."

So there truly was an invasion. They were at war.

The last thing she saw before Ivan pulled her around the corner of the alley was Pavlo herding the other released prisoners onto a waiting prison bus. Antonia recognized Krit behind the wheel. At the end of the alley, a black car was idling at the curb. Oksana was in the driver's seat, her hair tucked beneath a Soviet beret and a uniform jacket half-opened. Ivan flung open the passenger side and helped Antonia get in.

"Get her out of here. We'll follow as soon as we can."

Antonia did not even have a chance to thank him, to beg him to look for Viktor among the dead.

Oksana shifted gears and squealed out of the alley but Antonia pressed a hand to the window, the loss of Ivan like a vacuum.

"The Soviets are fleeing the city," Oksana said. She looked twice at Antonia, and winced. "Jesus. We need to get you cleaned up. Help me, will you?"

Oksana whipped the beret off her head and shoved it beneath her seat, then began unbuttoning the jacket with one hand. Antonia helped her shrug out of it.

"Toss it out the window," Oksana said.

They were on the boulevard, passing the opera house, and Antonia stared at the barricades. Sandbags and Soviet military vehicles were abandoned along the road. The Red Army was fleeing. Oksana suddenly slammed on the brakes and then sped up again, taking a sharp left. Antonia spun to the rear window and saw the reason. A German panzer rolled past the crossing.

It took some time for Antonia to realize that Oksana was maneuvering to the Mazurs' neighborhood.

"We have to get out of the city," Oksana said. "But we're taking your sister's family with us. We need to get there before the army sets up checkpoints." She quickly looked over at her. "The Ukrainian divisions are working ahead of the Germans. And they are on a rampage."

Antonia took in a deep breath and looked questioningly at Ivan's sister.

"Banderites," Oksana confirmed. "And we don't have time to explain ourselves."

People were running in the streets. In the distance, men in German uniform were setting up a barricade at the end of the road. Oksana stopped the car, backed up, and took a side street, tossing Antonia a meaningful look.

She was able to navigate their way to the art studio. Antonia gasped. A hole had been blown in the side of the building. There was smoke spilling out of the exhibition hall where Roman's paintings had been displayed. Still she could not find her voice. Oksana stopped the car outside the Mazurs' apartment building and Antonia whimpered at the sight of Lena in the window above. A moment later, her sister waddled out, clutching Roman's arm on one side and Konstantin's hand in the other. Roman had a single suitcase and Konstantin's face was slack with shock.

Antonia twisted in the seat as Oksana sprang out and opened the back door. When Lena got in, she stared at Antonia, and burst into tears. Konstantin released a soft whimper and Roman turned the boy's face away. Only then did Antonia find her voice.

"I'm sorry! I'm sorry! I'm so sorry!"

*

In Sadovyi Hai, Oksana and Lena took turns washing Antonia's face and body. The cottage had two bedrooms. The one that she had shared with Lena growing up, and her parents' bedroom next to it. Oleh had slept in the front room, which contained two benches and a table, a sofa, and an open stove for heating and cooking. Roman was in the front room with Antonia's parents and several of the neighbors, including the Derkaches and the Kovalenkos. They were speaking excitedly as someone fiddled with a borrowed radio.

Ukraine has not died yet! Not her glory! Not her freedom!

Recognizing the Ukrainian anthem crackling through, Antonia pushed Lena's hand away and drifted into the next room.

Our enemies shall dissipate like dew in the sun. And we too shall rule the land that is our home!

"What is going on?" she asked.

Her mother waved her over. "It's the leader of the Organization of Ukrainian Nationalists, they say. They're in Lviv, at the Prosvita building."

Lena stepped out of the bedroom, her expression shocked. "Andrij Melnyk is in Lviv?"

"It can't be," Antonia said. He was in Germany, unless he'd ridden in with the invading armies or the Nazis had brought him in. Oksana took Antonia's arm, but she shook herself free as a voice came over the airwaves.

"They're introducing Yaroslav Stetsko," Roman said over the static of applause.

Antonia frowned at Oksana. "Stetsko is not one of us."

A man's voice on the radio interrupted her. "As the first assistant to the leader of the Organization of Ukrainian Nationalists, I am here to declare our country's sovereign independence!"

Now a roar in the background and Stetsko raised his voice. "We honor the Ukrainian fighters who have lain down their lives to free us of the Soviet regime. With our declaration of war, this battle will take place on Ukrainian soil for Ukraine and Ukrainians first and foremost. We will free our rich lands until we are one sovereign nation from west to east, from north to south. Each and every true patriot must now stand up and help rid our country of all its enemies. Those from outside and those from within. Especially those who have betrayed our movement!"

Antonia and Lena stared at one another. Oksana clutched the table's edge.

"But our union is only possible when Germany recognizes Ukrainian independence and recognizes this government," Stetsko cried. "Here is our proclamation!"

Antonia went to the nearest chair, dazed.

"By the will of the Ukrainian people," the imposter on the radio continued, "the Organization of Ukrainian Nationalists under the direction of Stepan Bandera proclaims the formation of the Ukrainian State—"

"No," Antonia cried. "Not Bandera!"

Everyone in the room turned to her.

"Isn't this what you all wanted?" her father asked. "Isn't this what—"

"No," she cried again.

She stared at Lena, then at Oksana. Lena's face crumpled.

"You started this," her sister whispered. "You subscribed to it. You and the Organization's rhetoric have invited the worst assault on our soil. And by our own people."

Antonia turned away from her. Bandera's second-in-command was still listing the points of their proclamation. A proclamation that Antonia and Viktor should have attended. Their words, their vision. Their determination. Under the guidance of Andrij Melnyk. Of true visionaries. Not this.

"The Ukrainian People's Army, which has been formed on our Ukrainian lands," Stetsko shouted over the waves, "will continue to fight with the Allied German Army against Muscovite occupation for a sovereign and united state, and a new order in the whole world.

"Long live the Sovereign United Ukraine! Long live the Organization of Ukrainian Nationalists! Long live our leader, Stepan Bandera! Glory to Ukraine!"

Lena knocked the doorjamb with a fist. "There you go. We're a free country now."

This was not how Antonia had imagined it. It was a fascist-inspired regime that had taken control, founded on extreme nationalism. And she, as well as the others from the underground in Sadovyi Hai, were the mortal enemies Bandera's followers would come after.

CHAPTER 6

June 30–July 2, 1941

Lviv, Western Ukraine

Ivan turned off the radio after Stetsko declared Ukraine's independence and looked out the window of Pavlo's apartment. He turned at the sound of glasses clinking together. Yes, they could both use a drink, at least to settle Ivan's stomach.

Columns of black smoke rose around the city. Lviv was on fire even though there'd been little resistance to the German invasion. On the street below, jackboots pounded the pavement and several trucks blocked the road at the crossing. The two Ukrainian divisions, Nachtigall and Roland, had sent the rest of the Soviet regiment fleeing under the shadow of the Luftwaffe. Major Kiril Vasiliev and his crew had disappeared, but that did not stop the invading military from going on a door-to-door hunt for Communists.

"I'm not returning to police headquarters," Pavlo said.

There was no need to, unless the Half Cossack wanted to be arrested. By the time they had rescued Antonia and the other prisoners, and dumped the guards' uniforms in the tavern's cellar, Ukrainian troops had blocked off and seized all major buildings and offices. The military took over the police headquarters, Prison Number One, the secret police bureau, city hall, and even the opera house. From Kościuszki Park, he and Pavlo had studied the barricade set up along the university campus. Military personnel harassed the Jewish staff and escorted the milieu of professors in handcuffs, while Gestapo carried out boxes of confiscated materials.

Ivan and Pavlo made their way back toward the tavern and found that an angry mob had gathered outside Prison Number One. Word of the mass executions had leaked out. The crowd demanded to be let in, to go look for their families and friends. The German troops sent them away and said that, until the premises had been examined, nobody would be allowed in. It took several hours before the mob dispersed, the commander in charge having promised that they could return the next day to identify the remains.

The morning after Stetsko's address, Ivan returned to the tavern to find graffiti scrawled on his walls and on those of the adjacent buildings. The neighborhood near the Golden Lion was primarily Jewish and it was swarming with Wehrmacht. Numerous trucks were parked in the middle of the streets. A crowd of bystanders were watching at the end of the road as soldiers dragged residents out of their homes. Ivan clenched his fists as he watched one soldier drag a woman out by the hair, blue and yellow ribbons fluttering on his shoulder. So this was the Ukrainian division. The woman's dress was hitched up to her waist, and she was howling like a rabbit in the fangs of a dog. Someone fired a shot and Ivan pushed to the front of the crowd, just in time to see a young man in flight, the cap tossed off his head as he fell forward, the back of his head blown open. Ivan remembered Oleh and roared, shoving his way past the barricade. Two soldiers blocked his way.

"You're no nationalists," someone cried behind Ivan. "You're all traitors. Dirty bandits! Criminals!"

One of the soldiers charged into the crowd and laid into the protestor with his truncheon. A second soldier, shorter than Ivan but just as powerful, grabbed him by the shirt and demanded to see Ivan's papers.

Ivan glared at him and pointed to the trucks. An entire family—three generations—were loaded into the back like goods for delivery.

"Are you doing the Nazis' dirty work now?" he challenged. "Where are you taking these people?"

The soldier who'd demanded his papers tightened his grip on Ivan and sneered. "Communists and Jews. Most are one and the same. You got a problem with that? We're deporting them, like we should've done years ago. Now give me your identity papers."

Ivan growled but withdrew his documents.

We started this, he thought. *And we should have stopped Bandera sooner.*

Back when the Organization had been founded, long before he was a member, the statutes said no foreign entities would infiltrate the Organization. But by the time he and Pavlo were running the cadre, Melnyk had introduced a more tolerant vision. That did not mean anti-Semitism had ceased to exist within the group. It did. Antonia had worked tirelessly to help their faction bury its prejudices.

The soldier seemed disappointed when he handed back Ivan's papers. He barred the way again. "Go back to where you belong and leave us to it."

Ivan returned to the tavern just as another truck rolled past, stuffed with hungry-eyed Ukrainian soldiers. The blue and yellow ribbons pinned to their uniforms made him recoil once more. They were supposed to be an army that would free Ukraine, not terrorize its citizens just like the Soviets had.

From around the corner, Pavlo appeared and immediately urged Ivan inside.

"Did you see what they're doing down the street?" Ivan asked him.

Pavlo's face was dark, and it was not from the lack of light.

"Bandera's men will come hunting for his enemies," Pavlo said ominously. "They'll get rid of us the same way. We're not safe here. It's time to go underground."

Ivan scowled and punched the wall of rough brick. The sting-ing felt good as he shook out his hand. He swung back to Pavlo. "What's the word from the prison?"

"The Germans are opening it up to the public today." Pavlo looked at the clock above the bar. "In thirty minutes. But I can't go with you. I might be recognized."

Ivan nodded. "What about the provincial prisons?"

"I'll wait to hear from you. If you don't find Viktor, I'll start searching the other prisons. But you need to get back to Sadovyi Hai. Lay low."

Ivan did not hesitate. He gave Pavlo the keys to the tavern and made his way to Łącki Street. The crowd had gathered in front of the prison again. A half-dozen or so German guards were keeping them at bay.

Among the crowd, Ivan recognized one of the women who'd been in Antonia's cell. Her hands were bandaged, and she wore a cast on her right arm. She recognized him and introduced herself as Kira Laskava.

"This is my mother-in-law," she said, grasping an old woman's arm with her left hand. "Mother, this is one of the men who released us from the prison."

The old woman wiped her eyes and began thanking him. "My son. Do you know where my son is? Did you see him in there?"

Ivan put a finger to his lips. The last thing he needed was for anyone to think he'd been a real Soviet prison guard. Kira seemed to understand and she whispered into the older woman's ear.

The crowd suddenly surged forward as a German commander stepped out onto the top landing. A Ukrainian soldier stood next to him and it was he who spoke.

"The prison yard currently contains three hundred and twenty-two corpses. Ten people will be allowed to go in at a time. Anyone who can help with identifying the bodies. We ask you to register the names of those you are looking for first, and each group will have thirty minutes to examine the victims. Please report any identified bodies to the administrators located inside. If you are not able to find the ones you are looking for here, we have identified several provincial prisons where…" The man swallowed, before solemnly adding, "Where thousands more have been found."

The crowd gasped. Kira's mother-in-law moaned and cried into her hands.

Men began shouting. "Soviet swine!"

"Kill them all!"

The German commander's mouth flicked upwards for a second.

"I'm warning you, it will not be easy to find your families," the Ukrainian soldier continued. "In those other prisons, the Soviets murdered the inmates by tossing grenades into the cells. But we have recovered lists of names, and if you are unable to find your loved ones here, we will make those lists available to you."

Ivan chewed on the inside of his cheek and exchanged a look with Kira, but tears were streaming down her face freely now.

As if to spare her mother-in-law, she turned her head to Ivan and whispered, "He's gone. My husband is gone. They all are. If it hadn't been for you…"

"As for personal effects," the Ukrainian soldier called over the crowd, "they can be retrieved in the office upstairs. If we have a record of the items you are looking for, we will provide you with a receipt to claim them. Please consider what personal effects the victims"—he stressed the word—"might have had on them."

Ivan had to wait over two and a half hours before he was allowed in. By that time the wailing and the weeping had reached a crescendo behind the wall, and anger boiled over in the crowd. Neighbors and friends called to one another. A fight broke out between two families, accusations flying, sharp as knives. Another group prayed together. Everyone repeated curses against the Soviets. When it was time, Ivan took his place in line before a table to make his report.

"Dr. Viktor Gruber, professor at the university in Lviv."

"Age?"

"Thirty-four."

"Residence?"

Ivan gave the address. The policeman nodded but Ivan was studying him, memorizing his face, determining whether this man was friend or foe.

"We have a Dr. Viktor Gruber listed here. Are you family?"

"Friend."

"Any personal effects he might have had on him when he was incarcerated?"

Ivan had been thinking about it. "Possibly a gold locket. With a painting inside. Of a woman. Hand-painted. Cinnamon hair. Green eyes."

The soldier looked at him and Ivan realized how he must have sounded.

"There are personal effects for Dr. Gruber indeed listed. You'll go to the second floor of the building. Are there any family members here who can vouch for him?"

Ivan shook his head. "He's from Austria. His family is from Austria. My… sister. The one in the locket. She is his fiancée."

The policeman looked up. That one expression gave Ivan the final clue. Nobody had survived that prison. Not a single person other than those he and Pavlo had released.

"Was his fiancée," Ivan corrected.

Ivan entered the gate into the prison yard. The view that met him nearly made his knees buckle. One corpse after another was lined up in neat rows in the yard like some macabre exhibit. Family members were bent over loved ones, weeping. A priest swung a thurible over a dead woman with yellow hair. Another one next to her was wearing a violet dress. Women and men were half bent as they walked up and down the rows, their hands folded together, as if begging God not to reveal their loved one among those lying on the ground.

Ivan began the awful procession. One body after the other, some twisted from the wounds inflicted on them, others from when rigor mortis set in. He recognized those that had been bludgeoned. Stabbed by bayonet. Shot. Tortured. Expressions that revealed frozen shock, despair. Pain. Every single body looked broken. Every man and woman presented in that yard stoked Ivan's anger, his shock, his grief. He'd fled the prison with the women with hardly a glance at the dead strewn in the yard, but seeing them arranged like this—in neatly administered numbers and for this grotesque viewing—Ivan felt his insides clench again and again.

Three hundred and twenty-two bodies. He recognized their people. Wept over the students. Groaned over the couriers. But none of the victims in the yard were Viktor. Ivan wiped his face when what he really wanted to do was punch someone, kill someone. More specifically, he wanted to hunt down Major Kiril Vasiliev.

He found Kira kneeling next to her mother-in-law, the old woman spread over a young man as if to protect him from any further blows. They keened and prayed, the priest now with them. Ivan turned his head away to avoid intruding on their grief.

On the third floor, he took the receipt he'd received and stood at the table. There were angry discussions and Ivan only half listened. He handed over his receipt. Another Ukrainian dressed in Wehrmacht uniform took it from him.

"It's a gold locket," Ivan said. He muttered the details like a mantra. "Gold chain. A painting of a woman. Hand-painted. Cinnamon hair. Green eyes. Gold. A locket."

They gave him an envelope. A belt. Some change. A couple of banknotes. A tie. The gold locket. He pressed the envelope shut and walked out.

It was early afternoon before he returned to the tavern and dropped the envelope on the bar before Pavlo. "I didn't find him."

Pavlo looked inside. "This is standard procedure. They would have taken his things in when they arrested him. It means nothing. There are still the smaller prisons in the province."

"They threw grenades into the cells," Ivan said flatly.

Pavlo stared at him. "All of them?"

Ivan shrugged. "Some are saying they've already been to check. The Germans didn't take control of the provincial prisons until later. Thousands dead, Pavlo. But even harder to identify." He choked and covered his face. "Because they threw grenades into the cells."

"All right. All right."

He allowed Pavlo to lead him to a stool.

Ivan could not stop shaking and even when he heard the glassware, the muted pop of the stopper of a *horilka* bottle, heard the Half Cossack returning to the table and pulling out the chair, and pouring the liquid, still Ivan did not leave the darkness and space of his cupped hands.

Pavlo was silent. Ivan breathed heavily, the warmth and damp on his palms somehow calming. When he wiped his face dry and looked up at Pavlo, the Half Cossack had a determined expression.

"I'll go to every prison and keep looking. All right?"

Ivan stared mutely at the shot glasses, picked one up and downed it.

Pavlo poured again. "And you're going back to Sadovyi Hai. But don't tell Antonia anything. Just wait until I've checked them all. Wait until I get back. All right? There's still hope."

Ivan looked at him and Pavlo raised his eyebrows, then his glass.

"There's always hope," his friend repeated.

Ivan drank and glanced at the envelope still lying open on the bar. He rose, spilled the contents out and stuffed the locket into his pocket.

The next afternoon, he was at the Kozaks' cottage in Sadovyi Hai. He didn't have time to knock before Antonia—her cuts and bruises on her face in a variety of blues and purples and yellows—stepped out. Behind her, on the far wall of the cottage, was the portrait of Oleh hanging with an embroidered *rushnyk* around the frame. Ivan gazed down on Antonia, her eyes unmasked like he'd never seen before.

Tell me. Just tell me. Please, just tell me.

Ivan took her hand in his, pressed the locket into it and drew his arms around her.

CHAPTER 7

July 2–August 31, 1941

Sadovyi Hai, Western Ukraine

The locket didn't make sense. He'd had it on him. That's what he had told her. He'd had it on him when Kiril Vasiliev had dragged him out of the interrogation room. So how did it end up in the envelope of personal effects?

There was only one answer. Viktor had not been shot at Prison Number One.

Antonia met Pavlo at a prison in Sambir some thirty kilometers from Sadovyi Hai, and her hopes rose when he told her that many of those in Lviv had been transported on the same day as the invasion to Sambir, but at the scene before her, she fell to her knees amongst the others who were weeping and grieving. There was no hope in finding Viktor among the carnage here.

The prison yard was filled with locals and those who'd managed to travel from the surrounding cities and provinces. Every church was filled. Fights broke out. People marched in the streets of the villages and towns, cursing the Soviets and demanding the Ukrainian-German divisions bring them to justice. All along their routes, the Wehrmacht and SS lined up with impassive expressions. It chilled Antonia. Something was not right.

After four prison visits, there was no sign of Viktor among the dead, many of whom could not even be identified. By the time she returned to Sadovyi Hai, and it was clear that Viktor had not shown up there either, the slimmest thread of hope Antonia had left snapped in two and let her fall.

It was two weeks after she had escaped Number One that Lena came to her room. Antonia lay in her bed, staring at the familiar cracks and stains on the plaster ceiling. Outside, the sun shone brightly, a breeze moved the curtains, as if the summer had nothing better to do. Her sister rubbed her sides, her belly high. Konstantin was babbling in the background with his grandparents.

"I need to get back to the city," Lena said. "I don't want to give birth in the village here. But we'll come back, if we must. Or you could—"

Antonia looked at her sharply, then back at the ceiling.

"No." Lena sighed. "You're right. The arrests. Bandera…"

Antonia propped herself on her elbows and looked out the window. The orchard sloped down toward the valley, the woods beyond that, and then the mountains.

"It was too high of a price to pay," she whispered.

Lena perched on the bed opposite Antonia. "You mean Viktor."

"Everything. I can't believe he's gone."

"What does your heart say?"

Antonia looked at her, waiting. "I can't hear my heart."

"What does your head say?"

Antonia suddenly burst into tears. She curled up and lay in Lena's lap, sobbing. "Viktor is dead!"

Lena stroked her hair and murmured. "That was your heart, dear sister. That was your heart."

That evening, Antonia tried to talk her sister out of returning to Lviv, but Roman was also anxious to get back, to assess the damages to his paintings and to the studio.

As the shadows lengthened, Ivan returned to their cottage. She went outside and he followed her down into the orchards, silent. It was not until they were at the creek that she finally spoke.

"Lena wants me to go back to Lviv."

"You can't return to the university," he said. "They've arrested nearly everyone on the staff."

Antonia folded her hands behind her, maintaining the distance between them. He yanked up a long stalk of grass. They stopped beneath the shade of a cherry tree, three deer bounding across the meadow and into the woods. The sky was a dark blue-gray and thunder rumbled. He pulled two or three cherry stems off the tree and offered her the fruit. She declined.

"How many?" she asked.

Ivan took in a breath. His brown eyes were darkened with sadness. "Sixteen professors taken in. None seen since. Dr. Bodnar was with them."

She nodded and pinched the bridge of her nose. "What else do you know?"

"You're not on any list. Yet."

"Yet. But there's a record of my incarceration at Number One." She looked at him.

"Lay low," he suggested.

"Lay low," she mocked. "And you don't think they know I'm in Sadovyi Hai?"

"Of course they do. But Antonia, you established a good network, on all sides. That was your strength. You knew everyone, at every level."

"So did Viktor," she snapped. "That didn't save him, did it?"

Ivan rolled his head and turned to the creek. She stepped beside him. Right in front of her was the flat boulder where Oleh used to play. Where she and Lena used to listen to their brother while they lazily traced the water with bare feet, singing with him.

"Antonia, I'm sorry."

She gazed up at him. He had always been able to read her thoughts. "You saved my life. Don't say you're sorry."

He rubbed his reddish-blond mustache, his eyes on the locket around her neck. "I didn't save his."

A noise escaped from the back of her throat, not unlike a whimper.

"Antonia, we need to somehow negotiate with Bandera's administration."

"The Banderites," she scowled, "want to conquer. We wanted to liberate. That's the difference. We are under the wrong regime. I'm not negotiating with terrorists."

Ivan scuffed the earth. "I still believe in what we set out to do. Don't you?"

"Freeing Ukraine has been too heavy a price, one that I am no longer willing to continue paying."

Someone whistled in the distance. In the yard of her family's cottage, Pavlo was waving his arms wildly.

"There's news," Antonia said. She sprinted, nearly choking on the surging hope. Ivan was on her heels. When she reached the top, Pavlo caught her.

"Viktor?" she begged.

But Pavlo held out a newspaper and Ivan snatched it from him.

"I picked that up at the post," he said. "Everyone's talking about it."

She maneuvered to see the headline, her blood chilling. "Stetsko, in Lviv. Bandera, in Poland. All of them. The Germans have arrested the entire administration."

She took the newspaper from Ivan.

"The Germans wanted Bandera's men to rescind the proclamation," Pavlo said. "And they refused. The Gestapo came down on them and now—"

"The Nazis are creating a protectorate," Antonia said. Their supposed independence had not even lasted a full two weeks. She crushed the paper between her hands. "And they expect us to fight the Soviets under Hitler's command."

*

A thick wall was settling around the province in the form of gray-uniformed soldiers as the Wehrmacht, then the Gestapo, rolled into Truskavets, into Drohobych, and even appeared in Sadovyi Hai to patrol the area. The German language seeped into the administrative offices, into the post office, into the signs and posters and announcements and flyers, and onto the radio. The new governor—a German—made it clear that Hitler's armies were here to stay, and he expected the Ukrainians to assist in purging the Communists, the Jews, and anyone else considered a traitor to the Third Reich—and that meant the *Slavs* who did not cooperate.

Lena postponed returning to Lviv until Roman had investigated the situation. He wrote to say a few of his paintings were salvageable but the rest were gone. As if to compensate, he made a few minor renovations to the apartment before sending for Lena, and none too soon. She gave birth to a boy just a few days later.

Antonia took the bus to Truskavets with Ivan, Pavlo and Oksana in order to pick up supplies and to get messages to and from the couriers they had running again. As they neared the main square, the bus was rerouted to another street and stopped at one of the smaller city parks.

"There's another parade on," the bus driver announced.

Backtracking to the main square, Antonia and the others landed in the midst of the parade. German panzers, military vehicles, and soldiers filled the air with their war-drum cadence as they swarmed the streets. Swastikas and banners stretched between the buildings and over the passageways, some depicting the Führer, and the regime's stomach-curdling symbols. This was not the blue of the sky and the gold of Ukraine's rich fields, Antonia thought. Not the moon. Not the sun. This red, this black—it was death. The seal of Perun—of lightning, of thunder, of blood. Of dark nights to come.

Antonia stopped Ivan as they reached the square. An entire ensemble of Ukrainian women was dancing on a stage set up in the middle, their smiles bright, their heads adorned with *vinky* and colored ribbons fluttering as they spun. Men in *sharovary* were dancing the Hopak as the women encircled them, arms entwined, their smiles all alike, their beaming welcoming faces aimed at the enormous audience of Germans. When the dance was finished, three women approached a German delegation on the stage with a tray.

"With this presentation of salt and bread," a Ukrainian man at the microphone said, "we welcome the German Army, our salvation, our liberators of the Soviet regime!"

The crowd cheered. Antonia looked around her, dread squeezing her chest. A group of women were gathered together nearby.

"Why are you clapping and cheering?" she asked them.

One woman scoffed. "Did you see what the Soviet swine left behind? Our dead?"

"Our best hope is that the Wehrmacht does the job for us," another woman cried as she clapped. "Destroy the Soviets. That's what the Germans are here for. To help us."

Except they were not. They were not allowing the Ukrainians to determine their own fates against Stalin. Antonia studied the crowd around her, taking in their euphoric and angry expressions. Strange how cheering in ecstasy appeared to use the exact same muscles as were required to scream in fury.

With the uncertainties ahead of them, Ivan and Pavlo both gave up on Lviv and stayed in the village, but with hiding places nearby. In August, Antonia was in the orchards, helping to dry the late apricots, Oksana working next to her. They pitted the fruit, then dropped them into the big kettle over the fire to blanch them. She and Antonia took turns arranging the batches onto the drying trays.

"The German Ministry of Education reviewed my application last week," Oksana suddenly said.

Antonia put her hands on her hips. "And?"

Oksana tented a tray with cheesecloth to protect the fruit from insects. She fitted them out onto the frames in the sun before answering. "I'm young. Clean. No record. They've hired me. Did you manage new identity papers?"

Antonia nodded. "Father Bohdan helped retrieve my documents." She had not dared to return to Lviv. With administrators constantly being ousted and replaced, the village priest had taken advantage of the confusion and used a forged death certificate to claim her personal effects.

Stretching her back, she wiped the sweat off her brow then loosened the light scarf at her throat. It was a humid day in the valley. She saw that Ivan and Pavlo had taken off their shirts, their backs glistening in the sunlight. Her throat tickled and she coughed then pointed at the men.

"Those two are a pair, aren't they?"

"One and a Half Cossacks." Oksana chuckled. "Are you all right?"

"I'm fine. I just need some water."

They went to the table and Oksana poured them two glasses.

"What about the manifesto, Antonia?"

"Gone. It's gone." Like Viktor. Like everything. Everything Antonia had ever worked for was gone. She felt the familiar rising tide of grief.

"Ivan and Pavlo want to start over."

"With what, for heaven's sake?" Antonia asked. And what for? All their dreams were dead.

Oksana reached over and put a hand on Antonia's arm. "They're looking for a language teacher."

"Who?"

"The school in Dolyna."

"Your school?"

Oksana tugged the headscarf off her head, the waves bouncing as if relieved to finally be set free. "You could apply. The town has me in a lodge. I'd hate to be alone."

"German?"

"Yes. They need a German teacher. I thought of you right away, but I didn't know how… How to ask you."

Antonia sighed. "The Nazis won't want me to teach any more German than is required to read their orders and their signs."

Oksana cocked an eyebrow at her. "It's a job. In a quiet place. It might be… I don't know. Provide you with the room and time to think. To recoup?"

Antonia stared at her for a moment, then looked back up at the cottage where her parents were working hard. Two of the neighbors were helping to haul in the trees they'd felled earlier in the week. The *kolkhoz* was nothing for her. It had never been. Since the Soviets, it had been a silent agreement in the family that all the children were to disperse and be something other than farmers: Oleh, a musician. Lena, a writer, and she was so much more. Antonia, the academic. That's what they had worked for, her parents. That's what they had slaved for.

Antonia studied Ivan's sister. "He wants you to start a new cell in Dolyna, doesn't he?"

Oksana rubbed her nose and sniffed, then swatted at an insect. "Nothing's set yet. It's only an idea."

Antonia picked up an apricot she had sliced in half and used the paring knife to eject the pit. She inhaled the fruit then popped it into her mouth. She loved this land. She loved her country. But the fact of the matter was, she had no direction. Bless Oksana for trying to give her one.

When Antonia looked back, she saw Ivan striding toward them, mopping himself up with his tunic and then wrapping it around his head. His body was lean and muscular. He had to duck beneath the branches of the younger trees. His trousers were rolled up to almost the knees. He stopped at the table and took a swig of water straight from the jug, then wiped his arm across his mouth. He belched and smiled.

It was that smile. The one he reserved for only her. And it hurt to see it. Everything hurt now.

But when the smile faded, when Ivan looked over Antonia and up to the ridge, to her parents' cottage, Antonia whirled around. Her parents and the two neighbors had stopped working and were slowly walking over to men on motorcycles. Wehrmacht. Antonia turned back to Ivan. Pavlo was heading over, also looking up. Antonia stood before them both, pulling Oksana to block the view of the men as much as possible. They waited for a few terrible moments as the men on the motorcycles talked with the group above. But then the soldiers put their helmets back on, straddled their vehicles and drove away.

Not Banderites on the hunt then. But Wehrmacht was also no good.

Someone was calling Pavlo now. It was his father. He was hurrying toward them across the orchard, his expression one of sheer horror beneath a straw hat. Ivan and Pavlo met him halfway, and by the time Antonia had reached them with Oksana, Pavlo was unsealing a brown envelope. He unfolded the page. An eagle stamped on top. German. Grim, he crushed the page against his chest.

"Conscription," Pavlo said. His dimples were deep, his eyes dangerous slits. He faced the woods where the loggers were. "My brother is to report tomorrow."

"No," Antonia choked.

"We have to get him hidden," Pavlo said as if to comfort his father. "And if we hide him then…"

Ivan was shaking his head. "This is it."

"What is?" Antonia said.

He took two steps to her and grasped her upper arms. "Pavlo. Me. Everyone. We're going underground. Permanently."

"No."

"When I say everyone, I mean you, too."

"No." Antonia looked over to Oksana. "She isn't going with you. And your sister shouldn't have to do what the Organization expects—what you want from her—alone. I'm going with her."

"Antonia…"

It was that tortured look again. That longing. She could not stand it. Because she could not relieve it. He bent over her, so close, she could feel his breath on her cheek.

"It's an order," he said gruffly.

His grasp grew tighter and she gazed at him defiantly. It took all she had not to sway.

His hold finally relaxed. "I have failed you one too many times, haven't I?"

How was it possible for her heart to break so often in so many months? "Your wordsmith does not have the words for what is happening to her right now. But I do know this. Losing all of you? It's too much, Ivan."

There was a spark in his eyes—hope—but she wrenched herself from his hold and stepped to Oksana. "Tell your school council I'd be interested in that position."

She felt Ivan pull away from them, and when she dared to look, the sound of logging ceased and the forest was already swallowing up the One and a Half Cossacks.

PART TWO

1943–1944

Western Ukraine—
Carpathian Region—Slovakia

CHAPTER 8

Summer 1943

General Government of Galicia, Ukraine

A red kite called above Ivan's head as he steered the dappled gray mare into the valley of Dolyna. In the late summer dusk, the River Prut tumbled over boulder and bedrock. Ivan stopped for a moment to view the lay of the land from a hill. Like most mountain settlements, Dolyna's residents lived scattered about in the valley, marking off their properties and gardens with picket fences. Fields and meadows radiated up the slopes like a patched quilt lifted in the breeze. In the center of it rose a two-and-a-half-story wooden lodge—a villa from the days when the Austro-Hungarian Kaiser came for his hunting holidays. It belonged to the district now and housed the local schoolteachers. Four intricately latticed gables rose above the trees. A long alley of oak and maple led to the house, and the back opened onto a field of sunflowers. The Prut ran alongside the property, and a bridge led to the Hutsul-styled church that now rang its bells, signaling the end of evening vespers.

Maya followed the path down into the valley, but Ivan had to quickly pull her back. In the distance below him, a black sedan was turning into the villa's drive. It pulled up before the house and he recognized Oksana bouncing out onto the veranda, her hair loose. A Wehrmacht soldier and a man in a brown uniform—had to be a commander—followed Oksana into the house. She paused and threw an arm around the soldier.

"So, so," Ivan muttered. "This is what you do when I'm not around."

He kicked Maya into motion and steered the horse to follow the far riverbank. He reached the back of the lodge without being noticed. The veranda overlooked a vegetable patch and bushes of hydrangeas and roses. The sun was dropping between the dark green peaks. Crickets chirped in the coming dusk and the kite screeched once more, still suspended in the sky.

Ivan dismounted the horse and let her graze before walking around to the south side of the house. Beaded lengths of string hung before an open kitchen door. Antonia was in the middle of the room, a bread knife in hand. She was thinner. She coughed over her shoulder before gathering up slices of bread and putting them into a basket, then carried a tray out of the kitchen. Ivan took a step back. To the right of the kitchen was a large picture window and one of those Germans and his sister passed by it. A Hutsulian wool blanket hung on the far wall and gay music played. Then laughter. The top of Antonia's head briefly appeared before she returned to the kitchen.

She stopped and looked directly at him. Ivan's heart tumbled. Antonia removed her apron, and ducked through the strings of beads.

"This is unexpected."

"I came to see Oksana. And you, of course. To see how you were managing."

She threw a glance in the direction of the other room. His sister appeared in the window, her head tossed back in carefree laughter.

"What's going on in there?" he accused.

Antonia was down the steps in a flash and dragged him by the elbow to the back of the house. She shooed the horse away from the edge of the vegetable patch, then brushed her brow with a forearm.

"I need to speak to you," she said. "And then I want you to lead your horse to the front and pretend like you've just arrived, not like a thief or a partisan in the night."

"Why?" Ivan asked.

"Because our friends in there are nervous."

"You don't say." He crossed his arms. "I can't go in there. What if they ask why I haven't been conscripted?"

"Do you have your identification papers? Permission to travel?"

"I do. The permission is forged but a good one."

"Just follow our lead. They won't harass you."

He scoffed. "I can only imagine. Do I need to limp or something? Which leg?"

Antonia coughed and he reached to help her, but she shook him off, catching her breath again. "I'm going to tell you something and I want you to promise you won't get angry."

"Why haven't you taken care of that, yet?" He indicated her throat.

She ignored him. "This little area here? Oksana and I are surrounded by Bandera's supporters. And many of them have broken with the Organization entirely."

"It's one of the reasons I came. This Ukrainian Partisan Army under Bandera's command is out of control, and our people are running scared. We're having a hell of a time keeping ourselves organized. Pavlo and I have been lying low in Sadovyi Hai. But last week his parents' barn was set on fire."

Antonia gasped.

"Two days later, two of our people in Truskavets were found strung up in the forest." Ivan breathed in deeply, unable to shake the images of those men.

Antonia wrapped her arms around herself and stared angrily at the setting sun.

"Who are the Germans in the house?" Ivan asked.

"Protection," she said drily. "And a show of cooperation."

He looked at her, astounded. She had made such protests about collaborating and now this.

"Because we've been hiding members of our own faction here at the lodge," she explained. "Oksana and I offer refuge from the Partisan Army, then invite the Germans in order to put on a friendly face so the Gestapo will leave us alone."

"What is going on, Antonia?"

"Bandera's supporters are forcing us to put on this little show."

He pointed to the house, indignant. "Is that a show? My sister with that German soldier? What does that have to do with the other faction's renegades?"

Antonia's expression went slack. "No, Ivan, that's not a show. That is real. Oksana is in love."

He kicked at the grass and swore, then turned back to her. "How can you—"

"Stop being a dolt and listen to me. The Partisan Army decided to take the law into their own hands. You know how they are raiding Polish settlements, right?"

Ivan nodded. "And our people."

"Our people. Communists. Jews. Germans," she said impatiently. "Everyone who doesn't follow them. Right. But the Germans are scrambling to keep up. So, they send out squads in reprisal. None of us are safe because of this damned faction. Listen, Oksana and I have talked to the governor about countering that."

"How?"

"By organizing people loyal to Melnyk into an officially recognized policing unit. Get you all above ground again."

Ivan took in a sharp breath. It was a great idea, but he was grim. "What the hell has gotten into Oksana?"

"Your sister was harassed and threatened by some of Bandera's renegades."

He stepped back and folded his arms. "Explain."

"We were at a school festival in the next village," Antonia started, her voice low. "Oksana and one of the student's mothers had a real fall out. The mother accused Oksana of being a traitor. Next day, she showed up with her husband and his two brothers, and they harangued Oksana all the way home, telling her she better not fall asleep because the Konopliv clan was coming to get her. They threatened to hang her, Ivan."

He growled and turned the corner, but Antonia quickly pulled him back into the garden.

"It just so happens that the governor, who's in that sitting room right now," she said, "came along the road with his soldiers. Johan stepped in for Oksana and from there, well…"

Ivan scoffed. "How romantic."

"He cares for her, Ivan," she said tersely. "And he protects her."

"My sister." Ivan scratched the back of his neck. The mountains were turning a rich, dark blue in the dusk. "She's never needed protection."

"She does now," Antonia warned. "And that's your excuse as to why you're here today."

He stared at her, her features softening in the fading light. "What about you? Who's protecting you?"

"Oksana, of course." Antonia chuckled softly at her own joke.

"This idea of transforming our faction into a policing unit…" Ivan scuffed the ground with his boot again. "It's a good idea, Antonia."

"Governor Lasch says he would support it. The trouble is…" She sighed.

Ivan waited.

"Berlin doesn't want any foreign legions."

"What if Pavlo and I organize something? Can Lasch get us a meeting with the administration in Lviv?"

Antonia tilted her head. "At least with the administration in Truskavets, to start."

"Then introduce them to me."

She took that as an order, judging by how swiftly she moved, but Ivan halted her. "The command on the outside asked about you. They want to know whether you're redrafting the manifesto, whether you can get the newspaper started again. We need to reorganize and take action."

Antonia's laugh was strained. "Ivan, really? The manifesto? We're at war, with no end in sight. And the Organization is scattered all over the place. But yes, maybe the newspaper. I can imagine we could, but not yet. It's still too risky."

She meant her heart was still broken over Viktor.

"Lena is coming with the children tomorrow," she said. "Maybe for the summer. Just… Give me some time."

Antonia reached for Maya's reins and he followed her to the front of the house. The black sedan was parked in the drive. There were six birches in the middle of the front yard and a stone well. The German commander peered out the window as Ivan paused with Antonia beneath the trees.

She brushed a hand over the dappled mare's neck and indicated the house. "Go on, I'll put Maya in the neighbor's stables." She swung into the saddle. "I'm very glad to see you, Ivan."

He watched her ride away then found Oksana already waiting for him. She was wearing a dress with a red-and-black embroidered collar.

She smiled widely as he took the steps up the veranda. Her eyes were however filled with apprehension as he reached out to embrace her. He kissed the top of her head before whispering, "Antonia told me about him. Johan?"

His sister looked relieved. "He's a good man. I want you to meet him. But what are you doing here?"

"I heard you needed protecting."

Oksana nodded cautiously, her face rippling with emotion. "It's a good cover," she whispered, "and I'll explain it all later."

Ivan stepped into the large foyer of the lodge. A wooden staircase led to the second floor. To his right was a dining room and adjoining sitting room. The kitchen was off to the left, and the Germans were in the expansive parlor, with slices of goat cheese and bread lain out on the table. They rose when he walked in and greeted him politely, but Ivan sensed a mutual caution beneath the layers of courtesy.

She introduced the governor first—Hans Lasch, who saluted Ivan with a *Heil Hitler!* Ivan weakly raised his hand in return. The love interest was Johan Frank.

"The Cossack." The young man offered his hand instead of the salute. "Your sister has told me a lot about you."

In Ukrainian, Oksana muttered, "Only the least interesting things."

Ivan gripped hard, taking pleasure in the slight wince of the baby-faced German. They could ask for his identification papers, question why he was here. Why he was not on the front, anything that could land him in one of their detention centers, but to his relief neither did and he had to admit that maybe the women did have a good handle on things.

He turned back to Oksana.

"Why don't you show me to my room," he said. He steered her back into the hallway and nudged her up the stairs.

"You're not going to be a bully brother now, are you?" she tossed over her shoulder.

"I'm only here for the week. What you do with the rest of your time, I don't care."

It was not true, but he would wait until the Germans were gone to make his point. It did no good to admonish Oksana publicly. He'd learned that the hard way.

In a room overlooking the sunflower field, he dropped his bundle onto the bed. There were three mattresses set next to one another in a wooden frame.

Oksana picked at the collar of his embroidered shirt. "I think Johan might be intimidated by you."

Ivan grabbed her into a bear hug, unsmiling. "Let's keep it that way."

She kicked her way out, and smoothed her hair.

"What's this I hear about a run-in with some Banderites?" he said.

"The Ukrainian Partisan Army here is a mean bunch," Oksana whispered soberly. Below them, the door banged shut. Antonia had to be back. "Just wait until Lasch and Johan are gone. They've only dropped by."

Ivan pointed toward the corridor. He kept his tone casual. "Has she got one of those German boyfriends as well? That governor, perhaps?"

Oksana's eyebrows shot up in surprise. "Antonia? Are you joking? I will say this, they do have great respect for her. Lasch especially."

Ivan grunted. "She's too thin."

Oksana pursed her lips. "She doesn't trust any of the quacks around here. She was planning to go to Lviv to take care of her thyroid, but now Lena and the children are coming here."

"Antonia thinks all doctors are quacks. She's just making excuses."

He slipped off his shirt and Oksana's gaze landed on the scar on his right shoulder.

"The one who did that to you was a quack." With a tilt of her head, she left and went back down the stairs.

Ivan smirked. In the mirror of the dresser, he examined and touched the scar, wincing at the memory of the hot iron on his skin. Old remedies in a new age. He shook his head and put on a fresh tunic. As he reached the bottom of the stairs, the Germans were heading to the door.

"So soon, Governor?" Ivan asked.

Lasch shook his hand this time as well. "We only came to check on the women, brought some cheese. Duty calls, however."

Reprisals to carry out? Jews to deport?

Ivan watched Oksana escort Johan to the sedan. She kissed his cheek, then unwound herself from the German as the men took their leave.

Antonia turned on the lamp on the foyer table and stood with Ivan in the doorway. "Well," she said. "Have you had anything to eat?"

He had not. He followed her into the parlor and helped himself to a slice of bread and goat cheese. Above the large hearth, which was open to both the kitchen and the sitting room, hung several boiled deer skulls—one a twelve-point buck. There was a clock on the mantel. Scattered on the wooden floor were colorful wool kilims. The furniture was made of heavy wood, the upholstery draped in sheepskins.

Oksana returned with a plate of pickled herring and poured him a *kvass*, then threw herself into an armchair. "All right. You have something to say, I can tell."

Ivan shrugged. "I don't like him."

"Of course you don't. He's German, and the Germans have disappointed us."

"He is a good man," Antonia said again. "Very polite. Very proper."

"Very German," Ivan said, raising his mug to her. He took a good swallow of the *kvass*. "You want me to remind you of the rumors we've heard about their camps? What they're doing to the Jews? What they made our own people do to the Jews?"

Oksana leaned forward and narrowed her eyes. "Let me remind you what the faction out there is doing to our own people. I'm measuring Johan by his actions. You weren't here, Ivan. He was."

"Excuse me?" Ivan jumped up and spread his arms. "You were the one who wanted to come out here. You wanted to run your own cell. 'I don't need your protection, Ivan.' Remember telling me that?"

"Can we talk about something else?" Oksana cried.

"Yes," Ivan snapped. "Let's talk about how we're going to get rid of the Germans. Because he might have been chivalrous with you, young lady, but right now? He's out there murdering just like our secret police did, I can guarantee that."

Antonia made a noise. He glared at her. He knew what she was thinking. He paced back and forth between the door and the hearth.

"They were supposed to recognize us as an independent ally," he insisted, but the excuse sounded weak in his own ears. "They were not supposed to rule over us."

Throwing her arms up into the air, Antonia muttered, "God help us." Her scarf shifted upwards, revealing the growth at her throat.

"You don't want to talk about that either," he mocked. "So let's talk about how to get you a good doctor."

Antonia pointed a finger at him. "My health is none of your concern. Who do you think you are, barging in here, unannounced, and pushing us around?"

"Enough!" He slammed a fist against the doorjamb.

Oksana jumped up and tried to shove past him, but Ivan grabbed her by the elbow.

"What has gotten into you?" he growled. "A German, Oksana?"

"What has gotten into you?" she spat back. "You were the one who suggested collaboration from the start, and now you're behaving no better than a Nazi in the face of a Jew! You were not here," she repeated, "when our own Ukrainian men threatened me! Johan is a hundred times better than those people!"

There was a look on Oksana's face, as foreign as her behavior now. Ivan broke out into a cold sweat. His unflappable sister was terrified. Maybe she wasn't really in love, but she was serious about needing protection. His mouth went dry.

"What happened? Exactly?"

It was the look she shared with Antonia that made him realize there was more. Much more. Both women were quiet. Ivan went cold.

"Tell me what the hell you two are up to," he demanded.

Antonia scowled and looked away and out the window. Ivan turned on his sister.

"Somebody better start talking."

"Three degrees, Ivan, remember?" Antonia suddenly said. She whirled back to him. "But she has nothing to do with this. It was my idea."

He crossed his arms, still blocking the door. "You had better tell me what's going on. It's an order."

"I told you. None of us are safe here," Antonia said. "And Governor Lasch, well, he invites me over to eat with him at times—"

"And me," Oksana said. "With Johan."

"Or to parties," Antonia added.

Ivan stared at the two of them in disbelief. "You're fraternizing with the enemy. What else are you doing with them?" His tone was low and dangerous.

Antonia huffed. "What do you take us for?"

He shook his head, threw up his arms. "I don't know. What should I take you for?"

But Oksana whirled on him, pointing at Antonia. "She does it to steal lists. Lists from Lasch's office, lists that Johan somehow seems to accidentally leave lying about. Lists," she said meaningfully, "that contain the names of people who are to be deported."

Ivan dropped his arms. "But... but who? How? Where? Where did you find a window?"

"Hungary," Antonia said simply. "We've got a small network. We did it twice. Well, technically, maybe six times. I told you. People started coming to us."

"How many people?" Ivan blurted.

Antonia shrugged. But Oksana tilted her chin up at him. "Twenty-two. Twenty-two in just over a year. People who would have been deported to those Nazi camps. Jews. Poles. People from our faction. Got them out of range of those Bandera bandits. That's right, Ivan. Now what do you say about our German fraternization?" She stared him down, then nodded slowly. "That's what I thought. Excuse me. I need some air."

He was beat. He was still staring at Antonia and could hardly move as Oksana shoved past him. She snatched a wool vest off a peg in the foyer before storming out the door.

"Let her go," Antonia called. "She's just going down to the river. She'll be back soon."

Ivan watched his sister head for the Prut. Antonia was right. When Oksana was riled, it did no good to try and talk her down. She reached the bank, crouched down and tossed one rock after another into the river. When she looked over her shoulder, she scowled at him and moved to where he could not see her. As childish as when she used to stick her tongue out at him.

Ivan returned to his seat and sat heavily. "What has gotten into you? Why didn't you just tell me?"

"You got nowhere with Oksana and now you think you can pick a fight with me?"

He grunted with exasperation.

"Maybe you didn't ask the right questions," Antonia said. "Maybe it was how you asked the wrong ones." She poured herself a glass of *kvass* from the pitcher and raised her glass. "Anyway, we're done with that. It's gotten too dangerous. Lasch started suspecting there was a network, and Johan got scared."

"Now what?"

"It's become too risky. The SS is everywhere. We've done what we could, but to be honest, Ivan? We're scared." She took a seat across from him, stretched her legs. "Tell me, how are my parents doing? What's been happening in Sadovyi Hai?"

So he told her about his frustrations, how those who'd gone into hiding were flailing about in the forests, in need of leadership. Some had been captured and imprisoned, others killed. He and Pavlo were doing all they could to keep their heads low and their people out of trouble. In contrast, Bandera's rebel army were now so well organized they were formidable.

"We're hungry, we're tired, and we're constantly in hiding," he said. "They must be as well, but something is keeping the momentum going for them."

"Their hunger for power," Antonia said simply. "Sometimes it helps to be ruthless, I suppose."

"Their propaganda is strong, too. Even Pavlo's brothers were talking about switching to the other side." He rubbed his head. "He squelched that pretty quickly."

"How?" Antonia asked.

Ivan dropped his hands into his lap. "He sent them on a raid into a German base and we managed some weapons and a sow. That lifted spirits for a little while. But I don't know for how much longer. We were lucky nobody was killed. We need you. We need a plan."

Antonia was silent for a moment, then took in a breath and leaned forward. "Hungary is not the best option. They're in bed with the Nazis as well. Somehow we need to get you boys above ground." There was a flash in those eyes. She was beautiful. And he trusted her. He'd been a damned fool to accuse her of anything.

"Lasch said something interesting," she hurried. "He alluded to forest fighters putting a dent into Wehrmacht efforts."

"Which forest fighters?" Ivan scoffed. "The Soviet partisans? Bandera's army? Us?"

"We need leverage," Antonia said. "I told you, we have to convince the Germans to take us seriously, to form a security force that watches over our people. All of them. Imagine we offer to help fight off those forest fighters for the Germans."

Ivan nodded, still admiring the idea. "Security forces translate into power and leverage."

"Lasch seemed to take a liking to you." Her smile spread slowly. "Or at least he has a bit of respect. Who else could we bring together to help negotiate something like that?"

"Anyone here?" he asked. "You said you have a network."

"A few, but nobody with real clout. What about in Truskavets?"

There was someone. The idea excited him and he rose just as the clock chimed the hour. "Where is she? Shouldn't she be back?"

Antonia's face revealed slight alarm before she stood and went outside. From the veranda they called for Oksana, but there was no answer. He was already heading toward the river but Antonia went back in the house then returned with a lantern. The banks of the Prut were empty.

"With all you told me," he said when she caught up to him, "she wouldn't go far, right? Would she go to the church?"

Antonia's face looked drawn in the lantern light. "She usually just comes here, Ivan."

They followed the river to the bridge, but the church was locked.

"Let's get my horse, and we'll check with all the villagers," he said.

They knocked on all the doors of the settlement but nobody had seen Oksana. They hurried back to the lodge, Ivan hoping that she had returned, but the house was empty. He should have gone after her. He should have ignored her tantrum.

Antonia said she would call the police but when she lifted the receiver, the line was dead. "It happens sometimes," she said when Ivan tried himself. "It doesn't mean anything."

But he knew she was thinking what he was. Oksana would never make him worry like this. She was too level-headed for that. No matter which possibility he imagined, she was in danger.

"Now would be a good time to tell me exactly what happened the day she met the Konopliv brothers."

They stayed up all night together, often going out and calling for her again, but to no avail. When dawn broke, there was still no sign of her.

"I have to go into town," Antonia said. "Lena and the boys are coming on the first train. Come with me, and I'll drop you at the police station to report this. Maybe she went to Johan. And if she did, then we'll find her right away."

When they hitched a ride with someone, Ivan watched the vast wilderness they passed—wilderness that hid Bandera's rebels and renegade Soviet partisans. He begged God to keep his sister safe, and prayed that his pleas were not too late.

CHAPTER 9

Summer 1943

General Government of Galicia, Ukraine

Lena disembarked the train with Nestor in her arms, the toddler's shock of bright red hair melting Antonia's heart. It would likely turn the dark chestnut that she had but for now he was a true carrot-top. She hurried to her sister and embraced her, then took Konstantin's eager hand and looked for a taxi to take them back to Dolyna.

"Ivan is here," Antonia said. "He's at the police station."

"What happened?"

"Oksana went out for some air last night and she never returned."

Lena gathered Konstantin to her, her free arm shielding him. "What do you think might have happened? Gestapo?"

Antonia would not try to fool her sister. "I don't know what's gotten into our people, but, Lena, the worst of it would be if the Ukrainian Partisan Army got her."

Her sister's expression soured.

"They've been…" Antonia glanced down at Konstantin. "Persistent."

Lena snatched Antonia's hand in hers, her voice low and angry. "If you went to Lviv, you wouldn't recognize the place. I told you the Organization was going to ruin the country. Now they're carrying out pogroms against the Jews—how can any of you call yourselves Christians? And you, joined up thinking you could convince the leaders to reduce their anti-Semitic, anti-Polish—"

"Later," Antonia snapped.

But Lena was not listening. "I can't believe you were so naïve to think that you or Viktor could prevent the movement turning into this monstrosity. The minute Bandera stepped up—"

"Lena!" Antonia tore away from her and headed for the police station. Her sister said nothing more, and Konstantin began prattling on about this, that and the other thing.

They reached the station and Ivan came out just as Antonia was about to go in. He was gaunt. More hardened than ever from living in hiding. There were even flecks of white along the edges of his hairline. The way his chest expanded, she knew that there had been no good news.

"But no news might also mean nothing happened," Antonia tried.

"I asked them to locate Lasch and Johan Frank, but they're elsewhere in the district. I just want to know whether they have an idea of where Oksana could be. They're sending someone over to investigate and check the premises later today."

Antonia found a ride back to Dolyna and nobody spoke, save for Konstantin's constant chatter, as if he were trying to alleviate the tension in the vehicle. As they came up the drive, Antonia craned her neck to see whether there was any sign of Oksana. But there was none. She gave the driver a few Reichsmarks and Ivan helped Lena with her bags.

The house remained eerily empty, and Antonia was again filled with dread. She sent Ivan upstairs to sleep, then joined Lena in the kitchen, where she'd laid all the things out to make cherry dumplings. Konstantin and Nestor clamored around the table.

"I want to help," her older nephew said, already pushing a stool across the floor.

Antonia was glad for the distraction. "Bring me those cherries."

Her nephew cradled the bowl of fruit as he carried it to Antonia, Nestor waddling behind him. Lena kneaded and rolled out the dough, and with a clay drinking glass, Antonia showed Konstantin how to cut circles of dough while Lena spooned the cherries into the middle of them and pinched the edges together into half-moons. When they had used up all the dough and filling, Antonia brought the platter of *pyrohy* to a pot of boiling water and let Konstantin drop them in, one at a time. Like a spear fisherman, he stabbed at the dumplings with the slotted spoon until Antonia showed him how to do it properly.

He licked his fingers clean of butter and confectioner's sugar before they each took one. The tart cherry juice dripped down the boys' chins. Lena smiled apologetically and Antonia fetched a bowl of fresh sour cream. She ladled the *pyrohy* onto four plates.

"What about *pan* Ivan?" Konstantin asked. Then, "I thought *paní* Oksana lived here, too."

Lena winced. "Konstantin was hoping he could go to school here so that she would be his teacher."

Antonia absently ruffled his hair without answering, but Oksana's absence weighed heavily on her. When they were finished, Antonia shooed the boys out into the garden to play and warned them to stay within sight.

From the field behind the house came the call of a cuckoo and Konstantin called back before breaking into the children's song. Antonia stepped out onto the veranda and watched the boys, reminding them not to go further than the chicken coop. If it were not for the dark cloud that hung over the house, she would enjoy the carefree summer day.

Lena was in the kitchen, washing the dishes. Her sister seemed to be holding something back, but Antonia could not deal with any more bad news.

"I should go get some more water from the well," she said.

"Nonsense," Lena said. "I have enough here. Come and talk to me. Tell me what is happening."

Antonia took a plate from her and dried it. "First tell me why Roman's not with you."

Lena scrubbed harder. "Roman was caught in the middle of a protest and arrested."

"What?" Antonia frowned. "Why didn't you say anything?"

"He was only questioned and they released him afterwards. Right away." But Lena's face was pale.

"How did it happen?"

"He was on his way to the studio, but someone spoke out against him, said that he was a member of your organization. Him! His family is Polish, for heaven's sake." She made the sign of the cross. "It's one of the reasons I asked you never to involve us in your activities."

Antonio recalled Kiril Vasiliev, taunting her during the interrogation, threatening Lena and her family. What had the Soviet major had on her brother-in-law? Or her work with the art studio? What information was now in the Germans' hands?

The image of Viktor's face when he was brought to her in that prison made Antonia feel sick. She flung the towel over the sink and leaned against it, her back to Lena.

"Roman and I want to leave," Lena blurted.

Antonia spun around. "And go where?"

"West. Roman's been writing to friends, hoping that someone will read between the lines and arrange a work permit for him somewhere. We've written to a family we know in Switzerland. Roman thinks that if we can sit out the war in a neutral country, we can return afterwards and continue our work. Pick up the pieces and start again. But right now? He lost so many of his canvases in the Blitz, we have nothing at this point. All he can do is assemble what we have."

Antonia clicked her tongue. "And how do you plan to travel?" She knew she sounded patronizing, but her sister had no idea the difficulties that lay ahead. "You'll need a way to transport your things. You have two very small children, for heaven's sake!"

"I don't know. We don't know. But I can't stay in Lviv any longer. It's terrifying. Can't you do something?" Lena pleaded. "Can't you and Ivan help us?"

"Now it's convenient to have a sister in the Organization, is that it?"

"Don't talk to me like that."

Antonia sighed and shut her eyes. She was so tired. "Let me talk to Ivan. I need to lie down."

She was halfway up the stairs when she heard a vehicle coming up the drive. She went to the door, where Lena was already looking out. Ivan came down, buttoning his trousers.

But when they were both outside, she was disappointed to see that only one policeman had arrived.

"Captain Brunner," he said, barely touching her hand.

Antonia did not like the look of him. It was how his eyes did not quite land on her, how he seemed critical to find her there, and when they narrowed ever so slightly at the sight of Ivan, it was as if he were passing judgment on all of them. They were a waste of his time.

"So, this teacher. I heard she has a German boyfriend. You sure she's not just with him? Or someone else?"

"Her name is Oksana Kovalenko," Antonia said.

"Are you inferring that my sister is—"

Antonia snatched Ivan's arm and squeezed.

Brunner looked interested in Ivan then slowly walked up and down the veranda, raising his voice. "Why are you all so concerned about your sister, Herr Kovalenko?"

"My sister," Ivan said acidly, "was being followed and harassed by a family of brothers from…"

"From Berezi," Antonia filled in. "That's the next village south of here. The Konopliv brothers."

The captain's eyes flashed recognition but he looked at Ivan with dark interest again. "And you, Ivan Dmytro Kovalenko? You are not one of those fanatics with whom you all seem to be having troubles?"

"No, Captain."

Lena stepped behind one of the veranda chairs, gripping the back of it. She looked warily at Antonia.

"That is what they all say," Brunner said. "Why would those fanatics, as you call them, have a problem with anyone here? That's the question, isn't it?"

Antonia shook her head.

"These brothers, the Konoplivs," Captain Brunner continued. "They are wanted by the Security Division."

"For?" Ivan asked.

The captain winced and looked out onto the yard. "Murder."

Antonia froze. Lena straightened with alarm. Ivan looked as if he wanted to fetch Maya and gallop off to find the Konopliv brothers himself.

Captain Brunner sucked on his teeth. "It's unfortunate that your sister's gotten involved with them."

The boys suddenly came running from around the house.

"Uncle Ivan, can you come play with us?" Konstantin called. He stopped then and stared at the police captain.

Lena hurried to the children and bundled them into the house.

"You had better tell me everything you know." Captain Brunner prepared his notebook and a pencil.

Antonia began retelling the story she'd shared with Ivan the night before. In the background Lena scolded Konstantin before coming back outside.

"Would you like a drink?" Lena asked the captain. "We have some *kvass*. On a hot day like today, it's very refreshing."

The policeman turned to the well. "Just water, please."

Antonia watched Lena go and lift the bucket, but it was empty. Lena lowered it and Antonia returned her attention to the police captain.

"As I was saying, they threatened to—"

Lena's shrieks were blood-curdling. Antonia swung back to her sister, saw Lena hanging over the rim of the well as if she were about to jump inside, but then she slid down to the ground, still screaming.

Ivan and the police captain were running to her. Antonia felt her stomach clench as if someone had punched her. Brunner whipped the cap off his head and peered down the well, then withdrew a flashlight from his belt.

As if in a dream, Antonia gravitated to the group. She could not even help Lena, sobbing now, off the ground but watched as the policeman pointed inside the well with the flashlight. Ivan looked down and, in the next instant, released a deep, furious roar that made Antonia think of a wounded lion.

Bracing herself against the rim, Antonia followed the beam of weak light. Far below was the ghostly, swollen face, the purple bruises around pleading black eyes, the light-brown wavy hair, the embroidered collar of her blouse.

Antonia gripped Ivan. "No," she cried, over and over. She clawed at him, tugged at his tunic. Ivan looked away, as if he were trying to unsee what was inside that well. But he turned to peer down again and howled with such pain and fury that Antonia burst into tears and wailed with him. She wrapped herself around his arm. For a moment, she thought he would jump into that abyss after his sister, and it was all she could do to haul him away.

Lena suddenly sprang from the ground and raced in the direction of the house. The boys were heading for them and she tackled them both before they could reach the scene.

Next to Antonia, the captain was demanding to use the telephone.

"The line is dead," she said.

But Brunner was not listening. He stalked inside, searched the foyer, then lifted the phone. He was dialing. Brunner was dialing, and then he was speaking into the phone. The line was working again.

Another groan of agony from Ivan, and Antonia whirled back to the well. He was bending over the rim, so far and so small, she feared he would fall in. She pulled at him once more.

"Stay with me. Ivan! Stay with me. I'm here, I'm here, I'm here…"

It took the authorities an hour to fish Oksana's body out. Her hands were bound in barbed wire. From the back of her head to her feet, her clothing and skin were torn, shredded. One of the policemen suggested she had been dragged along the ground behind a horse.

Antonia sank to the ground, cradling and weeping over her friend's limp body, as Ivan raged and vowed vengeance on Oksana's murderers.

Father Bohdan swung the thurible over Oksana's coffin, his stiff robes rustling in time with his arm. The small church in Sadovyi Hai was packed with those who had come to pay their respects, but when Antonia took in the faces around her, she caught hostile looks tossed at neighbors, and the air was simmering with tension. Nobody here would admit to siding with one faction of the Organization or the other. Right now, the Kovalenkos were mourning the loss of their daughter, but Ivan's fists were clenching and unclenching in the pew before her, as if he were imagining exacting revenge on her murderers.

The Kovalenkos arranged for the coffin to be taken to the graveyard on sleds, as was the tradition. Lena and Antonia agreed to stay in the village, at least until the ninth day of the collective repast.

Before the wake, she returned with Lena to the farm, to leave the boys with their grandparents, then they cut through the orchards to the Kovalenkos' house. The apricots and plums were nearly ready for the harvest. In a nearby grove, Antonia saw Pavlo; he too was making his way on foot. She suddenly remembered him riding through those orchards on a black Arabian, but that horse had been commandeered by the Soviet collective farm. Before his parents' barn had been burned down, their two remaining horses had been requisitioned by the Wehrmacht. Now the Derkaches had nothing, and Antonia imagined that—like Ivan—Pavlo was also not only back for the funeral, but to organize a reprisal. It made her feel sick.

She and Lena waited until Pavlo caught up with them. "I came as soon as I could," he said, and greeted each of them with sad kisses on their cheeks.

He and the rest of their cell were dispersed and keeping low in the woods; in the villages they would have been at risk from Bandera's rebels and Gestapo raids. They climbed the slope to the Kovalenkos' cottage, which was sunken in grief when they arrived. Antonia felt the tears welling again, mostly from sheer anger. Ivan stood outside with some of their friends from the village but, at the sight of them, they stopped talking, and the men looked embarrassed. Antonia sent Lena inside to see to Ivan's other sisters, then whirled on the group.

"Let me guess. You're all planning to head to the next province and hunt down the Konopliv brothers."

Ivan threw pebbles at the chickens, and the others looked on in silence.

"Leave us," Antonia said. "Not you, Pavlo. You stay here."

Ivan jerked his head to the group, and once the men had departed into the house, Antonia leaned against the wall. "I'm done with this, boys."

Both Ivan and Pavlo huffed, but before they could open their mouths she added, "I want nothing more to do with the Organization. This is not what I fought for. These are not the people who are going to build up our country. These are not my countrymen, those who shed blood and those who go avenging our dead. It's a never-ending cycle. And it's a discredit to all that Viktor and I worked for."

"As if you are the only one who is angry," Ivan said with contempt. He whipped another rock, scattering the chickens. He stepped in front of her, tall, strong and angry. "They murdered my sister!"

"I know what they did, Ivan. I was there. I saw her body." She shuddered and took in a deep breath. "What they did to Oksana—believe me, I am furious. But I refuse to share any one of my ideas on paper for these idiots. And God forbid that you should become one of those idiots too. Pavlo, are you listening to me? You're included in this conversation. We saved dozens of lives for a much greater cause, and what have we proven? What? That if we are not beating each other on the heads like a bunch of barbarians, we have no right to civility? We have no right to run our own government and our own country!"

She wiped furiously at the tears. "My sister showed good sense, not getting involved with us. I want nothing more to do with any of it. As a matter of fact, as soon as Roman is here, I'm getting them out of this country."

Ivan looked dumbfounded and reached for her, but Antonia jerked away from his touch. "I know why Pavlo is here. You two and those men inside, you're here to go hunting down every Banderite you can find and sling them up by their ankles."

Antonia turned away and stalked out the gate, heading for the back fields. She heard the gate creak and bang again. They were both behind her. Before she reached the orchard, Ivan caught up to her, Pavlo on her other side.

"Tell Pavlo what you told me back in Dolyna, about convincing the Germans to permit a self-policing unit. We'll eradicate the Banderites legally then."

Antonia groaned. "Really? You know what I think? And if Viktor were here, he would confirm it. I think the Germans will play you against one another. They're all onto you—Banderites and Melnykites. They'll set up policing units with both groups and let you kill each other off."

"You can't be serious about leaving the Organization," Pavlo said.

"I am, Pavlo. I am. I've nothing to show for my efforts but loss. I've lost Viktor. I've lost Oksana and"—she whirled around to face both of them, the tears betraying her—"I refuse to lose you! Not to a vengeance spree!"

"It's not a vengeance spree. It's justice we're after," Pavlo argued.

"That's a thin line," Antonia bit back.

Ivan dropped his glare. "Pavlo," he said quietly, "could you please leave us?"

Pavlo threw his hands up into the air, but he turned on his heel. Antonia watched him as he climbed back up toward the cottage, the murmurs of guests and the sounds of eating and drinking spilling from the open doors. Suddenly Ivan grabbed hold of her upper arms. Before she could wrest herself away, frightened by the violent hold, he pulled her to him, his mouth on hers, hungry. Desperate.

Antonia tried to push him away, but he held on. She came down hard on his foot and he yelped. When he straightened, it was the tears on his face that really stunned her.

"You can't leave us," he said gruffly.

"Is that your way of apologizing?"

His hands were shaking and Antonia reached for them, took them in hers. She held her breath for a moment before looking up into his face and taking a step toward him. There were words jumbled in her chest. Words that made no sense, as if all the languages she knew were suddenly piling on top of one another, tripping over one another and trying to reach upwards and out. And when she heard what they were formulating, Ivan tilted his head, his gaze boring into her as if he could listen in. Antonia tore her eyes away and swallowed, but Ivan stopped shaking. He pulled his hands out of hers, turned her head to him, his resolve steady now.

This time, when he bent to her, she met him. This time, when he put those arms around her, she leaned against him, those words stirring once more in her. But she heard Lena again, in that kitchen in Lviv, the day Antonia had told her about Viktor's ring and Lena had expressed her doubts about Viktor being the right man for her. That Ivan was.

She yanked herself away. "Stop."

He frowned.

"Grief makes us do things we don't mean."

"But I most certainly do mean this." His eyes flashed. "I've meant it all my life."

He was her brother. Or like a brother. But no woman should feel this kind of stirring, this kind of desire, for a brother.

"I have to go," she said.

"Is it Viktor? Still?"

"Still?" She stared at him in disbelief.

"One thing is for certain," Ivan said bitterly, "Antonia Kozak always says what she means."

His jaw worked but he dropped his arms from her, and grief flooded her once again, wave after wave. Carried away by them, she left him like that.

That night, she dreamed of Ivan, not Viktor. Of apricots, and kisses, of bonfires and dances, of letting those words in her heart find their place in the world. And then she ripped herself from sleep, hot, anxious, her heart pounding. A self-defense force with the Germans' blessings was not the right thing for them to do. She was sending Ivan into the fires of Hell.

After breakfast the next morning, Antonia took the main road to the Kovalenko cottage, but Ivan's father had only bad news.

"Gone? Gone where?"

"Pavlo came and picked him up. He's left you this, though." He handed her a folded sheet of paper.

Antonia hesitated but finally took it. "Thank you."

She did not want to run into anyone on the main road, so she headed for the orchards. Outside the Kovalenkos' gate she stopped to read.

> *Pavlo's made contact with Colonel Sovchenko in Truskavets. He has the German Security Division's ear. We can meet them today. We're going to see about that self-defense legion. If we don't return before you go back to Dolyna, we'll come to you. We're going to find a way to set things right. We will find a way for the people to trust us again. Antonia, I'm very sorry. I don't know what I was thinking yesterday. I have no right to expect anything from you.*

Antonia carefully folded the letter, her fingers running slowly over the seams. She faced the orchards, the bees from the Kovalenkos' hives droning in the garden. So it would come to this: a voluntary collaboration with the Germans. Their men, above ground now, but no less in danger. She could not shake the feeling that she would have to question all of her convictions.

She pictured Oksana in that well. Her face. Her body when they'd pulled her out. The gag stuffed into her mouth. Antonia's anger rose hot and large.

Beyond that, a large swell was rising and she knew with dreaded certainty that the force of it would push her far from here and all that she had known. There was nothing she could do to prevent it from coming. But wherever she was heading, Antonia knew one thing: she did not want to go there.

CHAPTER 10

Summer 1943

General Government of Galicia, Ukraine

Pavlo shifted in the saddle behind Ivan as they rode Maya to Truskavets.

"So," he started. His tone hinted at teasing. "What exactly was that between you and our sister, Antonia?"

Ivan clicked Maya into a trot up the next hill in answer. Pavlo held on tight, and Ivan grunted when the Half Cossack did not press the issue. *What had happened?* What he had always wished would. To have her fall into his arms, to give into him. And yet now—with what he had to do just now—there was no chance for him to act upon it.

When the horse reached the top of the road, Ivan reined her in and leaned forward. Below them was a horse and wagon with crates and barrels scattered about. A man in a black uniform was poking through the back of the wagon with a bayonet. A gray-haired farmer was waving his cap angrily at the patrol. An elderly woman in a headscarf had her hands over her mouth. Ivan could hear her wailing all the way up here. The patrol reached into the wagon and yanked something out.

"Looks like trouble," Pavlo said. "That's police, though. One of ours."

"Yours?" Ivan twisted in the saddle.

"Not ours-ours. I mean, he's Ukrainian."

"Son of a…"

Ivan urged Maya forward and, as they cantered to the bottom of the hill, the policeman spun around, his scowl turning into surprise as he stared up at them. Ivan waved Pavlo off the horse then dismounted after him.

"Name? Rank?" Pavlo said with authority.

The stranger scowled. "Who are you?"

"Captain Derkach," Pavlo said simply.

"Officer Zenovich," the other said. "And?"

With Maya's reins in his hand, Ivan examined the wagon and road. A barrel of plums, crates of apricots and some vegetables lay scattered about. He studied the old couple and recognized them as one of the families that had joined the collective in Sadovyi Hai.

"Looks like you folks had an accident." Ivan tapped a crate with the tip of his suede boot. He kept the old farmer's gaze, who swung his head uncertainly. His wife covered her face, tugged at the edges of her headscarf.

"An accident." The farmer's eyes darted to the policeman. "Yes, that's what it is."

"Is that so?" Ivan asked Zenovich.

The patrolman looked eager. "Not an accident, per se. We have orders that no products be taken to or from Truskavets."

"Is that so?" Ivan muttered again. "We? We have orders. And why would that be?"

Zenovich tossed a nervous look over at Pavlo before answering. "What does it matter, the reason? Orders are orders. But if you must know, it's to prevent partisan weapons from coming into the city."

"Is that so?" Ivan said once more. He waited.

The old man pointed to the wagon with a shaky, weathered hand. His voice trembled as he explained. "We told this man that we are only looking to trade for some salt and oil, maybe oats if we can find some, in return for fruit from our orchards. That's all."

"Technically," Pavlo said, gesturing to himself and Ivan, "they are our families' orchards. But, yes, Officer Zenovich, this man is a farmer from our village."

The old woman muttered something and made the sign of the cross.

Ivan stalked to the other side of the wagon, checking the rest of the litter, lifting the hay. He remembered when the old man and his wife had come from the city to take over Soviet-appropriated property from the Derkaches.

"That by the way"—he pointed to Pavlo as he addressed Zenovich—"is the police captain from central headquarters in Lviv. At least he was until he was stripped of his badge by... well, we can only assume the same superiors you serve now."

Ivan motioned for Pavlo to help pick up the things and put them back inside the wagon.

To the farmer, Ivan said, "My companion and I will escort you to Truskavets. Prevent any further harassment from one of our own."

Without another glance at Zenovich, Ivan mounted Maya and moved to the front of the wagon, taking the reins of the farmer's horse. Pavlo climbed onto the rim then into the saddle behind Ivan.

Zenovich, meanwhile, picked up his bicycle and moved to block them. He pulled his sidearm and pointed it at Ivan.

The Cossack leaned over the mare. "I'd reconsider there, young man. There are no German guards here, there are no German officials. Nobody who is going to know what happened to you when they find you in the ditch. You're just here with *nashi*—our people. And our people," he glowered, "don't forget. Do we?"

"Nope," came Pavlo's voice behind him. He cocked his pistol and aimed his weapon over Ivan's shoulder. "We don't forget. Ever."

Zenovich looked at the gun, then at Ivan again. Ivan was twice his size. On the horse, four times. Weakly, he said, "These are the orders of the German gendarmerie."

"We understood that," Ivan said.

He kicked Maya, the horse and wagon surging forward with them. Zenovich jumped out of the way but only lowered his weapon when Pavlo taunted, "I suggest you make your way, comrade, before someone recognizes that your ass was kicked by the One and a Half Cossacks."

The back room of the tobacconist's had just enough space for Pavlo's contacts. Four men. Ivan took them all in as Pavlo spoke with them. The commander, Danylo Sovchenko, had a gray mustache, similar to Ivan's, and steel blue eyes. A long shiny scar on the side of his right face was purportedly from an unfortunate incident with a Prussian. Unfortunate for the Prussian at any rate. Even though he was all business, the old veteran soldier was pleasant, and that might have accounted for his soulful nickname—Dusha. But Pavlo had told Ivan the man had a reputation for being so stealthy and quiet in the woods that he was often the one who removed guards or sentinels before an attack. Spirit indeed.

The other three men were much younger but just as wary and tough-looking as their commander. They, too, had reputations that preceded them. Kvitka, a man Ivan imagined did very well with the ladies, was blond with green eyes. He stood in that stance as if he'd grown up in the military, legs wide apart, arms behind his back. But he was also the most genial in the group.

Terlytsia, next to him, was middle-sized and had dark hair and blue eyes. As a civilian, he worked as a journalist. In the underground, he led a well-disciplined and loyal group whose aim was to reform the more radical part of their faction. His smile, when he gave it up, was careful and slow. He was soft-spoken but exuded steely confidence. The last one, named Lys, was someone Ivan would not want to meet on a dark street, but he had surprisingly soft hands when he shook Ivan's. Lys was not any taller than Pavlo, but Ivan imagined he could bash anyone with just two quick jabs. He appeared to have a permanent air of suspicion around him, dark beady eyes, dark arched eyebrows, and his black hair was shorn close to his head. He was the kind of *gost'* who would ask questions only after he'd cut his victim's throat.

Pavlo reached up and clapped Dusha on the shoulder. "We worked together in Lviv. The cell here designated the colonel for the meet because he can speak with the *Nimaky.*"

"You speak German?" Ivan asked.

Dusha nodded.

"Me, too. A little." Ivan crossed his arms. "So, how did you manage to get this meeting with the Gestapo?"

"We sent them a letter telling them we'd be happy to help them fight the Polish and the Soviet partisans. But only under certain conditions."

He handed a sheet of paper over. Ivan read the list aloud.

"One, stop terrorizing peaceful and compliant villages. Two, release all non-criminal and non-communist political prisoners held in Galician detention centers. Three, supply us with light handguns and ammunition; and, four, hand over all civil administrative duties into the hands of the Ukrainians with Germans acting in supervisory roles." He dropped the letter onto the table. "And they're prepared to give you all that?"

Dusha rubbed his chin and smirked. "That's what we're meeting them for."

"And if they don't?" Ivan said. "I'm not going to be like that Zenovich out there. Either we are an independent force, here to protect our own people and give the Germans leverage to destroy the Soviets, or I return to the marshes."

Lys grunted and Kvitka smiled broadly. "We're all with you on this, Kovalenko."

"And if they don't agree to it?" Ivan repeated.

The colonel seemed to consider it. "If they don't, we'll be arrested. So we had better convince them to do our bidding."

Ivan shook his head. "How many of us are going?"

"They've asked that only two of us come."

"It's a Faustian deal, one way or another, Kovalenko," Terlytsia said. "Are you willing to bend a little to make this work?"

Ivan sighed and studied him.

"Here's what I believe," Kvitka said, relaxing his stance. "The Germans are less of a threat to our nationhood than the Russians. The Russians would absorb us, Stalin will destroy us. Our languages are too similar, our heritages too entwined. We are doing this for Ukraine's future. The Germans must win if we're to stand a chance at all."

Dusha inclined his head. "All right? Derkach? Kovalenko? Which of you two Cossacks wants to go with me?"

"I will," Ivan said.

Pavlo grinned a little. "Better you than me. You're much more intimidating than a scrub like me. Besides, my humor would be lost on those Fritzes."

On the way, Ivan mulled over what the men had discussed. He had argued the same not too long ago with Antonia, but he was not prepared to do the Germans' dirty deeds. He glanced over at the colonel. He knew the man's reputation. If he remained their commander, Dusha would make certain to vet their legionnaires and maintain strict discipline. Otherwise, they would be no better than the Ukrainian Partisan Army under Bandera's leadership, attracting criminals and lowlifes.

Dusha and Ivan arrived at the cemetery more than half an hour early. Shortly before five o'clock, a military convoy with four trucks appeared at the bottom of the hill.

Ivan scuffed the ground with the heel of his boot and watched them. "The Germans are punctual if nothing else."

"And paranoid," Dusha observed. "Come on."

He led Ivan to a mausoleum and unlocked the door. They slipped in and watched through an ornamental stone-cut window as the first four trucks were followed by at least half a dozen more. Minutes later, the cemetery was completely surrounded. From one of the vehicles, four men stepped out in officers' uniforms. Ivan saw that they only carried sidearms. They approached the cemetery gates and Ivan held the pistol Pavlo had provided him. Dusha was lightly touching his left pocket, and it wasn't the first time.

Ivan gestured with his gun. "What you got in there?"

The commander looked caught out. He reached in and withdrew a Soviet-issue grenade.

"I was joking about getting arrested. All I have to do is press the button and everything will blow up, including our chances of ever attaining power. Or finding the rest of our men."

Ivan stared at him then back at the Germans walking into the cemetery.

"Let's hope you have no reason to use it," he muttered.

The Gestapo broke into two groups: two stayed behind, near the cemetery gates, and two others continued forward. One of the officers called out in Russian and asked if anyone was in the cemetery.

Dusha glanced at Ivan. "You ready?"

Ivan raised his eyebrows. "Right here with you."

"We are here," Dusha called back.

"Come out where we can see you," the German hollered.

Dusha pushed forward and Ivan followed, raising his hands over his head, the pistol up in the air. He turned slightly to see Dusha was doing the same, but with no weapon in his hand. The grenade was still hidden. Ivan lowered the pistol onto the ground before him and the tension eased as the two officers approached. Their demeanor was calm as they introduced themselves. Ivan was taken aback by this, but even more so when they asked how many of them were there.

Quietly, Dusha told them that it was just the two of them, as instructed. After a few general questions, the officers decided that the men's German was good enough to get by without a translator. Although Ivan did not register the names of all the officers, the one who spoke Russian with them was called Strauss. He explained that he oversaw the political division in Truskavets proper.

They turned to the business at hand, and Strauss listened to their demands. On the first point—regarding the Gestapo-ravaged villages—they gave the men their word that they would call off any further non-essential "activities" conducted by the SS there. But in regard to the release of any prisoners, Strauss said that, though it was a possibility to satisfy this demand, it was not his department's responsibility. His superiors, however, were aware and they would call a meeting to discuss it further.

"As to your request for weapons, consider it done," Strauss said. "We'll get you as many weapons and as much ammunition as you need. And the last item, you are speaking to the wrong decision makers. The logistics of creating a unit of civil self-defense will be up to Commander Piz and Major Asmuth. It will require a meeting in Lviv."

It took the trip back to the tobacconist's shop for the events to sink in, more so because the Gestapo had let them walk away and seemed in earnest. They needed Dusha and his men, and that lifted Ivan's spirits. It could actually work.

Ivan clapped Dusha's shoulder at the front door and nodded. "This is going to be good for us. If we don't ruin our reputations like the Partisan Army, we have a chance of securing power in this country."

Dusha rubbed his mustache and narrowed his eyes. "I hope you're right, Kovalenko. I hope you're right. Stay here in Truskavets. We have much to discuss."

Ivan had hoped to get back to Sadovyi Hai, to perhaps catch Antonia before she returned to Dolyna, but he could not very well abandon the other men right now. Pavlo volunteered to return and let Antonia know what they were doing.

It took a week for the Security Division to make contact with them again and the invitation to visit the headquarters in Lviv finally arrived. Ivan took the train with Dusha. It was already growing dark outside when Captain Strauss escorted them to the three-story building where Pavlo had once worked. They were shown to a large meeting room where six Germans, including one of the captains who had taken part in the first meeting at the cemetery, sat around a large table. Strauss introduced Ivan and Dusha to the other five officers, one of whom was dressed in civilian clothing. He then introduced them to the heads of the Nazi's Security Division: Commander Piz and Major Asmuth.

Ivan had no sooner sat down at the table than glasses of champagne appeared before them.

Commander Piz, a beefy man with salt-and-pepper hair, proposed a toast to start the meeting. "To our new allies and to the success of our impending discussions."

Piz then turned to the issues discussed at the cemetery. "We have made our decision. In light of the General High Command considering a new Ukrainian military unit in Galicia—"

"Wait!" Ivan held up his hand. "The Wehrmacht is building up a new all-Ukrainian division?"

Major Asmuth folded his hands on the table. "We're taking on several thousand volunteers to form a division we'll call the SS-Galizien. Do you have a problem with that?"

A Ukrainian Waffen-SS division? Of course he had a problem with that. He could imagine Bandera and his army jumping at the chance. But catching sight of Dusha's stern face, Ivan said, "Not at all."

"It's good for you," Asmuth said. "It's the only reason why we're here discussing this idea of a legion."

"Turning to the issue of the political prisoners," Piz interrupted. He did not seem to notice the shift in Ivan's and Dusha's mood. "We will release a number of them, but not all." The commander slid a sheet before Dusha. Ivan peeked over but he was still too distracted.

Without looking at it, Dusha pushed the paper away. "There's no deal then."

Asmuth made a regretful noise and glanced over at Commander Piz, the older man clearing his throat, his fingertips tapping the table.

The major's frown disappeared and he looked admiringly at Dusha. "You're a good hustler. It's done, then."

Dusha took over the discussion and Ivan waited for a sign that the Germans had had a change of heart. This meeting could, after all, still be a trap. He touched the pocket on his right. Like Dusha had done at the cemetery, he was prepared to prevent the Germans from taking him or the colonel. He had Dusha's grenade right where he needed it.

"Your primary aim, gentlemen," Asmuth said, "is to protect the Wehrmacht from any further partisan activities. They are undermining the Third Reich's war effort and, as you know, if we lose, you lose."

Ivan smirked a little beneath his mustache, thinking back on that conversation with Antonia. The Germans would never consider a foreign legion, she'd said, but Hitler's forces had learned the hard way that forest combat and street fighting were the Wehrmacht's two primary weaknesses. No matter how well the army performed on the battlefields, the "forest fighters" caused the most damage. And what better way to fight forest fighters than with other experienced forest fighters?

When Piz raised the issue about assigning their roles to a policing unit, he folded his hands as if everything were clear. "Colonel Sovchenko, we'd ask you to accompany us to Berlin for a final discussion. We will establish all the details there."

"Certainly," Dusha said. "I'll go. But I want to bring my friend here as well. I think he would make a fine officer."

Ivan began to formulate his protests, but Commander Piz extended his hand to Dusha, grinning broadly. "Such a Don Cossack will only serve to impress the Führer and his men. I insist that Kovalenko join us. You will both receive training and return ready to lead."

"When should this take place?" Ivan stammered. He knew that he looked wild-eyed. His first thoughts were of Antonia and her intention to flee west with her family. "And for how long?"

Dusha frowned but then his face lit up. "Kovalenko here has a farm to tend to. But Pavlo can help your family while you're gone, right? Gentlemen, it's settled." He faced the Germans and raised his glass. "I propose we name our unit the Ukrainian Self-Defense Legion!"

Strauss, Piz and Asmuth all exchanged smiles before Asmuth raised his glass in return. "Yes, The USDL. That's very good." The officer in civilian clothing suddenly leaned toward Ivan. He wore a conspiratorial grin. "I've noticed you've got something in your coat pocket. Have you got a gun there? Or what?"

On the other side, Dusha nudged Ivan. "Go ahead. Show it to him."

Ivan withdrew the grenade and held it aloft, nearly laughing at the way the man's eyes bulged. All the Germans around the table froze. Ivan remained grim. The legion had been Antonia's idea, and in theory it was a good one, but had she thought through to beyond this point? That he would have to go to Berlin, laugh and drink with these demons, carry out their orders, and fight for his very soul?

Major Asmuth suddenly broke out into a broad smile. "You see, gentlemen, these people are not afraid to die. What better way to feel protected? Colonel Sovchenko, Herr Kovalenko, I do believe you will enjoy Berlin." The major's look landed on him then. "I think you shall rather enjoy having a bit of the law on your side now, no?"

Ivan peered at the major.

"Those Konopliv brothers," Asmuth smirked, "they are, after all, still on the run, right?"

The idea of arresting the Konopliv brothers, dragging those *vybliadky* to his men and serving up justice suddenly made Ivan relent. Slowly, he raised his glass to the Germans.

CHAPTER 11

Spring 1944

General Government of Galicia, Ukraine

Cloaked in a heavy robe, Antonia stood in the middle of the lodge's kitchen, watching as the Soviet partisans rummaged the half-empty larders. They smelled of the horses they'd ridden in on. Minutes before, she had watched from her bedroom window as their shadows stole out of the woods. But before they could come up on the veranda, she had gone downstairs, lantern in hand, and flung the door open. She'd had enough of them scaring the children and her sister. Instead, tonight, she let them in, hoping they'd do less damage this way.

"Leave something for the children," she warned. "Take what you need, but leave enough for the children."

Easter was the following week and they would have nothing to celebrate with. The ham was long gone, taken by the previous raiding party. The chickens had also fallen victim to the pilfering. In the meantime, the family had resigned itself to burying food, to leaving their stores low in the hope of keeping their losses minimal when they were found.

A smelly rebel with a long beard suddenly stood before her. He jeered and revealed a gap where two teeth were missing. "So, where have you buried your food this time?"

Antonia threw up her arms in exasperation. "Tell me exactly what it is that I should bury, other than your dead body? As soon as you're gone, the Germans come, accuse us of helping you and take what you haven't."

"Out in the garden," he said, as if she had not spoken.

"Go ahead then, go outside and start digging holes again. You can still be here when the Wehrmacht's panzers roll up first thing at dawn. They can help you look."

He growled and swept an arm over the kitchen cabinet, knocking off the bowls and platters.

She watched as the raiders deflated at finding nothing other than cold porridge and their last hunk of bread. A woman with a lantern stuffed the remaining loaf into her vest but Antonia rushed her, and stripped her of it. She gritted her teeth as she stared the woman down.

"I said, leave something for the children."

The woman had muscular arms, as if she felled trees for a living. She tried to snatch up the loaf but Antonia snarled and sank her teeth into the woman's hand. The woman bellowed and Antonia managed to hang onto the bread.

She tucked it beneath her arm and glared at the woman. "Come for me, and I will dig my teeth into your neck next time."

"Let's go," the bearded partisan called.

The raiders filed out, grumbling and cursing before galloping away behind the house and over the bridge.

She stepped into the foyer and cast a look up the stairs. At the top of the landing, Konstantin ducked away. Lena and Roman were also in the shadows. Roman had threatened that the next time the partisans returned, he would kill them with his bare hands before they got up the stairs. His remaining paintings and canvases were in the attic just above.

Antonia shone the lantern up the stairwell. "They're gone."

Roman put his arms around Lena and retreated with his family. It was not the first time that Antonia felt a brutal loneliness. She missed the One and a Half Cossacks. Pavlo was back in Lviv or Truskavets, and Ivan was supposedly back from Berlin, but she had not heard a thing from him and wondered whether he was keeping his distance on purpose.

The midnight raids guaranteed a follow-up visit from the Germans and they arrived in their scrabbling half-track panzers first thing in the morning, spattering the mud and erasing the horse tracks from the night before. The Germans questioned the adults about the Soviet partisans' whereabouts and balked at how easily the family had allowed the enemy in.

"What would you have us do?" Antonia snapped at one of the officers. "Shoot at them? With what? You've confiscated everything that we might have used to protect ourselves."

Only after the Germans had departed did Antonia go behind the emptied chicken coop, six paces to the left and dig up their stores. Konstantin startled her when she discovered he'd been standing off to the side. She opened the wooden box.

"Why is it all right to lie to the Germans," he asked, "but not when I lie to you?"

Antonia stared at her nephew, realizing the burden he was carrying. He had just turned eight. Old enough. How was she to explain to him that at times lies were necessary? How was she to explain injustice—how what one deserved and what one got rarely balanced out?

As she was on her way back to the villa with the boy, Roman appeared with two canvases tucked beneath his arms.

"I'm going to Truskavets to try to sell these. We need food. It's Easter next Sunday and we have nothing."

Lena prised one canvas away, and Antonia stifled her protest when she saw that it was one of her favorite paintings—*Hutsuls*

Working in a Field—which someone in Paris had commissioned. But the family had disappeared during the Occupation.

The second painting was a landscape of the Carpathians and included the field of sunflowers behind the lodge. It was a new one, but Antonia was sorry to see it go, knowing Roman would receive very little in return.

"I heard that Captain Strauss is a lover of art," Roman said. "I'm taking these directly to the Security Division."

Lena and Antonia looked at one another and released the canvases. There was nothing to argue about. Their situation was dire and everyone was trying to do what they could to survive.

It was on such days that Antonia wondered whether there was any reason left to fight for their cause. Ivan had written early on that, during his training in Berlin, he had connected with some of the Organization's commanders. He had even mentioned they were trying to reunite the two factions. When Antonia questioned the wisdom of that, Pavlo said that only a unified front, one that would remain strong after the war was over, would create an independent Ukraine.

"What about the manifesto?" Pavlo had asked her. "Have you begun rewriting what you and Viktor—"

"I don't give a lick about the manifesto right now," she'd cried. "The only thing I'm doing now is planning to get Lena and her family out." But in truth, she simply did not have the heart to do any of it. Not the manifesto without Viktor's input. And not making plans about going west if Ivan was too involved with the self-defense force to go with her.

To her relief, so far none of the Mazurs' contacts in the west had borne any fruit. Conflicted, Antonia returned to the kitchen and began cleaning up the mess.

"I think you miss Ivan," Lena said out of nowhere.

Antonia looked up from the dustpan but continued sweeping. "What do you know about it?"

"You've been moping since he left."

Antonia scoffed. "I have not."

"You have, too."

The boys ran into the kitchen and they shooed them out to a chorus of complaints about being bored.

"I saw the village boys playing in the woods. Why don't you go join them?" Antonia suggested. "But stay around the lodge."

She watched her nephew dart outside again, Nestor tailing after him. She heard Konstantin calling to Stasiu, the boy from the next farm, and a few other children from the village. Just a year ago, it had been all right for the boys to haunt the woods, the surrounding pastures, the fields, but now both she and Lena wanted them near the lodge. The forests were filled with vagrants on the run and trigger-happy Germans.

It was unseasonably warm by midday, and the puddles of snow in the yard disappeared. Antonia went into the large sitting room, moving a table beneath the window that looked out on both the front and the side yards. She watched as Lena wrested the pickets out of the empty chicken coop. Her sister was planting another vegetable bed in its stead. Antonia looked down at her notebook and then out the window.

The children—there were five boys and a little girl—were running about and shooting at one another with sticks and pointed fingers, playing war. Nestor was trying to stay with them, but Konstantin was shooting at his baby brother, and when Nestor did not die properly, Konstantin shoved him to the ground.

"You Soviet bastard," Konstantin cried. "Die!"

Nestor landed on his back in a puddle and began screaming. Antonia jumped up to intervene, but Lena was already hurrying across the yard, scolding Konstantin from a distance.

"Why?" Konstantin cried. "I thought the Soviets were all bad men. Soviets and Germans!"

Antonia groaned. They really needed to be more careful about what the boys picked up, especially from the neighbors' children. If the Red Army seeped over the front, such talk was mortally dangerous.

Before Lena could shake some sense into Konstantin, the older children all scattered. Nestor trudged after his mother to the garden, apparently not dirty or wet enough to warrant him changing into something else. What did they have, anyway? Hardly enough to cover their backs as it was.

It was mercifully quiet again and Antonia scribbled a few sentences, but her heart was not in it. She stared out the window once more. Chickadees and sparrows flitted between the branches of the six birch trees at the well. She had covered that well since Oksana's death. Nobody wanted to use it.

She watched the branches sway in a gust of spring wind. And then she realized the stillness was not a good omen.

Antonia pushed herself up from the table and craned her neck toward the river where she had last seen the children scamper off to. There they were, Konstantin in the middle of the group. He was cradling something in his hands and the others jostled alongside him, their envy plain. Whatever it was that Konstantin had, everyone else wanted a piece of it. She could hear their awe as they came closer, and the biggest boy, Stasiu, said, "You really think you could get a whole ham for that?"

Antonia frowned and drifted to the front door. She waited for the children to reach the veranda.

"I think it's an Easter egg," said the little girl.

"I think he could get two whole hams," the second boy pronounced with certainty. "Maybe even horses."

"Ham and horses," the third boy said, and he tried to reach over Konstantin, but Konstantin stopped short and pulled his hands back in.

"It's mine," he said. "I found it and it's mine."

Stasiu was a little bigger than Konstantin. He could snatch whatever was in her nephew's hand without any trouble but he turned to the house instead and now marched ahead of the pack. Antonia stepped out.

"Did you find a bird's egg?" she asked, both amused and saddened by the conversation.

Konstantin looked up, a little wary. The boys elbowed one another again, Stasiu still at the front.

"Not a bird's egg," Stasiu said. "Something metal."

He suddenly whirled on Konstantin and plucked the coveted object out of her nephew's hands. He held it aloft. "I wonder what this is."

Antonia saw the oval shape. Before she could order him to stop, Stasiu yanked off the metal spoon-like pin. There was a poisonous hiss. She threw herself down the steps so quickly, Stasiu did not have the chance to resist. She snatched the grenade from his hand, hurtled past the stunned children, and whipped it beyond the birch trees. It landed far up the drive but certainly not far enough. As if she'd grown eight arms, she threw herself onto the children and landed with them next to the stairs.

The children shrieked in surprise, but when the grenade exploded, they went mute with terror. Antonia, shielding them, looked over her shoulder as tree branches, pine needles, icy snow and mud rained down. She ducked her head again over the huddle of small quivering bodies. Nobody moved for some time until she heard Lena screaming from the garden.

"Mother of God," Lena cried, tearing for them. "Mother of God!" She repeated it over and over as Antonia leapt up and carefully checked each child.

"They found a grenade and thought it was an egg," she said, hardly believing it herself.

Lena grabbed Konstantin, and must have registered at least an idea of what had occurred. Voices were heading for the lodge as villagers also came to see what had happened. Miraculously, nobody was injured but Konstantin and the little girl had wet themselves.

Later, in the sitting room, Lena was cradling Konstantin, who was probably the most frightened. Probably because his mother kept on about how Roman would beat him raw when he came home. Antonia caught her sister's attention and gently shook her head. They both knew Roman would never do such a thing. Konstantin had been frightened enough.

On Easter Sunday, Antonia rose later than the rest of the house. The sound of distant artillery had caused her to suffer a week of sleepless nights. The front was closing in. Time was running out. They could not go on like this. With the Red Army having gained traction on some of the lines, Antonia was no longer certain the Germans would win, and even if Hitler's army did, Ukraine would never be rewarded for her collaboration. She had been wrong to think they could get the upper hand. The Nazis had proven they held only contempt for those they conquered. On the other hand, none of her family, and nobody from the Organization, could afford to be here if the Soviets regained control. But the children. They were still so very young. How would they manage to hide if they needed to? Often, Nestor cried for seemingly no reason, and nightmares plagued Konstantin. They had little money, and Antonia wished she'd had the opportunity to make plans with Ivan.

The boys were already dressed and downstairs in the dark before dawn. Konstantin complained that he did not understand all the fuss about going to church this early when their breakfast was going to be the same as every day anyway.

"It's just bread and a little butter," he whined.

"Today is the day that Christ rose again after dying for you on the cross," Lena chided. "He sacrificed far worse than what you must face this morning."

"Why don't you carry the basket," Roman suggested.

Konstantin lifted the embroidered towel that covered the goods they had blessed at the church the day before. There was a small loaf of bread, some lard—they'd found no butter—that Lena inserted cloves into to make a cross shape. Thanks to Roman's canvases, however, they had a half-dozen hardboiled eggs and salt. Nestled around the foodstuff were two hand-painted *pysanky* that Lena had rescued from their apartment in Lviv. Konstantin reminded them that he did not like eggs and he did not like lard, but Antonia squelched the protest by telling him that was his father's artwork in the basket next to his mother's hand-painted eggs.

"Good morning," Antonia said, scooping Nestor to her. "And you? Are you excited about Easter?"

Nestor yawned and fell against her shoulder, immediately turning his head and snoozing.

"Well then," Antonia said teasingly, "I suppose you are."

They locked the lodge, the first birds singing their songs as the family maneuvered around the crater in the drive. As they neared the bridge, Antonia saw two Soviet partisans lingering against opposite railings. The men had their rifles slung over their shoulders.

Antonia lowered Nestor to the ground. "With the Wehrmacht gone, they're getting rather daring," she said ominously.

"Must be," Roman muttered, "if they're patrolling out in the open."

Lena lifted the basket from Konstantin and clutched his hand. The rebels pulled themselves up in anticipation. Antonia took in a deep breath. There was no way to get to the church without crossing the bridge. The two men stepped together and blocked the way.

"*Kuda vyi ydete?*" one of them asked smoothly. Where are you going?

Antonia also replied in Russian. "It's Easter. We're going to church."

The two partisans glanced at one another and the second unslung his rifle and cradled it.

"*Da,*" he nodded. "Easter. But you know there is no God."

Roman said evenly, "We know. It's just one of those habits. A ritual."

"Habit," the first one sneered. "Ritual. I'll show you ritual." He removed his sidearm and aimed the handle at Konstantin. "Go on, take it. This is a ritual you will soon learn."

Lena pulled Konstantin to hide him behind her, but the soldier was faster. He yanked Konstantin by the shoulder and shoved the pistol's handle at the boy again.

"Take it," he taunted.

The child took one look at his parents before gingerly reaching for the weapon's handle.

The soldier chuckled and the other one jeered, raising his hands into the air.

"Who are we going to shoot today?" the latter mocked.

Antonia held her breath, remembering the day the boys were playing war out in the front yard, and Konstantin yelled at his brother to die because he was a Soviet soldier. Instead, Konstantin turned to his father, practically begging his father to take the pistol from his hand but Roman's expression remained impassive.

"Well, young man?" the first partisan prompted. "Who are you going to shoot today? Soviets or Germans? Go on, tell us."

Konstantin faced the rebels again. "The Germans."

The partisan with his hands up laughed and dropped them. The other one retrieved his sidearm.

"*Davai*," he waved. Go on.

Antonia took the first uncertain steps, and the men parted, leaning lazily on either side of the bridge once more. As Antonia passed them, the second one called, "Go on to your God. We've got plenty of bullets to spare and put into the five of you."

With Nestor back in her arms, and after reaching the other side, Antonia made the sign of the cross, and looked up into the hills. Where in heaven's name were Ivan and Pavlo? It was truly time to get out.

CHAPTER 12

Spring 1944

General Government of Galicia, Ukraine

Ivan watched the rolling landscape of the Carpathian Mountains below. A little turbulence jostled the airplane and he gripped the seat in front of him.

Next to him, Major Asmuth nudged his arm. "Hey, Don Cossack, you ever ride this many horses at once?"

"First time."

"You're awfully relaxed about it," Asmuth laughed.

Ivan pretended to appreciate the joke. He could not help but wonder, however, if this were a different time—if the man were not a Nazi—whether he would not like the major more. Secretly, he did admire him. The German officer was sharp, tactically and strategically brilliant, and he even had the kind of humor that Ivan could relate to. Asmuth had also proven that he kept his word. But it was what the man stood behind—the Nazi party, the Nazi tactics and the terrifying and vicious discipline Ivan had witnessed during the training in Berlin—which darkened his conscience.

He'd learned a lot during the police training, including how Asmuth's department achieved what they wanted. Terror was one tactic. Cruelty. When Ivan covertly reached out to some of the Organization's command in Berlin, he voiced his concerns—concerns Antonia had had from the beginning—and each of their leaders said the only way to get through the war was to continue playing the charade. Leverage power. Win the Nazis' trust. Then take control when the time came.

"Be sure," one of Melnyk's closest advisors had told Ivan, "of anyone you take into the legion. And keep checking that the Germans subscribe to our ultimate goal. You'll be walking a thin line, Cossack. Be careful."

But weeks later, Dusha shared a new order from the Organization. "We're to incorporate anyone we think might be wavering in their support of Bandera."

"Members of the Ukrainian Partisan Army?"

Dusha had sighed, also seemingly unconvinced. "Our faction sees the legion as a way to win back those who went to the other side. We reap the benefits if we remain in power until the end."

So even their exiled leaders had been lured by access to weapons and the Germans' tactical support. But only if the Soviets were defeated. And if they were not, the Ukrainian Self-Defense Legion would have a vastly different crisis on their hands.

Ivan turned to Asmuth. "I want to discuss what should happen if the Soviets invade the protectorate. The legion's superiors will need access to higher levels of intelligence than what you're granting."

Asmuth looked stunned. "Kovalenko, if the Red Army—"

"Listen to me." Ivan twisted in the cramped space between them. "We need access to all records. If Germany should abandon the protectorate for any reason, we cannot allow those documents to fall into the hands of the Soviet secret police. They will come after the legion's members with all they have. I was in Lviv. I saw how quickly they can and will execute dissidents. Stalin labels us traitors just for stepping outside the Soviet Union's borders. That's how it is. If there are any records of my visit to Berlin, for example…"

"Access to records is out of the question," Asmuth said.

"Come now, Major," Ivan reprimanded. "Not even the fall of the Reich is improbable."

Asmuth's face flushed red. "That kind of talk is treasonous, Kovalenko."

"Do you know how often our corner of Ukraine has changed hands?" Ivan challenged. "There's an old woman who has lived in four countries. In her eighty-some years, she never moved. The borders did." He studied Asmuth and remembered Antonia's words. "There are those who want to conquer. And those who want to liberate. I know what our men are. And you know what your regime is. You want our loyalty? Secure our access to records, and you'll secure our men's trust."

Asmuth scoffed and wiped his mouth.

Of course the major wouldn't answer his question but the German officer's indignation slowly dissolved. Suddenly he clapped a hand over Ivan's.

"You will have to take me at my word," he said. "We will leave no trace of you behind. No records. Not within your borders anyway. But I am very serious when I say that, if the time should come and Germany must abandon your territories, it will be too late for all of you. We're the only ones protecting you from the Soviets. And if we do not work together—if you should abandon this careful arrangement of ours, Kovalenko—it's a lost cause either way. You will be at the mercy of either the German High Command, the Reds, or the Ukrainian Partisan Army—whom I happen to know hold your faction in no great favor. But most of all, you should fear the German High Command."

Ivan took in a deep breath. He had seen it. Right before his eyes. Any subordination, any deserters, and the Nazis did not flinch at making everyone pay. It would only take one of them abandoning this arrangement for all of them to be wiped off the face of the earth.

He and the rest of their command had to sell it carefully, and one argument was that the Organization had a roadmap again. Specific instructions from their leaders, and real purpose. He and his men were now above ground, a legitimate unit in the eyes of the Germans. But if they were not careful—if the legion's command was not clear and slid over their own muddy moral boundaries—they would be no better than those they abhorred.

As the plane began its descent into Lviv, Ivan's anxiety about seeing Antonia grew. He had a promise to fulfill. She needed to get Lena and her family out of the country, but he had to find a way to convince Antonia to stay behind. He planned to ask her to head a propaganda campaign. Perhaps a concrete proposal was exactly what she needed. It could give her a new sense of purpose. Yes, a propaganda campaign, initiating a trust in the legion as those who were prepared to liberate the nation from Stalin's grasp and, eventually, Hitler's as well.

He had to give her a reason to trust him. At the very least, spark that earlier fire for the cause. She might never feel for him what she had for Viktor, but he was prepared to take anything she was willing to give as long as she stayed. And perhaps she would learn to love him. Perhaps.

The airplane rolled to a stop and Ivan followed Asmuth onto the tarmac. They jumped into a waiting black sedan. When they were back at the Security Division headquarters, Dusha—who had returned from Berlin a week earlier—briefed Ivan on the developments. Pavlo and Ivan were assigned as commanders to the western Galician units. Sergeants Kvitka and Terlytsia, and Captain Lys would vet new recruits. In the time that Dusha and Ivan had spent in Berlin, Pavlo and the others had organized small divisions. Asmuth was pleased with their progress.

"Once everything is running smoothly, I'm to return to Berlin," the major reminded Ivan. "And you'll be on your own."

He left the men to unload the weapons in Lviv, sort them out, and reload them into the convoys heading for Truskavets and the neighboring regions. In addition to numerous grenade launchers, each unit would be assigned one heavy machine gun, and every squad was allotted a number of semi-automatic rifles and grease guns. Ivan and Pavlo turned in their Soviet-issue Finkas, which the Germans replaced with full-automatic and semi-automatic guns. Every officer also received a Luger.

Ivan got into the truck to take the loads down to Truskavets and watched as Asmuth climbed into the back with him.

"There's a specific case I want to pick up in a village called Berezi," he told the major. "A band of brothers the local police have not been able to locate. They're suspected of murdering a woman last year."

Asmuth folded his arms. "Your sister. You forgot that I know about it. And you want to find these men?"

"I do. I want Pavlo with me, too."

"This can't be a revenge spree. I know you Slavs. You're forever stuck in a cycle of avenging the murders of your ancestors who stole the neighbor's goats."

Ignoring the jibe, Ivan leaned back on the bench. "Our guess is they are hiding in the mountains. Likely where your fancy equipment can't reach them. But Pavlo and I have horses."

Asmuth chuckled. "All right, Kovalenko. You and the Half Cossack grab a couple of ponies and ride off into the sunset together like in those American westerns. If you don't find your suspects, though, I want you back in Truskavets by the end of the week. If you do find them, and manage to capture them alive, then bring them to us. We have interesting ways of making sure they pay for their crimes."

Ivan tipped his head. "So do we."

Pavlo was the first out of the police building in Truskavets, and Ivan embraced him. He patted his shoulder, then led him to the back of the truck, where he lifted the flap to reveal their cache of weapons. He then pulled him off to the side.

"Have you heard from Antonia? Seen the Mazurs?"

"I was at the lodge not too long ago," Pavlo said. "Roman was here right before Easter, selling his canvases for money and food. They were asking about you."

Ivan winced. "I didn't think Berlin would take this long."

"They're having a rough time of it. Antonia is eager to go, but nothing has panned out in the form of a work permit or invitation. The entire continent is at war. It's not easy." Pavlo looked at him askance. "To be honest, I think she's waiting for you."

Ivan checked whether Pavlo meant it and saw that he did. "That's good," he muttered. It was really good. "What about the Konopliv brothers?"

"Still evading the local police."

"Asmuth will let us have two horses, but we're to bring the men alive." He jerked his head over his shoulder. "If possible."

Pavlo winked and clapped Ivan's arm, then jumped into the truck to help unload the weapons.

Ivan leaned in to help pull out a locker. "Pavlo, bring the horses to Dolyna tomorrow, will you? And see that you requisition some of the weapons for us."

"I can do that. What are you planning?"

"Borrowing the driver."

It was a forty-minute ride to Dolyna by truck. The air was crisp by the time they reached the pass. A band of rain had swept across the region, scouring away the remaining snow on the mountains, but the late afternoon sunshine was breaking through again, and the fields were dotted with the first spring flowers—primroses, buttercups, daisies and harebells. As the truck reached the top of the road overlooking Dolyna, Ivan tapped the driver on the shoulder and asked him to pull over. Ivan saw the lodge's gables, but it was what was around the lodge that had made him stop.

Smoke rose in five or six thin columns, and tents surrounded the yard. Through the budding trees along the lane to the house, small tanks glinted in the sun.

"What the…" Ivan muttered. "Who's bivouacking down there?"

The driver, still in the car, looked wary and Ivan touched his sidearm before getting back inside. They drove on, reaching the top of the drive, passing by the tanks. The driver swerved around a crater in the middle of the road, and Ivan peered at the milling soldiers, who returned his interest.

"Are those Hungarians?"

"That could very well be, sir," his driver said. "Probably on their way to support the Wehrmacht on the front."

Ivan wondered whether the whole lodge had been taken over by them and Antonia and the Mazurs had been cast out.

The truck rolled to a stop. Ivan walked to the side of the house when he saw Konstantin and Nestor zipping between the tents and cooking fires. Relieved, Ivan stepped in their way and the older boy came to a sudden halt. He recognized Ivan right away, but Nestor shied away behind his brother.

"What have you all got here?" Ivan asked. He glanced over Antonia's nephew, searching for a sign of her or the Mazurs. But there were just soldiers, going about their business, some hanging around on the veranda, soaking up the afternoon sun.

"Nestor and I were building a fort under the birches one day," Konstantin said puffing out his chest. "And then we heard this loud crunching sound and shining metal in the sun, and we thought that they were coming to get our food. But no, they are well equipped. That's what the *madiary* told us. They're well equipped."

"I see that," Ivan said.

Konstantin dragged him to where a large black kettle hung over a cooking fire. The men smiled at Konstantin and called him over, one holding out a tin plate and spoon. Konstantin waved Ivan over. "Look, Uncle Ivan. Goulash. We get goulash or tomato soup almost every day. The *madiary* keep the Red Army and the partisans out of the lodge, and we haven't been hungry in a long, long time."

Ivan nodded to the cooks as they handed Nestor a plate of goulash as well. When he faced the veranda again, Ivan saw Lena slowly coming out, shading her eyes.

"That is you," Lena exclaimed.

He embraced her, and near the back of the house, he saw Roman sitting on a stool before an easel. Opposite, sat a Hungarian officer in repose.

Lena waved a hand. "Roman paints their portraits. They pay." She smiled and led him toward the kitchen. "You're probably wondering where Antonia is."

"Is she all right?"

Her expression darkened. "The school let her go. They're not interested in having a German teacher in their midst now that the settlements are falling out with the Nazis. Those brothers—the Konoplivs—"

"They were here?"

Wide-eyed, Lena cupped a hand over her mouth and slowly nodded before explaining. "They were spotted by some of the villagers about a week ago."

Ivan led her inside and had her sit at the table. "Pavlo is on his way down tomorrow with horses. We're going to find them. Tell me what you know."

"Those men have been creating trouble at the school," Lena explained. "Then the Germans came and shut down the school because they thought we were harboring those murderers. The school council then told Antonia that we all have to leave."

"Where is she?"

Lena looked toward the kitchen door. "She's looking for a new place, or a new idea entirely."

Roman walked in from outside, a tin cup of paintbrushes in his hand. He greeted Ivan, but eyed the German-issued uniform critically. It was the first time Ivan realized how he must have appeared.

"Welcome back," Roman said cautiously.

"It's good to see you all," he said, but he felt the heat rising up the back of his neck.

"The *madiary* have been ordered to move out tomorrow morning," Roman said to Lena. "Konstantin's devastated. They're heading to the front. I'm not even close to completing the portrait."

"We needed whatever he was going to pay you," Lena said. "Every bit if we're all to go west."

Ivan was startled. "You're all going west? Antonia as well?"

The front door banged and Ivan turned to see Antonia rushing into the foyer. She pulled up just before the kitchen.

"Look what the cat dragged in," Roman called to her.

She was wearing a cloak and dress. She had cut her hair to shoulder length, that long, beautiful cinnamon brown hair now styled into something more modern. Western. He saw the conflict in her expression just before she masked it into something neutral.

"And?" she said, entering the kitchen. "Are you going to go after those men who killed Oksana now?"

Ivan gazed at her steadily. "Are you going west now?"

She turned her head away, but he saw her swallow. When she looked back at him, he recognized that look of determination. He feared it.

Lena stood up. "What did you manage?"

"An old bay horse and a cart, that's what. For my portrait and..." But Antonia's confidence was shaken. She looked at him and licked her lips. "Ukraine will be either in the hands of the Soviets—most likely—or the Nazis. You and I both know—we've seen how the Germans have behaved with us thus far—that they have no good intentions with us. And they are going to manipulate and use you. They'll toss you legionnaires into a ditch if they haven't killed you all by the time this is all over."

Ivan made to protest but she held up a hand.

"I started with the Organization to liberate our country. This is not how it will happen, Ivan. You have to come with us. And Pavlo."

He shook his head. Asmuth would have everyone killed. Dusha, Terlytsia, Kvitka. Lys. "You can't give up now. Listen, we need your help. I was in touch with the exiles in Berlin. If we can hold on—"

"You're all playing with explosives," she said.

"All right, Antonia." He raised his hands in surrender. "Then I'm asking you to go through this hellfire with me. I need you on my side when the time comes to take control."

She took in a sharp breath then softly said, "On your side…"

Something bloomed on her face. For a split second, Ivan thought she would come to him, wrap herself around him, but instead, her face darkened and her hand went to her throat. He saw it was not the lump she was checking. Between her fingers, she gripped the locket. Viktor's locket. With a faraway look, she took two steps back and fled up the stairs. By the time he reached the stairwell, the door to her room had slammed shut.

Ivan woke at dawn just as the Hungarian panzers rolled out, the soldiers marching eastwards in columns. He watched from the window before slipping on his tunic and going downstairs. Antonia was standing on the porch and turned to him, smiling slightly in the weak morning light. His heart collided with his ribs.

"And just like that, they're gone," she said. "Let's see if they've left anything behind."

Together, they walked down into the yard and went around the house. Ivan was amazed that the Hungarians had left only the scorched earth from the cooking fires, smoke still wafting from the ashes. They reached the kitchen side of the house and Antonia pointed to the stoop.

"They've returned the pots from the house." She lifted the lid off the nearest one. It was filled with soup.

"Konstantin will miss them," she said. "He swore allegiance to the Hungarians and tomato soup."

She carried a pot into the kitchen and he followed her, silently watching as she prepared *chai*. In the rooms above, the house was stirring awake.

Ivan gently stepped behind her and lightly encircled her waist. "Are you serious about leaving with Lena and Roman?"

She remained stiff. "Yes."

"There are some things I want to talk to you about," he said. "In private."

"Yes." She turned to him and took his hand, looking down at it in hers.

"You look terribly thin," he said. Even now, she wore a scarf around her neck and he reached over to it, his hand hovering. She nodded. He gently tugged the end of the bow and the scarf slid open and away. He tried not to look shocked. The lump now protruded visibly at the base of her neck.

"I have an operation scheduled in Truskavets. The iodine tablets are no longer helping. I can't sleep. I can't put on weight."

"When is it?"

Antonia sighed. "In a week. I have to vacate the lodge before then. And Lena and Roman must get out of the country. We found a note on the door one morning. It was addressed to

Roman. 'Bastard Pollack,' they wrote. With threats that they would string him up if he didn't leave the premises. I never showed it to them…"

Ivan frowned. "Lena said the Konopliv brothers surfaced. You think it's them?"

She nodded.

"Pavlo is coming with the horses today so that we can track them. Why don't you all go to Sadovyi Hai. Stay with your family until we return."

"Our enemies are everywhere, remember?" She put his hand to her cheek but before he could react, she stepped away. "We're going to sit this out in Switzerland."

Ivan swallowed hard.

"Roman has contacts in Geneva. He's certain that, if we can get there, the rest will work itself out."

"Where will you cross?"

Antonia shrugged. "We were waiting for our guide." She squeezed his hand and his heart leapt when she blushed. "I was hoping you would show soon."

Ivan reached into his holster and removed the Luger Asmuth had given him and some bullets. He would figure out a way to explain it. "Take this."

Antonia did not hesitate. "Thank you. But that doesn't answer my question."

It hadn't been a question but he understood what she meant. "Major Asmuth, my commanding officer… He would feel betrayed. And there's still something I need to do. There's still something you need to do."

"Me? What do I need to do? And who is this Asmuth to you?"

Ivan rubbed his mustache and glanced at the ceiling. "Let's just say that we have a mutual respect for one another. The Ukrainian Self-Defense Legion has made an arrangement. But I have no doubt that he will have me hunted down and killed if I desert now. And punish the others."

"And what is it you want me to do?"

Ivan told her about his meetings with the Organization's leaders and the need for a campaign to drum up their members and bring in new recruits.

She put a hand on his arm. "Ivan, I suggested this policing unit, but I was wrong. I've heard about the developments with the SS-Galizien, the Ukrainians who volunteered for the division. Some have fled, and their reports are horrendous."

But Ivan tipped his head and indicated the foyer. Someone was coming down.

"Ivan, you and Pavlo should come with us," Antonia whispered. "Save yourselves."

He stared at her, but Lena stepped into the kitchen, dressed and with Nestor in tow. The little boy babbled about the morning and the Hungarians, then asked Antonia about the horse.

"Pisok," Antonia said, but Ivan sensed her impatience. "Her name is Pisok."

"Can we see her?" Nestor begged.

Antonia threw Ivan a look before taking the little boy by the hand and leading him outside. Ivan watched her disappear to the back of the house.

Lena poured herself a *chai* and one for Ivan, then sat down.

"Antonia wants to come with us," Lena said. "And I think you should come as well."

"I've just been made one of the commanding officers of the legion, and Pavlo is on his way over here to help me track down the Konoplivs. I can't just up and leave."

Lena looked disapprovingly at him, then sighed. "Then she should stay here with you."

Ivan set his glass down.

"She's only using us—me and Roman—as an excuse," Lena went on. "She's afraid, Ivan. She's afraid of losing you. Like she lost Oleh. Like she lost Viktor, though I honestly believe he was never hers to have, and she knew it. Never."

"She's afraid to lose Ukraine forever," Ivan said. "That's all."

"And you…" Lena looked meaningfully at him. "You need to get that courage up and go after her. You'll have to reconcile with your demons later. But don't let her go in the process."

Lena looked over her shoulder and rose. "I think Pavlo's here."

Ivan met the Half Cossack on the veranda. "Brother—" He clasped Pavlo's arms and embraced him.

"Let's go get these boys, shall we?" Pavlo said cheerfully. "I've got some information on where we might find them."

"I need to see Antonia first. Go inside. Have a second breakfast."

Pavlo threw him one of those crooked grins and went in. Ivan hurried to find Antonia and intercept her before the crowd in the house did.

He found her on the back veranda with Nestor. He slid over next to them, the young boy stroking Pisok's nose.

"Promise me you'll wait," Ivan said. "Just give me a few days to track the brothers down and bring them to Asmuth. All right? And then—Antonia—please. Give me some time to come up with a plan."

"You've got a week," Antonia said. "That's when we have to vacate the lodge. A week. You understand?"

He did. He pointed to the Luger she'd lain off to the side.

"Be careful with that and use it only if you need to."

He suddenly imagined Asmuth cocking a gun to Pavlo's head, the Half Cossack cocking his weapon at Ivan. Asmuth ordering Pavlo to shoot Ivan for desertion.

"Ivan," she interrupted. "The note your father gave me. You're wrong about some things."

He frowned. He could guess what she meant and he would desert in a second if he was right. But if his guess was wrong, if she did not feel for him what he'd always hoped, proving he'd been a fool, then he would never find a way back to her. He had to make the legion work. He had to prove he was worthy of her.

"We'll talk about it when I return," he said hoarsely.

It was better to leave things unsaid than to have his hopes dashed.

CHAPTER 13

Spring 1944

General Government of Galicia, Ukraine

The vegetable patches were bare. They had four kilos of flour, a jug of oil, a sack of potatoes and a pouch of beans left mysteriously at the front door. One of the neighbors whose children Antonia had taught brought a chunk of smoked meat. Antonia did not ask what it was, nor did she want to know how they had gotten their hands on it. As the goat cheese would not last long on the trip, Lena had cooked it down to make a thick *mamalyga* with the last of the cornmeal. They were ready. Only Ivan was missing.

Antonia dragged her heels in packing up the cart. Roman and Lena said nothing, but she knew they were desperate to put the Red Army far behind them.

"Just one week in Sadovyi Hai," she begged them. "Only to spend some last days with our parents before we…" She could not say it. She could not express her certainty that they would never return to Ukraine if they left it.

But Roman's and Lena's sympathetic expressions revealed they knew Antonia was waiting for Ivan. Instead, Roman busied Antonia by poring over the maps again, looking for the best routes over the mountains and off the main roads. Partisan activity—the Russians, Bandera's renegades, and a variety of criminals made up of deserters from those armies—was a real threat, not to mention the creeping front. Three days earlier, one of the villagers had told them how an entire division of German half-track panzers had sped past, following the sunset.

No, they had to take the least traveled roads, the ones that she and Lena had grown up traversing on hikes and excursions. In higher altitudes, there was a good chance they would face the last of the spring snows, as well.

Roman had spent the last night dismantling and cutting his canvases out of their frames, rolling them carefully and packing them. In the meantime, Antonia fashioned a holster for Ivan's Luger to keep it close. By midday, the family had finished loading up the cart with the few things they had and the crate of paintings.

The next morning, the weather was on their side. They gathered in the yard one last time. Antonia walked around the villa, the River Prut still dark in the early light. The sunflower's dried stalks had been flattened by the winter's snow but the hydrangeas and rose bushes carried nubs and buds already. This house had been a refuge for her and many others. Much had happened here. But when she came to those six birch trees and the well in the front yard, Antonia shuddered.

"Let's go."

She took up Pisok's reins after Lena loaded the children onto the edge of the cart. It was rickety and Antonia was afraid it might fall apart by the time they trekked over any mountain roads to Sadovyi Hai. They had a pass to cross, after all.

It was not until after they had put Dolyna several kilometers behind them that Antonia realized she had forgotten all about the surgery in Truskavets. She opened her mouth and spun around to Lena behind her. Her sister looked quizzically at her, and Antonia decided not to mention it. Facing the road ahead, she touched the lump beneath the scarf. The growth now protruded enough to make people stare. She grew hot with the embarrassment. Once more, she had put off taking care of her own health.

The children suddenly shouted and pointed upwards. German planes sliced the sky high above, navigating eastwards. It was an abrupt reminder of the war in the otherwise peaceful wilderness. Later, when they reached the first slope, they found that it had been muddied by the heavy rains. The trail was narrow and one portion had been washed down by an avalanche and then the thaw. Lena unloaded the children and sent them up the trail before coming up front to help Antonia navigate Pisok. Roman secured the back of the cart's wheels with large rocks. The bay, for all her twelve years, was not only fit but had a good temperament. She was a sure-footed mountain breed. Konstantin and Nestor, waiting on the plateau above, cheered as Pisok reached the top without incident. The boys stroked her mane and hide, feeding her clumps of spring-green grass they dug up from beneath the patches of snow.

Lena was looking back at the trail, her eyes shaded against the glare.

"What in the good Lord's name are you looking for?" Antonia finally asked and just as quickly knew the answer. Her sister was hoping that Ivan would come riding up the mountain and snatch Antonia back in some romantic Hetman-like coup she could later write about.

"That's not where our future is right now," Antonia said. She pointed to the skyline ahead, the mountain peaks lined up on the horizon of the snow-patched meadow beyond the Ukrainian border. "There. That's where we're headed."

It was nearly dark by the time they reached the valley floor. The first village they came upon had a small church with a tin roof and a cemetery with fresh graves. A shallow river separated the northern and southern sides of the settlement. Antonia knocked at the door of the one house where candlelight shone through the windows. She had the others wait on the road.

A woman appeared with two little girls and a boy about Konstantin's age gathered around her. The boy's hair had been shaven off and his skull was dented and scarred.

"*Dobryi vechir*," Antonia greeted.

The woman glanced at the cart, the horse, and the four other mouths to feed behind Antonia.

"We have nothing left," the woman said and began shutting the door.

"We understand. We have food."

The woman swung the door open again.

"In return for a warm place to sleep," Antonia baited her.

The woman checked again. Konstantin waved at the boy, who shyly returned it.

Antonia added, "We have children. And a violin with us. My sister plays beautifully. We're only asking for one night."

The woman opened the door wider. "There is the barn, but your children can sleep in here. We have room for the boys."

Antonia doubted that the boys would agree to be separated from the rest of the family, but smiled and introduced herself and the others. The woman was Halka. Besides her son being Konstantin's age, Nestor and one of the girls shared the same birthday.

It did not take long for the woman to warm to them, especially when Antonia and Lena unpacked some of the cabbages and potatoes. Roman entertained the children with a game of *pesek*, and then told them a story. They shared a meal, and Halka told them about the situation in the valley.

"You won't want to go through the wilderness," she warned. She indicated the door. "The partisans are everywhere and they're all bandits. They'll take that cart and horse of yours and leave you dead in the process."

Antonia and Roman shared a look.

"What about the main roads?" he asked.

"You'll need to be careful about crossfire between partisan and German patrols," Halka said ominously. "And mines. We lost two of our men in the village to mines."

The next morning, after again studying the maps and possible routes, routes that created at least a one-day delay in getting to Sadovyi Hai, the family decided to risk the main road before taking a trail over the final pass. They said goodbye to Halka and the children, left her some of their provisions, and followed the river.

When they reached a stretch of flat land, the sound of artillery and shooting in the distance made Antonia jumpy. Roman stopped Pisok at the edge of a wooded road.

"That's all open ground," he said, pointing ahead. "I'm not going into that."

Antonia helped pull the horse off to the side and waited. The shooting suddenly stopped. They waited a little longer and then carefully eased Pisok and the cart into the open. Lena prayed aloud, begging that nobody would be hit by a stray bullet. It was slow going and the only village they passed was emptied. Antonia made Roman and Lena stay hidden on the outskirts and she withdrew the Luger, going from house to house. The hearths were cold. Plates, furniture, clothing, bed linen were in various stages of disarray in almost every cottage she went into. It was a ghost town. She thought of the massacres, the deportations, the rumors of those camps, the senselessness of it all.

Antonia returned to the family and announced they would not stay here. "We'll camp in the woods tonight."

"You heard Halka," Roman argued. "It's too dangerous in the forest."

But Lena stood at the edge of the village, her teeth chattering. "Antonia's right. This place is haunted. We camp in the woods."

They were several hours away from Sadovyi Hai the next day, just coming out from under the cover of the forest, when they heard the pitch and buzz of warplanes. The horse reared up as one airplane dipped down, low enough that Antonia could make out the pilot in the cockpit. Lena screamed behind her. The children shouted and Roman ran to help Antonia get Pisok under control. Around them, leaflets rained down from the sky. Konstantin dashed out and picked one up, Lena scolding him, but the boy handed Roman the paper and looked up with anticipation at his father.

Roman read grimly. "Do we have anything white that we can cover ourselves or the whole cart with? The Red Army will be bombing the area and they'll try to avoid hitting civilians."

The adults all stood around the horse and stared at one another. The Red Army. It was here.

Lena shook herself and instructed the boys to find everything and anything that was white. "Come now. We need to help the Russians aim at the right enemies," she said to the boys.

"Who are they shooting at if not us?" Konstantin asked.

"The Germans," Antonia said quickly. How far was the front, anyway?

In some twenty minutes, they hooked together light-colored clothing, towels, and sheets into a tarpaulin that nearly covered the back of the cart. Roman sternly told the boys to pull it over their heads if they heard planes. As soon as they were ready, Nestor cocked his head and pointed to the sky.

Several bombers flew over them. The magnitude and sound of the airplanes took Antonia's breath away and Lena shrieked as she gathered up the children. Both boys finally ducked beneath the tarp.

The sound of distant artillery fire echoed off the mountain walls. Antonia's knees turned to jelly and she leaned against the mare.

"We'd better keep going," Roman said.

No sooner had they reached the top of the pass when over a dozen men on horseback rode toward them over the meadow.

Wild-looking men, in an ensemble of bits and pieces from various uniforms—Slovakian, Russian, German, even the black armbands of Bandera's Partisan Army. Antonia desperately looked for a familiar face but found none. In addition to the mashed-up military and civilian garb, every one of them wore a bandolier of ammunition and carbines. Partisans, but whose? Antonia itched to reach for her Luger, but they were outnumbered, and she could already imagine all they needed was a single blow to her head and they'd possess the only real weapon the family had. Antonia pressed her arm against her side and watched them as they slowly surrounded the cart. Eventually one of them stepped forward. Their leader? In her wildest fantasies, she would never have picked him out.

Riding a chestnut horse, he was the oddball in the group. He was small but trim and muscular with fair and freckled skin. He had bright orange hair pulled back into a ponytail and Antonia thought he looked more like a poet than a partisan, though often there was a thin line between the two.

"*Ot čego ty bežiš?*" he asked in Slovakian. What are you running from?

Antonia braced herself, hands on her hips. "We are fleeing the Germans."

Konstantin sighed in exasperation and she pulled him to her. The child was trying to put two and two together. Yet she sensed that her nephew had long ago begun to understand that, whatever the elders said, that's what he had to go with.

"Are you Ukrainians?" The ringleader's gray eyes flashed with mischief.

There was a moment of hesitation before Roman answered in Ukrainian that they were.

The partisan then switched to Ukrainian and Antonia nearly sighed with relief. He introduced himself as Soletsky from a city several hours northeast of Lviv.

"Your group seems to have rolled right into the middle of our cocktail party." Soletsky laughed.

Antonia looked at the crowd uneasily. She wondered if these men had something to do with that ghost village they had passed. "You're a long way from home. What's the latest news then?"

Soletsky leaned forward on his horse and pointed toward the trail that would lead them to Sadovyi Hai. "You might want to have a look for yourself. You'll understand why we're here."

Antonia and the family followed him to the edge of the plateau. Before them spread a broad expanse of mountains and valleys, rivers and hills. On the northeastern horizon, however, columns of smoke, the air hazy and trembling with the thunder of war.

Soletsky moved next to her so that she had to face him. "Stalin gave orders to burn everything," he said. "*Everything*, so there is nothing left for the Germans to take ever again."

"I like to sketch a little here and there, myself," Soletsky said sincerely. "But certainly I am not very good."

"Perhaps you will show me some of your work," Roman offered.

The two men were carrying the crate into the Kozaks' cottage as Antonia spoke with her parents about the neighbors who might be able to take in the renegade Ukrainians.

"I would like that," Soletsky said, but his attention was on Antonia.

She shared an impassive gaze and he winked, then grinned. "One of our men shot a deer. You saw it, right?"

Antonia gritted her teeth, remembering the grotesque butchering of the animal. "Yes. The pregnant doe."

Soletsky opened his arms wide. "Beggars cannot be choosers. We'll build a bonfire, roast some venison, sing a few songs tonight and drink the Germans' *schnapps*! Make sure to invite everyone."

Several of his men were hanging about outside and chuckled when he stepped out, slapping his shoulder. One grinned toothily at Antonia.

That night, as the bonfire roared in the yard, Antonia was sitting outside between Lena and her mother on the bench against the wall. She watched Soletsky swagger over to Roman and pull her brother-in-law aside. Before Antonia knew it, Roman was in the house and, when she peeked through the window, was alarmed to see him withdrawing the crate with his canvases. She jumped up and went in.

"He wants to see them now?" she complained. She did not trust Soletsky. She trusted the man even less when two of his partisans wandered in, sick grins on their faces, bottles in their hands. "Roman, I wouldn't. They can wait until they're sober. Do it tomorrow."

But Roman looked helpless. "He said now."

He unrolled three of his canvases and Soletsky stepped over to nod over them, his chin propped on his fingers, eyes drooping.

Antonia laughed drily. "You're a satirist before you're some sort of critic," she muttered.

When the children ran in, chasing each other, she hustled them back out. One of Soletsky's companions raised a bottle to her and offered her a drink. Antonia declined and went to stand next to Roman. Her Luger was hidden in her boot, but still very much within reach.

Finally Soletsky spoke. "Listen, these are really good. *Very* good." Then he turned to the other two men with a solicitous smile. "But I didn't really bring you here to talk about painting."

Antonia moaned inwardly, and Roman looked alarmed.

Soletsky suddenly turned boyish. "It's your sister-in-law, here. I was hoping she would… I wonder…"

But Roman laughed aloud. "Antonia? You mean *Antonia?*"

"Why, yes. I mean… Look, what are you trying to say, old man?"

The great warrior-poet looked prepared to do battle but Roman pulled Antonia in front of him as if to offer her up, still laughing. "My dear boy, you would have better luck—and I mean this truly—you would have better luck catching and taming a wolverine than this woman."

Soletsky shook his head. "Now wait a minute… Such a mild-mannered, sophisticated gentlewoman."

"She certainly is that. She certainly is that," Roman guffawed and gave her a playful jab.

The partisan waved his bottle at them both. "I'm a horseman, my dear man, and I know a good breed when I see one. Your sister-in-law… she's the one for me. Do we have an agreement?"

"Horseman," Antonia cried.

Her arms itched to swing at the idiot, but Roman stepped forward. "Now look," he said, as if seriously considering the deal.

"Soletsky!" Another one of the Ukrainians stumbled into the cottage looking for the great horseman-warrior-poet-partisan. "We need you outside."

He clapped Soletsky on the shoulder and gave her a curt nod. Was that a look of sympathy on that man's face?

Soletsky threw his arms around Roman. "We have a deal then? You arrange it!"

He tottered off into the night for another drink and Antonia slammed the door on him.

Roman rolled his canvases back up. "You were being unusually gracious. I expected you to start a good, old-fashioned fist fight."

Antonia shook herself off, suddenly pining for Ivan. "One more move and I would have," she said. Then she grinned. "Maybe I could just learn to take a compliment once in a while."

Roman looked up and laughed.

The next morning, she was startled awake by an impatient knock at the door. Antonia sat up in bed. Lena, her long, auburn braids hanging loosely over her shoulders, cautiously rose and answered it. The pale light from the sunrise allowed Antonia to only see the silhouettes of the partisans in the doorway. There were three of them, including Soletsky. Roman got up and she threw him a look of disbelief.

"You think they're here—" he asked but she cut him off.

"Not for me," Antonia warned. "They better not be, or I'll raise the entire village with an alarm."

But Soletsky was sober as sober could be after the kind of drinking he'd done. "We've got an update about Red Army troop movements. I think your time is up. They're not far from Lviv. But we've got an idea. An escape route over Slovakia and the Tatra Mountains."

Without an invitation, he strode in and went to the table. Antonia rose and he threw her a penetrating look as she wrapped a blanket around herself.

"What makes you think we want you to escort us anywhere?" she challenged.

"Roman here said you were interested in getting to Switzerland."

Her brother-in-law looked sheepish. Shrugging, he made the sign that he had also had too much to drink last night.

"You could use our protection," Soletsky said. His gaze met hers and there was a flash of shyness before he looked away.

Antonia sighed, lightly amused, and decided to at least consider their offer. It would not be a bad idea to be surrounded by armed men, and obviously ones who had made it this far. Soletsky and the other two partisans traced a route over the Tatras. It was not at all far from the route Viktor had established. Her chest felt trapped in a vice. Antonia held her tongue, conflicted. After the night before, she was also not so certain she wanted the smitten Soletsky on her tail all the way through Slovakia.

"Let us think about it," Antonia said.

Soletsky began to protest but she held his look, and he deflated. "All right. Think about it, but—"

"We'll let you know," Lena suddenly said, her arm outstretched as if to sweep all three partisans off the table. She herded them back out the door and shut it, then turned around. She narrowed her eyes at Roman.

He raised his palms. "I didn't want to cause trouble, but I thought maybe they could be useful."

Lena put her hands on her hips. Roman looked about, called the children to him and escaped outside with them. Antonia watched them go, still leaning against the table.

"Time is running out," Lena said. "We need to move on."

The finality of it all—leaving everything and everyone else behind—without any idea of where she was going was just as sudden as the sob. Antonia clasped her hand to her mouth, her stomach contracting as if she were going to heave. She looked wide-eyed at her sister and shook her head.

Lena pushed herself away from the door and came to her, pulling her down onto the bench. "It's our men, isn't it? Ivan, especially."

Antonia buried her face in her hands.

"You're going to be the reason I lose every last hair," Lena said gently. "But you said it yourself. I'm an incurable romantic. We'll wait."

But Antonia sobered. If the Red Army reached Lviv, it would only be a matter of time before they overran the rest of the province.

"Just a day," Antonia said.

"Or two," her sister said.

CHAPTER 14

Spring 1944

General Government of Galicia, Ukraine

It had taken Ivan and Pavlo over a week to get information on the bandits' whereabouts. Ivan got nowhere in their German garb so he and Pavlo had managed to get their hands on Ukrainian Partisan Army regalia. For days, they rode around the countryside south of Dolyna in disguise, going from village to village. Finally, they met a drunkard who was desperate for Reichsmarks and recognition. They quickly won over his trust and the stranger led the One and a Half Cossacks to Vedmid Mountain.

"The German police lost the Konoplivs' trail," he told them. "But I know they're hiding out at a friend's hut up there. Friends to the Konoplivs," the man clarified. He spat and wiped his stubbled beard. "Not mine. They're no friends of mine. None of them are."

"All three of them are there," Pavlo confirmed.

"That's right." The scarf around the drunkard's neck was stained with sweat marks. "The big one, he's Markian. Then there's Denys and the youngest is Askold."

"All right," Ivan said and dropped a short stack of Reichsmarks into the man's hands.

The drunkard grinned and tugged at his shirt collar before Ivan sent him away.

"Amazing what you can exchange for a few sheets of paper," Pavlo muttered.

"Not loyalty," Ivan said.

"No," Pavlo chuckled. "Definitely not that."

When they reached the lower foothills, they stopped to take a look at the mountain ahead of them. Maya snorted and Ivan stilled her before lifting the binoculars back up. Vedmid Mountain, with its thick forests and craggy ridges at the top, had a few bald spots of pasture. He swept over one on the far left, and grunted at the sight of a shepherd's hut on the edge of the forest.

He handed the binoculars to Pavlo on the horse next to him. The black band around the Half Cossack's arm read UPA.

Ivan pointed out the pasture. "The hut's up against the trees. It's perfect. You'll come from the back. I imagine they're keeping watch from that crag of rocks just above."

Pavlo's mouth worked itself into a grin. "You're only a few days late, but if this all works, we'll be heading over to Sadovyi Hai by tomorrow."

Ivan twisted in the saddle. "You really think she's there?"

"Where else would she wait for you?"

The Half Cossack kicked his horse and Ivan ripped off his Partisan Army band. They stuck to the edge of the woods until they were in a spot where the Konopliv brothers wouldn't be able to see the Cossacks if they crossed into the open. Carefully, the horses climbed the slopes, navigated over forest brush, and Ivan swore when they hit a wall of rock. They picked their way back down and around, and finally located an easier trail. Before reaching the top, they slid off the animals and scouted the far side of the mountain. Ivan pointed out a narrow trail, probably made by sheep and goats.

"If you follow that, you can come back around and into those woods behind the house."

"The outcrop, first," Pavlo said. He was referring to where at least one of the brothers was likely watching out for intruders.

"You'll have to kill him," Ivan said. "You sure you don't want me to go?"

"Because a giant Cossack like you won't get noticed out in the open?"

Ivan clicked his tongue. "Right. Do it quietly."

"How else would I do it?"

Ivan grasped him by the elbow. They couldn't know. As a policeman, Pavlo was no stranger to violence but neither had ever had to do anything like this, to sneak up on someone and take a life without warning. They had lived like animals, hiding, running, surviving. Now they worked for the worst kind of animal, and Ivan was not certain he wanted to deliver Oksana's murderers into the hands of the Gestapo. This was personal, a matter between *nashi*—his own people. And Ivan wanted to make certain the Konoplivs understood why he was coming for them.

As if reading his thoughts, Pavlo nodded and went to his horse. He swung the rucksack onto his shoulders. "An eye for an eye. This has nothing to do with Asmuth or anyone else."

He turned his back on Ivan, and Ivan opened the bag, making sure the bottles of alcohol were well packed and wouldn't make any noise.

"You're set," he said.

Pavlo grinned, but his blue eyes remained somber. Ivan gave him a slight push up the slope and led the horses several hundred meters from the pasture before tying them up. He slowly made his way toward the clearing. One if not all three brothers would be patrolling and keeping a lookout, and he had no way of knowing where they were. Some distance from the clearing, he began scouting the vicinity with the binoculars. Ivan had to locate all three before he could feel secure.

The hut had a front door and a small window to the right. He was not in a position to determine whether there was a second exit or other windows, but Pavlo would manage that once he made his way around. Finally, Ivan detected movement. Two of the Konopliv brothers appeared out of the hut. They were armed with Soviet-issue rifles. To his advantage, Ivan had a semi-automatic. He swung the binoculars to the outcrop above the clearing and after a moment spotted the third brother. A stony creek and several large boulders divided the pasture between Ivan and the hut. Relieved to have all three in his sights, Ivan settled into keeping an eye on them and watching for any sign of Pavlo. The Half Cossack would take it slow, be cautious.

The late afternoon shadows pulled in the dusk. Ivan calculated that the brothers took turns every hour or so to walk up the slope and relieve whoever was guarding the outcrop. By now he knew who was who, thanks to the information they had gathered. Markian was the biggest and the eldest. Denys, the shortest of the three, was stocky and long-haired. Askold was the youngest, but like Markian, he had bulk in both height and girth.

Ivan shut his eyes at the thought of those three with their hands on his sister. His mind tortured him with images of Oksana sitting on the banks of the River Prut—just meters away from the lodge in Dolyna—angry with Ivan. He imagined the three brothers sneaking up on her. Overtaking her. Stuffing her mouth with a gag.

Ivan's breathing grew louder and he stayed low to the ground, trying to still it. He squeezed his eyes shut. But it did not help. The cocktail of rage and grief rose from his gut into his chest.

He saw Markian strangling her. Denys wrestling her to the ground. Askold binding her hands with the barbed wire while the other two tied her feet to one of their horses. Ivan looked up but he saw only Oksana's mangled body. Which of these brothers mounted that horse? Which of these brothers had dragged his sister through the forest until she died?

Wait. Just wait.

When darkness fell, smoke rose from the narrow chimney of the hut and clouds veiled the stars. Soon snowflakes began to fall. His legs were cramped, his back hurt, but his pain was nothing compared to what his sister had gone through. Training his binoculars on the outcrop, Ivan waited. Askold, the youngest, was at the lookout now. Pavlo would slit his throat, killing him in silence so as not to alert the others, then the Half Cossack would have to move behind the hut and get the other two brothers to run out without coming in the line of their fire.

And then it came. The call of a screech owl. Their signal. Askold was dead. Ivan's heart galloped. This was really happening. Pavlo was positioned somewhere in the dark near the building. Ivan moved. He scrambled over to a large boulder near the creek and returned the signal before lifting the semi-automatic and aiming for the front door.

The sound of breaking glass rang out and then *poof!* The first flaming bottle was tossed in. Now Ivan could see Pavlo's shadow and make out the clinking of the remaining glass bottles. Pavlo lobbed the next one in. There was a muffled cry of surprise from inside and then outraged curses. The front door flew open. Markian and Denys had thrown something over the flames because it was dark, but smoke billowed out. The third bottle was tossed in from the other side of the house. Shots fired out of the window, but the Half Cossack was sprinting already, back into the dark woods. The third Molotov cocktail caused an explosion. Pavlo's toss had hit something, quite possibly whatever had been used to douse the flames from the other two bottles. It worked, because the brothers were now making a run for it, shooting wildly toward the creek.

Ivan took aim and pulled the trigger.

Too high. Denys halted, arms in the air. He swung toward Ivan, his eyes wide in the light of the flames.

"Is this about the woman?" Denys taunted. "About that German's whore?"

A bullet smashed against the boulder. Markian.

Ivan ducked, his ears filled with the sound of his rage. When he looked around the rock, Denys was running toward him up the creek. Ivan raised his rifle, pulled the trigger. Denys fell. First man down. With a growl, Markian turned and retreated down the slope. Without thinking, Ivan leapt up and swung his aim on the eldest of the clan. He pulled the trigger again.

Oleh. He flew like Oleh had. He disappeared when he hit the ground.

Ivan strode far enough to look. A groan from the wounded man, still angry. Still defiant. But he was down. The Cossack bowed his head and took in a deep breath. He marched back to the horses, untied them both, and swung onto Maya's saddle. He had the rope in one hand, Pavlo's horse's reins in the other. When he returned, the hut was ablaze, feeding on whatever the Konopliv brothers had had inside. He trotted to Denys' body. Dead. But Markian was on his stomach, crawling toward the rifle, still some distance away. The ground beneath him was slick with blood.

Ivan jumped off the horse and strode over to the rifle and picked it up. Markian gurgled and spit into the grass. Ivan heard movement behind him, did not turn around. He stood over the last Konopliv brother. The leader.

The wounded man looked up at Ivan, his grimace betraying his recognition. "The bitch deserved it."

"Her name," Ivan said, his voice rumbling like thunder, "was Oksana Kovalenko. She was my sister." He slowly got onto one knee, then the other, his fury seeping from every pore as he leaned in close.

Pavlo took the rope from Ivan, dropped down next to Markian and tied up the big man's hands behind his back. Ivan rose and positioned the horses then waited until Pavlo secured one end of the rope to his saddle, then the second end to Ivan's. Like they'd done to Oksana. But worse.

The saddle creaked as Pavlo mounted his horse. Maya whinnied.

With the Konopliv brother on the ground between the two horses, the grassy slope before them, all it would take was one hard kick to their mounts.

Pavlo was waiting, and though it was dark, Ivan knew the question on his friend's face.

Markian's eyes rolled wildly as Ivan moved to his mare.

"Go ahead," he gasped. "I should've done the other woman, too."

It was enough.

Ivan swung the rifle at the man's head and finished the job.

Justice. Vengeance. He'd straddled both sides of the line on Vedmid Mountain and was unsure whether the distinction was large enough to defend himself. As if to mock Ivan's dark mood, the birds were singing with exceptional cheeriness and a bee hovered near the curtain, aiming for the primrose in the window box before darting away. With all this innocence, Ivan could not look Antonia in the eye as he sat down at her family's table.

"We have food," Antonia said, her brightness grating him even further. "Are you hungry?"

She placed a dish of thickly sliced ham and four potatoes before him without waiting for his answer. He was grateful for the distraction. Just before he was about to cut into the meat, a man—frizzy hair pulled back from his face—knocked at the open door. He was a pale-skinned, freckled carrot-top, and wore an embroidered tunic.

"This is Oleksander Soletsky," Antonia announced with feigned lightness. "He's from Lutsk."

Soletsky's glance nicked Ivan, and returned with wary interest to Antonia.

"This is Ivan," Antonia said. "The Cossack."

The stranger reluctantly stepped forward and offered a hand. Ivan took it, made sure to grip it fast, and Soletsky retreated behind the table once more. Ivan forked a piece of meat and chewed with intentional disinterest.

"Well, I came to…" Soletsky started uncertainly. "To see how you are all doing."

Antonia's smile was cool. No answer.

Ivan's knife slipped and clattered on the tin plate.

Soletsky looked as if he'd just lost his footing. "Actually, to confirm our offer to escort you and your family over the border."

"That won't be necessary," Antonia said.

"I've been reviewing the best routes," Soletsky insisted. "You could at least follow us. We'd keep an eye out."

Ivan looked up and forked half a potato into his mouth. "Do show us." He looked away from Antonia's glare.

Soletsky gestured to the table with his saddlebag and Antonia moved a pot of dried flowers off to the side. He then arranged a roll of maps, one on top of the other. Ivan focused on cutting his ham steak.

"I suggest that your party make its way through the Red Mountains," Soletsky said.

"Yes, we've been through that." Antonia pointed out the towns and cities in intervals. "Around Luborka, Mikulas, then through these here to Bratislava."

"Then you are all set," Soletsky said weakly.

"Then we are all set," she confirmed.

There was nothing else the poor partisan could do. He rolled those sheets up and struggled to get them back into his bag.

"Goodbye, my dear lady. It has been a pleasure meeting you…
and your family."

With a great sweep and a bow, Soletsky kissed her hand. Ivan
smirked. Soletsky's freckled face flushed to a beet color. He bowed
to Ivan slightly and walked out into the farmyard.

Ivan, his fork poised over the last potato, watched the man
go out the gate.

"I wonder what he was thinking," Antonia said. "We've already
been through the maps."

"*Mamo ridna!* What a woman! That's what he was thinking,"
Ivan said and tried to laugh.

"Men are so jealous," she huffed.

"Of him?" Ivan pointed out the window, still trying to tease
but not quite hitting the right note. "Did you want me to be?
Because you'll have to try harder."

Antonia shook her head and her smile turned into something
softer than he'd ever seen. "Are you done devouring your meal
now?"

To his surprise, she reached over and ate his last potato with
her fingers, tipped his plate and silverware into the washing pot
and took his hand.

"I want to show you something," she said.

When she hooked her arm around his elbow and led him
out to the village outskirts, Ivan saw Soletsky speaking with one
of the farmers along a logging trail. The stranger eyed him with
envy. Ivan turned his head to Antonia. No, he was not jealous of
this Ukrainian partisan. The only man he'd ever had to compete
against for Antonia's affections was Viktor. And he—may God
rest Dr. Gruber's soul—was not here. Even if she still wore that
locket, it could never bring him back. And as soon as he told her
about what he had done, he'd probably lose any chance in hell at
winning her affections.

*

"That strange partisan is right about one thing. We need to get you and the Mazurs out," Ivan said.

They lay in the grass next to one another beneath a cherry tree. The earth was warm from the afternoon sun. He was still avoiding the issue of whether he and Pavlo had found the Konopliv brothers.

Antonia rolled over onto her side. Her hair had grown out again but she wore it in a simple chignon instead of that trademark crown of braids.

"Then we go over the Ulychka River," she said. "Like we used to. And we'll ask the people in Ulič to take us in for a while."

Crickets chirped as the shadows lengthened. A roe deer barked somewhere below them in the woods. Her fingers played with the grass.

"But what about you?" she asked. "Will you come with us? To Switzerland?"

He licked his lips and breathed in deeply. She would never accept him now. "I was born to fight, Antonia. I'm a descendent of the Cossacks. And you—" He bit his tongue. He could not accuse her of not doing enough.

"My family needs me. Two small children…" She laughed mirthlessly. "Can you imagine Lena or Roman holding that Luger of yours?"

He sat up and took her hands into his. "I'll send Pavlo back to Asmuth in Truskavets and let him know what I'm doing. We were expected back. We were supposed to…" They were supposed to have brought the Konopliv brothers to the Security Division.

He sighed and bowed his head.

But she knew. "You got to them."

He closed his eyes. A bumblebee buzzed over his head. For a split second he saw the hut on fire, the brothers running out. Heard his breath as he marched to Maya, with the intention of making sure that Markian Konopliv felt what Oksana had felt.

Antonia's hand on his mouth startled him. "Shhh. You're breathing so hard."

He stared at her. He'd murdered those men. He'd been responsible for Oleh's death. For Oksana's death. Hadn't gotten to the prison fast enough to rescue Viktor. But this—this murder—his emotions had gotten the better of him, and he had done what he'd done with full intent, regardless whether he'd served a swift death in the end.

Antonia was on her knees then, her face was over his, her green eyes steady, a flicker of concern, but mostly steady. He turned away from it, but she forced him to look back at her. She tried to hold his gaze and every time he tried to shut his eyes, she made a noise, said, "Look at me," until he had no choice but to do so.

"You," she said stressing the word, "are not responsible. You did not kill Oleh. You did not kill Oksana. You did not kill Viktor."

Ivan tore himself away, and nearly knocked her over with the momentum. He jumped up and took three steps to the creek before facing her again. "I'm not a free man, Antonia. Neither is Pavlo. But we were that night. I was free when I delivered justice."

She blinked, her face drawn and pale. "What do you mean?"

"We killed them. All three of them. I wanted to drag them behind the horses just like they had done to Oksana."

Her eyes fell closed for a moment and when she opened them, he saw a flash of anger. "They gagged her. They raped her. They tied your sister to a…" She stopped and tipped her head. "You didn't though, did you? You didn't use the horses."

Ivan dropped his head. "I still have a great penance to pay."

She reached for him and he offered his hand, helped her to her feet. Her eyes shone with remorse. "The legion? You're going back to them, aren't you?"

"Do I have a choice?" he snapped.

"I did this to you," Antonia said slowly. "It's my fault."

He grasped her hands, angry and grieving, and wanted nothing more than to find something—anything—that would take them back to the beginning. So that he could do things differently. Starting with that first kiss.

She placed a hand on his cheek. "Then make sure the legion works for what it was intended."

He saw her swallow, her eyes expectant. What? What did she expect from him, then? She was letting him go, in more ways than one.

Beneath the scarf around her throat hung Viktor's locket. He stared at it. When he released her, she rocked back on her feet.

"It's time to get you across," he said and stalked across the field.

The villagers of Ulič in the Slovakian Tatra Mountains initially met them with suspicion. Lena, Roman and the children waited near the cart as Antonia and Ivan tried to find their "friendlies." Finally, someone came forward and said they'd known Dr. Gruber.

They were welcomed with kind gestures from everyone after that—from the widow who made room in her cottage for Antonia and the Mazurs, to another who organized food and supplies.

Ulič looked much like any other village. The houses were lined up close together along the main road, with the settlement surrounded by fields of barley, rye and wheat. Half-hipped roofs were either covered in tin or wooden shingles. Wooden shutters were practical as well as decorative and most contained boxes of geraniums or frankincense. As the barns were larger and longer extensions of the main houses, all the properties were rectangular in shape. Chickens ran about on the pathways and in the gardens, shadowed by seemingly disinterested cats. Interspersed between parcels of fields and around the area were the thick forests, the thin streams, and a strong, wide river. A single chapel stood forlornly at the crossroads.

That evening, as the children kicked a home-made ball and Lena played her violin, they sat around the bonfire, discussing the German occupation, the Slovakian government, and the East Front creeping over Ukraine.

"My sister and her family lived further west from here, in the plains," one man said in broken Russian. "She fled back here and told us of entire villages emptied because the Germans are sending women and children to slave labor camps."

Ivan and Antonia exchanged a look and Lena covered her mouth and stared at them.

"On our way to Sadovyi Hai," Antonia said, "we passed a village that had been completely emptied."

Another woman nodded. "Exactly."

Ivan knocked on the table. "Then you're not safe here either. What is different about Ulič?"

The first woman looked surprised. "We're well tucked in the mountains here. The German patrols come, but rarely."

One older man raised a finger. "And our local rebels let us know in advance if they do."

Ivan allowed himself a slow grin and Antonia matched it before squeezing his wrist. This was a good place to hide away, for a while at least.

Before he left, she took his face in her hands and kissed his cheeks.

"Come back as soon as you can. Let me know what is happening."

"I will. I know where to find you. For the time being." This time he did kiss her hands, held them against his cheeks where her lips had just been. It was his last chance. "Antonia, think about it. Get your sister and Roman a good, trusted escort and come with me. Come with me and rejoin us."

Her breath hitched and she slowly withdrew. "I'll think about it."

He had to return, or Asmuth would really believe he'd deserted. Ivan would not be responsible for any further deaths.

"Ivan?" Antonia was plaintive. "You think me a coward, don't you? You believe I'm just running away with my family because I'm a coward."

He swung to her, his heart breaking. He'd burdened her with his request. He'd asked her to share his penance when she had the chance to be free. He groaned as he took her into his arms, kissed the top of her head, and he could feel her heart pounding, the sobs shuddering deep within.

"By God, woman, no. You are not a coward," he whispered. "I am the one who has to atone for what I have done."

She was about to say something, argue further, but he pressed her to him, kissed her forehead and both her cheeks. He left her before she could finish breaking his heart.

As soon as Ivan returned to Truskavets, Dusha and Pavlo were eager to see him.

"We've got orders," Dusha said. "We're to patrol and clear the western regions of partisans. The Germans are running. They don't want to get squeezed between rebel fighters and the Red Army."

"In other words," Ivan said gruffly, "they want us to clear a path for their retreat? Leave the Soviets to us, is that it?"

When Asmuth stepped out of the administration building, clean gloves, spit-shined boots, freshly pressed uniform, Ivan narrowed his eyes. The German officer had a bemused expression as he looked Ivan up and down, and Ivan could imagine the condition Asmuth saw his Cossack in.

"And?" the commander asked. "Is it clear what your orders are?"

"To help the Wehrmacht run," Ivan said acidly.

Asmuth tilted his head. "I'm going to pretend I did not hear that. Did you find those criminals you were out hunting for? Those three brothers? You were to deliver them to us."

Pavlo pulled faces behind Asmuth.

"No," Ivan said. "We did not."

Asmuth's mouth twisted left, then right. His eyebrows jerked. "*Schade*. I was looking forward to helping you bring them to justice."

Ivan nodded. "*Schade*."

Oksana had been Ivan's sister. It was his story. It had been his responsibility to bring those men to justice. As Asmuth walked away, Ivan was convinced he'd done the right thing. He was prepared to die before falling to their level. Yes, there was a difference between justice and vengeance. And then there was sheer cruelty, as exacted by the Nazis for their sadistic pleasure.

He looked at Sovchenko and the others.

"We need a code of conduct."

The colonel looked curious.

"Yes," Ivan continued, "a code of conduct and we make sure everyone agrees to it." He threw Pavlo a look, that grin already spreading on his friend's face. "And make clear what the consequences will be if our legionnaires do not follow it."

CHAPTER 15

Late Summer 1944

Ulič, Slovakia

Ulič was so tranquil that Lena and Roman postponed moving on to Switzerland, knowing full well that the long trek would require them to cross into dangerous, war-torn territories. Regardless which route they took, they would run into raging battles. With news that the Allied forces were making progress in Italy, Antonia was not certain what the future held. Shortly afterwards, Roman discovered that the villagers were renovating the chapel, and he decided to help restore the frescoes as a way to repay for the many kindnesses shown them. Even so, food trickled in as payment, which delighted the old widow they lived with.

The local insurgents brought regular word about the war and had endeared themselves to Antonia and the Mazurs. They were good men. Brave men. They brought news when Minsk was taken. When the Red Army took Lviv. They'd told them about the uprising in Warsaw. Based on the information they provided, which heavily contradicted Axis propaganda, Antonia began to suspect that the rebels were well connected to Allied ops. She only wished that there was news from Ivan. Once, a Ukrainian family purposefully made the detour on their way to Budapest just to bring news from the One and a Half Cossacks. They were fine.

That was all they could say. They were fine and waiting anxiously for one or the other to be granted a short leave.

As in Sadovyi Hai, some of the farmers in Ulič had bountiful fruit orchards. As the late summer days turned to early fall, Antonia pitched in and helped at a neighbor's apricot orchard. They were pruning and cleaning up the fallen fruit. She and Lena remarked how nice it was to be working with the trees, to be doing the kind of tasks they had grown up doing. Nature was healing. Antonia's communion with it was a balm for her weary soul, but the scent of one particular pile of apricots delivered a memory so vivid and clear, it left Antonia reeling. She remembered the carelessness of that sweet, perfumed juice running down her chin. The feel of Ivan's finger catching that drop and putting it to her lips. The kiss that followed had released a longing that Antonia much later attributed to simple curiosity and the rush to grow up. Back then, she remembered telling Lena that the kiss had lasted a lifetime, but some months later, when Ivan tried again, Antonia decided it could lead to something like unveiling the magic behind Christmas. St. Mykolai was nothing more than a village elder dressed up as the saint, after all, and the kiss was nothing other than lust dressed up as love. That was what she had convinced herself of for years.

"We were so young," Antonia now muttered. "We had no idea how much more was to come."

Lena looked up from where she was working, regarded her sister solemnly and said, "I think you should return to him. They're certainly in need of nurses or fighters. You could fight. I know you have a weapon."

Antonia gaped at her.

Lena waved a dismissive hand. "Don't pretend like you're surprised about my knowing what's on your mind. You know that I always do."

"I wouldn't even know where to look for him," Antonia said. Besides, Ivan's last gestures—the way he had left her—made her uncertain as to whether he wanted her with him at all.

Frowning, Lena put her hands on her hips. "You? Of all people? It takes one word from you and they'd hand-deliver you to wherever he is. The war is no reason to stop living your life, not when there is so little to take pleasure in. You could at least give yourself what joy you are due."

Antonia looked out over the rolling dales and when Lena came to stand next to her, she put an arm around her sister's shoulder and hugged her close.

But Lena was not finished with her yet. "Go find Ivan, do what the Organization requested of you. You can send for us when the war is over."

"I'm going with you." She turned to her sister, came eye level and checked that Lena understood the decision was final.

"Don't do this to yourself." Lena eyed the swinging locket between them. "Love only comes around—"

"Twice?" Antonia laughed sadly. She straightened, the locket falling back against her breastbone. "I've been in love, remember?"

Lena hung her head. "I remember that you were in love. I do. But not like this." She pointed to the eastern hills, but her gaze was soft. "Not like this, Antonia. And you have denied yourself long enough."

Antonia put a hand on her sister's cheek and kissed her, then made her way with the basket of fruit to the wagon. A sharp, long whistle—a reminiscent signal—made Antonia look up the slope. A man was approaching on horseback. At first glance, she thought it was one of the Slovak rebels, but then she noted the height of the rider and the dappled gray coat of the horse. He was in civilian clothing.

Ivan. He'd come back to her.

Lena made a satisfied noise behind her. Sparing herself her sister's smirk, Antonia dropped the basket of apricots and ran up the hill to meet him.

A flock of starlings swayed and rocked across the sky. Maya nickered softly and Antonia stroked the horse's face. Ivan was sitting in the saddle, watching Antonia intently and she tried not to laugh. They were supposed to hold very still, look very authentic, but the blanket around Ivan's shoulders that should have been a cape, and the sheepskin hat which should have represented one from a Cossack made her giggle, and those giggles—so unlike her!—made her laugh. She could still hardly believe that he was here, Ivan. That she was standing with him, so near, with just a horse between them. That made her laugh more.

As if infected by her gaiety, Ivan made mocking expressions of stoicism. A drop of sweat rolled down the side of his brow, and Antonia had to scratch her scalp beneath the itchy headband of flowers she wore. Her wool vest was also too warm. Before Roman could scold them for moving, Konstantin burst out from between the oak trees shouting at the top of his lungs. Nestor was on his heels. Antonia jumped and had to still Maya. Both boys were riding stick horses. Ivan reached down and sent Konstantin's tied hat flying off his head.

"Would you all hold still," Roman exclaimed from the easel. "How am I to get anything done here with all this commotion?"

Behind him, Lena looked up from the grass where she was writing in a notebook. "I'm going to write a song about this scene."

Antonia had to stifle another laugh.

The boys ran around Roman's easel and he threw his hands up. "What are you? A couple of bandits?"

Konstantin stopped and, blinking, put his hands on his hips, looking just like his mother. "We're *hetmany*, like Mama told us from her stories."

Antonia hooted at Lena's proud expression, but when Roman exclaimed a string of Polish curses, Ivan also doubled over with laughter.

It took a moment, but Antonia collected herself and stepped back into her position, urging Ivan to do the same. A Cossack and Hutsulka. That's what Roman wanted to paint, that's what they were all dressed up for.

"Just let Roman get the sketch down," Antonia whispered. "And then we'll get out of here. I've packed a picnic for later."

Ivan raised an eyebrow, a gesture that reminded her of Oksana, and sent a dull stab of grief through her.

It took Roman a while before he released them from their poses. Antonia came around the easel to have a look and heard Ivan's intake of breath. The lines and the scene were all filled in, even a small boy with a hat had been penciled in. Antonia and Ivan stood together, the horse between them, gazing at one another. It was only in charcoal and pencil, but Roman had it down. Somehow, he'd captured the emotion. Antonia's shy surrender. Ivan's quiet victory. Between them, the longing. And something more that distance and time had forged.

"That's going to be beautiful, Roman." Antonia draped herself over her brother-in-law's shoulders to give him a kiss. "Isn't it, Ivan?"

Ivan blinked and she was astonished to see that his eyes were wet and shining. He wiped his mustache and turned away.

"I still have to paint it," Roman said. "But you two are done. Thank you for your patience."

Antonia gestured for Ivan to follow her and took Maya's reins herself. As they walked past Lena, she checked to see whether her sister would ask where they were off to, but she appeared oblivious. Antonia knew better. The corners of her sister's mouth twitched up although she was writing away.

The basket, in which Antonia had packed a blanket and some food, lay in the grass and she snatched it up. Ivan followed her through the orchard, then into a small forest of oak and birch before coming out onto a beautiful knoll that overlooked the valley. A creek cut a zigzag through the meadow. The village was off to their left and almost hidden from view save for the very tip of the chapel's cross.

Antonia stripped off the warm clothing and slipped off her shoes. All around them, violet forget-me-nots bloomed and she reached down to pluck a few, but then remembered Viktor's bouquet that one Easter. She released the stems without plucking them.

"What's wrong?"

Instead of answering, she stepped in front of Ivan, smiling. Impulsively, she kissed his cheek.

He had a hand in his satchel, his dark brown eyes alight. "I brought something for you." He withdrew a canvas sack and she recognized the type.

"A half kilo of dried apricots from Sadovyi Hai," he said. "I know that you have apricots here but, well, these are from home."

"Ivan." Antonia drew the sack to her and put her nose in. The last time she'd dried any was with Oksana, when Ivan and Pavlo had been working the orchards with them. It was the day the men had all disappeared into the forest. "These are definitely ours. From home."

"Then you are pleased."

The tears were gathering behind her eyes. "It's one of the most romantic gifts anyone has given me."

He moved to her, that longing all over his face. Antonia turned away and yanked a long stalk of grass. She was about to step into the creek but felt Ivan's arm encircle her waist. He twirled her to him, causing her heart to knock about in her chest.

"You've been laughing a lot today," Ivan said. "A lot. Are you nervous?"

"About a picnic?" Antonia teased, but there was still a hint of sadness.

He brushed over her arm and gently plucked the stalk of grass from her hand. "Antonia," he warned. His voice was heavy with emotion. "There is no time. We are not children. I love you. I have always loved you and I am not worthy of you, and now I ask myself what would make me—"

She reached up, pulling his face close to hers. "Shut up."

It was like before, their kiss. It was exactly like before, except now she had something that grounded her; experience that made her realize that all this time, this man—Ivan Dmytro Kovalenko—her best friend, had been right in front of her, and was her life. Yes, he'd been her brother, but the way any warrior was one's brother. The way any woman could be a sister. Friend. Brother. Lover. Now lover. The reason for Christmas presents was to share the joy of giving. There was no need for magic. Love was an act. A choice.

When they pulled apart, she rested her head on his chest, so afraid that she held on tightly. So afraid too about never being able to catch up on all the lost time she had spent on pursuing anything but him.

She laughed, but the tears were in her mouth. He was trying to tip her head up, asking why she was laughing, and she laughed harder, the tears now streaming down her cheeks.

"Lena was right." She laughed. She touched the locket around her neck. "Lena was always right. She's going to be so happy when I tell her how right she was."

With her head propped on his middle, her hand entwined in his, he talked about the pain between them that was Oleh. He told her about the Konopliv brothers, again. He wept, holding out his hands to her, the hands that had pulled the trigger and killed two men. He told her of the Russian partisans and how conflicted he was about fighting for the Germans.

Lying on her side, her finger outlining his ears, his chin, the jawline, stroking the reddish gold of his mustache, she took him back to Sadovyi Hai. To the village dances, and how they had danced with anyone but each other, though she'd never wanted to dance with anyone else but him. He told her how he'd dreamed of her every night since the first night in the swamps, since that kiss in the orchards. How he'd stood at the back of the cottage outside of her window, courageous enough to build up a resistance cell, to lead rebels, but too frightened to ask her whether she, too, had been affected by that kiss. She told him she'd seen him there, had watched his agony beneath the moonlight. She told him what she had whispered about his kiss to Lena. She reconciled the journey she'd taken, reconciled with having left her heart behind all those years ago, of what she had denied herself.

As dusk fell and a sliver of moon rose higher and higher, as the crickets played a lazy orchestra and even the buzz of mosquitos brought back the memories of summer nights far before their lives had turned to nothing but battle, they cocooned themselves—one silver-threaded story, one carefully woven memory, after another—until Antonia was convinced that nothing could touch them. To prove it, she rose from the grass and stood before him, pulled the tunic over her head, removed the rest of her clothing, and in the moonlight, she let him look at her.

Ivan got onto his knees, then onto his feet and she watched him shed his layers. The two of them stepped toward one another, like the first two people ever to enter the world.

CHAPTER 16

Late Summer 1944

Ulič, Slovakia

The thought came to him slowly. Piece by piece, with every stroke of his hand over her head.

With her.

I am.

The man.

I am meant to be.

Antonia looked up from his bare chest, the curtain of hair, the blanket over her back, tenting them. "What are you thinking?"

He thought the words through once more and grinned. "I think I've just composed a poem."

She chuckled, her fingers teasing the hairs on his chest. "And are you finished? Is it ready to share?"

He shook his head. "I'll let you know when it's done."

It was getting dark but he could still make out her features, her details, the crinkles around her eyes as they melted away with that smile. He sensed she was slowly coming back to the truth of their situation, and he was not wrong. He only regretted that it was necessary.

"What now, Ivan?"

"We get married. Isn't that what normally happens after?"

She nibbled his skin and he jerked, regretting it because she rolled over and sat up, drawing the blanket over her shoulders, but covering his middle with one end.

"We need to leave soon," Antonia said. "I know it's been quiet, but it can't last much longer. We have no idea what we'll meet as we head for Bratislava."

"Bratislava. You keep saying *we*. But you don't mean with me."

Her hand reached for his and she snaked her arm through his as he sat up. She encircled his knees with her arms. He leaned against her shoulder.

"I don't know what to do, Ivan. Lena. Roman needs help with Lena and the children. She is doing all she can to keep herself together but…"

"That's not the impression I get of her." His tone was too rough.

Antonia turned her head and he flinched when he recognized that her expression had once again been carefully arranged. "I catch her crying, just so. Roman does what he can, but it's me she leans on. It's me she goes to when she needs strength."

"That's quite a burden you're putting on yourself, Antonia."

"I want to get them to Switzerland safely." She gazed at him, but he sensed the question beneath.

"I won't be in Switzerland."

She nodded.

"There's a war on. One of us might—"

"Or both," she said softly.

She faced the dale below. Now, more than ever, he was certain that Antonia's place was by his side, but he could not force her. If she could not have the Ukraine she wanted, then she would rescue her family. Find her freedom. And again, somehow, he had no place in this mission of hers. He had only ever been a cog on the wheel that brought her to where she needed to go.

She turned to him suddenly, her face unmasked. As if to soothe him, Antonia lay back onto the grass and drew him to her. He gazed at her, trying to see the green in those eyes of hers but the darkness was nearly complete. Her hair was fanned out on the grass. He lowered himself onto her, kissed the nape of her neck, along her shoulders, and he made love to her again, this time to relish every stroke of her fingers, every touch of her skin, consciously burning it into his memory because he knew—he knew—she would not return with him. And that made his mouth fill with salt, with bitterness, with despair.

Afterwards, he stroked her bare breast and she rolled into his arms, her warm breath on his chest, but he burned.

From the village came the sounds of closing up for the night. Some of the villagers would sit outside and talk in the dark. Most of them went to bed early.

"When the war is over," Antonia said in that determined voice, as if she were giving orders, "I will move mountains, heaven, earth, whatever it is that I have to, to be with you again."

He sighed and pressed her closer to him. She was talking about things that were far away, mistaking her vision for something she could check off a list. A vision was a star, one that could never be reached.

She moved her head so as to meet his look. "Promise me you'll do the same. That you'll look for me?"

"You know I will."

"And if we—I—cannot return to Ukraine, for whatever reason? I will do what I can to bring you to me. Everything. Everything to bring you to me."

Ivan had to swallow several times to avoid weeping. He stroked her hair, pressed her head into his chest and kissed the top of it, his lips trembling.

With a sideways look, he watched her hang the locket over her neck again. They walked back toward the village together, arm in arm, and Ivan stopped her along the way to kiss her, to feel her, to have her in his arms. He'd never experienced Antonia so vulnerable, so absolutely pliable and willing, and he both cherished it and wanted to hang on to this moment for as long as possible.

"When do you have to go?" she asked, pulling away. Not the locket, not the horse, but the war between them again.

"Day after tomorrow. Major Asmuth is back in Berlin, but Dusha expects me." Maya nickered as they reached the end of the forest path. They were on the rise just above the village. Ivan took Antonia once more into his arms and buried himself in that long, loose hair, knowing that as soon as they were amongst the strangers in the village or Lena and the boys, they would be forced into a propriety that did not speak of their newfound intimacy. She pulled her hair together and bound it.

The air suddenly shifted. Something was not right. Ivan cocked his head and listened. There it was. In the distance, the hum and buzz of engines, the crunching of shifting gears. Then headlights cut through the dark on the road below them. Ivan pulled Antonia and the horse back into the trees. One after another, a convoy of nine vehicles rolled into the village.

The SS.

The motorcade broke apart, encircled the outskirts. Four drove into the middle of the village. The engines continued running, like panting, waiting wolves. Candlelight and lights appeared in the windows. Then the sound of gunfire.

They were distant pops. Far too distant. And they were coming from the woods opposite where Ivan and Antonia stood. Directly below them, the Germans shouted angry commands. Ivan heard the drum of hoofbeats, the yelp of war cries. Those damned Slovak rebels were riding out to meet the troops.

He moved to Maya's side, gripping the reins.

"No," Antonia cried. "You are not riding down there."

"I'm police. I could help."

Antonia blocked his way again. "You're not anywhere near your jurisdiction!"

Bullets from both sides sliced through the air now, and sparks flew from the circle of SS patrols. Ivan heard cursing, saw the Germans' silhouettes jumping behind the trucks to give themselves cover. The searchlights on top of the trucks were thrown on. And then the machine gun. The Germans mowed down the partisans the moment their horses were illuminated.

An animal screamed below. Maya whinnied, nearly jerking the reins out of Ivan's hands. One of the partisan's mounts skidded sideways before one of the Germans' trucks, the rider tumbling with it. A soldier marched out where he'd taken cover behind the vehicle's open door. Ivan saw the flapping trench coat, heard the single pistol shot and the horse stopped screaming. A second pistol shot, and Antonia—gripping Ivan—groaned.

Over the cries and shouts from the villagers came the crackle of orders over a loudspeaker.

"We are moving you to another village!" The lie was so heavy the air pushed down on Ivan.

A command followed to pack personal belongings and come outside.

"*Raus! Alle raus!*"

Ivan whirled Antonia to him, his grip so hard she cried out. "They aren't moving them anywhere. You have to come with me."

But she was shaking her head. "I can't. I can't just leave them!" She wrenched around to face the scene.

The house where Antonia had been living was lit up by one of the trucks, and he recognized Lena and Roman escorted by one of the patrols. He could hear the plaintive cries of Antonia's sister all the way up here.

Antonia pointed ahead of her. "The children."

Again she tried to wrench herself free. Ivan wrapped his arms around her, let her fight as she kicked out and even bit his forearm. He gritted his teeth and held on.

"They won't survive without me." Antonia was hoarse. "Ivan, let me go. Let me go, or I'll scream and they will know you are here, too."

"I'm coming with you."

Now she was sobbing, furious. She shoved him back so hard, he marveled at her strength. But then she rushed back at him, taking his face in her hands, so near he could make out all her features.

"You were right," she said, her voice heavy and urgent. She placed a palm over his heart. "I should be with you. By your side. Finish what we were supposed to do, Ivan. Finish it so that I can come back to you. But my family. I can't leave them like this."

Antonia reached up and kissed him. In his ear, she whispered. "Promise you'll survive. All of you. Heart and soul."

And then she was gone. Slipped away like smoke on the wind.

"I'll find you," he cried after her. "I will follow them and I will find you."

But Antonia was running. She was down the hill and heading straight for that circle of burning light.

Ivan grabbed the reins, flung himself onto Maya's back but Antonia suddenly pulled up, still outside the circle of light. He saw her turn. She was coming back. She was coming back! He spurred Maya forward.

"*Halt!*" The command was followed by a single pistol shot.

Antonia screamed. Ivan shouted her name. Maya reared, nearly knocking him off as he whirled her in circles on the ridge.

But Antonia was still standing. She was still alive. She spun back toward the village, slowly she raised her hands into the air, and strode into the center of vehicles. A patrol snatched her by the arm and herded her at gunpoint to the middle of the village.

Ivan beat his breast, gasping as he pleaded. *Please. Please, dear God. Don't let them shoot her! Please.*

The locals from the village were beginning to spill out, not of their own accord. One after another, they were loaded into the trucks. Beneath him, Maya's muscles flexed, waiting for his command. Ivan held her back.

Antonia! She was in the truck. Another five, six, seven people were loaded in with her.

But there was excited chatter from the patrols below, search-lights scathing the field, inching their way up to him. Another call to stop. That command that, when not immediately obeyed, usually proceeded with a final bullet. He could still charge them. Still try and take his chances. But then the machine gun was being redirected.

The report of a pistol shot, the bullet whizzing just past his head and splintering the trunk of a tree behind him. The *click, click, click* as the automatic was locked and loaded into place.

The only way he could rescue her was if he stayed alive. Ivan roared, whirled the horse toward the ridge and kicked her hard.

Behind him, the bullets sprayed the field, but he had already galloped over the hill.

They hunted him for some time, and even sent a truck to track him down. Once he was in the thick woods, he got off the horse, slapped her rear and scrambled up a rock face. In the dark, he would be safe. One man against an entire troop of SS soldiers. He'd been a fool to draw attention to himself.

By dawn, the adrenaline had caused his muscles to cramp. His jaw hurt from grinding his teeth. He'd cut himself in several places. None of this mattered compared to his grief. He walked to the village, expecting it to be burned down. However, only two of the houses were on fire. The bodies of the partisans and their horses lay scattered like felled trees in a storm. He found four villagers, shot in the head. Ivan wept.

The house where the Mazurs and Antonia had been staying was intact. He stepped through the entryway. Their items were strewn about. Roman's paints and brushes scattered on the floor. Lena's notebook, tented beneath the table. The sketchpad Roman had used.

Ivan bent down, flipped it open. Landscapes in charcoal. Faces in the corners, not quite complete. A pond. A birch tree. And then the drawing of the Cossack and the Hutsulka. Ivan's hands shook, staring down at the sketch of him, the outline of Konstantin flying past the lovers, his hand over his hat. It was not how it had been. Ivan had knocked that hat off but Roman had redrawn history here.

Next, he picked up Lena's notebook, and it fell to a page. The first draft of a stanza. A song about a Hutsulka and a Cossack. He took in big gulps of air, pressing the pages to him. She had said she would write one.

Something clattered to the ground in the back room and Ivan crept toward it, withdrawing his sidearm. A white cat shot past him and out the door. Sighing, he lowered his weapon and checked the rooms again.

Why? Why Ulič after all this time? At the sound of a soft whinny, Ivan pressed the sketch pad and notebook to his chest and went outside. Maya nodded her head and snorted in greeting. In the middle of the road, an old man with a cane appeared from the smoke rolling between the two burning houses. Ivan hurried to him, the man's fist trembling, the cane trembling.

"I was in the chapel," the man said. "In the chapel's belfry. I was hiding in the chapel."

"Why did they come?" Ivan begged. "Why?"

The old man's head wobbled and he pointed to the north. "Commander Jan Golian."

"Who?"

"Golian. Slovakia was preparing for an uprising for a long time," the old man said. He lifted his cane toward the field of slaughter. "Including our rebels. He gave the order. And if the Nazis were here, we were not successful."

Ivan stared at him. So this had been a retaliation for an organized rebellion. With an exasperated sigh, he rubbed his face and collected himself.

"Where can I take you?"

The villager looked Ivan up and down, and seemed to have lost his strength. He sank toward the ground. Ivan helped him, sat down next to him.

"Where can I take you?" he repeated. "I have a horse. Let me take you somewhere."

But the old man sighed heavily and hung his head. "I know nothing but Ulič. This is my home. This is where I will stay."

To get to the self-defense legion's camp, Ivan had to trek across the Polish territories. He started to put a plan in place. The Germans were very good at keeping records, this much Ivan knew. As soon as he was back with his men, he would send word, have Asmuth look for her. Find her. It was a mistake. Neither Antonia, nor the Mazurs, had anything to do with any Slovak uprising.

It was raining when he crossed the border. The road was strewn with debris from soldiers who'd been this way. He found a metal cigar tube and got the idea to secure Roman's drawing better. The Cossack and the Hutsulka. Beneath a canopy of forest, he rolled up the sheet, and capped off the tube to keep it dry. It fit into Ivan's breast pocket.

At the sound of an engine, he withdrew further into the woods. A German half-track panzer drove wildly past him and he spun Maya out of the way and watched them disappear into the stand of trees ahead. A moment later, an explosion rocked the ground and Ivan slipped off the horse to take cover. A cloud of smoke rose over the tree crowns and the forest crackled. A mine. Two figures suddenly burst out, on fire and running as if their arms were windmills. Each man collapsed before they reached him. Ivan watched in horror as they died, their screams of agony extinguished moments later.

If they had not come, if they had not overtaken him, it could have been him and the horse instead.

Ivan rode on tenterhooks after that. Ahead of him the sky was black with greasy smoke. As he closed in on the source, it was a large town built around a factory that had been razed to the ground by the fire. The tracks indicated that an entire division had been here. Germans. They were reversing Stalin's scorched earth policy, burning everything in their wake so that the Red Army would have nothing left.

Just half a kilometer from where he'd last seen the legionnaires, Ivan ran into patrols. Four men stepped out of the woods and surrounded him.

"It's the Cossack," someone called. "Let him through."

A large man with a long beard, someone Ivan did not recognize, shook his head. "Not without the password. Orders are orders."

"That's right," a voice called from behind.

Ivan turned on his horse, emotion welling so suddenly that he had to take a deep breath to steady himself. In all his life, he had never been happier to see the Half Cossack. Ivan dismounted Maya and strode over to Pavlo. His friend clapped him into an embrace and the grin wavered.

"What's happened?" Pavlo said.

Ivan took up Maya's reins and began walking slowly toward the well-hidden camp.

"He has to give the password," the sentinel shouted after them.

"Shove it," Pavlo threw over his shoulder.

On the walk to the gates of their stronghold, Ivan told Pavlo about Ulič. "I need to get a hold of Asmuth."

"I'm sorry, Ivan. He's on tour and we're getting orders to move again. They want us to hold back the Polish Home Army. He'll meet up with us eventually, but not for a while."

Everything in him resisted the idea of doing anything to help the Nazis. Pavlo seemed to sense it.

"Ivan, now's not the time. It will come. Dusha says as long as we stick together, keep things on the up and up—"

"We're in the midst of a war," Ivan growled. "And on the wrong side. I need to see Asmuth as soon as he comes."

From his coat pocket, Ivan withdrew Roman's sketch, unrolled the paper carefully and handed it to Pavlo. "Please tell me this is not all I have left of her."

Pavlo knitted his brows together, the dimples were deep. "She's a strong woman, Ivan. Strong enough to admit she'd been wrong about the two of you. She's going to survive this. I feel it." The Half Cossack shook him gently. "We need you to feel it, too. I need you to feel it."

Alone in the legion's cramped office, Ivan removed the sketch one more time. He did not really have to look at it, because he had memorized the drawing. That constellation of images—from Antonia's first laugh, to the moment she gave herself to him, only to be ripped from him—would be forever burned into his brain. The drawing was black and white, but Ivan knew the green of her eyes, the flecks of gold and brown. He'd been a coward. He should have gone with her. Given himself up. And at the same time, he saw those Nazis mowing down all the Slovakian partisans. He'd never have been given the chance to explain why he was there. They'd never have waited long enough for him to take the papers out.

PART THREE

1944–1945

Germany and the Eastern Front

FINLAND
HELSINKI

SWEDEN

LENINGRAD

BALTIC SEA

ESTONIA

LATVIA

LITHUANIA

MINSK

RUSSIA

WARSAW

BERLIN

POLAND

KIEV

GERMANY

PRAGUE

KRAKOW   LVIV

CZECHO-
SLOVAKIA

VIENNA

BUDAPEST

HUNGARY

ROMANIA

BELGRADE

BUCHAREST

YUGOSLAVIA

BLACK SEA

BULGARIA

━━━━ FRONT LINE JUNE 1944
━ ━ ━ JAN 1945
◄━━━ RUSSIAN FORCES

CHAPTER 17

Fall 1944

Wilhelmshagen, Outside of Berlin, Germany

The slam and click of the cattle car door was barely audible over the screams of those captured inside. Antonia clung to Nestor's hand as the toddler wailed. She hoisted him into Lena's arms, her sister's face revealing her sheer panic. Antonia put a protective arm around her as the train lurched and shrieked against the metal track. A collective gasp, then people began calling the names of family members, Lena among them.

"Konstantin! Roman," she wailed. "Did you see them? Are they on this train?"

Antonia did not know.

Next to her, an old woman sobbed. Urine splashed off her mismatched shoes. She stared at Antonia, her pupils dilated with fear, her headscarf hanging around her neck. Antonia bent down, found a handkerchief in her pocket and tried to help her. Other women joined. There was no water, no toilet that Antonia could see in the crowded car. She found a place for the old woman to sit, the train picking up speed, the wheels chugging and occasionally clacking as if to tick off the kilometers toward their destination. To Hell. It could only be.

Nestor's whimpering moved Antonia to action. His teeth were chattering and his skin was cool and clammy. She removed her sheepskin vest to cover him. Lena began weeping over him.

"Lena," Antonia said, "you need to pull yourself together. You're scaring him. He's going into shock."

Antonia negotiated a spot where she and Lena could sit down with Nestor. A stench began to rise in the cattle car—of fear, of sweat, of others who had lost control at the realization that they were trapped. The earlier screams turned into sobbing and groaning pleas. Five women prayed together. Antonia stared at them, remembering Prison Number One, remembering Kira. Viktor. Ivan coming to save her. Ivan begging her not to leave him.

"Hail Mary, full of grace," Antonia whispered. "The Lord is with thee. Blessed art thou among women…"

Later, someone pointed out a single canister meant for them to do their business. Women began producing food from pockets, satchels, their valises. An apple here, a half a loaf of bread, a bunch of grapes, a bit of cheese. But something had shifted. Reality, Antonia decided, for the men began guarding their food, ignored the desperate looks of those who had brought nothing—had not had the prescience to pack food when the Germans ordered them to leave. But it was the women who—succumbing to guilt, or the instinct to nourish, to protect—insisted on sharing at least a little of what they had.

Antonia watched Lena cradling Nestor like an infant, her head hung over him as if to shield him from this very car.

"I've brought a few potatoes, the ones that were cooked," Lena whispered. "I packed them with a bit of cheese and two apples. But…"

"No," Antonia whispered back. "We shall wait. For when we really need it." She reached into her dress pocket and felt the burlap sack that Ivan had given her. She produced five of the dried apricots, gave two each to Lena and Nestor, then ate the remaining one. It was leathery and the sweetness caused a flood of memories and regrets.

When Lena looked questioningly at her, Antonia swallowed. "Ivan brought them from Sadovyi Hai."

Lena's own tears rolled down her cheeks.

The night turned into morning and the train stopped. Light had begun creeping up the slats of the cattle car before the train moved again. Thirst plagued them all next. As Christian as they all might be, as neighborly as the prisoners in this car wished to consider themselves, Antonia knew that if she and Lena did not take care of themselves first, did not protect what they had and make sure that Nestor had enough to eat, they would not survive this journey. As discreetly as possible, Antonia used a razor she found among her sister's toiletries, and began pulling apart the seam along the inside of Lena's valise. When she had managed a big enough hole, she sliced Lena's apples and wrapped a few individual pieces in the burlap she had with her. She did the same with the potatoes, giving Nestor a piece of cheese and a slice of potato before storing the rest along the inside. Less bulk, less suspicion.

When Lena saw what she was doing, Antonia said, "In case someone tries something... Or if we need to try something." Food was always a commodity when money was not available.

Before anyone could tell what she was doing, she quickly slid her hands behind her neck, undid the locket and dropped it into the valise's hiding place.

And by evening, as she had feared, people revealed their true selves. Individuals pleaded, bribed, and even threatened for bits of food. A couple of the men looked angrily at the women and one even snatched a piece of bread from a little girl. Three women protested and one shoved the man back against the cattle car. Another threw a punch at him and snatched the bread back before handing it to the child.

"We might be in a cattle car," the woman cried in Slovakian, "but we are not animals!"

Antonia was trying to work out the districts this train was passing through. Wherever they were going, they were taking a roundabout route. More often than not, the train stopped. Once, they heard either new cars being attached, or ones that were being removed. People crawled to look between the slats. Beneath them, the ground trembled from bombings, and artillery shells whistled in the distance. A sickly sweet smell of decay hit Antonia's nostrils. Only when it was quiet again, and dark, did the train stutter forward, carrying them onwards.

By the second day, Antonia and Lena, together with Nestor, had eaten a portion of the provisions. Antonia shared some of her potato with the elderly woman with mismatched shoes. The woman gave her an open-mouth toothless smile that might have been mistaken for a grimace of agony.

Weeping, Lena placed the rest of her potato back into the rag. When Antonia asked her why she was not eating, Lena answered, "Roman and Konstantin have nothing. They have nothing to eat."

On the third morning, Antonia awoke from dozing with a start, her heart hurting with the realization that she was very likely riding inside her own coffin. As the wheels continued to churn and the light faded into dark once more, her head screamed in rhythm. *What have I done? What have I done? What have I done?*

And then they stopped again, but this time it was different. This time, further up the train, they heard the sliding of those doors. Voices. Harsh, jeering commands. Dogs barking.

Eyes wide, Lena took her son and held him close. "Nestor, listen to me. Stay with us at all times. No matter what, do you understand? We have to find your father. We have to look for your brother."

Antonia grasped her sister's hand. In her heart of hearts, she feared they would never see Konstantin or Roman again.

As footsteps approached their car, everyone's heads rose. Some people clambered toward the doors. Shouting and pleas broke out again, some moaned for water. The old woman who'd been standing next to Antonia at the beginning of their horrific journey now lay in a heap on the ground. Two other women were trying to move her body out of the way.

"Is she dead?" Lena's voice was high-pitched. "Did she die?"

One of the women nodded. Antonia thought about that bit of potato she'd wasted but shook herself and clasped Lena's hand as the door was yanked back. The platform, the sea of bodies, the barbed wire, the guard towers off in the distance. Men in black caps with swastikas smack in the middle of their heads like bullet holes. Armbands that read SA on them. Side arms. Truncheons. Orders. The passengers were swine. They were rats. It was time to unload the meat. Dead meat. *Untermenschen.*

It was as Antonia had feared. They were at a camp. The dreaded camps. But none of the rumors had come close to this, nothing could have prepared them for the nauseating stench.

In the background, megaphones announced that, if they worked, they would be free. Walk orderly. Be orderly. Stand in line. Move. It was like entering the arena of a Roman colosseum filled with roving lions, snarling and hungry.

Antonia straightened, staring the SA man down as she jumped onto the platform. She retrieved Nestor from Lena, gave Lena a hand and then they were shoved by a guard with a truncheon toward a low-ceilinged barrack. Several tables were set up and women sat behind those tables, their faces impassive as they took down names, examined the items that were brought in, and then issued a prisoner number and a barrack number. The typewriter clacked away, as fast as a speeding train.

"Where are we?" Antonia asked in three languages.

The woman who was registering them glanced up when Antonia asked in German and finished stamping a document before answering, "Wilhelmshagen. It's a transit camp, but you will be expected to work until you are transferred."

"Transferred where?" Antonia begged.

The woman shrugged and beckoned to Lena.

"We're family," Antonia said when the woman threw her a scowl.

"Name?"

They were told to line up again. A photographer provided each person with number cards. They had to hold them up as he took headshots. Antonia was handed her numbers, a 29, a 72 and then the letters BLN and the date—04.09.44. She was told to move along and sent to another room at the back. Someone pressed something into her hands, but she was looking for Lena, for Nestor. God forbid she lose sight of them.

The room was watched over by a large woman who towered over Antonia. She had light-brown hair, hard eyes, and high cheekbones that were much too pink.

"Please help us," Antonia said. "We're looking for our family."

She peered down at Antonia. "Your German is very good. Where are you from?"

"Lemberg," Antonia said, using the Germanized name for Lviv. "We're all from Lemberg. We were fleeing the Red Army."

"And what is it that you want?"

"Where are we?" Antonia asked. "Where is Wilhelmshagen?"

"South of Berlin. You will work here until the Germans decide what to do with you." She pointed with a truncheon to a cluster of huts. The ground was sandy. Three birch trees grew in a V in front of it. Antonia's eyes widened at the sight of a beautiful, serene lake far behind the chain-link fence and barbed wire.

"Your barrack is over there. Now go on." The woman shoved her off.

"I need to find my sister's husband," Antonia pressed. "And her son. Whether they were on the same train. Whether they are here?"

The woman rolled her shoulders back, the truncheon now a threat. "Do I look like a concierge to you? Do you think you're on vacation here?"

Antonia felt someone pulling her away from the woman and she spun around to face a tall girl, dark curly hair, wearing a worn dress and shoes so threadbare Antonia could see her socks at the toes.

The girl urged Antonia to follow her off to the side then whispered in Russian. "You better get a move on. And you had better learn very quickly that information is never free. Ever."

Antonia was about to be dismissive but studied the stranger more closely. She'd been here a long time with those threadbare clothes. A survivor. "I need to find Lena and my nephew, Nestor."

The guards were herding the new arrivals behind the barbed wire now. When, again, Antonia tried to linger, craning her neck to see whether she could find any sign of Roman or Konstantin back on the crowded platform, another guard scowled at her, matching the snarling German shepherd on his leash.

The dark-haired woman pointed behind the SA man. "Is that them?"

To Antonia's relief, Lena and Nestor were heading toward her and, even better, they had all been assigned to the same barrack as the woman.

"I'm Regina," she said and winked. "I'll be your tour guide today."

Regina eyed the plate and spoon each of them was carrying. It was the first time Antonia registered she had anything at all besides the valise of personal belongings.

"Listen to me," Regina said. "If you're crafty in any way, you make sure that you find a way for those items to attach themselves to your body. Permanently."

Antonia stared at her, clearly remembering what had happened on the train.

"And that was Kapo Horák you met," Regina added. "You'll get to know her personally soon enough, but if I were you, I'd find a better way to deal with her. And I mean, deal."

Antonia narrowed her eyes. She understood.

Regina led them to a row of bunks and tapped the frame of one set. "Welcome home."

Nestor was moving as if in a trance. He sat on the edge of the lower bunk and watched as Antonia and Lena took in their surroundings. At least they had some of their personal belongings. And they had the valise with the secreted food. The locket, however, she would find a separate place to hide. And it would have to be soon, because if people were prepared to kill for spoons and plates…

A woman that Antonia recognized from Ulič smiled shyly from the bunk across the way.

"Are you all right?" Antonia asked.

The woman shook her head, then nodded, then shrugged. "I'm Livia," was her answer. With her cardigan clutched in one hand, she gestured to a group of gaunt and pale girls with dark circles beneath their eyes.

"They're from a town near Bratislava," Livia said. "They arrived a month ago. I asked them what people do here."

Antonia bent toward her as Livia was keeping her voice very low. "And what did you find out?" she asked.

"Some workforces get sent outside the camp. Some inside. They said they're assigned as laborers in a workshop on the camp's grounds. They're assembling some sort of electronic components and need magnifying glasses to do it. Radios maybe? Anyway, they say they have to work by lamplight even during the day, because the windows are blacked out to avoid bombings at night. They said they have to write down how much work they got done, and if they don't meet a certain quota, women immediately get sent somewhere else. They said something about Auschwitz-Birkenau."

Antonia frowned. "In Poland?"

The woman shrugged. "How should I know?"

"Did you come here with family?" Antonia tried to remember exactly where in Ulič she had seen the woman. She was young but maybe if her family had come, she had a chance of finding out where Roman and Konstantin might be.

"My husband and I were together. I don't know where he is. My parents are maybe here? I don't know. I just got married before you and your family arrived in the village." She seemed hesitant, then blurted, "There was talk that your friend, the one in German uniform—"

Antonia eyed her. "Ivan is—"

"A collaborator."

Antonia backed away but Livia reached a hand to her. "I don't believe it. I don't. And I think we need friends here. Not enemies."

Antonia returned her attention to her sister. Lena was hunched into herself. She had two tasks now. Keep Lena and Nestor alive, and find Roman and Konstantin. She would definitely need friends for this.

That night, Antonia remained awake, once in a while dropping her hand to Lena, who clung to it as if it was a lifeline. Women coughed, and Antonia had a fit herself, pulling the thin blanket around her throat, and massaging the lump. At some point she fell asleep, awaking to a hiccupping sound. Several women were weeping in their beds, and Lena was wracked by sobs below her. Hoping that nobody would hear her, Antonia gave into the despair, biting her arm to keep herself from screaming, to keep Lena from knowing.

The next morning, they were ordered to roll call, and stood in line as Kapo Horák announced the work details. Antonia was relieved when they were assigned to a factory.

Horák stalked over to her and tugged hard on the end of Antonia's scarf. "Take that off. What do you think this is? A fashion show?"

She undid the knot and Kapo Horák snatched the scarf from her, but her eyes landed on Antonia's lump. She wagged the tip of her truncheon for a moment, Antonia holding her gaze. Her eyes darted to Lena then back to Antonia.

"Tomorrow, you'll be shoveling coal," she said, and stalked away as a camp guard ordered them to the manufactory barracks.

"What am I to do with Nestor?" Lena pleaded.

One of the women from their barrack said matter-of-factly, "The children stay where they are. Sometimes they are there when you come back. Sometimes not."

When Lena turned in horror to the source of information, the SA man brought his truncheon down on her arm with a sickening crunch. Lena cried out and Antonia threw her arms over her. Her sister shook, but did not make another noise for the rest of the way to the workshop. In terror, they spent half the day assembling the electronic parts before another group appeared to take over. When Lena and Antonia returned to the barracks, they found Nestor cowering beneath the bunk beds with both of their blankets, fast asleep.

"Let me see your arm," Antonia said.

Lena shook her head, her mouth trembling. "It's not broken. I swear it. But if Nestor wakes up and sees it…"

The next morning, Antonia found the place where she could hide her locket safely. She was sent to scrub the floors in the washroom, and it was a mouse that revealed the hole behind one of the toilets. At her next opportunity, she returned with the locket. Ignoring the scum and her own disgust, she dropped to the floor and slid the locket behind the wall, making certain she could still touch it, find it, and retrieve it. With the stealing, the daily inspections, the lack of humanity she had encountered in just the last few days, Antonia would keep her most precious item safer this way. She hoped.

Later, she spoke with a group of women, and one said, "Many of the Nazis left the camp some weeks ago. Since then, the guards have stopped doing daily selections. It used to be that every day they would pull out the weaker ones, the sick ones, and send them away. But that has stopped. Now everyone must work. The SAs that are left here, the Kapos, they've gotten—I don't know how to say it. Desperate?"

"They're on a power trip," another said and trailed off. "Especially Kapo Horák." She exchanged a knowing look with the others. She had such thin skin, Antonia could see the blue of her veins.

"If you don't work," Regina said, "they'll club you to death or just shoot you out back, though Horák says the guards have been told not to waste bullets."

"Kapo Horák?" Antonia had learned that a Kapo was a shortened term for a camp captain.

"Doris. Yes."

She referred to Horák by her first name. This was interesting. Antonia narrowed her eyes. "What is she like? Who is she?"

The blue-veined girl shrugged, her eyes drooping as if she would fall asleep sitting up. "She's like any of us. Except that she chose to be a bully and the Germans made her oversee us. For that, she gets to eat sausages and sauerkraut while the rest of us get by with rotten potatoes and this gruel they call soup."

And make-up, Antonia thought. She gets make-up. Another interesting bit of information. Doris Horák was vain.

Over time, she asked the other women about the Kapo and nearly yelped with delight when one woman, rolling her eyes, said, "Yeah, I know her. She claims to be an art historian from Prague."

"Why is she here?"

"Political prisoner."

"Is that so?" Antonia muttered, trying not to smile. She gave the woman a slice of apple.

*

Fall overtook the night and hinted that even winter would conspire against the inmates. In a matter of days, temperatures dropped to the point where it was impossible to see out the frost-covered washroom window. Even the inside window ledges were iced over, and it was only early October. Nobody at Wilhelmshagen received enough calories to keep themselves warm, unless they wore a black uniform, or were Nazi administrators. And like the Kapos and administrators, winter was pursuing a vendetta against the inmates.

As newcomers, Antonia and Lena were assigned to a hard labor force with some thirty others, including Livia. They were loaded onto buses and driven almost an hour outside of the camp where the women were then instructed to help clear a woodland. Some men chopped trees, but the women had to clear thick tangles of brush. Lena and Antonia looked at one another. This was work they had done on their orchards, work that was familiar to them.

Antonia was soaked in sweat from the exertion. There were beautiful lakes to be seen, and the birds were singing. A flock of geese competed with a warplane in the sky. The ground was sandy and soft, but soon she felt as if her nose, her mouth and ears were full of sand.

Suddenly aware of a rhythmic beat close by, Antonia looked up to see a guard kicking a prisoner who was lying on the ground.

"I said, faster!" The guard's cap flew off his head as he laid into his victim.

The other prisoners were off to the side, heads low, shoulders hunched. When another guard looked her way, Antonia turned back to work, but her jaw hurt from clenching it.

A vehicle screeched to a halt and an officer jumped out, his boots sinking into the sand as he marched up to the line of men waist-deep in one of the pits. Antonia could not tell what they were doing in there, none of it made any sense.

The officer teetered on the edge of the pit, his legs apart, his hands on his hips.

"Is this what you all call work?" he screamed. "Kapo! Have them dig to the count! Spades up—spades down! Spades up—spades down! One—two! One—two!"

Before Antonia realized what was happening, the officer was charging about in a fury, randomly kicking and punching the inmates who were still above the pits. The more he bellowed, the greater his rage. Antonia frantically searched for Lena and spotted her sister behind her, just a few meters down the line.

Where could they hide from him if he came after them? Behind the bushes? Run to the lake and swim? A few meters away, there was a stack of large branches. She could grab one of those and club him to death, perhaps inspire the others in her line to do the same. To fight back.

The officer suddenly stopped, his eyes on the line behind Antonia. He raised his truncheon and barreled straight for her. Antonia scooped up the brush near her, and swung the bundle of thorny branches around to face him. She moved straight in front of him, as if by mistake. He halted, lowered the truncheon, and squinted at her.

Antonia dared to look at him. She knew that shine in the eye, those signals as he took in her face.

"So." He sneered and proceeded to walk slowly around her. "So, so, so, so. What have we here?"

When he was standing before her again, Antonia took him in, from the small ears, to the sharp chin, the narrow eyes, the crooked mouth. He removed his cap, his hair shorn close to his head and more white than blond.

"You don't miss a thing, do you?" he muttered.

His truncheon swinging limply in his hand, he stepped around her, and Antonia swung with him, prepared to defend Lena if she had to. Instead, he raised a gloved hand to the detail and pointed with the truncheon. "Work! All of you. Get back to work! You're not here to eat for free!"

On the bus back, Antonia whispered to one of the other women. "Those men who were digging. What were they digging for?"

The woman shrugged tiredly, and closed her eyes before answering. "Who knows. Everything we do can be destroyed on the whim of any of these beasts. Might we find all the brushwood we cleared right back where we'd collected it today? Of course."

Antonia never found out because the next day, she and Lena were called to stand in the main assembly as several bosses from a munitions factory came to select inmates for labor. They checked for manual dexterity, hearing and eyesight, received certifications from the camp doctor, and chose Lena to go. Antonia, in the meantime, anxious about being separated from her sister, was sent to work in a potash mine. It was located a half hour outside of the camp. The only thing that made the trip less harrowing was that Kapo Horák was on that bus with her.

Antonia took a seat not too far from hers, close enough so that she could lean into the aisle and speak with her. "Horák," she said. "Is that Slovakian or Czech?"

"Czech. Why do you ask?"

"It's interesting. I learned that your first name is Doris."

The Kapo raised an eyebrow but nodded. "It is."

"Huh." Antonia sat back and crossed her arms. She looked out the window, her brow furrowed in concentration. "Where did you say you were from in Czechoslovakia?"

Doris crossed her arms as well, also narrowed her eyes. She resembled an opera diva more than a prison guard. "I didn't."

"Because, my brother-in-law," Antonia said, "might have mentioned that when he was in Bratislava, he knew of an art professor... I think it was Bratislava... Anyway..."

Doris continued to peer at Antonia suspiciously but Antonia shrugged and leaned back into her seat.

A moment later, Doris turned to her. "Prague. I'm from Prague. At least that's where I worked. Why would your brother-in-law know me?"

"Wait. Are you a Renaissance expert? It might be a coincidence as well."

"The Impressionists," Doris said, her smile triumphant.

Antonia thrilled. "Impressionist. That's it. Of course. I should have known. Now, I remember... yes."

"Who is your brother-in-law?" Doris asked again.

"Mazur. Roman Mazur."

When the Kapo's eyebrows shot up, Antonia leaned into the aisle. "You two do know each other."

Doris shook her head. "I've never met him. I never knew that he was in Prague. But I do know his work. My colleague collects folk paintings, especially from the Carpathian region. And she took me to a gallery where some of his work was exhibited."

Antonia's luck could not have been better. She sent a short prayer of thanks before she shot Doris a pleading look. "He's the one I asked about when we arrived. Roman Mazur and his son, Konstantin. I have nothing to give you for your help... Nothing of value, anyway."

Doris's eyes roved over her. There was nothing.

Antonia sighed with exaggerated disappointment. "All those portraits."

Doris's eyes skidded over her.

"Saved us all before. Painting portraits."

"He's certainly not painting where he is now," Doris said, but there was the slightest tone of interest. "I can assure you of that."

Antonia winced. "No. He wouldn't be. And it's a shame."

It took another moment before Doris turned back to her. The bus was pulling in through the gates of an enclosure. "Portraits, you said. Do you think he'd—"

"Paint yours?" Antonia nodded. "I'm sure he would."

Doris nodded. The bus screeched to a stop and she jumped up, hustling everyone off. As Antonia passed her, she said, "I'll let you know tomorrow."

The work at the mine was exhausting. From morning until afternoon, the women worked in rows along the pits, breaking down the potash, then carrying buckets and wheelbarrows to the elevator. Now instead of sand, it was the dust that irritated Antonia's throat, and she coughed frequently. When it began to rain, she took shelter from the deluge beneath a leaky tarp, huddling with the others until it let up a little bit. Their clothing was soaked. Antonia still wore the same blouse and skirt she'd had on when she and Ivan had made their picnic. That had been many weeks ago, but she was now a lifetime away from that grassy knoll in Ulič.

By the time Antonia returned, it was dark and their detail was the last to arrive at the camp. They were given a piece of bread that was meant to sustain them for dinner and for breakfast the next day. They received gruel as well. Antonia's legs, arms and back ached so much, every step was agony. She reached the barracks, relieved to see Lena and Nestor already there, unharmed. They had all survived another day. She embraced and kissed them both, then perched on the edge of Lena's bunk. She did not dare tell her sister about her conversation with Doris; getting her sister's hopes up for nothing would devastate all of them. Lena would have to find comfort solely in her prayers a little while longer.

That night, women complained when Antonia broke into a coughing fit. She was unable to stop and her throat was raw and burning by morning. She'd had little sleep and the idea of returning to those mines made her weep. But when Doris returned to their barracks to pull together the detail, she did not call Antonia's number. Instead, the Kapo strode over to their bunk, flashing the light into Lena's face. Antonia bent down, ready to protect her sister, but Horák yanked her back up by the neck and peered down at Lena.

"Are you Mazur?" Horák barked.

"Yes," Lena cried, her arm over her head.

"Your husband is in the men's camp, but your son Konstantin will be brought to you here."

"*Dyakuvaty Bohu*," Lena sobbed. "Thank you. Thank you!"

Doris looked at Antonia. "Apparently, your brother-in-law was looking for someone who might find you useful, just so that he could locate you."

"How's that?" Antonia asked.

"He's recommended you for a translator's position. You are to report to Kommandant Fitzwald after breakfast."

Antonia's scrambled brain tried to remember whether she'd ever seen the Kommandant.

"How is my husband?" Lena asked.

Doris scoffed. "The first thing he offered to do was paint Fitzwald's portrait. I'd say he's doing rather well."

Antonia clasped her hands together. "Thank you, Kapo Horák."

"You're welcome, Professor." Horák nodded, satisfied. "That's right. I asked about you, as well."

When Antonia arrived at the camp's administrator's office, she hoped to see Roman but did not. Instead, when she was ushered into Kommandant Fitzwald's office, Antonia was taken aback when she recognized the closely shorn head of white blond hair. The man she'd tried to protect herself from with the armload of brambles.

He turned away from the window, arms behind him, his head slightly tilted. "So. So, so, so."

Any hopes Antonia had harbored were quickly replaced by dread.

CHAPTER 18

Winter 1944

Carpathian Mountains, west of the Russian Front

From the office in the cramped administrative building, Ivan heard hammering muffled behind the high walls of their enclosure, or maybe it was an axe ringing in the cold. The clock read noon. A line would be forming outside the mess hall soon. He tossed his brief into the desk drawer and was about to close it when the cigar tube with the sketch inside it rolled forward. *Antonia.* Just behind it, the edges of Roman's sketchpad and Lena's journal. He pulled out the metal cylinder but stuffed it into his breast pocket when someone knocked on the door.

A young boy stepped in and snapped a salute. "Captain Lys requests to see you at the gate, sir."

Ivan dismissed him, picked up his wool cap and strode out of the headquarters. The air was crisp. White drifts were piled everywhere. The forest was locked beneath ice and the roofs of their few buildings creaked beneath the burden of snow. A squad was coming through the high wooden gate at the same time as another group went out, their breaths colliding in the air.

The legion's camp was situated on a large, isolated ranch in a remote part of the Carpathian Mountains. The twelve hectares of thick forest protected them and served as excellent grounds for tactical training. So far, the Ukrainian command had staved off the Germans from turning them into a combat unit but even as a security force, Ivan and the others kept both the men and women in good fighting condition.

Ivan saluted the young men guarding the gates. Their coats were ill-fitted—sleeves too short, or collars too big. Gone were the days of German-supplied uniforms for each of them. Most of their supplies came at a trickle now, at best. Ivan had already argued he preferred it that way. Less reliance on the Germans meant more independence to make their own decisions. They had grown in number, with both men and women flocking to their gates. But the Ukrainian commanders also needed to be more careful about who they allowed in.

The hard winter had drawn a flock of Ukrainian Partisan Army deserters reporting that their cells were breaking up. They came with what they had on their backs, some saying they could no longer carry out the orders of their radical commanders and wanted to swear loyalty to the legion instead. They claimed the legion had an honorable reputation but Ivan suspected their motives were much simpler: the Partisan Army had run out of food and supplies.

His suspicions proved justified when a group of deserters were sent out on a joint patrol with one of Ivan's own squads. Knowing there had been tensions between his men and the newcomers, when they did not return Ivan went out with some of his most trusted men to search for them. They found that every one of his legionnaires had been slaughtered, along with a group of Polish women and children. The Ukrainian Partisan Army deserters were not among the dead. Ivan immediately ordered a manhunt and found the rogues in a swamp, nearly frozen to death. He showed no mercy.

Off to the side of the main gate, two women—dressed in long coats and once-bright headscarves, were speaking with Captain Lys. They carried baskets tucked under their arms, and made excited gestures. One was a dark-haired woman, petite and handsome with large brown eyes. Ivan recalled her name was Nadia and that she came from the Volhynian province.

Lys was scowling—an expression which Ivan had since learned was a sign of concentration rather than perpetual dissatisfaction—and indicated the women when Ivan arrived.

"I sent these two to sell odds and ends in some of the villages and gather intelligence."

"We learned about two Partisan Army camps," Nadia said when Lys prompted her.

"Just over fifteen kilometers from here," Lys said.

The second woman had a full moon face, a splatter of freckles across an upturned nose, and clear, gray eyes that were as mischievous as a fox's. She reminded Ivan very much of Oksana. He had never seen her before, but she stepped up to him as if they were old friends.

"One of the combat units," she said, as if she were selling a secret, "is camped between two gullies. The second is about three kilometers further northeast."

"That's nearly in Poland," Ivan said, drawing away from her.

"You think they're trying to push the Polish insurgents back?" She suddenly stuck out her hand, cornering him in the open space. "I'm Maria, by the way."

"I'm Lieutenant Kovalenko," he said. "And if you're right and the Ukrainian Partisan Army is engaging the Polish Home Army, then that's one problem we don't have to concern ourselves with."

"We should inform Dusha," Lys said. "He'll want to know. I'd hoped he would be with you."

Ivan shook his head, and watched Nadia hugging herself against the cold. "The colonel is at the clinic, taking inventory. Ladies, thank you for your good work. I think there's borscht in the mess hall waiting for you."

But Nadia straightened and checked her companion. "If someone's taking inventory, we should be there."

Maria brushed by Ivan, fluttering her eyelashes. "Follow us."

Lys fell into step with Ivan as they followed the nurses at a distance. "I do believe Maria was flirting with you," he teased.

"Tell me something I don't know," Ivan muttered.

Lys let out his usual laugh: a single, abrupt guffaw. Maria turned, checked over her shoulder, and winked at the two of them.

For the second time in a matter of minutes, Ivan yearned for Antonia. He had to get through this war and find her. And he would do all he could to make good on his promise.

They found their commander at the clinic, and the two women repeated their information before taking over the lists of inventory.

"Where are you getting supplies?" Ivan asked Dusha.

"I'm sending some of the men to meet with Major Asmuth in Moroczyn and take whatever they can with them."

"Moroczyn? That's in Poland," Ivan said. He had not seen Asmuth since he'd returned from Ulič and had been desperate to speak to him about Antonia's situation. "Let me go to him."

Dusha looked apologetic. "I need you here."

Lys was indignant. "What's in Moroczyn?"

"They requisitioned an entire town," the colonel explained. "They've set up a base for us to go to if we need."

"We're not running away," Lys growled. "And we're not joining forces with the Wehrmacht."

Dusha clapped the man's shoulder but Maria, her eyes dancing over Ivan, squeezed between them to get to the medicine cabinet.

"We need aspirin, some knives and other surgical instruments," she announced with authority.

"We are especially low on morphine and antibiotics," Nadia added, but more cordially.

"We need everything," Maria stated matter-of-factly. "Anything we can get, except…" She lifted a box from the dresser below the cabinet with what looked like bottles used for home brews.

"Nadia brewed this antiseptic and it's as good, if not better, than what you get at the pharmacy."

Ivan lifted a bottle out. "What is it?"

Nadia blushed a little. "I stripped birch buds off in spring and soaked them in *horilka*."

Ivan studied her. "Bet whoever's liquor you took didn't appreciate it."

She ducked her head but not before he saw an embarrassed grin. "My father was not pleased, but I did the old man a favor."

That surprised him, how forthright she was. He liked it.

"I'm resourceful as well," Maria chirped. She reached around him to produce another box, this time from the makeshift examination table. "I spent two weeks scrounging up old fabric and wrapping these bandages." She showed the large box to Dusha next. "So, Colonel Sovchenko, the other things I listed, I'd say those are critical."

Dusha put away his list and thanked them, then ushered Ivan and Lys out.

Lys nudged Ivan. "You know," he grumbled, "if you're not interested in that Maria…"

Ivan clapped him on the back. "I'll stay out of your way."

Back in his office, Dusha pulled off his hat and gloves, the long scar on his face taut from the cold. "Men, we all know the war is winding down. It's time we prepare the legion to take a real stand, and set up a security force on the Galician borders. For that, we are going to need more people. I want to investigate these two Ukrainian Partisan Army camps and see whether we can convince them to unite with us. It's time we lock the Organization of Ukrainian Nationalists back into one common force."

Taking in a deep breath, Ivan scratched the back of his neck. After that incident in the Polish settlement where Ivan had lost his men, they had sworn to take no further Partisan Army rebels. He could not imagine they had anything left in common.

"Two or more battalions will make us formidable," Dusha said measuredly. "Let the Germans fight the Poles while we concentrate on our own territories. But we'll need Asmuth to step up supplies if I'm to negotiate for those rebels' loyalties."

"I don't trust them," Ivan said.

Dusha winced beneath the gray mustache. "I understand you. It's noted. You have a better idea?"

Lys was up in arms. "Those sons of bitches will take you as soon as they see you. At least exchange hostages."

But Dusha was not convinced of the danger. Instead, he dismissed them, then strode out, his gloves and hat in his hands.

Ivan heard him call to someone to saddle up his horse. He looked at Lys. The captain's expression was dark. Ivan shared his reservations, so when the door to the office opened, he hoped Dusha would appear and say he'd changed his mind. But in came Pavlo, together with Lieutenants Kvitka and Terlytsia.

Pavlo shook himself out of his coat and took in Ivan and Lys before lowering himself into a chair at the conference table. From his canteen, he poured something steaming. "You two look as if you've been sent to sit in the corner."

"I think you should all go," Lys blurted to Ivan. "You, Pavlo, Kvitka—"

"Go where?" Terlytsia asked. He wiped frost off his dark mustache and dropped a satchel on the table.

Kvitka opened it and with a charming smile pulled out a half-dozen fire-roasted potatoes. Terlytsia tossed one to Ivan.

But Kvitka presented one to each of the other men as if he were handing out flowers, bent at the waist, one hand behind his back. "Here you are, ladies."

Ivan placed the potato on the table and paced the floor, as he told them all about Dusha's plan to negotiate with the Ukrainian Partisan Army and his own reservations.

"Would you stop?" Pavlo complained, holding out Ivan's potato. "You're making me dizzy. Sit down."

But Terlytsia was already moving to the maps. Kvitka, his potato stuck in his mouth, looked over his shoulder.

"You'll stay here, Lys," Terlytsia said. His black eyes were alight. "Take over command of the camp and let the rest of the men know where we are."

Nadia, the nurse, suddenly popped her head in. Ivan nearly barreled into her.

"Hello, there," she said with surprise. Cheeks ruddy from the cold, she took a few steps backwards.

Pavlo jumped out of his seat and caught her just before she landed against the wall. "Hello, there," he said, his arms firmly around her.

"Hello," Nadia said again. The rest of her face turned a lovely shade of rose.

Ivan cleared his throat. "How can we help you?"

She ripped her gaze from Pavlo's. "I didn't mean to interrupt. Has the colonel already sent someone to Moroczyn?"

"Talk to Lys over here," Ivan said. "He'll get you what you need. Boys?"

Terlytsia and Kvitka rolled up one of the maps and headed out with Ivan.

"Bye, there," he heard Pavlo say behind him.

"Bye, there," Nadia called.

Ivan led them to the stables, and Maya nickered softly. "Not today, girl. You're still a bit lame."

Within minutes he had another horse saddled and was riding out the high wooden gate. Their intention was to tail Dusha from a distance, just in case. But several kilometers up the road, the colonel's trail suddenly disappeared into the forest, and no matter how many times they tried, they could not pick it up.

"Now what?" Kvitka said, removing his cap. His blond hair stood on end.

Ivan looked about, threw his arms out. "How does he do this in the middle of winter? With all this snow?"

"We keep going," Pavlo said. He clicked his tongue and steered his horse onwards.

Not a half kilometer later, the colonel suddenly stepped out from between two large boulders. Dusha. A spirit indeed. But this one had a furious scowl etched into the lines of his face.

"I thought I was clear about going alone."

Ivan looked at the other men but their gazes remained intent on their commander.

Dusha pursed his lips but, after a moment, he silently swung back onto the stallion. Now a group of five, they rode on to search for the two partisan encampments.

Exactly as Maria had described, the first encampment was located between two gullies, difficult to reach other than on foot or on horse. They were alerted by kits clanging and echoing off the steep walls. Ivan caught the whiff of smoke and boiled cabbage.

Ivan and Pavlo volunteered to scout out the premises and scrambled up one of the slopes, eventually picking their way through underbrush that turned into a forest of browned ferns and dried pine needles. Ivan pointed to the thin trail of smoke rising in the distance and removed his binoculars.

"What the...?" he muttered, glassing over the premises. Large black dots moved against the snowy landscape but there were no more than a couple dozen men.

Pavlo echoed Ivan's confusion. "Where are the rest? That camp is large enough to hold maybe forty, fifty men."

"I spot only a few guards on duty," Ivan added. "And they look hungry."

"Good reason to join us, then," Pavlo teased.

Ivan glanced over at him, but a feeling of dread cemented his middle. "Let's go tell the others."

They were just beginning to move when bullets suddenly spattered the trees behind them. Pavlo released a muted howl. Ivan spun around to see the Half Cossack writhing on the ground. Blood seeped around the edges of his fingers where he clutched his shoulder. Ivan bolted back up the path, the bullets flying again.

"Now we know where their patrols are," Pavlo gasped. His lips were pulled back from his teeth.

"No time for jokes," Ivan said. Another bullet zinged past them.

"Not a good time to be a tall guy," Pavlo quipped back.

Ivan grabbed Pavlo and lifted him up, both of them sliding down the forest floor. They stumbled back out onto the lower road, Pavlo hobbling against Ivan.

"Christ," Terlytsia cried. He and Kvitka rushed to help them.

"Get his horse," Ivan called. He lifted Pavlo onto his mount, took a split second to assess the wound and was relieved to see that it was more of nick than anything else. "You're going to live, you asshole." He slapped the horse's rear and Pavlo rode off.

Ivan got onto his horse and rode up to Dusha.

"It's their patrols. They know we're here."

Terlytsia and Kvitka spurred their horses after Pavlo. Dusha swung his mount in front of Ivan.

"What about the other camp?" he asked.

"I don't like any of this one bit," Ivan said. "That one is mostly empty, they can't all be situated in the woods, can they? It's a trap. We should leave the other one."

Shots rang through the forest above them again. The renegade army was on the move.

Dusha nodded. "We return to our camp."

The ride back was tense. Ivan expected partisan rebels to surround them at any moment, to come riding out and attack them, at least harass and question them. He galloped to get nearer to Pavlo, and Pavlo grinned at him then winced.

"Flesh wound?" Ivan asked.

The Half Cossack nodded. "I'm hoping so."

"Where the hell are they?" Ivan said, slowing down. The other officers glanced over at him as they drew up.

The Half Cossack shrugged. "Maybe it is just a small band. Maybe they're just keeping low because they don't have the numbers."

But Pavlo was just shooting blanks, and he knew it.

As they reached the top of the road leading to the camp's narrow valley, Ivan pulled his horse to a stop next to Dusha. Kvitka's mouth dropped open. Terlytsia cursed under his breath, but it sounded like a prayer. Ahead of them, coming from the grove of trees, they saw smoke and flames.

"Christ," Ivan breathed. He stared in Pavlo's direction in the rapidly coming dark. They'd been tricked to ride out.

They kicked their horses and galloped down. The huge gates were standing wide open. Three trucks were parked in a semicircle, illuminating a group of wounded on the ground.

Bodies were strewn from the gates to the mess hall. Ivan crouched next to one, then the other, checking pulses. He looked up as Dusha strode over to them.

"Those *ublyadky* set us up," the colonel growled.

Ivan grabbed the lantern from him. The kitchen and mess hall were on fire, the clinic as well. Suddenly there was an explosion and he ducked. Ivan pictured Nadia's bottles of home-made antiseptic. And the two nurses. He sprinted toward the burning building.

The doctors were outside, dead. One shot through the head. And Ivan bent over another shape before him, lifted the lantern and moaned. It was Maria, her face scratched and bleeding, a bullet wound to the stomach. Behind him, Ivan heard Lys's voice and he rose. Through the gates, and out of the wreckage, some people were coming back in. He recognized Nadia with a boy. Ivan hurried to her and put an arm around her just as Lys strode over to the boy.

"What happened?" Dusha demanded when they reached him.

"Those partisan bandits," Nadia gasped. "They surrounded us. Everyone panicked. They captured the men out on the training grounds and were holding them at gunpoint. We had to open the gate. They insisted that we give up all our weapons. Captain Lys tried to talk them down. Everyone was screaming at each other."

Ivan led her to where the survivors were congregating in the light.

Lys, his voice heavy, reported to Dusha. "I gave orders not to shoot, but tensions rose. We were outnumbered. They wanted our weapons. I gave orders. I told them not to shoot, but someone shot and then it was mayhem."

The boy stepped up next to Lys.

Ivan reached out to him and recognized the cadet who'd come to his office on Lys's request. "Are you all right?"

"This is my brother," Lys said.

"Kulka," the boy said.

"Little scrapper," Lys added, "but a good shot."

"How are you doing?" Ivan asked.

"I was hiding in the forest and started picking off some of the bandits. They got scared. Whoever was left took off. They took about twenty or thirty of our people with them, just kidnapped them."

Ivan glanced over at Nadia. She was holding herself, shivering in the middle of the assembly of wounded and dying. Ivan was filled with shame. If this was how Ukrainians were going to work together, then Antonia had been right about wanting to leave. He shook himself at the sound of Dusha hollering orders.

Ivan walked over and put an arm around the small nurse.

"Nadia," he said, "are you able to help?"

Her teeth were chattering as she spoke. "What if... what if Maria and I led them straight here? What if we weren't careful enough in our inquiries? What if..."

"Shhh..."

But her eyes were wide, and she shuddered violently.

"Listen, my friend, Pavlo Derkach, he's been shot," Ivan said. "You know? The little guy you saw me with earlier? If I know him, he won't be feeling a thing yet, but when he comes off the adrenaline, he'll be screaming murder. Just get him bandaged up, okay, and then tell him I told him to help you. Do what you can? All right? He's good at helping with wounds. We're all going to have to split up later and find places to hide out. These assholes will be back, I promise. But we need to work fast, and get ready to move out. Understood?"

"Yes." Her teeth chattered. "I understand."

"Good, go now."

Ivan growled with frustration as he looked around him again. They would have to flee to Moroczyn now. The damned Partisan Army was forcing the legion to hightail it straight to the German High Command. The last thing the Ukrainians needed to do right now was admit they needed the Nazis' protection.

He suddenly remembered Maya and swung around. The stable was miraculously still standing. Lys's little brother zipped past him, and Ivan called him back.

"Kulka, you know anything about those horses?"

The boy ran back to him breathlessly. "They took them. They're all gone."

Sprinting away, Ivan headed for the stables to check for himself. It was empty and Maya was gone. Ivan yanked his cap off and bellowed with rage then remembered something else. He ran out and watched the flames that had engulfed the administrative office. Roman's sketchbook. Lena's journal. He wept. Sometimes it was the little things that finally broke a man.

CHAPTER 19

Winter 1944–45

Wilhelmshagen, Outside of Berlin, Germany

As another night fell behind the frosted-over windows, Antonia and Livia spoke, their breaths lifting like the last of a heavy fog. They were waiting for Lena to return. While they had all worked, the children in the barracks had used their fingernails to scratch drawings onto the windowpanes—Christmas trees, words in several languages, stars, candles and snowflakes. In one corner, they had blown onto the patches of ice and left kiss marks. Antonia went back to the children and huddled under the blankets with them, wrapping her arms around Konstantin and Nestor to keep them warm as she retold the story of Jonah and the whale, their favorite.

The days and weeks had passed painfully by. Once or twice a week, Kommandant Fitzwald called Antonia in for a perverse game of boss and secretary. On the other five or six days of the week, Antonia was assigned to labor in a factory or on the campgrounds, most often wherever Lena was not. They all dragged themselves to work and back, shivering in their thin clothes and worn shoes. Breakfast was the second half of the bread they received at night. There was watery tea at midday, occasionally with something that looked like aspic. Sometimes it contained pieces of ice. The diet was hardly meant to sustain them. Beyond the hunger, the rate of illness had risen exponentially, as did the work accidents. Regardless, the guards were brutal with them. Those who stumbled, or fell, or dropped their tools, or whose movements were uncertain because they were weak, received punishing blows with the end of a rifle butt or with the truncheons. The men in the camp shared incidents from construction sites, about those who'd fallen from scaffolds, or of those who worked in the mines, loading coal. Some had been bludgeoned to death by the guards, others had stumbled in their exhaustion and been crushed beneath the wheels of trains. The numbers of the dead were so high that, Antonia observed, they no longer aroused much emotion in her. The collection of corpses became as routine as the daily roll calls, as routine as the work itself. And it was this indifference—when she caught herself thinking it—that made her head hurt. Who could blame them, however? She and the other inmates of Wilhelmshagen were officially referred to as simply "material." Even when she worked in the office, which to some of her barrack mates appeared to be a luxury, Kommandant Fitzwald treated her as his own personal object to play with as he liked.

Fitzwald tasked Antonia with some of the accounting, among other things. Sometimes this included recording the number of Reichsmarks companies paid for using the camp's "material." Four Reichsmarks per inmate per day was standard. And Fitzwald once argued that this was fair, for it was exactly what any other unskilled laborer received, and therefore, Antonia assessed, nobody could later complain that the Nazis had exploited the inmates. It was a surprise, then, and a revelation, when Fitzwald had her fill out a pass for one of the inmates to see a doctor in town. The pass contained an exact amount of time the inmate could leave the camp, and he was to bring back a report from the doctor each time.

An idea had begun to form in her mind.

The barrack door opened, followed by a blast of winter air before a group of women, bent against the cold, shuffled wearily in.

This was the work detail from the Friedrich tunnel. Lena appeared moments later. Her eyes were dark with exhaustion, her wrists swollen and her fingers black from her work in the munitions factory, but Antonia knew that, more than anything, Lena was distressed about how, some weeks ago, Roman had been moved to a satellite camp near Magdeburg, two hours away.

Wordlessly, Lena motioned for Nestor to come to her. The body, Antonia thought, was a miraculous thing. Lena had taken to breastfeeding both children. It had been a gradual process to convince her system to lactate but it worked. At least a little bit. But there were some days when she was no longer producing milk, and now they tried to keep Konstantin fed on what rations they received. Both boys were wasting away. Konstantin's skin was gray. His head was grotesquely oversized for his body, and it lolled back onto Antonia's chest.

"I'm hungry, too," he whimpered.

But Lena's look of despair already signaled Antonia that her sister did not have enough milk even for Nestor.

Antonia shivered, unable to prevent an image of herself and Lena being lifted one morning from these very bunk beds and dropped like stones onto the cart used to collect the dead. They'd be wheeled away to the back of the washrooms, where the other corpses were stacked like firewood until the ground thawed enough to dig the mass graves. And Nestor and Konstantin would be left alone.

Nobody, Regina had once warned, ever escaped suffering.

When the Kapos came by the bunkers to call lights out, Antonia was waiting for Doris Horák. She never knew in which kind of mood the former art professor would be in. She truly did not do anything without pay, and sometimes even then she did not come through, such as when Antonia begged her to have Roman's detail in Magdeburg cut short. The woman had only laughed and asked Antonia who she thought she was. But Antonia never stopped trying because sometimes—*sometimes*—Horák came through, just like she had when she'd found Roman and Konstantin for her and brought Konstantin to the women's barrack.

"Lena is ill," Antonia now said to Doris. "What will it take to get my sister on a work detail in the kitchen? Her body can't take the rigor."

Doris pursed her lips. "The kitchen detail? That will cost you. What have you got left to offer me?"

Countless times, Antonia had considered the locket, still hidden in the washroom. Countless times, she had considered whether the situation was dire enough to give it away now. She was close. She was terribly close. And still, she resisted. The moment that she would apply its value there would be nothing left. She had even considered dividing up the locket into three parts: the chain, the locket itself and then the miniature painting, and determined that the locket was only valuable whole, and if she began to give away the pieces, someone would come to the conclusion she was hiding more. Lives depended on this one piece.

She looked back to where the boys were huddled with Lena beneath the blankets. Lena handed Konstantin a crumb of bread. No. Not yet. Things could still get worse. Though it was hard to imagine. And as long as Roman was not back in the main camp with them, she could not just give away the locket because she had another idea for it.

The following morning, Antonia was summoned to the one-storied administrator's building for work. Cold, crisp snowflakes drifted from the sky as she crossed the main assembly grounds. Through the window of his office, she could already see Kommandant Albert Fitzwald waiting for her. When she arrived, he clasped his hands behind his back and rocked on his feet, his eyes trained on the camp's activities. A pair of women's high heels—beige and nearly new—were planted by the door. Antonia slipped out of her mud-spattered shoes, picked up the stranger's pumps and stepped behind the office door to put on the dress Fitzwald hung on the back for her each time. Today, it was a soft, green wool dress, intended to fit her, she guessed, but she was losing weight nightly. She took off her worn clothing and changed. Though she could cinch the waist, the dress was still too loose for her. When she brushed her hands over the front, she felt her hip bones. Next to the door was a sink with a mirror and a small shelf that contained make-up and a brush. She washed her face, dried it, and applied lipstick, rouge and some mascara. She combed her hair. Fitzwald had had her hair chopped off the second time she came to work for him. It was shoulder length now. At first, the Kommandant had tried to have her use curlers, expressly in fashion with fancily pinned updos and rolls. However, after a few days of this, where Antonia's straight, thick hair would not cooperate, and it was logistically impossible to put her hair in rollers overnight in the barracks, Fitzwald hung a poster next to the mirror. It was a movie poster, featuring Hilde Krahl in *Dreaming*. He told Antonia to make her hair "look like that." She now tied and pinned the bun at the nape of her neck and smoothed the hair behind her ears.

Antonia stepped away from the mirror and took her place at the desk perpendicular to his. That was when Fitzwald moved away from the window, and bowed slightly before her.

"Good morning, Fräulein Kosaken."

He had Germanized her last name as well.

"Good morning, Herr Kommandant. What is it that I can do for you today?"

Antonia prepared to take notes, but Fitzwald strode to her desk and placed a hand over the book. His fingers spasmed, as if itching to reach out and touch her.

"I was reminded that Christmas for the Slavs is tomorrow," he said. "Is that correct?"

"Yes, Herr Kommandant. Christmas Eve is on January the sixth."

He took in a breath and straightened, his living hand hidden behind his back again. "I should like to arrange a gift for you. Every good employer presents at least a small gift to his employees. Especially his most"—his eyes narrowed in that look that chilled Antonia—"valued employee. So. Fräulein Kosaken, what is your greatest desire this day? What is it that you would wish the Christ Child to bring you?"

Antonia did not hesitate. "My brother-in-law to be moved back to Wilhelmshagen."

Fitzwald's eyebrows jerked upwards. "Your brother-in-law?" He wheeled to the portrait of himself on the wall, the one that Roman had done for the camp commander since Antonia had gotten Horák to locate him. "Where did we send him?"

"To the satellite camp, near Magdeburg."

"And what should I do with him here?"

Antonia did not think long. "He could paint the posters you need for the camp, but there is also the munitions factory in the Friedrich tunnels—"

"Where your sister is?" Fitzwald smiled coyly and wagged a finger at her. "So that you may perhaps make a Christmas present for your sister?"

Antonia was not certain how to respond but Fitzwald raised both hands as if in surrender.

"Right," he exclaimed. "Done. Then that shall be the first thing you do today. Put in a work transfer for Roman Mazur and set him on the same work detail as his wife tomorrow. And on Christmas Day, as well. Yes, I like that. And afterwards, reassign him to the foundry."

It was a trick. He was teasing her. Fitzwald was torturing her, as he often could. But when the Kommandant returned to his desk and opened a file folder, Antonia did not waste a second. She filled in the work orders, rose and stood in front of his desk. He glanced up at her, a slow smile where the mouth did not turn up. Not once. He extended his hand for the sheet and Antonia could imagine that he would laugh contemptuously and tear up the document, slowly and many times, until it was nothing but confetti.

But Fitzwald took it, signed it, and stamped it. He waggled his fingers. "And the one for the foundry."

She handed it to him, still unbelieving. When he returned both documents intact, she waited even longer.

He cocked his head then took in a breath and smiled before returning to his file. "Yes, yes. Extra rations as well. For all of you. Merry Christmas."

Dazed, Antonia returned to her desk. It was not until shortly before noon that he pulled the shades over the windows and came after her to take his reward.

The Tower of Babble. That's what the barracks reminded Antonia of every time she walked in but today the women were clamoring and shouting in the middle room. Before Antonia could see what was happening, Nestor and Konstantin hurried to her, terribly excited and with great grins on their faces. Konstantin coughed deeply, and Antonia felt that inevitable itch in her own throat.

"What is it, children?" She tightened the rag she used as a scarf.

"It's Christmas already," Nestor cried.

Antonia looked for Livia or Lena for an explanation but could not find either. Instead, when she moved to the door of the middle room, she saw Doris Horák surrounded by excited women. The Kapo held a box with a Red Cross emblem imprinted on it. Antonia's mouth dropped as she recognized what the commotion was about. The Kapo was handing out tins of food, biscuits and apples. Even chocolates. The inmates were nearly hysterical, reaching for the next item.

But Doris unhitched her truncheon and whacked one of the pillars of the room. "Back off! You're all behaving like animals!"

In one corner, two women were going at each other, scratching at one another and pulling one another's hair. Antonia recognized them to be both Ukrainian women, who had once briefly spoken with her but then had kept to themselves.

"Stop it, you two," Antonia shouted. She charged between them. Regina suddenly appeared, all black curls and spunk, and she shoved herself in between the group. But the woman that Antonia gripped spit in her face.

"Get your hands off me, you traitor."

Shocked, Antonia released her. "What did you say?"

The woman's face screwed up into a look of disgust, her eyes flitting between Antonia and Regina. "I know who you are."

The second woman scoffed and wrested herself away from Regina before pushing herself into Antonia's face. "Don't act as if you're one of us. As if you were the same class as us. You're part of the old elite, the ones who never believed in a free country unless you could be running it."

Incredulous, Antonia asked, "How do we know each other?"

The first woman's lip curled. "You tried to recruit my son once, *shanovna*. He told his father all about it. That's right. Your sister's married to a Pollack." She pointed to Regina. "And you're running around with a Jew."

The second woman jabbed a finger into Antonia's breastbone and Antonia slapped it away.

"People like you ruined our country," the woman accused. She threw her hands up as if to get the rest of the room into her corner. "Sneaking our best people across the border to run things. Ukrainians for Ukraine! Let the real people run the country. But you all, you just wanted to hang on to your power."

"That's right." The first woman jeered, as if the two of them had not just tried to kill one another over the tin of sardines she held.

Antonia clenched her hands. "I'd understand if you were saying I'm a Communist and I'm the one who caused your brothers and husbands to get murdered by the secret police, but this? It's more than disgusting. You're disgusting. Take your tins of food and knock each other over the heads with it. And Merry Christmas."

She turned and headed out of the room, but one of the women screeched after her, "I wouldn't sleep tonight if I were you."

Regina caught up to Antonia. "What on earth was that about?"

"Politics," Antonia cried.

"I'm half Italian. Not a Jew," Regina said softly.

Antonia halted and swung back to her. She opened her mouth, then reached for the little woman and took her into her arms. "I wouldn't care if you were Jewish."

When they crossed the barrack back to their bunks, Antonia pulled up at the sight of Lena with the excited children. She hurried to her sister and hugged her from behind, still trying to squelch her outrage.

"I have such good news," she said instead.

Lena turned to her and held up a tin of meat and an apple, one in each hand. "Did you see this? Did you?"

Antonia nodded. Somehow, she had the idea that Fitzwald would have allowed this before he'd violated her; that he had already authorized the Red Cross goods. Her cheeks flushed with shame.

"Lena, listen. I have something to tell you. Today I—"

Konstantin suddenly shot out from beneath the bunk bed, stumbling and catching himself just before the door. "Father!"

Snow swirled across the barrack floor as Roman strode in, practically swallowing Konstantin out of sight in his hug. His hair had thinned, his face was drawn, but his eyes were alight as he crossed the room to Lena. He stroked her hair, kissed the top of her head, and Lena broke into sobs, dissolving into his arms.

He smiled at Antonia. "They let me come back. I have no idea how. It's a miracle."

He reached for Antonia's hand and drew her in, Nestor and Konstantin clinging to his legs.

"It's a miracle," Antonia agreed and buried her nose in Lena's hair to fight off the nausea and aches in her own body.

The next day, after Lena and Roman spent the day in the munitions factory, he returned to their barracks with several of the other men. The women in Antonia's section of the barrack had collected what remained of the Red Cross donations and put together a Christmas feast. Traditionally, they were not allowed to eat until after midnight mass so they held vespers together and prayed, delighted when a priest from another part of the camp arrived to bless them all. He made Communion of their crusts of bread and by evening, when the first star appeared, the group sat down to feast.

The Slovakian women broke into a Christmas carol. The Latvians followed. Antonia led a small group of Ukrainians —nothing like the two women in the other room of the barrack—into *Nova radist stala*. Then it was Roman and the other Polish members who broke into a Carpathian carol that the Ukrainians also knew. The children in the barracks brought in the crown of a fir tree they'd found, and decorated it with twine from a sweater. Someone lit a candle. There was laughter and more singing, tears, and shared stories with many gestures to convey the meaning of foreign words. These attempts left them laughing all the more.

Before Doris Horák could appear and call lights out, Antonia asked the family to gather around her. The boys were nearly asleep, and Konstantin—unable to keep his eyes open— crawled into the bunk, and curled up on his side.

"Lena," she said, "cannot go on like this. Both of you have wasted away. I asked Horák about how we might get Lena onto a kitchen detail. But I have nothing left to give…" She swallowed and looked away but finally submitted. "That's a lie. I do have something."

Roman frowned. "I don't understand."

Antonia whispered so softly they both had to lean very close to her. "I have Viktor's locket here. Hidden. But I want to use it to buy our escape."

Roman turned his head to her and Lena covered her mouth. Both stared at her in silence.

"Is that even possible?" Roman asked.

"I don't know. I'm going to try, though. Lena needs food if she is to sustain Nestor and Konstantin…"

Roman nodded. "I still have half a dozen small sketches."

"Half a dozen?" Lena whispered. "Where do you have them hidden?"

Roman hesitated, then cupped her chin in his hand, his look tender. "That's my secret."

Horák walked in. Antonia straightened, muttering to Roman, "Give Doris one of her choice. Tomorrow."

Roman squeezed her hand, kissed Lena on the forehead and left the barracks.

Konstantin rolled out of the bunk bed, clutching his stomach. "Father! Don't go!"

The child suddenly dropped onto all fours and retched. The women around them rose.

"That food was too rich," one woman scolded.

Another complained that it was a waste. A third admonished Konstantin as well, but Roman dropped down next to his son and tried to clean him up. Horák hovered over them, her hand flexing and unflexing.

"You better make sure he takes it easy," she warned. "I've seen too many like this before they go."

"Go," Roman said absently. He was wiping Konstantin's face, the boy's eyes were fluttering. "Go where?"

But Antonia shook her head angrily. *Konstantin is not going to die. He can't die.*

Horák sucked in breath between her teeth, tapped the truncheon against the wall and walked away. "Mazur, get to your barrack and let the women do their jobs."

The next morning, Konstantin said he was feeling a little better but he was hungry. Lena and Roman did not stop fretting over his health.

The following week, when Fitzwald called Antonia into his office to type up further reports on Soviet intelligence, he left her without telling her where he was going or for how long. She watched as he passed by the window outside. There were two buildings for the administrators, and Fitzwald occupied the larger but on occasion someone would use the front room. When she checked, it was empty. She continued to listen. The ticking clock. Muted voices and the tops of heads as they passed by the yard outside. A dog barking.

The telephone on Fitzwald's desk loomed large. Off to the side, was the register he used to place calls to other military leaders within the Reich. Trembling, Antonia pushed away from her typewriter and went to his telephone. She lifted the receiver and dialed the code that Fitzwald used to access an outside line.

A woman's voice answered. "Berlin Central, who would you like me to patch you into?"

Antonia gave the name of the second-in-command for the Organization of Ukrainian Nationalists.

No answer.

Antonia dialed again. Gave another name. No answer. Where were they all? Where were all the people she had helped cross into the west for the very purpose of *being* there when they needed them?

She alternated between the door and the window, straining to listen to both the operator and for Fitzwald—anyone—coming. After a third failed attempt, Antonia got desperate.

Ivan. Would he even be listed in the register? She threw it open but the operator was demanding an answer.

Antonia blurted, "Major Asmuth, please."

"I'm sorry." The woman was snappish. "Asmuth? First name?"

Antonia racked her brain. What was the major's first name? She ran her finger down the register, flipped through the pages. It was a big book.

"Which department is that?" came the woman again. "Hello?"

Antonia stilled herself. Straightened and spoke with authority. "I'm calling for Kommandant Fitzwald in Wilhelmshagen. I'm afraid he has just left me for a moment. Are you able to find out, please?"

The operator sighed. "One moment." She took agonizingly long before returning. "I have one Major Asmuth at the Security Division."

"That's him," Antonia breathed.

The line buzzed twice and a man answered. Outside the window, someone hollered and Antonia's heart almost jumped from her chest. She craned her neck.

The man's voice on the other end of the line was impatient. "Hello? Who's calling?"

"Major Asmuth?"

"I'm sorry, the major is currently in a conference. Is it urgent? May I leave him a message?"

A message? Antonia was prepared to drop the receiver into its cradle. She watched the door. "Yes. Tell him that Ivan Kovalenko is calling, please."

"Pardon?"

"Ivan Kovalenko." Antonia choked, tears springing to her eyes as she added, "No, tell him that Antonia—Ivan's fiancée—is at Wilhelmshagen Labor Camp."

"Could you please repeat those names, ma'am?"

But it was too late. Through the window, Antonia spotted Fitzwald and he was almost at the door already. She replaced the receiver just as she heard him enter at the other end of the building. Antonia fled to the sink and quickly smeared away the streaks of mascara from beneath her eyes. As Fitzwald walked in, she bent her head to drink from the tap, then used the towel to pat her face dry. Before he could ask her anything, she took her seat again and began typing away.

"Have you been crying?"

"I had a coughing fit," she said. "Please excuse me. I was choking."

His eyes went to her throat. "You really ought to see the camp doctor about that." He waved a hand toward her desk. "Fill out a pass for yourself."

He caught her off guard so much this time she really did choke. She collected herself in a hurry, went to the row of filing cabinets, produced the booklet that contained the passes and tore two out and slipped the second one into the pages of the accounting book as soon as it was safe.

The next time she saw Roman, she pulled him around the corner of the barrack.

"Who do you know in Berlin? Someone who might help us?"

He looked baffled but she continued urgently, "Fitzwald left me alone in the office for over half an hour. Thirty minutes with access to the telephone. I tried a number of the Organization's contacts, but whether they've been arrested by Gestapo, whether they're anywhere in Berlin still, I don't know. So, I need someone neutral."

"Edward Jacek," Roman blurted. "A very well-known sculptor."

Antonia clasped her hand in his. "Good." Her plan was slowly coming together.

CHAPTER 20

February 1945

Polish Territories, west of the Russian Front

Ivan stood at the third-story window, watching dawn creep over the horizon. The guards—a German squad—were moving about, rubbing half-frozen hands, shrugging their rifles back onto their shoulders, or yawning in anticipation of the next shift that would soon relieve them. Not only the guards were changing shifts. There was something greater at play here in the Polish town. Here, the Germans were in command, and the Ukrainian officers were tense with anticipation. There were rumors about transforming the policing unit into a German military combat unit. It was exactly what the Ukrainian Self-Defense Legion had refused from the outset. If they were combined under Wehrmacht command, there would be no way to separate their activities from those of the Germans.

Slowly dressing, Ivan mulled over the dilemma. They needed the Germans. They needed their supplies, from food to ammunition. Ivan—after five months of being unable to connect with Asmuth—also needed intelligence about where Antonia and the Mazur family might have been taken. Until he could get that, the Cossack had to play the charade. When he glanced outside the window again, he saw that men were beginning to gather for the general assembly. He hurried to join them.

The Germans had created a comfortable base out of Moroczyn. They were established in the town's administrative buildings, while the school, hospital and gymnasium housed the legionnaires and their activities. What had been unsettling since their arrival was that Berlin had ordered a program for the legionnaires. The German officers claimed it was to keep them occupied during the winter, but the Ukrainian commanders saw the curriculum as a Nazi indoctrination program. Their German counterparts filled the days with mandatory lectures, and lessons on geography, history, ethnography, and literature, as well as some German language training. Couriers from the radiating networks around the territories delivered mail, newspapers, and messages sticky with Nazi propaganda.

But one had to be blind to not see the shape of things to come. Aimed for Berlin, the Red Army was making great advances and if it had not been for the early thaw, the Soviets would have already managed to get over the Dukla Pass. As it was, they were trapped in the mud and heavy rains.

After musters and breakfast, Ivan waited for Pavlo outside the clinic as the Half Cossack kissed Nadia goodbye. She waved and smiled at Ivan, then gave Pavlo another kiss, quick but nonetheless tender. When he then jogged down the steps of the building, Ivan swore his friend's feet did not touch the ground.

"I'm going to marry that girl," Pavlo said, and raised his chin to the pale sun.

"When?"

"Before Lent."

"But Ash Wednesday is next week," Ivan blurted.

Pavlo bounced up and slapped Ivan's back. "And you're not busy, so you'll be my best man."

"Are you serious?"

"Deadly. Except she wants to get married over there." He pointed at the picturesque park next to the headquarters. There was a creek winding through it and willow trees lined up along the banks. A wooden covered bridge would certainly make a nice pavilion, Ivan thought, but it was still damned cold and the sky had not revealed anything above the washed-out clouds in what seemed like weeks.

Ivan said as much.

"She wanted a spring wedding," Pavlo started. His grin was mischievous before delivering the punchline. "But I told her, 'Nadia, my love, I can give up drinking for forty days, but I cannot give you up.'"

Ivan laughed and ruffled his friend's hair, trying to dull the stab of envy. The sudden longing for Antonia was so strong it constricted every muscle, as if his body was urging him to flee, to run, to go find her. *Now.*

They reported to Dusha, and the colonel had news for them. "Major Asmuth is due to arrive anytime. It seems, gentlemen, the entire command is getting promoted."

Ivan scoffed. "They think they can win us over with pins and titles."

He did not sleep well that night and he arose before dawn once more. With Roman's sketch of Antonia and himself in his breast pocket, he strolled off the main grounds and into the sur-rounding countryside, the air milder than it had been in days. They were surrounded by hills, and he climbed one, knowing that he would end up looking over an abandoned German colony. The sky was just lightening when Ivan spotted Kulka hiding behind some brambles. Lys's brother had proven to be one hell of a sharpshooter. He had a rifle propped up and was following something in the sights. Ivan scanned the area but couldn't see what the kid was aiming at.

Kulka, a cigarette rolling in his mouth, slid the bolt without looking up. "Lieutenant, if you want to enjoy your breakfast today, then you had better take cover."

Alarmed, Ivan dropped face down next to him. Kulka squinted behind his rifle. Before Ivan's face, several blades of grass pushed through the last crusts of snow. A crow called nearby.

Kulka, his finger on the trigger, and smoke wafting into his eye, didn't even blink. Then the boy fired. Ivan peered where the boy pointed. In one of the abandoned yards lay a dead chicken.

The kid took a hard drag from his cigarette and tossed it into the grass, then strode away, returning minutes later to drop the dead chicken at Ivan's feet. He took up position again.

Ivan scratched his neck and looked around. Weeds strangled the untended and overgrown gardens and Ivan saw no sign of life, no farm animals, and no chickens for that matter. He squatted down next to Kulka, who was lighting another cigarette.

"There's another bird over there by the fence, sir. Permission to fire, sir."

"There's nothing there, Private."

The boy exhaled and handed the cigarette to him.

"No, thanks," Ivan said. "You know I don't smoke."

"Apologies, sir. I meant for you to hold it. I don't want to waste a perfectly good cigarette. Do I have your permission, sir?"

Ivan scowled, but he took the cigarette just as he caught a movement in the brush. "Fire away."

Kulka's rifle rang off another shot.

This time, Ivan followed the boy to retrieve the bird. "How the hell are you shooting so far without a scope?"

"Carrots," replied Kulka, swinging the twitching fowl by its feet.

"Pardon?"

Kulka raised an eyebrow and repeated, "Carrots, sir! My mother always said carrots were good for the eyes."

When they returned to the ridge, Ivan asked for a chance to shoot. They waited a few minutes, Kulka smoking easily. He pointed out the next target, not three hundred meters from them.

Ivan took aim, shot, and the chicken jumped, half-flew over a log and back into the grasses.

"Damn it," Ivan muttered.

"Carrots," Kulka punctuated. "Sir."

Some time later, they returned to camp with half a dozen birds.

"Best sharpshooter we've got," the cook said.

Ivan looked around the field kitchen. "Got any carrots for that soup? Make sure we all get plenty."

The next day, at assembly and prayer, Ivan promoted Kulka to squad leader. When he saluted the boy, he saw a black sedan pull into the perimeter.

Major Asmuth was back.

"Volia narodiam! Volia liudyni," the legionnaires chanted. Freedom for nations! Freedom for the people!

Major Asmuth and Colonel Sovchenko saluted one another and the rest of the men and women were dismissed.

"Gather your command, Colonel," Asmuth said. "It's time to meet."

Ivan followed the other officers into the room containing the largest table and Asmuth took the head, waiting until they had all arrived and were seated.

"I am authorized to promote you all here on the condition that you take the oath to the Führer," he said abruptly.

Across from Ivan, Kvitka's look of anticipation turned into one of dread. His eyes flicked over to Ivan. Not a day earlier, he'd sworn he would never do this, and Ivan had agreed with him. Pavlo cleared his throat and Lys shoved his chair back some. Terlytsia and he were both smoldering.

Dusha took them all in with one sweeping gaze. "And if we do not agree?"

Asmuth glared at him. "Why would you not?"

There was silence and the major then folded his hands on the table. "Gentlemen, let's be realistic here. You all know what will happen if you do not."

Concentration camp. Execution. It was a short distance to both. Ivan hung his head, rubbed his face. He at least sensed that the major, who had always kept his word, was not thrilled by these developments either. But the Ukrainians were trapped.

"There is another matter." Asmuth's tone was contrite.

The Ukrainians all looked up again.

"They want to split you up. Three divisions."

Lys pounded a fist on the table. Kvitka, not one to show any insubordination, ever, cursed in Ukrainian. Asmuth seemed to have closed his ears to their grumbling, and allowed them at least that. He rose and went to the maps hanging on the wall and waited.

"Believe me when I say that you prefer to hear this from me than from anyone else," he said. "Colonel Sovchenko, you will be given command of a new unit in Warsaw."

Dusha dropped his head.

"Warsaw?" Terlytsia said acidly. His face darkened. "So that if we lose, you can take the whole lot of us and execute us, is that it? Lump us together as enemy insurgents with the Polish Home Army?"

Asmuth swung back to the table and pounded it with a fist. "We," he growled dangerously, "will not lose."

Everyone took in a deep breath. Asmuth smoothed his hair and glanced up at the ceiling before doling out the rest of the bad news.

"Terlytsia, Lys, Derkach and Kovalenko here will take over command of a combination of new and old forces. You'll march out over Slovakia to the Austrian border and meet up with what's left of the SS-Galizien."

Terlytsia glanced over at Kvikta. "And Lieutenant Kvitka?"

"Kvitka," Asmuth said, glancing at their most genial lieutenant, "will be transferred to Krakow."

Terlytsia opened his mouth but Asmuth pointed at him, then at the rest around the table. "One more word out of any of you and I'll see to it that you are all split up. These are my orders and they will be followed."

Pavlo puffed out his cheeks and exchanged a glance with Ivan. Kvitka and Terlytsia, separated? They were just as close as the two Cossacks.

Asmuth looked furious as his glare seared each of them. "I expect to hear nothing but the highest of praise about each of you. Oberst Biegelmaier will take over command here."

Ivan stared at Asmuth. Nobody here had ever heard of any Biegelmaier.

The major slowly sat back down. "I'll be meeting the Oberst tomorrow morning, and then I will be back to conduct the ceremony for all your promotions, and," he punctuated, "your oaths."

"Are we dismissed?" Ivan asked coldly.

Asmuth's face gradually smoothed. He nodded at Pavlo. "I understand there is to be a marriage ceremony today. I assume I am invited."

Pavlo's neck bent only slightly. Maybe it was a nod.

"Good. Then, if that is all gentlemen." Asmuth rose. The rest of them took a long time to stand up, chairs slowly sliding against the parquet floor, as if they were all hoping the major would crack open a big smile and say this had all been a very bad joke.

It did not take long for the six officers to gather in the park afterwards.

Ivan scuffed the ground with his boot. "Now what?"

"We make a run for it?" Kvitka tried. "Go underground."

Lys's mouth worked as if he were trying to form the words but he spit in the space between them instead. His actions, as usual, spoke louder than any words could.

Kvitka pursed his lips. "Who knows? Maybe they'll assign me to accompany the women behind the front lines." But his tone was strained beneath the light attempt.

Because—to make matters worse—he'd just reminded them that the women would be transferred far behind any lines. Far from the men.

His face rippling with dark emotions, Terlytsia remained sullen. Ivan understood and sympathized. After all they had been through, he could not imagine being separated from Pavlo just now.

"The Germans," Dusha said, "are scared."

Ivan peered at him. "Go on."

"Look what they've done. Look at what they are leaving behind if they lose. We've heard about these camps. We've witnessed the executions. If the Fritzes thought the treaties and reparations from the last war were bad, then you can imagine how the international community will make them pay for this one."

Lys grunted, and the others also perked up with interest.

"But they will drag us through the mud with them," Pavlo said ominously.

He was right. If the legion was found to be involved in any of it, the Allies would make Ukraine pay as well.

"They won't be able to pull apart who did what," Ivan said. "Ukraine would have to prosecute its own people as accomplices."

"Collaborators," Pavlo said softly.

Dusha sighed heavily and gestured to Pavlo. "We have a wedding to prepare for. We all have the day off for this and I say we reconvene in the morning to figure out what our options are."

"I say we stand our ground, boys," Terlytsia said, unrelenting. "Tonight, we make sure every one of our men is behind us. We need to convince them to take a stand. The Germans won't get anything done if the morale is low. But we need to agree to this. Now."

He was suggesting insubordination. And this under a new commander nobody knew. But everyone nodded, Ivan included. They had stuck together this long, their legionnaires would also balk at being pulled apart. Then Kvitka put his hand out in the middle of them. One by one, each of the men grasped the other's wrists. But they all had to know they were trapped. This was just a show of bravado. There was no way to get out of this without each of them getting a bullet to the head.

Dusha walked up to Ivan as the group dispelled and pulled him aside. "If nothing else, and you get anywhere near the Austrian and Yugoslavian border, you take the chance, take the risk and find Tito's partisans."

"Tito's partisans?" Ivan asked.

"They're Communists, but a mixed band," Dusha said, keeping his voice low. "You'll find sympathizers among them. Ivan, what I'm saying is, you need to be on the right side of this war when it's over without falling into the hands of Stalin's commanders." Dusha jerked his head at Pavlo, who had turned to wait for them. "Both of you. All of you. Don't worry about me. I'll be fine."

Over the last months, Ivan often found himself standing before a deep pit, the tug and pull of it stronger with every loss, with every catastrophe. Oksana's haunted figure below the water's surface beckoned to him now, inviting him to jump in.

"I need a drink," he mumbled.

Dusha shook his shoulder. "Hey, Cossack. Pavlo's getting married today. You make sure it's memorable. A little light in this fucking hellhole. That's an order."

Ivan forced himself away from that tempting darkness. He strode over to Pavlo.

"You nervous?" he asked the Half Cossack.

"Ha! You?" Pavlo wiggled his eyebrows in jest, but the earlier spark was gone. It was a good chance that tonight was one of the last nights he would have with Nadia, too.

"I'm not the one getting married," Ivan said softly.

"Not yet," Pavlo said. "Not yet. And I plan to be there when you do."

As they pieced together the celebration, the men steered clear of the discussion, trying to get their spirits back to the festivity at hand. The bottle of cognac they scrounged up helped dull their senses.

That afternoon, a priest from the nearby town arrived, as big and bushy as a bear. The camp gathered for the wedding in the park, the temperatures having warmed quite a bit and even the sun came out. Nadia's dress, with flowing, embroidered sleeves and a wide collar, had been pieced together by the women from white tablecloths they'd scrounged together from an abandoned banquet hall. She wore a crown of ivy leaf, and Ivan remembered with great pain the night of the midsummer festival back in Sadovyi Hai. He had fished Antonia's wreath from the creek, held her hand as they sprang over the bonfire. Their kiss in the orchards.

Again, that dark pit yawned. Ivan was standing at its edge.

As Pavlo stepped up to his bride, Ivan decided Nadia was not just handsome. She was beautiful and he wanted nothing more than to make sure that the two of them would make it through the war. To give them the light that Dusha spoke of. Ivan drew in a deep breath and steeled himself.

The celebrations took place in the mess hall. Someone had found an old mandolin and a harmonica. Kulka had shot two pheasants for the couple and a few more of those feral chickens to go with the dumplings. Asmuth, always well stocked, shared his case of cognac, but it was not going to compensate for the gray cloud he had pulled over them.

As the party got underway, Ivan sought the major out, and Asmuth cautiously toasted to the couple with him before Ivan leaned against the wall.

"How are you?" Asmuth asked. Despite the shots of cognac they had drunk together, he looked earnest, as if he were trying to make up for the meeting that morning.

"Well, Major, considering your news, considering the war and the fact that I haven't been home in what feels like decades…" Ivan swallowed, realizing he was slurring a bit. He sighed. "I don't even know whether there is a home to go to."

"Kovalenko," Asmuth seemed to be testing the waters. "You have no choice but to go out there and get your country back."

He raised the bottle and poured again. "*Slava Ukraini*," he said and drank.

Ivan stared at him. "Glory to Ukraine," he repeated.

"So," Asmuth said, as if all was now well between them. "How's Mrs. Kovalenko?"

Ivan flinched and shoved away from the wall.

Asmuth's polite grin faded and he looked genuinely sorry. "Ivan, I was only asking. I never followed up after you escorted her to Slovakia. I just assumed you were successful…" The major looked him up and down as if he could not believe Ivan would ever fail at such a mission.

"The village where they were staying…" Ivan tensed. "They were surrounded by the SS. They deported the entire village. Asmuth, I've been wanting to… I know I shouldn't be asking for any more favors, but…."

The major tipped his head, his expression unreadable when he said, "That was around the time of that failed Czechoslovakian uprising."

"She saw her family loaded into those trucks," Ivan said measuredly. "She was with me, Asmuth. I had her. And she said she had to go with them. She…" He sighed. "She gave herself up. I have no idea where she is."

The expression on the German officer's face looked regretful, even admiring. "Interesting."

The major stepped away from the wall and faced Ivan. He looked as if he were trying to decide whether to tell him something. His chest rose. "I think I might know where she is."

Ivan's mouth dropped open. "What? How?"

"Not long ago, my secretary told me a woman called. She was terribly nervous, spoke German well but he noted she had a slight accent. She said something about an Ivan."

"Where?" Ivan begged. "Where is she?"

But Asmuth's look was cold. "Why would she be calling me, Kovalenko? And how would I know where she is? I have been wondering since who you think you are. All of you here." He waved an arm at the dancers on the floor then jabbed a finger into Ivan's breastbone. "Because you all have a very, very high opinion of yourselves and I would like to remind you that you need us. It's time that you all start repaying Führer and Fatherland. You are the reason we're here in the Polish territories. These are your failures. Not ours. We have provided you with everything that you needed to make this campaign a success. By God, we should have already had the entire eastern territories of Ukraine!"

Ivan stared at the major, and fell back against the wall.

Asmuth's face smoothed out and he brushed a hand over his head. He reached up to put a hand on Ivan's shoulder, his mouth twitching into some kind of encouraging smile. "She's alive. And if she has access to a phone, the Reich has probably put her to work. If I am correct, she is also committed to destroying the Red Army. She is doing her part. Now, Kovalenko, you—all of you—finally do yours."

The major then refilled their glasses and raised his to the wedding party. "Heil Hitler, you crazy Cossacks."

Numb, and not from the shots, Ivan placed the glass on the table next to him, and strode out into the fresh air, the door slamming behind him. He heard it creak open again and spun around, prepared to confront Asmuth, beg him, but it was Pavlo.

The Half Cossack strode over to him. "What's that all about?"

Ivan wanted to tell him, but it was his friend's wedding. He clapped the Half Cossack on the shoulder. "Nothing, scrub. Nothing that can't wait until tomorrow. She's a great woman, you know? That bride of yours. What are you doing out here with me?"

Pavlo frowned, his face briefly illuminated by the moon before another cloud passed over. "Because I worry about you."

"Come on Derkach," Ivan said dismissively. "You got other things to worry about now."

"Nothing's changed between us, Ivan," Pavlo said soberly. "And it won't. We're in this together until the end."

No. Not between them, perhaps. But everything had with Asmuth. And Asmuth could find out where Antonia was. Information that Ivan could not possibly get if he did not obey the man's orders, march southwards, far from where she might be located because the Ukrainian Self-Defense Legion had become an inconvenience.

Pavlo lightly kicked Ivan's shin with his boot. "I know when you've got something brewing in that mug you call a brain. What happened in there?"

But Ivan knew what would happen if he told the Half Cossack that Asmuth had information about Antonia. Pavlo would get riled up, possibly—the way he was swaying now—march in and start a fight with Asmuth, and then he wouldn't be able to reconcile with himself all night long. For all his weight and height, Pavlo's heart was too big to let go of something like this.

"Let's talk about this in the morning."

Nadia appeared in the doorway and stepped out into the night. "Is something wrong?"

Ivan gave Pavlo a little push, but his friend turned around.

Suddenly, he threw an arm around Ivan's waist. "That woman, right there? If anything should ever happen to me? I want you to make sure you take care of her. You understand?" He hiccupped, then tottered away to her, leaving Ivan feeling adrift.

"Come back inside, Kovalenko," Pavlo called then. "It's time for the *Hopak!*"

But Ivan did not feel like dancing. He needed time to consider Asmuth's demands. He needed time to come up with a plan to locate and get to Antonia. And it infuriated him that it was during Pavlo's wedding that he had to do it, but he would make it up to the Half Cossack. To the Half Cossack and his wife.

He awoke in his own bed, although he did not remember ever returning to it. Ivan groaned, the call to musters clanging through the fog in his head. Then he sat up suddenly, remembering the plan he'd formed before passing out. Ivan jumped up and threw on his tunic as he looked out the window. The legionnaires were gathering and Dusha was at the front.

"Damn it," he muttered. He was likely too late. Asmuth had probably already left to pick up the mysterious and unwanted Biegelmaier.

He was right. Asmuth had left bright and early. Ivan got through musters, climbed into a truck and took his squads, together with Kulka, on patrol. On the way back, Ivan caught up with one of Pavlo's groups and found the newlywed wearing the green face of a bad hangover.

"You doing all right?" he asked him.

Pavlo wiped his mouth. "I'm a happy man. Don't I look it?"

Ivan chuckled and bent down a little as they rolled back into the camp. Slowly, he unraveled the information about Antonia to him.

Pavlo's eyes grew wide. He was vehement. "Son of a bitch! No! Ivan, you get that son of a bitch to find out where she is, make sure it's accurate and tell him that you and I will do what the damned Germans want. At least for a little while longer. At least until we find a way to get the hell out of this."

Before Ivan could protest, Pavlo grabbed him by the tunic and twisted. "We'll keep the morale up. Tell the son of a bitch, we'll do whatever this Biegelmaier wants. I'll even take the damned oath if that means we can save her."

"The others will not be pleased," Ivan said.

"To hell with the others. This is you and me. You and me, Ivan. Just like always. For Antonia, anything."

Ivan let out a long sigh.

"All right," Pavlo said, checking. He slowly released Ivan's tunic. "All right? You've got my support. But only if the bastard gives you the information and only if it's accurate."

Ivan smiled sadly. The Half Cossack was already one step ahead of him.

As they crossed the assembly area, Ivan braced himself. Dusha was striding toward them from the administrative building. Asmuth and Biegelmaier had probably arrived and by the look on Dusha's face, he'd received his transfer papers. But the commander dropped his head when he reached them, and pulled his cap off, twisting it in his hands.

"I'm afraid I just received terrible news." The colonel looked up. "Major Asmuth's convoy was caught in Polish and Red Army crossfire. He and his driver were killed."

Ivan swayed, his knees weak. It was Pavlo's hold that stopped him from buckling.

Dusha was silent for a moment. "Right. Regardless of what he did, we all kind of liked him. Felt protected by him. Anyway, Biegelmaier is coming with another transport. Assembly at twenty hundred hours."

Ivan stared after Dusha as he made his way to where the other officers were coming into the camp.

When Pavlo moved in front of him, Ivan could not bear the look of pity from the Half Cossack. Antonia had slipped from him so many times before, but this time—this time—it was different. This time nothing could prevent him from falling into that well of darkness.

CHAPTER 21

February 1945

Wilhelmshagen, Outside of Berlin, Germany

While January had been torturously cold at Wilhelmshagen, February began with a sudden thaw and temperatures rose as if it were already spring. Rivers of mud weighted their shoes and soaked their feet. As Antonia and Livia returned from the foundry, two men whispered amongst themselves that, with such a thaw, the Red Army would never reach the Rhine Valley. It must have put out the last light of hope in Livia because the following morning, when Antonia tried to wake her up, she found the young woman from Ulič curled up on her side, her eyes and mouth opened, as if she had awoken, seen something horrible and instantly froze.

Regina appeared and leaned against the bunk bed's frame.

"How are we to survive this?" Lena sobbed.

Regina snatched her chin between her fingers. Antonia was about to intervene but the dark-haired woman glared at her before gazing at Lena. "It's the little things that keep us alive. The routine. The predictable meager rations of soup. The knowledge of how hard we have to work. But it's the big things that make us fight for survival. Your children. Your husband." Regina looked at Antonia. "Love."

She released Lena and pointed to Livia's body in the bed. "She had none of that left. Everyone she knew was gone."

"And you?" Antonia said, because Regina had also lost all of her loved ones. At least that was what she had told them. "What keeps you surviving, then?"

Regina snapped her fingers. "Hate."

She helped Lena and Antonia carry Livia's body to the cart. Antonia followed it around the barracks. At the far end of the camp yard, she saw the diggers. The washrooms would soon be cleared out. Regina might be right, but Antonia was not going to take her chances. They had to escape.

The German propaganda that Fitzwald had Antonia type out and announce over the camp megaphones touted the Wehrmacht's victories and glories on all fronts, but nobody could fool the inmates about what was truly happening. Bombers scraped the skies, creating a dull, rolling thunder in clear weather. Days later, the news trickled into the camp that Dresden had been severely bombed by the Allies, and nearly annihilated.

"The Allied forces are all going to meet here, in Berlin," someone whispered.

Lena's detail in the kitchen had cost Roman two of his sketches. She peeled black potatoes and cooked the rotten grain that comprised the camp's allowance of five hundred calories per person, per day. Nestor stayed nearby with a group of other young children who were too young to work. Konstantin, meanwhile, was in a kindergarten aimed at indoctrinating him in the ways of the Nazis. Since Christmas, his health had deteriorated at an alarming rate. More than once, Lena's desperation was greater than her fear and she took the risk of smuggling some of the better potatoes for her son via a small network of "friendlies," a network that cost Roman his remaining sketches.

When Antonia had gone to see the camp doctor about her thyroid, she had also brought Konstantin, trembling over the forged pass she'd made for him. But the doctor was dispassionate. For Antonia, he gave her a few iodine tablets. For Konstantin, he washed his hands and said he could do nothing. Her nephew was dying.

To prevent Lena from further despair, Antonia and Roman shared their anguish in secret.

"He needs a real doctor," Roman wept.

Antonia went to the hiding spot and considered the locket. Since her attempt to reach Asmuth and send word to Ivan of where she was, Fitzwald had not left her long enough to make any further phone calls. She wondered whether this was the moment she had been waiting for. With the Allies closing in, they might be liberated soon anyway, but Konstantin had too little time.

Even Kapo Horák had found some iota of compassion and allowed Roman into the barrack after curfew for nothing in return. He knelt next to Konstantin's bunk. The boy's stomach and face were swollen. He was retaining water and Antonia knew that this was one of the last stages before death. They all prayed, but Antonia knew she had to do more.

That night, as Konstantin's breathing thickened, she did not sleep. As soon as the women gathered for roll call, she begged Horák for permission to find Fitzwald.

"You can go, but he's not going to help you," the Kapo said. She scrutinized Antonia, as if examining her state. "I can't imagine why he would."

Antonia thanked her anyway and went to the washroom to fetch the locket. She carried it in her pocket to the administration building. Fitzwald was just coming out and when he spotted her, his eyes had a curious shine but he jutted his chin out.

"Inmate Kosaken, what are you doing here? Who gave you permission to approach?"

Antonia lowered her eyes. "I wish to speak to you, Kommandant."

"I'm listening."

Her eyes flicked over the other guards and Fitzwald motioned for them to leave.

"What is it, Fräulein?" he asked, his voice now dangerous. "I did not send for you."

"I am here to beg for mercy."

His chuckle sent shivers down her back. "What have you done?"

"It is a matter of life and death."

"This whole camp is about life and death. What is so special about your situation?"

He was right. What was so special about her situation?

But he motioned for her to follow him into the building. She did and, when he closed the door, he stood behind her.

"Take off your clothes."

Antonia stifled the whimper.

"You're filthy. You stink. Take off your clothes."

Shakily, she bent down to grasp the hem of her dress and pull it over her head, and just as she did, Fitzwald shoved her forward.

Antonia rose on all fours, her heart knocking wildly in her chest. He strode around to her front, and she slowly raised her head, willing herself to lock gazes with him.

His smile spread across his face, as if taking pleasure in her defiance. "Who is dying?"

"My nephew. He's starving. The camp doctor said he needs a specialist. And there is one in town."

He rolled his eyes then studied her, his sneer oozing disgust. "I want you to beg. Like a dog. Like the animal that you are."

She dropped her head. But suddenly, she had an image of him knocking that locket out of her hand, then taking it and her at the same time. Because that would not be punishment enough, he would also likely have her killed for hiding valuables in the first place. She was nothing to him but a toy. And when he broke her, he'd discard her in a corner of the camp and find himself a new one.

"Beg," he said through gritted teeth.

Antonia had been so close to this with him before. She had always feared he would push her to such sadism. And now, here it was, and perhaps it could really be this simple. She shifted so that she was on her knees only, and her hand brushed against the pocket of her dress.

"Please," she said, raising her eyes to his. "Please help us."

With narrowed eyes, Fitzwald cupped her chin, and when she was standing, he lowered the shades of the window.

At the sight of the pass, Lena dropped to her knees to thank God right there then wrapped her arms around Antonia. Antonia flinched, her body battered and bruised, but that was nothing compared to the pain inside her. When Lena realized how Antonia had managed the pass, she had no tears left by the end of the night. It was Regina who led Antonia away and gently washed her.

"Bury it," Regina said. She looked up at Antonia from where she was dabbing at the scratches and bruises. "Bury it deep inside if you want to use it later. And it will feed the hate as it has in me. Or, give it up and put it in His hands to carry. It's up to you how you want to live when you leave this place."

The pass—which contained all of the family's names on it—allowed one member to leave the camp with Konstantin in order to see the specialist in town. Roman was the first to go to Dr. Hagen, returning with Konstantin and medication. Dr. Hagen had said that Konstantin's brush with death had left him in critical condition, and for the next few weeks at least, he needed to be brought in for daily visits to check his progress.

"The boy's heart is drowning," Roman continued. "These pills are to help rid his body of excess water. He must be kept on a strict diet, but under no condition should he be allowed to drink any water, and no salt. Salt retains water."

He showed them a slip of paper upon which Dr. Hagen had jotted down a list of foods that Konstantin should eat if he was to survive. Antonia nearly crumpled it with frustration. Where were they to get eggs, vegetables, meat or milk? Fitzwald would likely thrash her with glee if she asked for this.

But Roman grabbed Lena's hands. "Dr. Hagen said that I should bring Nestor as well, and he will provide food."

With the list in his hand, Roman then pulled Antonia aside.

"Look, I was in town. There is a square and a park at the center. There are buses going back and forth to Berlin. Not regularly, but they are still running. And there is a train. Across the park from the doctor's office, there is a small jewelry and antique shop. It sells all sorts of things."

Antonia nodded, understanding. Together, they continued making their plans. They would need papers. They would need money. They would need a phone. Antonia would try to reach Edward Jacek, as Roman knew the man had a summer cottage outside of Berlin. In the meantime, Antonia would attempt to locate someone from the Organization who might help with funds and documents.

The doctor's pills made Konstantin rush to the toilet frequently. Some of the women in the barracks assisted in taking him, or cleaning up after him if he was not fast enough. He was horribly weak, and much too small for his nine years. But as the days passed, the camp doctor examined Konstantin once more and declared that that boy was out of immediate danger. Dr. Hagen, however, would have to continue seeing him.

When it was Antonia's turn to leave the camp with Konstantin and Nestor, she walked gingerly out of the gates and was again taken aback by Wilhelmshagen's beautiful landscape. Behind that high wall surrounding the camp, they were living in hell, while here the townsfolk were surrounded by beautiful birch forests and lakes. Birdsong and the scents of spring beneath the thaw jarred her so much it nearly made her weep. Antonia grasped the boys' hands and turned her attention to inspecting the town.

At the bus stop, she watched a German patrol get on board one of the buses. She imagined the same would happen on the trains. Public transport would be too risky. They needed another way.

As Roman had described, Antonia found the antiques and jewelry shop he'd scouted out. She warned the children not to say a word and not to touch a thing in the shop. With the locket in hand, she went inside and lowered Nestor to the ground. The air smelled of dust, silver polish, and old books, something that might have normally brought her comfort. A man in a brown suit and smeared spectacles came out from the back. The cuffs of his sleeves were frayed, the buttons mismatched. He watched her with suspicion as she placed the locket on the counter. She hesitated for a second before uncovering the piece, popping open the clasp and revealing the miniature painting of herself inside.

The shopkeeper jerked his chin at her. "*Sind Sie an eine schwere Zeit geraten?*" Did you fall on hard times?

"*Wie wir alle,*" Antonia said. Like we all have.

Konstantin clutched the counter with dirty hands, peering up at the man. He was still awfully pale, his eyes still puffy. The shopkeeper considered the children—both very subdued—and his stern resolve seemed to melt a little. He lifted the chain, examined the locket, and offered Antonia twenty Reichsmarks. The locket itself was certainly worth ten times that amount but she quickly calculated how far twenty Marks would get them. They needed money to offer someone for petrol, they needed food, a place to sleep. They needed identity papers for five people. She wasn't even sure whether the Organization would fund only her or the entire family. It was not enough. Not nearly enough.

"Sixty," she countered. She did not want to speak too much should he catch her Slavic accent and turn her away altogether.

The man protested, placing the locket back on her side of the counter. "Twenty, or nothing."

Konstantin coughed, and leaned against her.

"Fifty-five," she said. "Please."

The shopkeeper pushed himself away from the counter. She spotted the telephone in the back office. She needed access. She needed to reach someone who could help them.

"*Passt*," she said. It's fine. "*Zwanzig*."

With twenty Reichsmark in her pocket, the first thing she did was go to a shop and buy a little food to hide on her person. Then they hurried to the doctor's office. As Konstantin and Nestor waited outside the examination room, she begged the nurse to watch over the children and left in search of a public telephone. Her hands shook as she dialed the number for the Berlin operator and requested Roman's artist friend.

A man answered the telephone right away and identified himself as Edward Jacek. When Antonia told him who she was, his first question was, "Are you able to get out of the camp? All of you?"

Antonia told him they were trying. "There are five of us. But *pan* Jacek, we must at least save the Mazurs." She winced at the thought of Fitzwald taking out his revenge on her. "We have a little money. For petrol. We'll need papers. Public transport is too much of a risk with the patrols onboard."

"Let me handle this. I'll find someone who can fetch you."

"I have friends who will get funds together for us," she said. She told him a few names from the Organization he should call to assist with that.

"Just tell me when we should come," Jacek said.

Antonia turned to the road where the doctor's office was, her thoughts straightening out as if the last piece in the puzzle had fallen into place. It was perfect. With a car, the risk of being found out by any patrols on the bus or train was eliminated.

She turned her attention back to Jacek. "This is the third time one of us has left the camp. We have to prove we're trustworthy. They allow us to leave between two and four in the afternoon. That is all. The doctor said he still has about two weeks before he's done with the boys' treatments." Feeding them. Treating them. In their situation, they were the same things.

Jacek asked what her plan was, and she explained, so tense her jaw ached. She told him about the park she had seen, where someone might wait for them.

"Please have someone here starting within a week. Just in case. I will do all we can to get us all out of here."

Jacek promised that he would follow her instructions.

When Antonia returned to Dr. Hagen's office, he asked her to come in alone. "The boys, they will be fine. But… Would you like me to examine you?"

Antonia shut her eyes. He was not talking about her thyroid. *Let it go.* "I'm fine," she said. "Thank you."

What else could she need? She had taken the first step to setting them all free.

Over the next week, each of them—Lena, Roman and Antonia—left the camp three more times. Each time, the same two Wehrmacht guards were at the gate to stamp their pass and, as the days progressed, they hardly looked at either the document or the adult who accompanied Konstantin and Nestor.

By the second week, and as she had arranged with Jacek, Antonia spotted a man in the park where she had instructed someone to wait. He was wearing a camel hair coat, brown hat and a dark green satin cravat. Something about him simply made her think he was waiting for them. She veered across the road and approached.

"*Guten Tag,*" she said cautiously. "*Haben Sie vielleicht die Zeit?*" There was a clock tower just beyond the park but the man looked at his watch then back at her.

"*Shanovna* Kozak?"

The relief overwhelmed her.

The man regarded her and the children with mild shock before offering his hand. "Edward Jacek."

"You came yourself?"

He smiled. It was a warm smile. "I'm the only one I trust."

"It must happen soon. Konstantin is, thank God, feeling better and that means that the pass will no longer be valid. The doctor sends back a report with us after each visit that I must hand in to the camp administration."

"I will be here every day from two to four o'clock," he said. He took her hand again, then brushed each of the boys' heads. "Every day."

It took all of five minutes for the doctor to tell Antonia that Konstantin was better, and that the boys could be seen to by the camp's doctor from here. She and the Mazurs had run out of time.

Dr. Hagen slowly handed her the report. "I'm sorry. It is all I can do for you now."

On the way out of the office, the nurse pressed a small sack into her hand. "It's additional food. Dr. Hagen has written that it is required. Good luck." Then very quietly she said, "It's almost over. Be careful."

Antonia held the report and the sack. She was to bring the document to Horák as always, who then passed it along to Fitzwald's office. They were done for. There was no time left to see their plan through. It was only a matter of days before the meager camp rations would send her nephews to the brink of death again. Outside, pulling the boys by the hands, Antonia quickly returned to the park. To her relief, Jacek was still there.

"This is it," she said, nearly breaking down. "If we do not escape today, we never will."

"Come with me." Jacek ushered Konstantin and Nestor to a mint green car, and when Antonia climbed into the passenger seat, she was overwhelmed by the sense of freedom and security the vehicle provided.

The artist slowly got into the driver's seat and turned to her. "I could take you and the children. At least the three of you. Right now."

Antonia took in a sharp breath. A tear rolled down her cheek. She stared at Jacek. Lena would want this. She would say yes immediately. Roman would insist. Antonia knew that. She reached for Konstantin in the back seat, and grasped his bony knee then touched Nestor's leg. Wide-eyed, they gazed back at her, frightened by her tears.

But, Fitzwald. She remembered the pain he caused her. His sadistic nature. Lena would never survive it. Brushing her eyes dry, Antonia looked out the rear windshield at the town clock. It was quarter to three. Her chest constricted, the lump at her throat, rock hard.

"Drive me to the camp," she choked. They were so close. She and the children were so close to escaping. "Just drive me to the gates of the camp and I will make the decision there."

Jacek nodded and started the ignition. The camp pulled into view some minutes later and Antonia leaned forward to peer at the guards, wondering how she might wheedle Lena and Roman out. There was a plaza opposite the drive and Jacek turned left and parked alongside it. Antonia helped Konstantin and Nestor out of the back seat.

"Wait here," she said to Jacek. "If I do not return within the next half hour or so, I have failed."

She walked up the drive to the gates, Konstantin's and Nestor's hands in hers, her heart pounding. As she neared the guards, her steps faltered. These were not the same men she'd encountered over and over. They were younger, much so. Fresh. Inexperienced. And, therefore, possibly more difficult to handle.

She turned back to the vehicle, to Jacek, astonished. He was leaning against the driver's door, watching her. Antonia spun back to the camp gates, and quickened her steps.

When one of the guards opened the gate, she presented him with only the pass, containing all the family's names. He looked at it and validated it. A new confidence quelled her jitters.

"I need to return to town with my nephew," she said. "It's very urgent. I'm here only to get his parents. The doctor wishes to consult with the parents."

The young guard frowned at her and stuck out his hand. "Do you have the doctor's order for that?"

"Order?" she feigned confusion. "I did not get any order. As you can see here, we have until four o'clock, and the doctor wishes to see them right away. So I've hurried back to fetch them. It's regarding the children's conditions."

"I'll have to ask the commander of the camp," the guard said. He went into the barrack and she saw him lift the phone. Antonia's heart hammered in her ears. Fitzwald would never let it happen. Never. He'd already broken her. She was no longer interesting.

"Kommandant?" the guard said. "Sorry, I was looking for the Kommandant. Yes, Oberleutnant. I have a woman here"—he looked down at the document. "Lena Mazur, or Antonia Kozak, I'm not sure which one it is. But a pass signed by the Kommandant." He went on to explain Antonia's story.

When he hung up, Antonia looked down at Konstantin, who was biting his lip.

"The Kommandant is at one of the work details. The Oberleutnant is coming to check on this."

Antonia shifted on her feet. She turned slightly to see that Jacek was still waiting. Her feet itched to run with the boys back to the car, to turn around and flee to Berlin now. When she faced the soldiers again, she saw the Oberleutnant coming around the corner of the administration building.

A moment later, he threw her a cursory look before taking the paper from the guard. "The doctor is supposed to provide you with a report each time you return. Where is that report?"

Antonia took in a deep breath, her middle lurching so much she could hardly focus on the young Oberleutnant.

"My nephews," she said unsteadily, "and so many other children here, are dying senselessly. Is this your plan to defeat the Soviets? By killing the very manpower that should and could fight for you? By killing the children you are educating to love Führer and Fatherland? The ones you have invested in making loyal soldiers out of? Kommandant Fitzwald understood the dire consequences of my two nephews here. That is why he issued the pass in the first place. Blood and soil! That's what you all call for. Keep killing these children and you will only have blood and nobody to protect all that hard-won soil!"

The guards stared with dismay at the Oberleutnant. Fitzwald's second-in-command lowered his glare a moment. It was all Antonia needed.

"This boy"—she shoved Konstantin forward, her voice shaking—"is prepared to serve for you in just a few years and you're killing him! Go on, then. Shoot him. Shoot me. Shoot all of us for wanting to preserve the 'material' that will help you win this war." She snapped a salute. "*Heil Hitler!*"

Konstantin stared up at Antonia for a moment, then turned and copied her. "*Heil Hitler*," he croaked.

As if it were a game, Nestor followed.

The Oberleutnant grew wide-eyed. The guard who had checked her in shuffled uncomfortably. The other began to raise his rifle, but the Oberleutnant waved him down.

"Where are the parents right now?" the officer demanded.

It took Antonia a moment to understand the question.

"Well?" he asked impatiently.

"Lena Mazur is in the kitchens. Roman Mazur is at the foundry."

"And you? What does the doctor need you for?" the lieutenant asked.

Antonia yanked down the collar of her dress and exposed her throat. "It's either I go with them, or your Kommandant Fitzwald will have to find someone else fluent in four languages."

The Oberleutnant scowled but snapped his fingers at the guards and jerked his head. The one who had placed the call to him went back into the guard's booth and, once more, picked up the telephone. She heard him asking for Lena to come to the gates. Then put in a call for Roman.

Konstantin finally dropped his hand, and looked to her.

"Did I do the right thing?" he whispered in Ukrainian.

Antonia tipped her head back and blinked the tears away. She stroked his stubbled hair. "Yes, darling. Yes, you did."

When Lena appeared and saw the boys and Antonia with the guards, her face went slack. Antonia motioned for her to stand next to her and said, "Just wait for Roman. The doctor wants to see us all together."

Lena did her best to mask her astonishment, but Antonia saw her grip Nestor's hand, the whites of her fingernails showing. When Roman approached, Antonia was brisk about it.

"Come, Dr. Hagen wants to speak to you and Lena. Hurry. Before the office closes." She cautiously checked the Oberleutnant's look. "We'll be back by four o'clock."

As if moving under water, Antonia turned her back on the camp, aware of each person behind her and next to her as they walked the stretch of plaza. As soon as she saw Jacek take off his hat and scrabble to open all the car doors, she grasped Konstantin's and Nestor's hands in hers and this time she did run.

CHAPTER 22

March–April 1945

Berlin, Germany

The air-raid sirens screamed throughout Berlin. Antonia squeezed into the shelter's entrance, with crowds of other people. Ahead of her was Petro Stefaniuk, the first Berlin contact she'd located. They had barely sat down to review her situation and the documents he'd arranged for the family when the sirens sent them and what seemed like the entire population of Berlin into the underground passages of Kleistpark. Fluorescent markers on the bomb shelter walls glowed in the dark, pointing the way to supposed safety. Stefaniuk shouted for Antonia not to lose sight of him. With the impact of every explosion rattling and echoing through the air vents, Antonia imagined that there would be nothing left when they crawled out. A small child, about Nestor's age, was half-running, half-jumping like the stuffed rabbit she was clutching. The plush floppy ears and long limbs were grimy but the little girl held on to it as if her life depended on it.

They reached the end of the tunnel and had to go right, but people were pressing and pushing into the rooms along the corridor, their cases banging against the brick walls. In the search for empty bunks, they were causing a human traffic jam. The squabble of several languages—and that unique Berlin dialect especially—did not serve to make things easier. Stefaniuk finally broke through into a room, the light bulbs flickered on and Antonia tried to prevent a crush from following them in.

There were two bunk beds, three stories each, with three mattresses laid out crosswise. Eighteen people were meant to bunk in this room no larger than a storage closet. There was one sink and signs that indicated the men's and women's toilets were somewhere back where they'd come from.

Antonia leaned against the sink, watching as sixteen more people claimed the remaining mattresses. "My sister and brother-in-law are at the Jaceks' summer cottage outside the city."

Stefaniuk nodded. "They should be all right."

"I didn't think we'd end up like this," Antonia said, remembering how she had helped the journalist flee over the Soviet border years ago.

"This is how Berlin has been for some time," Stefaniuk said. "Sometimes we wonder whether we will ever see the light of day again. Everyone curses the war, but nobody has yet considered cursing and overthrowing Hitler."

"German propaganda," Antonia whispered, casting a look at the others in the room. The air was thick with suspicion and mistrust amongst the crowd of strangers. "But you were saying that the Red Army is already across the Oder."

Stefaniuk bent his head. "The Americans won't beat the Soviets to Berlin."

"Then we can't stay here. My entire family is surely on their blacklist. They will send us to the gulags before they send us anywhere near Galicia."

"The Allies need Russia," Stefaniuk said. He shifted to stand in front of her as another shudder vibrated through.

Antonia wrapped her arms around herself as Stefaniuk continued, "They have no idea what they will unleash if they win. You and I have had enough experience with the Soviets to know that they will secure measures after the war with lies and falsehoods, false promises. None of us," he stressed, "none of us should be within reach of them when that time comes."

Antonia rubbed her eyes. "Where can we go? Is there anywhere? We tried to reach Switzerland but…"

"Do you know anyone further west in Germany?" He lifted the small valise that was still gripped in his hand. Inside, the identification papers she needed. "I've got Roman a job permit here. All we have to do is adjust it. But you should head west. And hope it becomes American or British occupied territory."

"Roman gave me a name for that very reason. Myron Kosar in Bavaria."

"That's perfect. What does he do?"

"He's working for a newspaper, as a propaganda cartoonist."

Stefaniuk frowned. "And he's to be trusted?"

"Do we have a choice?"

It was a day later when they were finally allowed to leave the shelter. As she passed one of the emptied rooms, something caught her eye beneath one of the bunks. She stepped in and whisked out the plush rabbit, the tip of its ear crusted as if the little girl had chewed on it. She took it with her, searching for the child owner but she had no idea what the family looked like. She'd only seen the rabbit and the back of the little girl's head.

Above ground, Berlin was on fire. Entire facades had collapsed into heaps of rubble. Fire brigades were working on putting out the flames, but Antonia could not imagine anyone finding anything left of their homes.

It was a long hike before she and Stefaniuk found a bus that could take her back to the Jaceks. By that time she was ravenous. He opened the valise and produced the papers he'd been holding for her. She did not dare to look at them in public.

"Is it all there?" she asked.

"As you ordered." Stefaniuk kissed her cheeks three times. "There's a little money as well. Listen, I asked about the Ukrainian Self-Defense Legion."

Antonia looked up, hopeful. She had nearly forgotten in the stress of the bombings. "Ivan Kovalenko. Pavlo Derkach. Any word on them?"

"Our own command is scattered everywhere right now. Those who I did manage to reach said they lost touch with almost all the cells within Ukraine. The last time anyone heard anything about them, they were somewhere in Poland under the command of an Oberst Biegelmaier. The Ukrainian officers had been split up and integrated into combat units." He finished softly, as if he recognized that he was causing her great distress.

"Anything else?" she asked.

He shook his head.

As soon as she was on the bus, alone in the back, she withdrew the papers from the envelope. Roman was Polish, that had been easy, and his and Lena's and the boys' papers were as legitimate as could be for forged documents. For herself, she had asked for a Polish name—Zieleńska—identifying her as a professor of German literature at Krakow instead of Lviv. As the bus took her down a country lane, and she savored the flat landscape and peaceful setting, she mulled over every morsel of news Stefaniuk had shared. If the One and a Half Cossacks fell on the front, it would be her fault. She should have stayed with them. She unsnapped the bag next to her, reached in and withdrew the grimy bunny rabbit, hugging it to her.

Back at the Jaceks' cottage, Antonia took a day to recover from the ordeal in Berlin but insisted that Jacek get them out as fast as possible. He escorted the family to the main train station. Antonia's heart sank at the pandemonium before them.

The bomb shelters had been nothing in comparison to the flood of humanity fighting to board one of the few trains running out of the city. Men and women clung to the sides of cars, and people had to hang their luggage from the windows as others pushed their way into the compartments. Antonia watched with horror as one man, dressed in military uniform, shoved a woman into an overcrowded carriage. The passengers were trying to push her back out, but then she turned around and the man lifted a toddler from the platform. The woman took the child into her arms and one by one, the passengers reluctantly left her alone. The man made no sign of going with her.

From the carriage in front of Antonia, a suitcase fell from the window and onto the rail below. The young woman who'd dropped it screamed, her hand groping at mere air. Roman jumped down between the car and the rails and retrieved it, scrambled back onto the platform and held it up to her until she had hold of it again. She thanked him over and over in German, her dark hair falling into her face as more people pushed her up against the window. Antonia could not watch. She was certain the woman would suffocate before her very eyes.

Lena knitted her brows together, as if scolding Roman. "We're getting on the next train. We're going to be the first ones on it. And I don't care where it goes, as long as it's west."

Except, Antonia thought, that was everyone's plan. The mayhem on the platform did not cease even when that train jerked and pulled out of the station. General kindness and good manners blew away like the ashes of Berlin in a strong wind. She was roughly pushed aside as two men launched into a fist fight right next to her. Antonia noted that the boys had also been stunned into silence. Nestor's widened eyes absorbed the scene before him as he furiously sucked at the bottle Lena had handed him. The plush rabbit was crushed against him with the other arm. Konstantin was trying to hide in the folds of Lena's coat. When the next train pulled in, the crowds rushed it, but Lena did not hesitate. She snatched the boys' hands and barreled into the crowd. Nestor dropped the stuffed rabbit, but Antonia scooped it up and shoved it into the sleeve of her coat.

Her nephew twisted away from Lena.

"I've got him, Nestor. I've got him. Go with your mother!"

Roman was pushing Antonia forward. "We have to stay together. Get on the train."

By some miracle, they were onboard, and Antonia could hardly believe how she relished the feel of the train's floor beneath her feet. When Lena realized that they were all still with her, she seemed even more bolstered by her courage and—without mercy—she shoved herself into one of the cars, turned around and yanked Antonia in with her, then Roman after that. Outside the grimy window, the platform was heaving with bodies; Antonia wondered how they had survived that crush. The desperate faces looking into their carriage reminded her how she'd felt as she realized they weren't going to make it onto the previous train.

Apparently the stationmasters had learned their lesson with the last train; they blew their whistles almost immediately. With no chance to push inside, many sprang off at the last second.

Nestor began to cry, and Antonia plucked the rabbit out of her coat and gave it to him. After all, she understood the pain of losing beloved things.

In Nuremberg, the family had to spend the night huddled near Königstor with hundreds of other refugees after the trains to Munich had been canceled. The next morning, the station managers were running a better system. When Antonia and the family arrived, they were directed to the correct platform at the correct time, and got on the train to Munich. But just north of the city, in the middle of the countryside, the train stopped. Antonia and the other passengers peered out the windows to see what the delay was about. The horizon was black with smoke and the sky was swarming with black dots, like circling vultures. The train conductor passed through the car, announcing that they would not be able to make it to Munich.

Roman and Lena looked at one another. Along the track was a country road. The exodus of refugees had continued all along the rail lines from Berlin to here.

"I think we should get off here and walk to Rosenheim," Antonia said.

"It's seventy kilometers from Munich," Roman said.

But Lena was already collecting their things. "We're walking. I don't want any more stations and I don't want any more cities with air raids. And no trains."

He took some persuading, but eventually Antonia managed to talk the conductor into letting them off. Several other passengers also decided they did not want to be rerouted elsewhere in Germany. Across the tracks, Antonia stopped a slow-moving vehicle before realizing the family was fueling the contraption with wood.

"Do you know the way to Rosenheim?"

They showed Antonia their map and she gathered up the family before leading the way.

Not two hours later, they neared a field where two farmers were working down rows of dirt mounds.

"Are those potatoes?" Lena asked, shading her eyes.

"Might be," Antonia said.

Lena stepped onto the edge of the field. She scanned the broad expanse. One of the men rose from the ground, scrawny in a blue overcoat and rubber boots.

"*Was wollen Sie?*" he called. What do you want? His head turned to the other farmer, but the second one had his back to them, unaware.

To Antonia's surprise, Lena marched up to the farmer who'd called to them. She beckoned for the crate on the ground. He shook his head, but she reached into the crate despite his protests, dropped onto her knees and dug a hole, then covered the potato. Lena raised her head and took the next potato. The second farmer had spotted them and was now heading over. He was beefier, with a red face and a gray, cone-shaped hat on his head.

"*Wir suchen Arbeit*," Antonia called to them both. "*Wir können helfen.*"

She indicated the rest of the family but the first farmer began protesting again. Antonia went to him.

"We just want to work," she said again. "Look, you have this huge field to harvest with just two of you, and we could help."

Lena was nodding, still on the ground, burying another potato with her bare hands. Roman slowly came forward with the boys. The second farmer now crossed over the rows, and though his stature and coloring were the opposite of the first man, Antonia determined they were brothers. She pleaded to him as well.

"In return for a place to sleep tonight," she said. "Just in your barn, that will do. We have to walk to Rosenheim and that's a long way."

The farmers seemed at a loss for words.

Antonia tried once more. "Look, we'll help and tomorrow we'll be gone. What do you say? One meal. One night. We'll work for the rest of the afternoon."

The second farmer lowered his head as if it were too heavy, and mopped the nape of his neck with a handkerchief. He looked up and down his field and then at his brother. The scrawny one pulled his shoulders up nearly to his ears.

"You stay the week," the bigger brother said. "Maybe two? Help us with this and with sowing the other fields, in return for food and shelter. We have a house. It's nearly empty. And when you're done, we'll take you to Rosenheim in the wagon. There's no gasoline, so it will have to be by horse and wagon."

"*Gut!*" Lena cried. She got up and brushed herself off then stuck out her hand for each of the farmers to shake on it. "*Sehr gut!*"

CHAPTER 23

May 1945

Bavaria, Germany

Edgar Huber removed the long rubber apron and washed his hands. Antonia leaned against the stall. There was a consistent ache in the middle of her back but no matter how much she rubbed or tried to stretch, it would not go away. As Antonia changed the straw around the heifer, the farmer gradually helped the red and white calf to its feet. On unsteady legs, the newborn got beneath its mother and searched out a teat.

"You don't keep the bull calves, do you?" she guessed.

Edgar mopped his face and replaced the gray hat over his protruding brow. "When the boys wake up, you should let them know there's another one for them to squeal over." He was apparently unwilling to confirm that the calf would be slaughtered come fall.

Antonia washed her hands in the bucket then extinguished the lantern. Outside the barn, the sun was just coming up, the sky swathed with pinks and oranges.

"Mighty thankful for your help," Edgar said shyly. "You have animals back on your farm in Poland?"

"Only a few goats. Nothing this big. We were fruit producers."

Edgar had a habit of always tilting his head down when he spoke. "Well, looks like spring has sprung. That makes three calves in just under a week. I suppose, now that the planting is done, you folks will want to head on to Rosenheim."

Antonia nodded, still rubbing the spot on her back. "Yes, if we're no longer of use to you."

"You said you have an acquaintance there. Is that still the case?"

"My brother-in-law does, yes. He will arrange work for Roman when we get there."

Edgar looked up at the brightening sky. Blackbirds and larks made a ruckus in the woods off to one side of the farm. "Today's a holiday," he said. "First of May. Labor Day. And the *Maibaum* is up. We usually have a festival in town."

"Then you won't want to make the trip to Rosenheim today," Antonia said.

Edgar swung his head a little just before opening the door for her. "If you folks are in a hurry and all." He looked doleful when he raised his eyes again. "Otherwise, there's dancing and such…"

Antonia smiled, though she was deathly tired after three nights of having slept so little. "That sounds positively charming. I'll tell the others."

Lena was in the kitchen, already making coffee. "Another calf?" her sister chirped in Ukrainian. She threw Edgar a look. "You're returning to your farming roots, sister. Keep it up and he'll ask you to marry him." She stroked Antonia's waist. "You could use putting on some fat and color on those cheeks."

Antonia pinched Lena's cheek and kissed her. "We're going dancing today. All of us."

Before Lena could finish protesting, the back door burst open, and Konstantin and Nestor charged in and chased one another around the kitchen table. Roman followed in with Norbert Huber, the latter throwing Edgar a questioning look.

"That's three," Edgar told his younger brother. "And they're all coming to the festival with us."

"The calves?" Norbert asked.

Antonia laughed. "No, we are."

Norbert raised his eyebrows and took a seat at the table. The children followed suit. He swiped at Konstantin's nose, holding his thumb between his index and middle finger. "Look, what I have Nestor. It's Konstantin's nose."

The boys giggled and Konstantin mocked indignation, touching his face. "You do not. It's right here."

Antonia placed the basket of bread and butter on the table and examined her nephew. "Your German's getting better."

"I'm so glad I don't have to go to school today," Konstantin declared in Ukrainian. "The kids make fun of me. They call me a stupid Russian—"

"And what do you say?" Roman asked hurriedly.

Konstantin sniffed and shrugged.

"What do you say?" Lena repeated sharply.

Edgar and Norbert appeared to note the change in tone and quietly buttered their bread.

Konstantin still did not answer. Silently, he pleaded with Antonia.

"Go ahead. Tell them," she said.

Defeated, Konstantin said, "I tell them I'm a Pollack." Then he grinned. "A *stupid* Pollack."

Lena and Roman were stunned at first, and then both of them burst out laughing at the clever joke. As long as he said they were Polish, it didn't matter.

After breakfast, the boys went to go see the calves, Nestor giggling every time one blew on his face, and giggling when he touched the moist pink noses. Edgar hitched up the horse and wagon and Norbert and Roman rounded up the boys and gently tossed them into the hay in the back. They then helped Antonia and Lena climb in. The Huber brothers sat up front.

"Why aren't they married?" Lena asked. "They're both so kind."

They were, Antonia thought. But they were also very quiet, did not share much about themselves, and they worked all day, every day. Edgar had the old family house, and Norbert had taken over the property and home of an unmarried uncle who'd died in the Great War. They kept to themselves, and even when neighbors came inquiring about the refugees helping in their fields, they had responded with hardly more than a couple of words, their shrugs underscoring their reluctance to waste any.

When they pulled up into town, the first thing Antonia saw were people coming out of their houses, their faces pinched with excitement. The residents were chattering and gesticulating wildly with one another outside of the church. One man, his face in his hands and his shoulders shaking, appeared to be weeping. Antonia caught the brothers' wary glance at each other before Edgar slowed the wagon alongside a man and a woman heading for the village center.

"Martin," Norbert called. The man stopped. "What's happened?"

"Hitler's dead!"

Antonia clapped a hand over her mouth. Lena grabbed her by the elbow, and Antonia shushed her.

"When?" Norbert asked.

"Yesterday," the man answered. It was difficult to read his expression. "They just announced it on the radio."

The brothers looked at one another and then at Antonia. She nodded that she'd understood before telling Lena and Roman. "It's true. Hitler's dead."

Everyone seemed careful about how to react. Antonia wanted to shout out with happiness, to scream with relief. This meant that the war would finally end. However, all of them got out of the wagon soberly, eyes shining but a cautious mollification coursing through the village. The people crowded into the square where tables and benches surrounded the Maypole with fluttering blue and white ribbons. A band started to play and Edgar leaned over to her.

"Our village here," he said quietly, "is a bit… different. Most of it anyway."

On the seams of the square, a group of men scowled at the revelers but Lena came and tugged her toward the church with Roman and the children. They filed into a pew. Several others were drifting in. A priest joined them at the front and led the congregation in the Rosary.

When they were back outside, the Hubers pressed a mug of beer into everyone's hands and bottles of sodas into the boys'. The dancing began, yet Antonia sensed everyone was on tenterhooks. Edgar, head low, offered his hand to Antonia and she took it even though her legs felt heavy. He led her into a polka accompanied by an accordion, a trombone and two horns. Smiling, she spun with him, astonished and pleased to find that he was a very strong and able dancer. When they were finished, he was grinning with embarrassment and mopped his brow. He nodded at her once, and led her back to the table.

Next to her, Norbert leaned in. "My brother likes you."

She smiled warmly. "And we appreciate you. All of us do. Who knew that my sister's determination would win us such a friendship?"

Norbert glanced at Edgar, who looked away and sipped from his mug. "He's a good man, my brother. When the war ends…"

Antonia put a hand on his arm and squeezed it. "When the war ends, there are people we must find. People I must find." She captured his gaze to make sure he understood. "People I love. And a country we must at least try and return to."

Norbert sighed sadly. "Do you believe Poland will fall into Soviet hands?"

She kept her emotions in check. Despite their kindnesses, none of the family had admitted to being anything other than

Polish. "It is our ardent wish that it does not. And I will continue to make it my life's work to see that it remains free."

The farmers looked at one another, and she saw the most imperceptible shake of Norbert's head. Edgar's eyes dropped and he twisted again to the crowd in the square, looking more solitary than ever.

True to their word, the Hubers drove Antonia and the family to Rosenheim the next day, only to meet a blockade of U.S. troops at the city's entry. The mayor, they discovered, had handed the town over to the 12th Armored Division that morning.

"*Papiere*," one guardsman motioned.

The Hubers withdrew their identity papers, and Antonia nervously presented hers and the rest of the family's. She shifted in the wagon, the pain in her back still needling her.

"Finish?" she asked one soldier in English. He was examining the wagon. "*Der Krieg?* Finish?"

The soldier—he looked no older than twenty—looked at her warily, reviewed her documents and showed it to a man with stripes on his lapels.

"You're Polish?" the officer asked. "Refugees? *Flüchtlinge?*"

Antonia nodded. "Polish, yes."

"You don't have permission to be here," the officer said in German. "It's dangerous. Still dangerous."

The Hubers were being asked to abandon the wagon now. They stepped down, hands raised above their heads. The other guards were patting them down and searching them.

"Good," Antonia pointed to the brothers. "No soldiers. Good mans."

The American officer nodded dismissively. "Yeah, they all say they're good now. They're all anti-Nazis now, aren't they? You have to go back. *Zurück. Zurückfahren.*"

Roman tried to explain that they had a friend in Rosenheim. "Myron Kosar," he repeated, shoving the paper to yet another sentry.

Antonia mixed up English and German. "Friend. Myron Kosar. He's a resident here, a friend of the family. My brother-in-law has a job."

But the soldiers and the officer were not listening. They searched the entire wagon, even removed all the hay and scattered it onto the ground. When they found that they and the wagon posed no threat, the officer again told the Huber brothers to turn around and go back home.

Inside the city, something exploded, and there was the distant rattle of gunfire. Edgar and Norbert, released by the guards, climbed quickly back in and Edgar took up the reins.

"I don't think the townsfolk accept the mayor's decision," Norbert said drily.

The soldiers, their weapons still poised at the ready, helped steer Norbert's wagon around.

When they were up the road and in the countryside again, Edgar leaned back, calling over his shoulder, "We'll go back to our village and ask the postman for a telephone. You can call your friend and let him know what's just happened."

Antonia thanked him and settled back against the boards. Everyone was quiet. The war was far from over. Not for the first time, Antonia's thoughts turned to Ivan. Where was he? Had he heard the news? She clutched her hands and looked off into the distance. This time, she prayed with all her heart.

After a night of loud and vivid dreams, Antonia awoke in her bed shivering. It took her a long while to remember where she was. Norbert's house. The bedroom above the front yard. Bavaria. Her eyes were burning, and her bedding and the mattress were soaked. She felt as if she were encased in cement. Weakly, she tugged the blankets up to her chin and rolled onto her side, trying to get out

of bed. As soon as she had one foot on the ground, she shivered
violently and withdrew it back beneath the blankets.

"Lena," she called feebly.

There was no answer. Outside the window, she could hear
Nestor giggling, no doubt playing on the rubber tire Norbert
had hung from the walnut tree. Konstantin was probably on his
way to school.

"Lena?" she called again. "Roman?"

Antonia's teeth chattered and she coughed, recalling that she
had been coughing more often over the past week. Her throat
did not hurt, neither did her lungs. She pressed her fingers to
the lump, protruding as large as a plum, and coughed again.
Something was terribly wrong, and she feared that her fever was
related to her illness.

With great effort, she gathered her strength and will and thrust
the duvet off of her, swung her legs to the floor, and stumbled to
the window. Relieved to see Roman with Nestor at the walnut
tree, she tried to open the window, her hands shaking. She rapped
on the pane, unable to utter more than a squeak.

Roman looked up, and Antonia slumped as she beckoned for
him to come upstairs. With one hand, he interrupted the swinging tire and urged Nestor to get off. Relieved to see him heading
into the house, Antonia fell into the bed, her back burning as
she pulled herself beneath the covers again.

Her brother-in-law strode in and touched her forehead. "Jesus
almighty. Antonia, when you didn't come to breakfast, Lena
thought you needed the sleep after all that calving."

"Get the doctor," she croaked.

Soon, she heard Roman calling for Edgar in the barn, heard
voices outside the bedroom window. It was Edgar who checked
on her next and she was so surprised when he whisked her out
of the bed and carried her to the bathroom that she did not even

protest. The slip she used as her nightdress clung to her, damp with sweat. Edgar lowered her into the bathtub with Roman's help, then turned on the faucet.

"We need to reduce her fever," he said.

Roman seemed to understand, but Antonia whimpered when the ice-cold water crept up her thighs. Her teeth ground so hard they were squeaking.

"You wait," Edgar said in slow German to Roman. "Stay. I will get the doctor."

He was gone and Roman took a washcloth, dipped it into the water and pressed it to Antonia's head. She closed her eyes and let the darkness take her.

Voices. Many voices. One man's, in German, soothing. A sharp prick in her arm. Numbness. More voices, and the sensation of floating. Clicks. More clicks. Wood upon wood. The sound of horse hooves. A cuckoo. The scent of forget-me-nots. The taste of apricots. Ivan's kiss. *Search for me. Find me.* The lights slicing through the darkness. The hiss and click of the cattle car door. Her body seized up. It remembered everything then.

Again the darkness.

Again the light.

"Hail Mary, full of Grace, the Lord is with thee. Blessed art thou among women and blessed is the fruit of thy womb, Jesus…" Reaching to Antonia, over and over again, like someone dangling a rope to help her out of a deep well.

Oksana.

Lena's voice. The soft knocking of wooden beads. Norbert's rosary, which he'd loaned to her the first Sunday they all went to church together. The scent of incense. The laugh that bubbled up. Pavlo and Ivan as altar boys, having shaved the sides and backs of their heads and brushed their hair forward like two Cossacks.

One and a Half Cossacks. *Pavlo. Ivan. Ivan, if you're alive, hang on. Hang on. I'm coming to you.*

Antonia groaned and awoke, relieved to find herself dry beneath the blankets, warm and not shivering. Yet every joint ached, every bone—to the marrow—felt bruised.

When her eyelids fluttered open, Lena's silhouette came into view. Outside the window, it was late afternoon.

Lena paused in her prayer and took Antonia's hand.

"Am I going to die?" Antonia croaked. She swallowed. "You told me… to see the doctor… to take care of the…"

"It's not your thyroid," Lena said. "Though he did say you should have the growth removed. You have a kidney infection. And your fever was dangerously high."

"Edgar."

"Yes," Lena said, brushing a tear away. "Edgar saved your life. None too soon, either."

She pressed something into Antonia's hands. "He wanted me to give this to you."

Antonia looked at the book. The Holy Bible. "For me?"

"He said he wants you to keep it."

Antonia placed it next to her. "What day is it?" she asked hoarsely.

Her sister rose and lifted a glass to Antonia's lips. "It's still Tuesday. It's still the same day. But…"

Antonia drank the water then lay her head back onto the pillows. "But what?"

Lena's face appeared above hers, somber. "The Germans have surrendered. The war is over."

She was too weak. Antonia could only close her eyes and smile, and tears slipped down her face. She patted Lena's hand, and clutched the Bible to her chest, crying until she fell back to sleep.

It was another week before Antonia felt well enough to go outside. It was a warm day, the walnut tree spreading out its new leaves, and sparrows and redbreasts pulling up worms brought up from last night's soft spring rain. She sat on the bench outside the door, watching Konstantin and Nestor playing on the swinging tire when a vehicle appeared on the road opposite the farm. A black sedan, shiny and menacing. Antonia straightened. The sedan turned into the farm's drive, swerved to miss a puddle and then rolled to a stop before the yard.

"Boys, get over here." Antonia then called for Norbert.

Konstantin stopped, threw a look at the car and then came to her, pulling Nestor along.

Both farmers came around from the barn where they had been working on the fence posts. Roman was with them. Norbert's long face was drawn taut and threatening. Edgar swung his head low, like a prowling lion.

Antonia grabbed the children to her as two men stepped out. Both men wore suits and hats, and both men looked anything but German. She was reminded of the plainclothes secret police.

But Roman suddenly surged forward, his hand extended to the passenger. "Myron! Myron Kosar! By God, it's good to see you!"

Antonia let go of Nestor's hand. Lena came out of the house, a dish towel flung over her shoulder and embraced the stranger, then the driver.

Edgar swung his head to Antonia. "Time to go home?"

She reached over and hooked her arm around his. "Maybe," she said. "At least, we're going to try."

CHAPTER 24

April–May 1945

Eastern Front—Austria—Yugoslavia—Italy

A team of medics was carrying out the two snipers who had been wounded in Feldbach's tower—the building's guts and shaved-off sides lay piled around the smoking ruins.

Ivan cheered when he recognized Kulka propped up on a gurney. The boy's face was writhing in pain, but he was alive.

"Hang in there," Ivan cried and grasped the boy's hand. "I'll let Lys know where you are!"

Kulka lay back down, groaning. His head was bandaged, his right arm in a sling. Ivan scanned the premises but all he saw were shocked men, milling about, checking on the wounded, identifying their dead comrades.

Ivan saw to it that Kulka was put into the first ambulance.

"Where are you taking him?" He surveyed the destruction around him for some sign of the boy's brother. Bombers rumbled back behind the lines and Ivan covered his ears.

"Likely Tyrol," the medic shouted before slamming the truck shut.

Ivan stepped away as the vehicle roared to life.

"We'll find you." He banged on the door. "We'll find you, Kulka. Hang in there!"

Ivan stopped in the middle of the ruins and watched the truck pull away, his words echoing in his head. He'd promised many people he would find them. Keep them safe. Kulka. Terlytsia. Lys. The Half Cossack. Antonia. But as Ivan turned around, observing the wreckage around him, his promises were nothing but empty words now.

The Styrian town of Feldbach had been the Wehrmacht's last stronghold, hit so hard by the Soviets, Ivan wondered how it was possible he—unlike some of his men—was walking away. The enemy had not retreated, though. The Soviets were likely only taking a moment to regroup after the Luftwaffe had ripped massive holes through their lines.

Two days earlier, Ivan's division, together with the remnants of the SS-Galizien, had marched into an intact town. The 14th SS-Waffen division and parachute troops had been waiting for them. Now, St. Leonard's church was burning. The priest's rectory was damaged. Café Mayer in the Burgstrasse and Leitner Leather and Shoe store were shells of themselves.

"Kovalenko!"

Ivan spun around. He could not believe the sight before him. Covered in chalky dust, smeared with dirt, Terlytsia, Lys and the Half Cossack were striding toward him through the gates at Torplatz.

They surrounded him and—after relieved greetings—shared how they had narrowly escaped.

"Kulka's been taken to hospital," Ivan told Lys. "Somewhere in Tyrol. I think he'll be all right. He's in pain, but he'll live."

Lys chewed on that news. Ivan turned at the sound of several German soldiers creating a ruckus. They had surrounded an older man. Ivan recognized him as a member of the town's council.

As Ivan drew up to the group, the local man ripped his hat off, face twisted in anger or grief. "You'd better run like hell before the Reds find out and come back."

"Find out what?" Ivan turned to a Scharführer just as Pavlo joined them.

"Germany's capitulated," the Scharführer muttered. He strode away, calling to those who remained in his squad.

Ivan shoved Pavlo around and they went back to the other two Ukrainian officers to share the news.

"We should have joined the Yugoslavians when we had the chance," Lys said. "I'll find my brother later. Right now, we go back and fight those Soviets with men who are still able to."

Before Ivan could react, a pistol shot sliced through the air. Several men cried out and three soldiers sprinted to where their commanders had taken shelter in an air raid bunker.

"The Oberst," one cried. "Biegelmaier's shot himself!"

Terlytsia shoved Ivan toward the gate. "We need to go. Now."

Ivan did not manage to ask where. They were all jogging after Terlytsia towards a military truck parked nearby. Ivan threw Pavlo a quick look, but the Half Cossack was already moving to the passenger side and scrambling inside. Ivan leapt into the back with Lys just as Terlytsia slammed the truck into gear and began rolling.

They passed the wreckage of the battle, the broken railway tracks, the fields of grapes and rapeseed, the undulating road, heading south. Wounded men limped out of the ravines. Bodies were strewn about on and along the road. An ambulance sped by. A motorcycle and sidecar were tipped over in a ditch.

Ivan turned his attention to Lys. "Where the hell is Terlytsia going?"

The captain fixed his dark gaze on Ivan. "I think he's finally fulfilling Dusha's orders to make a run for it."

Ivan gaped at him, then at the back of Terlytsia's head. The truck didn't slow down until they had reached Spielfeld. Weeks before, they'd requisitioned farmhouses and homes in the surrounding Styrian hamlets. The River Mur was the only thing separating them from the Yugoslavian territories.

Ivan recognized the farm that Terlytsia was pulling into and rubbed his head as the Half Cossack turned, half-grinning, half-frowning.

The old farmer—belly protruding over his grimy trousers—cautiously came out of the house. Terlytsia turned off the ignition and he and Pavlo got out of the cab. Ivan followed Lys into the yard where Pavlo stuck his hand out to the farmer.

"Max," Pavlo called as if in warning. "We need that *slivovitz*. *Bitte*."

Ivan also shook the hand of the farmer they'd befriended weeks earlier. It was time for him to make good on his promise and prepare a delivery of plum schnapps across the Mur. The Ukrainians were going to locate Tito's partisans.

Max told them he would make contact, then sent them into the hayloft of the barn, warning them that some of the generals were ordering that every man fight to the death regardless of the official surrender. They were also shooting deserters, which meant the Ukrainians—if caught—would be considered fair game.

Ivan and the others stripped off their uniforms, washed and dressed in the clothing Max provided them with. When night fell, the farmer returned.

"At two a.m.," was all he said.

Ivan turned to Pavlo, nervous but putting on a brave face. "Hey," he said, clasping the Half Cossack's arm.

"We're going to make it," Pavlo said. "We really are. I feel it in my bones."

Ivan was not as certain. The word was that the Chetniks and Tito's partisans had banded together, although the two parties followed vastly different ideals. It was sure to be a rough-and-tumble bunch, neither side trusting the other. Throw a bunch of Ukrainians into the mix, and Ivan could imagine they were headed for an explosive finale. The Germans had been predictable thanks to their ordered discipline. The group across the river had the reputation of men who would slit someone's throat for the most trivial thing.

The barn was just light enough to make out Pavlo's grin. "I know what you're thinking," he said. "We need to do this. What choice do we have? I want to be alive when this is over, my wife and that child she's carrying back with me."

"You'll be a whole Cossack soon enough," Ivan said.

"After we get Nadia out of Austria, we'll help find Antonia."

Ivan drew in a deep breath. "Let's get some sleep."

An hour before they were to meet the partisans on the river-bank, Max returned to escort them. He told them that there was a raft on the other side of the river that Tito's men would use to pick them up. Ivan spotted the rope stretched taut between the trees on each bank. At 0200 hours, Ivan was alert but there was no sound. No signals. No dipping or slithering of any raft in the water. Only the distant rumble of what sounded like whitewater downstream.

At 0220, Ivan rose out of hiding. "They're not coming."

"What are we going to do?" Terlytsia hissed.

"Ivan, come with me," Pavlo said. "The rest of you stay here. I'll be right back."

Ivan followed him to the edge of the bank, and Pavlo nudged him.

"Lift me up to the rope."

Ivan frowned but did as Pavlo asked. The smaller man grabbed hold of the rope and swung his legs up, head pointed toward the river. Without another word, he shimmied along the stretch, and was swallowed by the darkness before he was halfway across. Ivan chuckled and softly whistled. Terlytsia and Lys soon joined him. They heard the pop of a gun on the other side then the clang of metal. The men ducked, Ivan concerned only until there was the sound of a soft splash followed by the jump and tug of the rope. The raft must have been chained up, and Pavlo had used his weapon to break the lock.

They were all grinning when the Half Cossack showed up. Ivan clapped him on the back and pulled him in for a kiss. Terlytsia and Lys also got onto the raft, and Pavlo pushed them off. On the Yugoslavian bank, a dark figure suddenly rose.

Ivan saw the flash at the same time as he heard the gun's report. There was a splash, a surprised cry, and Ivan saw Pavlo in the water. Ivan belly-dropped onto the raft and grasped the Half Cossack's arm.

"Are you hit?"

Pavlo sputtered and coughed in answer.

"Don't shoot," Terlytsia shouted in Russian. "We're here to help!"

Ivan felt Pavlo slide deeper into the water. "I'm pulling him up," he cried. "Help me pull him in."

Terlytsia and Lys tried, but the raft tipped dangerously. They would capsize. On the riverbank, he vaguely noted shadows scrambling downriver. Ivan rose to his knees, saw a lantern and one man cranking his arm.

"Rope," Ivan shouted. The end of the rope flew into the air and he reached to grab hold as Lys and Terlytsia both snatched Pavlo's arms. The raft yanked beneath him and Ivan jerked forward before steadying himself in the center. Slowly, the partisans fought the current and hauled them in. Behind him, Pavlo was releasing a very long list of choice words.

"You fucking crazy Chetniks! We're here to fucking help! Thanks to you, I lost your goddamned schnapps!"

"Are you hit?" Ivan asked again.

"No," Pavlo cried. "But one of the bottles exploded."

Ivan was so relieved he was laughing as the strangers pulled them in. Pavlo shook himself like a wet dog, but they sobered when six men encircled their party. Each had a weapon pointed at the Ukrainians.

"Welcome to Yugoslavia," one man said. His round glasses reflected the light of the lamp he held. He looked like a miniature Trotsky, grave face and all. "I'm Major Josef. You're here to help? I believe it's we who had to help you, and you thought you could just take our raft all the way down to the Mediterranean, or what?"

"Is that why you were shooting at us?" Terlytsia cried. "You knew we were coming."

"You stole our raft," the man said simply.

"You were late," Ivan defended.

"We're late because we received orders to move out. Immediately. Except quite a debate ensued about whether to pick you up first."

"Move out? Where?" Ivan and Pavlo asked at the same time.

"Udine. Italy."

Terlytsia stopped wringing his tunic. "Italy?"

Major Josef shrugged. "We go wherever I say we go. Either you're with us, or you're against us." The soft clicks of six rifles taking closer aim.

Next to Ivan, Lys grunted.

"We're with you," Ivan said, raising his hands over his head. The others followed suit.

"I might," Pavlo said, "still have a bottle left here…" He slowly reached into his soaked coat and withdrew one of the smaller bottles of schnapps.

Major Josef stepped forward and snatched it from him. He pulled the stopper with his teeth and took a long drink, beard quivering. He plugged the bottle again and sighed. "Good old Max." Then, as if he'd just noticed the four Ukrainian officers, he added, "The Allies are counting on us to beat a path to Trieste. The most fanatical Nazis are hell-bent on holding their last access to the Mediterranean."

The commander jerked his head up the bank. The other partisans shouldered their rifles and led the way. Ivan shoved Pavlo ahead of him, but made sure to keep the Half Cossack within reach. He prayed Pavlo's gut instincts were right, that they were going to make it, but the thought of facing the Germans in battle made his blood run cold.

The world was in chaos as mortars and grenades rained upon the open meadow. In the brief moment of respite, Ivan flung himself out of Terlytsia's foxhole and sprinted to Pavlo's pit. He jumped in, hit the wall and pushed himself to the opposite side where Pavlo was taking cover. Another grenade sent a shower of earth and rock cascading over their hole.

"Lys is ten meters from here." Ivan jerked his thumb. "We need to pull back, but the trap's been set. Get ready for some very pissed-off Germans."

Although the Führer had killed himself and one Nazi officer after another was reported having committed suicide, the war was still raging in a mess of last stands and desperate battles. The Soviets on one side and the remnants of the German army on the other, with Tito's partisans and the Chetniks trying to hold off both without killing one another in between skirmishes.

For over a week, Ivan, Pavlo and the other two Ukrainian officers stumbled from one battle to the next, shelled first by artillery, then by mortars.

Pavlo was suddenly yanking on Ivan's sleeve.

"Let's go! Let's go!"

Ivan raised his head, followed him, scrambled out of the pit and made a run for it. The panzers were rolling in. He threw a look over his shoulder. They were heading straight for his booby traps. The fireworks were about to start.

Earth suddenly broke loose beneath his feet. He was ready to fling himself into the next foxhole but, at the sound of a distant explosion, Ivan pulled up. Half a kilometer away, the farmhouse he'd passed hours earlier was now aflame. Pavlo screamed at him to jump in as another mortar shrieked across the sky.

Ivan dropped and his ankle twisted grotesquely beneath him. The pain was so sharp and sudden, it took his breath away. Fourteen more blasts by mortars. Then more grenades, one after the other.

"Those sonsofbitches," Ivan screamed beneath his folded arms. "When are they going to hit the booby?"

"Those are Soviet," Pavlo shouted. "They're here, too! We've got to make a run for it! Let them do each other in."

There was only one way to go and that was downhill. There was a village a kilometer away. If their partisans all pulled back, it would be there. But could he make it? Ivan stretched his foot out in the boot, the pain searing up into his upper thigh. But it was not broken. He was sure of that. They were up and over the pit, scrambling toward the woods. Ivan rose and hobbled as fast as he could on his bad ankle. He was nearly at the treeline. Ten more meters. A blast exploded near him and Ivan was rocked off his feet. Something hit his back, burned right through it and he imagined a huge crater in the middle of his chest. He raised himself, his head ringing as if he were inside a huge cast-iron bell. He spotted his rifle, reached to pick it up, but his right arm was not working. It was dangling from its socket. Over his shoulder, he saw fire. It had to be the booby trap he'd set. But the panzer must have gotten one last shot in before it had met the explosives.

Somewhere behind him he heard screaming, then wet gulping, then screaming again.

Ivan opened his mouth to shout after Pavlo, but he couldn't get any breath. The roiling black smoke made it impossible to see anything but he did see the blood spurting from his shoulder the moment he tried to move his arm again. He finally managed to suck in some air, grasped his arm and screamed Pavlo's name in pain. Huge, long cries that emptied his lungs each time.

Finally, the ringing in his head receded somewhat. He stumbled to a tree and leaned against it, but the field was still exploding up ahead. The Soviets were here, coming from the river. Ivan forced himself to take another breath.

"Pavlo! Derkach! Where are you?"

He blinked and swayed, bouncing from one trunk to the next. A branch was burning overhead, sending down a cascade of embers. Ivan scrambled back for his automatic rifle, picked it up with his left hand and, bent over, limping as he searched for Pavlo.

"Derkach!"

Someone was suddenly pulling and yanking him by his good arm, making him run in the other direction.

"Keep up, Kovalenko." It was Lys. Lys was holding on to him.

Ivan continued shouting for Pavlo. After the treeline, it was a hard climb up a steep ridge, and Ivan tried to twist away, to turn back for the Half Cossack.

Suddenly Terlytsia's voice sounded on the other side of him. "I've got Derkach. I've got him. Keep going!"

Ivan tried to focus. Terlytsia was carrying a huge backpack. No. A man. Pieces of a man.

Then Lys's voice made it through the din in Ivan's head. "We're almost there, Kovalenko."

The back side of the ridge was steeper and higher but they were going down now, not up. Below them, a cluster of houses with smoke rising from their chimneys. Everything hurt, and then it didn't as Ivan struggled to keep the gray curtain from closing around him. He just wanted to sleep. Just rest.

He heard shouts of help coming from a distance and forced his eyes open.

Again the cry for help, but he knew it was not coming from him.

A door opened. Fire crackled in an oven. The world teetered and Ivan sank down, a wood-beamed ceiling swimming in and out of focus above him. He was on his side. The strangest thing was that there were no more blasts, no explosions. No more noise. No more screams of mortars in the air, no more panicked commands. Ivan blinked but his vision was growing gray again. Then a woman bent over him. Her cinnamon brown hair. Her green eyes with the brown and yellow flecks.

"Antonia…"

The face swam before him. He lifted his hand, but grasped nothing but air as Antonia's face disappeared and someone else's took its place. The stranger lifted his head, tipped a bottle to his mouth. After he drank, he gasped. They were lowering Pavlo's body, broken and bloodied onto the table next to him. The Half Cossack's face was charred. His left arm was gone.

Pavlo was breathing, though. In thick, wet gulps. His eyes were wide open and rolling like a wild animal's. Then he turned his head to Ivan. With his good hand, Pavlo reached across the space between them and Ivan fastened onto it. Pavlo raised his head from the table, his eyes finally still and focused on him.

"Na. Dia."

Ivan shook his head, clutched the blackened hand harder. "You're going back to her. You're going to see your wife and you'll meet your son."

But Pavlo was not listening. He lay his head back down and his chest struggled upwards one more time before it caved in. Ivan bellowed, his body drawing into itself. Curled up on his side, he clung to the Half Cossack's hand.

It took hours before they could pry them apart.

PART FOUR

1945–1946

Allied-Occupied Territories of
Germany—Austria—Italy

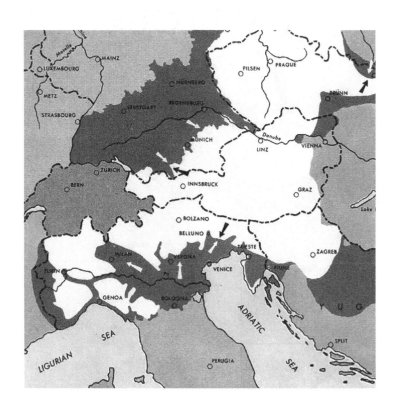

CHAPTER 25

May–June 1945

Bavaria, Germany

If anyone had told Antonia that it would be more difficult to get "back to normal" than to adapt to the horrific conditions she'd experienced in prison or in Wilhelmshagen, she would not have believed it. There was something more jarring about settling into a routine of peacetime than there might have been when she'd been tossed in like freight with hundreds of others and deposited at a slave labor camp.

Maybe because peacetime was a fragile illusion, a flimsy paper compared to the very real horrors enacted on their bodies and minds. The Bavarian countryside was so splendid it hurt. How was it that late spring could bloom so beautifully out of the ruins of war? And here, in Hitler's Bavaria, most especially? The meadows of flowers, lush and colorful like Roman's paint palette, were as impossible to look at as the sun.

The Chiemsee was dotted with sunbathers, and warm-weather revelers. Shops sold souvenirs as if Antonia had arrived on holiday instead of ending up here like debris after a brutal storm. Stands served beer and sausages again. People ate cake. Roman was painting on the pier—a scene of the Fraueninsel—his easel and paints set out as if he had not lost every single one of his canvases for ever and ever. No, he had gone back to work, and had even taken to painting some of his older studies from memory.

Meanwhile, sitting at a picnic table, Lena was writing again. She had a notebook and was filling pages upon pages with her beautiful longhand. The week before, she'd composed a song to the Carpathians. It had flowed out of her, she'd said. One minute she'd disappeared into a convent garden, the next she was presenting Antonia with a full page of lyrics. It was a love song filled with longing and hope but also with an undercurrent of anguish. They all knew—every single one of them—that they would never be able to go home as long as the Soviets controlled Ukraine's future.

Antonia watched the boys playing in the water. Konstantin was occasionally moody and very much disliked school. He would wake up at night, crying and distressed, sometimes having wet his bed. Antonia understood what he was going through. Homesickness and the anxiety about the future filled her as well. Most nights, she awoke in a cold sweat, the scum of war and trauma layered upon her so heavily she could barely breathe. Her escape then was the Bible Edgar Huber had given her. She clung to Scripture like someone thrown overboard clings to driftwood.

The only one who seemed unscathed was four-year-old Nestor. He was active, and energetic now that he had put on some weight, and seemed to shed the war the way he had cast off the donated pullovers when warm weather hit.

As she stared out onto the water, Antonia yearned for her roots, for her purpose. In a bookshop in Rosenheim she'd found a copy of *All Quiet on the Western Front*. Not even Remarque could soothe her now. Perhaps it was the chapter about Paul Bäumer's return home, where he went through all his books on his shelf hoping for solace and finding none in the old words. Her life was summed up in those lines; like Paul, she wished she could return to something more familiar. Even if it was the familiarity of a front.

Was this what she had fought for? They were all drifting. Simply drifting. She had risked everything for her country, and now she could not even return to it. Neither she, Lena nor Roman could be who they really were. According to their papers, they were Polish nationals now. The Americans, the British, the French, overwhelmed by the sea of traumatized refugees seeking a lifeline, were allowing Mother Russia to scoop out "her people" and return them to the "homeland." Those very same people were begging the Allied forces to resettle them anywhere but Soviet-controlled territories.

Everyone wanted to go to America. As if the promised land meant a promise to wipe out all the bad memories and problems just by being there. But the refugees Antonia had run into were repackaging their pain, their bitter histories, tying them into safe little bundles and stashing them deep inside themselves and close to their hearts. Every few days, there were new Ukrainians washing up in Rosenheim, and they were all looking for the same thing: connections back to the fold, *their* fold. Except all that brought were the old problems, the old fights, and there was a hefty need for vengeance amongst them, thanks to the unresolved politics.

When Antonia looked over her shoulder, Myron Kosar was walking toward her. She released her hands from the mounds of pebbles and sand she had formed around her. Her feet were in the water but now she drew up her knees.

"*Shanovna*," he greeted her. He sat down, rolled his trousers up his shins and slipped off his shoes. He was a handsome man. Perceptive green eyes, an elegant nose over a thoughtful mouth, a high forehead and wavy brown hair. He was also exceptionally well connected and informed.

Antonia wrapped her arms around her calves and lay her head sideways to give him her attention.

After a moment of watching the lake, he said, "I'm inviting some people over to the house tonight. I'd like all of you to come."

"What kind of people?"

"I think the kind that you would like. A group of *nashi*—our people—who found one another in Munich. They're coming for a little reprieve from the dust and rubble in the city. Their bus will get here late this afternoon."

"Where will they be staying?" she asked.

"I've got them quartered around Rosenheim and in the villages in the countryside here."

"Like us?"

"Like you. Except their stay is limited. They are here to paint, or write, or simply refresh their spirits. I'll be holding a few meetings at the house to discuss our future, to organize ourselves. You should be there."

"I think my sister and brother-in-law are better suited for this. I will watch the children."

Myron reached out as if to stroke her arm but withdrew his hand back to his side. "I wish you would reconsider. I think it would be worth your time."

Antonia faced the lake again, her chin resting on her knees. "I'll think about it."

She only said it so that he would go away.

Antonia and the Mazurs were staying in two farmhouses outside of Rosenheim. Herr Koch, like the Huber brothers, grew potatoes, but he had hectares of beans as well. When Lena found that out, she declared they would never go hungry again. Her sister's number one concern was to never starve again. Ever.

Herr Koch's neighbor across the road was Frau Wechsel. She took Antonia and Konstantin in, giving them the spare bedroom which overlooked the road and Herr Koch's yard. In return, the Mazurs and Antonia helped with chores on the two farms. It was an altogether pleasant arrangement. Herr Koch was a man of few words but of good heart. He treated the family fairly and often left them to their own devices. Frau Wechsel, a reedy woman, was Herr Koch's age. When Frau Wechsel offered Lena and Antonia a glass of her cherry cordial one evening, she explained that Herr Koch's deceased wife had been her best friend since childhood. Whether it was the spirits or Lena's insatiable need for romance, Antonia's sister decided immediately that Frau Wechsel and Herr Koch should marry. Antonia was more annoyed than Frau Wechsel, who tittered and blushed, and sipped the cordial as if she knew a secret they did not.

Frau Wechsel was outside hanging laundry when the family returned from the lake in Myron Kosar's car. Myron spoke with the German woman in low tones. Antonia shooed Konstantin into the house to change clothes, eat and say his prayers before going to bed. When she was downstairs again, Myron was still outside.

"What is it?" Antonia said.

"Frau Wechsel will watch the children if you would like to join us this evening."

Antonia sighed. "Really, I'm not up for it." The excursion to the lake had put her in an awful mood.

Frau Wechsel, however, insisted that Antonia go up and change. "The world is waiting for you to rejoin it."

Reluctantly, Antonia put on her other dress and tied her hair into a chignon. With Roman and Myron up front and Lena next to her in the back, they drove along the winding roads past rolling spring-green fields and meadows. The sun dipped down behind the alpine peaks. Myron pointed out the Watzmann, and he and Roman immediately made plans to take out a boat and paint on the Königssee with a number of others who were arriving from Munich that day.

On the back bench, Lena squeezed Antonia's hand. Though the men were busy chatting up front, she kept her voice low.

"You don't look well. I thought the excursion would do you good, but you look tired. More than ever."

"And melancholy," Antonia said. "I'm terribly, terribly sad today."

Lena did not let go of her hand, but her eyes went to the bright blue scarf around Antonia's throat. "We should take you to a doctor. Why don't you ask Myron to recommend one?"

Antonia shook her head. She knew she was being unreasonable but the fewer people she needed to show her falsified documents to, the better. "I'll be fine. I'm just—"

"Homesick," Lena said at the same time as she. "That's why we're going to this gathering. It will help. I'm sure it will."

When they entered Rosenheim, Antonia noticed that workers were rebuilding the demolished train station. They'd cleaned up the rubble and piled it into neat mounds. Some of the track had also been restored.

Myron lived in a house in the center, a three-story medieval structure with polished wood floors and a large oriel window that hung out over the narrow street. It was a comfortable home with plush couches and Oriental carpets, dark wood furniture, a grandfather clock and stand-up bar. Myron had done well for himself before the war, and during the war—something Antonia had found difficult to digest until he revealed that drawing propaganda cartoons for the Nazis had only been a cover. In truth, a Ukrainian émigré had recommended him to British intelligence, and he'd fed information to them. She now held him in the highest regard.

Antonia had been to his home several times before, but now the rooms were filled with strangers. Or so she thought. From a group gathered near the oriel window, she saw a man with a shock of white hair. A white mustache. She nearly fainted.

"Dr. Bodnar!"

The dean from the university in Lviv smiled broadly. Like all of them, he was thinner, more gaunt and seemed to have aged decades rather than four years.

He opened his arms to her and Antonia ran into his embrace.

Unbelieving, she clutched his arms. The last she'd heard, he'd been arrested shortly after the Blitz.

"*Shanovna* Kozak, when *pan* Kosar told me you were here, in Bavaria, I could not wait to surprise you."

She whirled to face Myron, who was beaming a few meters away. He mouthed, "Surprise," and turned his attention to the wine he was passing out to guests. Across the room, Lena had also found an acquaintance—a poet Antonia knew from Lviv as well, a woman for whom Lena had written music.

Antonia led the dean to the nearest sofa. Kosar offered them each a glass of wine. "How did you come to Munich?" she asked.

"Tereza and I left as soon as we could," Dr. Bodnar said. "We traveled to Munich via Poland. It was not easy. My sons and their families refused to go—they joined the underground instead. We have yet to hear from them.

"It was an awful time, *shanovna* Kozak," he continued. "We lived as best we could on what little we had. As I imagine everyone here did."

Antonia's hand fluttered to the growth on her throat.

"And you? What about you? What happened to you and Dr. Gruber?" He looked around the room as if expecting to find Viktor. She had not anticipated the question and it shocked her that in all this time she had constantly thought of Ivan but had hardly spared a thought for Viktor.

"Professor Kozak," Dr. Bodnar said gently. "I'm so sorry. I didn't mean to—"

Antonia drew in a deep breath. "He was murdered. In Lviv, days before the Germans came."

"Dear God. I knew you had both been arrested. We attempted to intervene, but that Vasiliev…"

She closed her eyes to the images of those victims, the prisons.

"To be honest," Dr. Bodnar said quietly, "I did not want to believe it."

Dr. Bodnar made a sympathetic noise and waved his wife over. Myron Kosar caught Antonia's eye. He appeared to be pointing her out to a small group as Tereza came to join them. Like her husband, Dr. Bodnar's wife also had white hair and bright blue eyes, and that stance women of academia seemed to always have—an air of polite patience and careful curiosity.

A moment later, Myron approached with a tall man in tow. He was gray-haired and had a gray mustache and a long shiny scar on the side of his face.

"I'd like to introduce you," Myron said. "This is Colonel Danylo Sovchenko. He was the commander of the Ukrainian Self-Defense Legion—"

"From Truskavets." Antonia sprang to her feet. He heart hammered.

"*Shanovna* Kozak," Sovchenko said. "When Myron Kosar told me you were here… Well. I knew Ivan Kovalenko and Pavlo Derkach. We were last together in Poland."

"Last together?" She felt faint and had to reach out and hold his arm to steady herself.

"Yes," he said. "I was reassigned to Warsaw, but we were all together until early this year."

"And then," Antonia stammered. "What happened after that?"

Gently, he led her to a corner so they could speak in private. Antonia's expression must have concerned Lena, because her sister stopped talking and began excusing herself from the poet.

"Where are they?" Antonia turned back to the colonel. "Do you know how they are?"

"We were separated. Most of us, anyway. The legion was absorbed into several different German divisions. Many of my men escaped into Germany toward the end of the war and went into hiding. Last I heard, Ivan and three others—including Pavlo—were sent to the southeastern front, to Austria."

Antonia leaned against the wall, her head spinning. She was holding her breath and her lungs hurt. "What else?" she breathed. "What else do you know?"

Sovchenko smiled a little. "There was a wedding."

Antonia tilted her head. "A wedding?"

"Pavlo married one of our nurses. Her name is Nadia. Last I heard, they too were separated, but she was also sent southwards. So maybe they were not too far apart?"

"How do I even begin to find them?" Antonia's mind was frantically running through the possibilities. Maybe they'd been caught by the Soviets? According to reports from the refugees, the final battles had been devastating, with deserters on all sides being killed.

Sovchenko pointed to the Bodnars, now occupied with someone else. "We are doing our best to organize ourselves, with the help of the Red Cross and the refugee organizations. Again, Nadia is a nurse. You could start there. But, in the meantime, many of us are drifting from one place to another, and we're collecting names. Asking if anyone knows of so-and-so. And…"

"And?" she asked testily. The idea of finding people through hearsay and word-of-mouth alone was daunting.

"We're making appeals to the Americans and the British. Arguing against repatriating our people to the Soviet Union. I understand that many Ukrainians in the west are indebted to you and to those"—he chuckled warmly—"One and a Half Cossacks. We need to convince them that it is time to repay that debt. A list, perhaps, of well-known intellectuals amongst these refugees that our emigres in the west could sponsor. You understand? Something that would persuade these countries that we are not coming to take up space but to add value. First, we have to share our stories, our experiences under the Soviet regime. We must get the Americans and the French and the British to listen to us. They must understand the threat Stalin poses to our peacetime."

Lena was approaching. "Would you please excuse me?" Antonia said.

But Sovchenko raised a palm, his expression pleading. "We could resurrect *Our Nation's Voice* to share that message."

Antonia nodded. "I'll consider it."

When her sister reached her, Antonia fell against her. Lena put her arm around her and the two of them hurried down the corridor. Lena opened a door, a bedroom, and lowered Antonia into a chair in front of a writing desk.

"This is not good news," Lena started. "What—"

But Antonia interrupted her and related all that Colonel Sovchenko had told her.

"I promised I would look for him." She ground her palms into her eyes, swiping away the tears. "How can I, when I cannot even tell the authorities who I really am? What if he is dead?"

Lena crouched next to her. "You are going to do all it takes to find him, Antonia. I won't let you sabotage your happiness any longer. Even if it means… Well. Let's just assume that both of them are alive."

They were interrupted by a light knock on the door. Myron Kosar, followed by Roman, stepped in, closing the door behind them.

Kosar was concerned. "I'm sorry if I've upset you. That was not my intention."

"It's fine," she said. Though she was far from fine.

"Colonel Sovchenko has already had several meetings with the American military in Munich," Myron said. "They are listening, or at least beginning to. The British are more responsive. And they are setting up camps for displaced persons."

"I'm not going to any camp," Antonia cried. "No more camps."

Roman looked sympathetic and turned to Myron. "If we admit to being Ukrainian citizens," he said, "we might be digging our own graves."

"One step at a time," Lena said. "First we try and find our people—Pavlo and Ivan, for starters."

"How?" Antonia pleaded. "How am I to find him now?"

"I'll help you," Lena said. "We'll go to the Red Cross tomorrow. We'll start by looking for Nadia Derkach."

Antonia had to laugh at this. Lena with her chopped-up German and side-dish of English. But she loved her sister for it.

"Then let me do it," Kosar said. "It does not have to be your name. We'll put in a request to find the three of them. How's that?"

Antonia nodded, and a fog began to lift. She was almost prepared to call it hope.

CHAPTER 26

June 1945

Udine, Italy

The ward at the 56th Evacuation Hospital in Udine was a warehouse of wounded, ill, and malnourished patients pleading for help in a whole mess of languages. One of the American doctors flipped through Ivan's medical records, but Ivan turned his head away. They could do what they wanted with him. He didn't care either way.

The doctor tapped the clipboard on the metal frame of the bed before hooking it back on.

"You. Good," he said in broken Russian. "Good to go."

Go where?

From what he knew, the Yugoslavians had begun turning in all the non-Yugoslavians to the Soviets. The Americans were repatriating Ukrainians, Lithuanians, White Russians, and anyone else from the Soviet-controlled union, back into Stalin's hands. In other words, straight into redoctrination camps.

Which was why Ivan could not understand Terlytsia's grin and Lys's familiar scowl when they strode into his ward.

"What's so amusing?" Ivan asked Lys.

Terlytsia scoffed. "How can you tell anything by that guy's face? He's only got the one expression."

"When you spend enough time with him, you can tell the difference," Ivan joked. "There's a slight variation in the wrinkles of the brow."

The corners of Lys's mouth twitched upwards and he drew a thumb across his throat. Ivan smiled, but every time he saw these two he was reminded of Pavlo dying on that table.

"Are you done enjoying your spa?" Terlytsia asked. His joke also fell flat.

Ivan shrugged his right shoulder, flexed his arm and checked that everything was in working order.

Then Lys jerked his head toward the ward entrance. "Surprise," he grunted.

Ivan looked over and had to sit up to believe what he was seeing. He pushed himself off the bed and raised his arms as she came to him. She had a valise in one hand and a Red Cross rucksack slung over her other shoulder.

"Nadia." His voice was thick with affection. "Good Lord, Nadia. It's you. It's really you."

She dropped the valise and rucksack on the floor and clung hard to him. He felt her strength and he felt her sadness beating against his chest. Ivan swallowed hard before saying the words he needed to say.

"I tried to find him, Nadia. We all tried to save him." He closed his eyes against the burning behind his eyes, remembered Pavlo's wounds, remembered the Half Cossack's last breath. *Na. Dia.*

Tenderly, she kissed Ivan's cheek. "I know you did."

He stepped away and rubbed her upper arms as he examined the extended belly. She looked down.

"He's still here," she said. "And I'm going to make sure he or she knows all about their father and the Cossack. We have to understand where we came from if we're to forge ahead."

Ivan brushed a tear away and kissed her forehead.

Lys was all business now that his surprise had been delivered. "We need to go, Kovalenko."

"Where?"

But Terlytsia was already gathering Ivan's few belongings together. Ivan reached for his coat and checked the pockets, relieved to find the sketch of the Cossack and Hutsulka safe in there. Him and Antonia.

"There's a group of *nashi* heading to Austria," Nadia said, as if reading his mind. "They're drawing up a list of people whose families are trying to find them, and I put Antonia and the Mazurs onto it. And Ivan…?"

He looked into her eyes.

"We found Kulka. A nurse who came down here looking for her husband had seen Kulka in a hospital in Tyrol. He's now in Salzburg."

Ivan looked at the grinning faces around him. Even Lys was wearing an actual smile.

"Are we allowed to just walk out of here?" Ivan asked.

"Nope," Terlytsia said.

Ivan frowned. "Then how are we supposed to leave?"

They ushered him outside the ward and walked out the front doors of the makeshift evac hospital. Before them was a truck. *Not again*, Ivan thought. But Terlytsia jumped in, the others climbed in after Ivan, and the engine roared and sputtered before Terlytsia threw it into gear.

They were in the mountains of Austria when the truck spasmed, coughed and eventually came to a complete stop. The black smoke told them the story. Oil. Terlytsia tried to get her going again but it was no use.

"Can't we fix it?" Nadia begged.

Ivan studied the road ahead. They'd been in the American hospital. They'd been in a British Zone. Now they could be anywhere: Red Line or American. They had no idea. But Salzburg was still some distance away. And the highway that led there was certain to be crawling with armed men from both sides. Their chances of running into the wrong star—the wrong insignia—were no better than fifty-fifty.

Resigned, Ivan ordered everyone to pile out. Terlytsia threw open the hood anyway, as a token more than anything, but they all knew they were in for a long, and dangerous, hike.

The panorama of bluffs were marbled in shades of green as the dark old pines blended with the green of new buds on poplars and linden. Here, as with every mountain range, the area had its own character. These hills were soft and rounded, but beyond—toward Salzburg, where they needed to go—the high Alps were still covered in snow.

The night drew in, cold and bitter, and they froze in the small shepherd's hut they found. The next day, they crossed into the province of Salzburg. They slipped over rocky trails and fought through the uneven terrain. Often their weight broke through the crust of snow and they sank in deep. Ivan's feet were soaked and freezing. None of them were dressed for a hike in alpine snow. Nadia was only wearing a Red Cross uniform: navy culottes, thin gray shirt and a wool blazer with the Red Cross badge. They had thought it would be a good cover should they run into any troubles along the way.

When they stopped to see what they could do to combat the cold, Nadia poked Ivan as he handed her more dressing to wrap her feet in. "How's your arm? Your ankle?"

"I'm fine."

But she was shivering. He slipped off his military jacket and draped it over her shoulders, ignoring her protests. Eventually she gave in, flashing him a grateful smile.

As darkness fell, they heard the gushing of waterfalls. Deep lines in the mountain's face had been carved by years of melt now pouring into the ravines below.

"Look," Terlytsia called from the other side of the ridge. "There's a village down there."

In the valley, they saw several winking lights. Ivan pulled Nadia into him.

"That's where we're going," he said. "Down there, there's no more snow."

But it was almost another three hours before they finally reached a homestead. The night was silent save for the occasional cowbell clanging from the attached barn. Without further discussion, the men hung behind while Nadia knocked. Each of the men had a pistol but they were not going to threaten anyone unless absolutely necessary. There was no answer except for the bellow of a cow and the sound of something knocking against the stall box, then the swish of water dumped on the ground. Terlytsia motioned to follow him to the barn.

"You go first," Terlytsia told Nadia.

She pushed open the door. "*Hallo? Hallo? Ist jemand da?*" Is someone here?

They startled a middle-aged woman from her chores. She scrambled back so quickly, she almost tipped over her pail of milk. There were only two cows in a stable that could have held twenty.

"*Nicht schiessen,*" the woman cried. Don't shoot.

Nadia raised her empty hands and pointed to her Red Cross patch.

The expression on the woman's face was still doubtful as she took in the three men behind Nadia. Her eyes flicked, untrusting, from one to the other. Nadia removed her pack and held it out to the woman.

"*Alles gut?*" she asked. Everything all right?

The woman nodded, but she looked briefly over her shoulder, then at Nadia. There was such intent in her gaze that Ivan unholstered his pistol.

"Who else is here?" he said in a low voice.

The woman looked frightened again.

Terlytsia and Lys were also on guard.

"*Nicht schiessen. Nicht schiessen.*" The woman kept her hands up but bent toward the bucket of milk, keeping her eyes on Ivan.

"There's someone else here," Ivan said.

The Austrian woman shook her head and lifted the pail, tipped it to show the milk, then beckoned to Nadia. Nadia stood her ground. The woman stepped to her, gave her the pail and dipped a cup in, offering it to her.

"Drink," Ivan said. But he kept his eye on the dark barn behind the woman.

Nadia took it and drank. The woman's eyes flicked to the Red Cross bag, then to the men. She beckoned the men to have a drink as well.

"*Russen?*" The woman asked, her voice shaking.

"*Ukrainer*," Nadia corrected. "*Nicht Rote Armee.*" Ukrainians. Not the Red Army.

The woman hesitated, her eyes shifting over them all again.

Ivan went around her, but the woman began whimpering. "*Bitte.*" And again begged them not to shoot.

Lys was not having it. He was with Ivan. They took a lantern off the hook and headed to the back of the barn. The woman was crying now. Terlytsia called for them to be careful, but the barn was empty. Only slightly reassured, Ivan gave in and drank some milk, as did Lys, while the woman continued speaking to Nadia. Her accent was so strong Ivan could hardly understand, but it was clear from the way she kept indicating Nadia's medical bag that she was pleading for help.

"She says she wants to take me somewhere. Someone needs my help," Nadia said.

"Not alone," Ivan said. Not on his life.

The Austrian woman's face fell when she understood the men would go with them. Throwing on a faded blue work coat, she beckoned for the lamp from Lys and urged them to follow her. They fell in behind her as she led the way across a rickety bridge over a stream and along to one of the shepherd's huts they had seen earlier.

From inside the hut came the stench of rotten meat. Nadia covered her nose, gagging. It was bad enough for the rest of them to smell it, but Ivan had forgotten that Nadia would be extra sensitive with the pregnancy. He led her back out and she vomited the milk she'd just drunk.

Terlytsia called from inside. "It's her son. An old wound—it looks like he needs to have it cleaned."

Ivan went back in. In the lamplight, he could make out a huddled mass under a blanket. From the smell in the room, he'd have assumed it was a corpse. Then Nadia pushed her way in, hand clasped over her nose, and uncovered the young man. He was indeed in a bad way.

The woman went on about how she had to hide him here, not telling anyone, because she could not trust anyone in the village. When Nadia repeated that the war was over, the woman shook her head.

"*Der Krieg ist nicht vorbei. Nichts ist vorbei.*" The war is not over. Nothing is over.

Ivan looked at the poor boy again. He was in his early twenties, and his face was deathly pale. Ivan and the others helped Nadia, who had to go outside several more times for air. Lys and Terlytsia cleaned the straw. Ivan helped Nadia to drain the wound and change the bandages. When they were finished, Lys and Terlytsia convinced the woman to bring her son to the house where he would be warm.

Nadia then asked her who the occupying forces were in the area. She looked from one to the other before answering: "*Die Amerikaner.*"

When Terlytsia let out a little cheer, the woman smiled uncertainly. Nadia told the woman it was a good thing, and Ivan asked the woman for directions to Salzburg.

They were finally able to get some sleep, taking a bit more food in, and careful what they ate. The woman offered them some smoked bacon, but Nadia warned the boys that the fatty meat would only make them sick after so many days of near starvation. Dipped in a little sugar, they only sucked on the rinds.

The next morning, they checked on the young man and Nadia said his fever was down. Eager to get going, Ivan led the group out of the valley and they collected food as they went, trading aspirins and bandages for supplies. Then, some twenty kilometers before Salzburg, as they were making their descent to the main road, Ivan heard engines.

"Back," he shouted. "Everyone back."

The group scrambled back up the slope and took cover, Ivan bracing himself for Soviet military vehicles. But when two jeeps appeared from beneath the canopy of trees, they were painted with white stars, not red. American military!

Ivan sprang out of hiding and ran to the middle of the road. The first jeep shuddered to a halt and the soldiers inside pulled their weapons on him. Ivan slowly raised his hands above his head.

"Salzburg?" he called in German. "Take us to Salzburg?"

Terlytsia, Lys and Nadia also cautiously appeared, their hands raised in the air. Then he remembered what Nadia had said. Refugees. Displaced People.

"DP camp?" Ivan asked.

There was a lot of talk that none of them understood, but they were loaded into one of the jeeps. Elated, Ivan grinned at the Americans, and mimicked their chewing. One gave him something wrapped in foil, and Ivan unwrapped it and put it in his mouth. It was sharp and strange. The soldier who had offered it to him, opened his mouth and showed him a ball of something, then chewed vigorously. Ivan copied him and the thing became gummy. Another soldier offered Lys a cigarette. One American took off his coat and handed it to Nadia. Another one handed her his canteen. But when they arrived at a military base, the banter and niceties ceased and they were each escorted inside and separated. Ivan realized they were going to be questioned. He was not sure how he felt about that.

A private led him down a corridor. As they passed a window, Ivan saw hundreds of people lined up in front of tents. Perhaps they were at the refugee camp. Perhaps Kulka was out there now.

Ivan tried again. "DP camp?"

"No. No, camp," the private said. He led Ivan into the room, gestured for him to sit, and closed the door.

When another soldier came in, he began drilling Ivan with questions. Name. Rank. Country. Ivan hesitated at that.

"*Bist du mit der SS-Galizien gewesen?*"

Ivan understood that. Had he been with the SS-Galizien? There was no way he was going to be able to explain this.

"*Übersetzer,*" Ivan said. Translator. He needed time to get his story straight. At least a little. He hoped that, with so many people being subjected to questioning, it would be some time before an interpreter was available. He was right.

He sat in that room for hours, looking out the window at the refugees passing by. Women. Children. Old men. Soldiers. A whole world of castaways, floated up to this American shore in Austria, and everyone hoping for the same thing: a life that could be better than even before the war. He scanned their faces, hoping for a glimpse of Antonia, the Mazurs, her nephews...

There was a knock and Ivan turned away from the window. A man walked in. Dark hair swept over the brow. Round glasses. Where once there had been a scruffy beard, there was now a deep scar on the chin. Ivan's limbs went ice cold.

They spoke each other's names at the same time.

"Kovalenko?"

"Dr. Gruber?"

Ivan fell back against the wall. He knew he was gaping. Either he was insane, had lost his mind completely, or he was speaking to a ghost.

Viktor took a step forward, but Ivan moved away.

The Austrian slowly moved behind the desk. Ivan drew comfort from the fact that the Austrian professor looked as shocked as he felt. So this was not a cruel trick.

Viktor opened a drawer. With shaky hands, he withdrew a packet of cigarettes which he held in his left hand. The tips of the fingers on his right hand were missing. He was gaunt, his body slightly bent as if he were carrying something heavy on his shoulders.

"You were dead." Ivan shook his head. "We were certain of it."

"Yes. Quite possibly I was. But not the way you think." Viktor extended the pack over the desk. "I know you don't smoke…"

Ivan took one. He slowly eased himself into the chair.

When Viktor reached over to light his cigarette, Ivan shook his head.

"I'll just…" He put it in his mouth.

Viktor lit his and exhaled. There was a knock on the door and an American officer hustled in but pulled up at the sight of the two of them. He spoke with Viktor in English for about a minute, then nodded at Ivan and left them alone again.

Viktor turned back to him, his face lit up. "I understand there was a woman with you—"

"Nadia. Pavlo's wife," Ivan said.

Viktor looked down. "I see. And Pavlo is…?"

Ivan studied Viktor, still disbelieving. Finally, he relented. "He fell in battle. In Udine."

Viktor sat down and stubbed out the cigarette in an ashtray. "Antonia?"

"I lost track of her," Ivan said.

There was silence. Viktor was waiting for more, but that story was sealed deep inside of Ivan and was his alone. His grief to keep. Sharing it with a man he'd thought was dead was not an option.

Ivan placed the cigarette on the edge of the table. "Before we start any inquiries into my story, I think you should answer a few of my questions first."

Viktor looked resigned. "All right, Kovalenko. We've got ten minutes before Sergeant Harris returns."

CHAPTER 27

Summer 1945

Bavaria, Germany

In the beginning was the Word...

Words mattered. Words gave meaning and words could create meaning but most of all, words could start and they could stop wars. Words could liberate. And they could conquer. Words gave hope. And they took it away.

America. That was the one prayer on everyone's lips. The land of the free. And one single word would break open new possibilities. *Yes.*

And if it was *No*?

In German, the word *unterwerfen*, depending on the formulation could mean to subdue or to subject. To subdue the world, as her copy of the German Bible had it, or to subject it? These were the thoughts that Antonia wrote into the brown leather-bound notebook. Myron offered to loan her a typewriter but Antonia declined.

"I need to connect my hand and my head again," she said. Or, as Lena would say, her head to her heart.

The journal contained blank cream pages where Antonia could formulate her ideas in unconfined lines, the ends of which curved upwards like the inflection at the end of a question.

Sometimes, she would stop at the end of a sentence and look up, half expecting to see Viktor there, hearing his voice, his ideas, his corrections, his arguments. Sometimes, she would close her notebook and gaze at a landscape that had nothing to do with Bavaria but with an orchard, a grassy knoll, the Carpathians, those swamps outside of Sadovyi Hai, and a tall Cossack on the horizon.

Don't second-guess yourself, Ivan had told her. A million years ago.

She had nothing left of either of them. Nothing of Viktor's—not even a book. Nothing of Ivan's that brought him closer to her. Made him materialize for her. Viktor was dead. Ivan? It was the not knowing that drowned her in melancholy. As long as the refugees floated on the currents of a war-torn Europe, how were they to get word to one another? Her first trip to the Red Cross had underscored the enormity and the sheer futility of trying to find anyone. Everyone was armed with fake identities, some stolen from people, dead or alive.

What future did any of them have when it was clear that Ukraine was back in Stalin's grip? He had the country by the neck now, jaws locked, slowly breaking the vertebrae one by one. This time, Stalin would not let go.

Sticking out from between the pages of her journal was a thin sheet of paper, carefully folded. She did not have to open it. It was a letter from Dr. Bodnar. She used it to mark the pages.

> Come to us, Antonia. We are prepared now and organized. We have a plan. Come to Munich. Help us to help.

Every parent teaches their child that, if they should get lost, they had to stay where they were. If they kept moving, the chances of finding them were harder.

Kiril Vasiliev's voice suddenly resonated in her head. *Every author leaves a fingerprint.* Antonia shuddered.

They did not need her in Munich. She could send them her articles. She just had to start writing again and hope that somewhere, somehow, Ivan recognized her voice in the crowd. Antonia turned to a clean page and wrote the words *autocracy* and *democracy* the way one might write the cardinal directions for east and west. *Words matter.* She had promised to look for him, to do everything to find him.

She began writing.

Frau Wechsel brought her flowers and a jar of honey from one of the neighbors, neighbors that Antonia had never met because, as the days went by, she stayed closer and closer to the Koch–Wechsel properties as if she were on a small island. It took all she had to get into Myron Kosar's car when he came round. But now Frau Wechsel was bringing Antonia greetings and presents from people who had never met her.

The Germans, as shell-shocked, as shamed as they were, were proving to be a decent folk. It was not always so. Konstantin still complained of being teased and harassed, and sometimes he got into scuffles with the children at the school. But in general, she and the Mazurs had been offered many kindnesses from people like the Hubers, Herr Koch, Frau Wechsel and Myron Kosar, so Antonia was prepared to say that people were—by and large—inherently good.

Myron Kosar continued to bring in groups of Ukrainian refugees to the area for excursions and soon enough, a clique made up of a dozen artists, including Roman, became known to the locals as the *Chiemsee Künstler*—the Chiemsee artists. Sculptors, painters, woodcutters, poets and authors came to Myron's home, and Antonia began doling out tidbits from her journal, testing them. A phrase here. A theory there. When Dr. Bodnar returned for a visit, a good Riesling loosened Antonia's tongue and they spent the entire night debating and discussing how the potential future might look. And what they had to do to get there.

"We should rally the Ukrainian parishes in America and Canada," Tereza Bodnar suggested. "They could set up sponsorships and at least get an immigration program together for our people."

"Sure," Lena said brightly. "If the parishes could guarantee shelter and arrange work permits, it might allow people to obtain green cards."

"We'll make a list of our best-known supporters," Dr. Bodnar said, "and begin there."

Antonia was cushioned between large pillows on Myron's carpet. She opened the middle pages of her journal and together they began drawing up a list of names—who was where, who might help, and who needed help.

The Bodnars returned to Munich and immediately took action, writing letters, delegating Antonia to resurrect *Our Nation's Voice.* As news slowly trickled in via the refugee organizations, Antonia could put some ticks next to the names of the people they were looking for. And then, while working in his study, Myron delivered another letter from Dr. Bodnar.

> You were looking for Pavlo and Nadia Derkach. We've just met a nurse who was in Carinthia, in Austria. She knew Nadia.

Antonia's heart raced with renewed hope, but then plummeted to her stomach as she read on.

"I'm so sorry," Myron said. "It's bad news?"

She lowered the page, and closed her eyes. "It's Pavlo. He fell in Udine, Italy."

Myron took a step toward her. "And Ivan?"

But she quickly folded the letter into the envelope. "I have to go. I have to get back. Please take me back."

She wanted Lena. Now. She wanted Lena and to get away from Myron's question. Not knowing was better. Not knowing.

The One and a Half Cossacks. If they had been together near the end... She could not imagine one without the other.

Myron returned her to Herr Koch's immediately and Antonia burst into the kitchen. She dropped the letter on the table and held her breath. Lena wiped her hands and carefully opened it, read it and then gently put it back into the envelope.

"Is there anything? Anything about Ivan?" Antonia said softly. Lena shook her head.

Antonia fell onto a stool. Mercifully, Lena did not say a word. Not a single word about how Antonia needed to stay hopeful, about how Antonia had to pray, that certainly Ivan had not fallen. Not a single word. Her sister crouched down next to her, took Antonia into her arms and mourned Pavlo with her.

After church on Sunday, the day after midsummer's eve, Antonia and Lena joined the party of artists on a trip to Königssee. There was a man who rented rowboats, and that afternoon Lena and Antonia got into one and glided under the shadow of Watzmann to the small island and the pilgrimage church of St Bartholomew. There was a *Gastgarten* where visitors could sit outside on benches and picnic tables and drink mugs of beer, eat fresh pretzels and inexpensive bowls of broth with *Knödel*.

The Chiemsee artists liked to paint and work on the far side of the island. They were not the happiest lot. There were traumatized refugees whose art depicted the monsters and horrors they'd encountered in the war. They painted the ghosts of their friends and their families, of fires and famine, of torture—transferring the scars from their souls onto something outside themselves.

Antonia was not an artist. She wanted to conduct her own ritual of release and cleansing, and she wanted to do it with Lena. On the banks of the lake, the sisters collected flowers and long grasses and branches, then found a secluded spot where they wove *vinky*, like they had as girls back in Ukraine.

From a rucksack, Antonia fetched and lit tiny candles that Frau Wechsel had used for last year's *Christbaum*. She arranged them in the wreath. Lena wiped her tears and began to sing the song for Kupala. Antonia choked on the words at first, found her strength and then her voice and, holding the wreath, walked waist-high into the water. Gently, she placed it onto the surface of the lake. It floated toward the sunlit shore.

When she was a girl, sixteen and old enough, she, Lena and the village girls had done this in Sadovyi Hai at the widest part of the creek. Antonia had woven daisies and campanula, lungwort, spurge and forget-me-nots. She inserted small beeswax candles to make a crown. Barefoot and dressed in their embroidered tunics, their aprons, the ribbons in their hair, the girls had spent the afternoon singing and gossiping about their hopes, and the boys they thought could fulfill them.

Everyone except Antonia. She had made the *vinok*. She had participated. But she had no aspirations that superstitious folklore would choose her husband. She had her own mind, she'd claimed, and she would select a husband for herself, if any. Not some silly boy picking up a wreath.

In the evening, when the girls had built a large bonfire and released the candlelit wreaths into the water, the young men arrived and lined up on the opposite bank of the creek. They took turns singing, the banter and laughter lengthening the game. First the girls sang—inserting the boys' names into the lyrics—then the boys teased out the individual personalities of the girls into the verses. There were peals of delight, the boys pushing and shoving one another in jest, the girls giggling like drunkards when their name was part of the song.

And then the boys rolled up their trousers and went into the creek, each one intent on retrieving the wreath of their sweetheart. Woe to those who chose the wrong one.

Ivan had picked hers.

She'd ignored the superstition even then, even when everyone cheered just because they had not let go of each other's hands as they jumped over the bonfire. Afterwards, she had let him kiss her beneath the apricot tree, but for the rest of her young life, she had ignored what God put directly into her path. *Ivan.*

Antonia stepped from the water and onto the bank. She and Lena held hands as they watched the wreath float away. No. Not knowing was not an option. She would find Ivan, no matter where he was, or what had happened. She had given her word.

And words mattered.

Roman returned from one of his painting excursions, flushed and excited. Antonia, Lena and the boys were in Herr Koch's kitchen, preparing dinner.

"Look," he said, waving two green bills. "Two dollars! Two American dollars!"

Lena snatched them from her husband's hand and stared at them. "For what?"

"I was painting—just painting—and an American commander approached me and started speaking English. Then German. I was terrified. I thought he wanted my papers, so I stood up and produced our Polish papers. But he was pointing to my easel. He wanted me to paint him. And I'm to do so at the American base!"

While Lena was laughing and hugging her husband, Antonia saw only problems. "How are you getting there?"

"He'll pick me up," Roman said.

"Here? At Herr Koch's?"

Roman's smile wavered then faded.

"They'll know we're here, Roman," Antonia said. "They're putting all the refugees into camps now. DP camps. I told you, I am not going to any camp ever again. Not with Americans, not with Poles, not with Ukrainians, no camp."

"Calm down, Antonia," Lena tried, but Antonia pushed past her and ran across Koch's yard to Frau Wechsel's house.

Despite her warnings, Roman went to the American base and the dollars multiplied. He bought new paints and brushes, and soon he had a long line of American officers and commanders who wanted their portraits painted by a Chiemsee artist. For the next two weeks, it appeared the Americans truly had no interest in who Roman really was, or that an entire group of refugees was living in a Bavarian hamlet. Until the day they did.

The American military police came wearing white armbands. The SA men in Wilhelmshagen had worn black. The American military officers wore stars pinned to their caps. The Nazis had had skulls. Eagles. Swastikas. Antonia fought the interrogating American commander the way she had fought Vasiliev. The way she had struggled with Fitzwald. She tried to arrange her expression, tried to veil what was going on in her head behind her eyes. But her hands would not stop trembling. She dug her fingernails into the skin of her palms. Her feet burned at the memory of those toenails being yanked out.

"Your name," the American administrator repeated. He wore round spectacles and had soft eyes. His Polish sounded anglicized. "It's all right. You're safe now."

She could not roll her shoulders back. She could not sit still. Her teeth chattered.

"Zieleńska. Anna Zieleńska."

"From Krakow."

She blinked. Licked her lips. Surely he would notice. But no, he was typing in her name.

"Profession."

He never asked questions, she realized. He always made statements.

"Professor of German literature."

"As it says in your documents."

"Yes."

He removed his glasses and suddenly in Ukrainian, he said, "You really are safe now. There is a temporary hold on repatriating Ukrainian refugees back to the Soviet Union."

Antonia blinked. "Pardon?" she asked in Polish. Trust no one. Your enemy is everywhere.

The man gazed at her, sighed and put his spectacles back on. In Polish again, he said, "I shall put in your request but there is no guarantee."

She rose. "Is that all?"

"That's all. There will be a bus taking you all to Neubeuern at two o'clock."

Neubeuern. She had seen road signs for it around the countryside, recalled a village with a large castle on top of a hill. It was nearby then. Perhaps he was telling the truth. Perhaps they were safe now, and would remain in the American zone. Antonia saw herself out but his voice was calling her.

"Professor Zieleńska?"

Now he was questioning her.

She turned and in the way he swiped those spectacles off his face once more, Antonia was reminded of Viktor. But this was an American and apparently with Polish or Ukrainian ties, but she dared not ask him why he could speak her languages now.

He put a thumb and forefinger around his throat. "I think you should have that checked."

Antonia stared at him, her hand automatically going to the growth at the base of her neck. She had no scarf on. She had forgotten. "I will."

But he waved her back in. Her legs leaden, she returned to stand before his desk as he wrote on a form. Those passes, like the ones at Wilhelmshagen. Was he going to give her one now?

She uttered a one-syllable laugh. "Ha."

He tore it out of the pad and looked up at her, extending it to her. "It is mandatory."

Antonia stared at the sheet in his hand. Slowly, she reached for it, the paper burning hot between her fingers.

"It's now noted in your file," he said, looking up at her, challenging her, "and we shall require the report from the examining physician."

Antonia put the paper into her pocketbook, clicked her heels and raised her right hand. "*Jawohl, Herr Kommandant!*"

Outside the dormitory rooms, the wooden floorboards creaked from the staircase to the corridor as if they were on a ship. The others—displaced persons, as the Allied forces designated them—were heading up from the dining room. Some had spent the evening playing cards, or the old guitar from the music room. Others had sat in the castle gardens and listened to the crickets, thanking God they had survived. Or, more likely, wondering why they had. The children were being children. Instead of parents covering their mouths to hush them against discovery, or to prevent a beating, or capture by Nazis or Soviets, these children and their parents now loudly negotiated the brushing of teeth. Tomorrow, they would live to see another day, and that was why they pursued the frivolity with such passion.

As the boys fought to turn the next page of the picture book, Antonia tuned into the symphony of Eastern European languages. Polish, Latvian, Lithuanian, Czech, Russian and Ukrainian all intermixed in this old castle in Bavaria—just a short drive to Berchtesgaden; a short drive to Hitler's bunker—now secured by American troops.

Antonia coughed and the boys gave her room, but the irritation quickly passed. Out of habit, she ran a finger beneath the thin, cream-colored scarf wrapped around her neck, and half-consciously checked the size of the growth at the base of her throat. Before she could assess it further, someone knocked on the door and Lena appeared.

"Mama," Nestor called to his mother. "Aunt Antonia is reading to us."

Lena did not seem to hear. She raised her hand, revealing an envelope. But it was the expression on Lena's face that made Antonia close the book in her lap.

As her sister's gaze locked with hers, Antonia was again whisked back to Sadovyi Hai. They were back in their village orchards, back to the first days in the secret underground organization. Lena's and her first fight but not their last battle. In the time it took Lena to close the space between the doorway and the bed, Antonia relived the torture in the Soviet secret police interrogation room and the terror of being captured by the SS. Lena's eyes embodied the value of unconditional love. Forgiveness. And freedom's heavy toll. Antonia's heart clenched at the fear of breaking again.

Lena knelt by the side of the bed, as she did when she said her prayers, then extended the envelope, but Antonia had already seen the Red Cross emblem. She already understood that another one of their men had finally been found.

The words jumped off the paper and glowed. They meant something. *Udine, Italy. Discharged. No trace since.*

No trace, but he'd been alive. At the end of the war, Ivan Dmytro Kovalenko had been alive.

CHAPTER 28

Summer 1945

Salzburg, Austria

"All right, Kovalenko," Sergeant Harris said. "You're free to go. You've checked out. Here is your pass, your papers, and the information you need for the DP camp in Gnigl." He turned to Viktor, standing behind him. "I still can't believe you two knew each other and under those circumstances."

The sergeant then gripped Ivan's hand. "Don't go far, Kovalenko. We'd really be interested in talking to you more about your work with the Organization of Ukrainian Nationalists. All right?"

Ivan nodded to Harris after Viktor translated then went out into the corridor. Terlytsia, Lys, Kulka and Nadia were waiting on the benches outside, the corridor jam-packed with refugees. Nadia pushed herself up, her eyes wide and questioning, one hand around her belly. Ivan raised the documents and she gave a little cheer before hugging him.

"We should celebrate," Nadia said.

Kulka grinned mischievously. The boy was up to no good again. "I made cognac."

Even Lys laughed.

"You made cognac?" Viktor said.

"Yes. There was a bombed-out university building in town and I found some jars of formaldehyde—well, they had specimens in there, but that's no matter—and what you do is you take sugar and... What?" Kulka peered at his brother.

Lys's scowl was so deep, his eyes were just slits. "You don't actually expect us to drink that."

Kulka looked miffed. "But our uncle taught me. Remember? And it doesn't give you a hangover."

When nobody took up his offer to try his formaldehyde cognac, he promised to put together a more edible and appetizing menu. As a dishwasher in General Patton's kitchen, Kulka had access to goods. Food. Medicine. Clothing. Anything for "a favor." And there was always someone who owed him a favor.

Viktor pulled Ivan aside. "I put in some calls to Berlin. I think I have an idea of where the Mazurs and Antonia might have been."

It was a double-edged sword. Ivan waited.

"Some of our people have managed to find a man who was forging papers. Antonia was with a journalist. Stefaniuk—"

"I know the name," Ivan said. He watched Viktor carefully.

"He's gone but she was with him. She picked up papers—legit for the Mazurs but a false identity for herself. He said he can't remember under which name."

"But that's good," Ivan said. "Right? They were all together, so that is something."

"It's something, but it's not enough to go on. Anyway, he contacted me again. He said he remembered that Antonia talked about a place outside of Berlin where there are lots of summer cottages. And something about an artist, though she could have just meant Roman."

"Not necessarily," Ivan said. "Roman knew a lot of other artists all over the place."

Viktor nodded. "That's what I thought, so—" He reached into his breast pocket and withdrew a sheet of paper. "I put some names together. Any of these look familiar?"

Ivan reviewed the list of five names. He knew none of them.

"All right," Viktor said. "The search continues. I didn't have a chance to locate any of them, but that would be the next thing."

"What was she doing in Berlin?"

Viktor's expression turned contemplative. "They escaped a slave labor camp."

"Escaped?" Ivan's chest swelled. But then he pictured Antonia in one of those camps, the conditions of the camp Viktor had been in, the torture he'd undergone. Ivan had done that to her. He'd let her go.

"We need to find her," Viktor said. *We.*

The Cossack put his hand on Viktor's shoulder, his voice heavy. "I'm not going to stand in your way, Viktor."

"I can't stand another minute in this building," Nadia called to them. She was at Ivan's side, linking her arm through his and tugging him toward the entryway.

But Viktor's expression had soured. "I think she should make that decision, Ivan. I mean… If there is a decision she must make?"

Ivan dropped his eyes and took a breath. He tried to smile down at Nadia. "Let's go get that mountain air."

Along with the rest of the entourage, they waited outside the base until Kulka joined them. A bus took them all to the Kanzel. Mindful of Nadia's condition, they got off at Aigner Park and looked for a spot that did not require a strenuous hike but still provided a view of the valley. Kulka unpacked tins of something called Spam, oranges—unheard of this time of the year—fresh bread, cheese and then, with a flourish, produced bottles of beer and one bottle with a caramel-colored liquid.

Ivan pointed to the last bottle. "Is that…?"

Kulka grinned. "I'll drink one with you, Lieutenant, and you can see for yourself."

"No," Ivan said. "Cognac is made of grapes, not formaldehyde."

But Lys was gesturing for the bottle. He pulled the stopper and sniffed. His eyebrows shot up and he looked at Kulka with amazement.

"I'll be…"

"I told you." The kid grinned.

"Our uncle taught you this?" Lys tipped the bottle to his lips. Everyone stared. He swallowed, wiped his mouth and looked at the bottle again. "I'll be damned."

Now everyone wanted a taste, except for Nadia who said someone would have to explain what had happened when they all dropped dead around her. But the concoction was delicious. Smooth. Sweet. And very similar to cognac.

"One taste is enough," Ivan said, handing back the bottle. "I didn't survive the war to be killed by cognac. Or whatever this is."

Terlytsia leaned back on the blanket and put his hands behind his head. "Kulka, you're going to be a rich man."

When they'd had their fill, Ivan and Viktor climbed the trail up the Kanzel. He wanted a few moments alone with the professor after the rigamarole of interrogation and investigation. He might have been issued with the documents, but Ivan did not feel he was a free man, not in his bones. He knew that the Americans were looking for something in return.

They reached the lookout and Ivan gazed over the valley. Austria was beautiful. From here, far away from the rubble and construction of Salzburg, he had an idea of how idyllic it was. Church bells tolled the hour, accompanied by cowbells from the high meadows above them.

"Do you think any of us will eventually be repatriated to Ukraine?" Ivan asked Viktor.

Viktor turned his back on the view and leaned against the rails. "You know, Austria's getting away with this pretty easily, right? The Allies are not stupid. They labelled us as victims of the

Reich, but Hitler had plenty—don't be fooled—plenty of supporters here. And now those people will repress that or use their
victimhood status to explain away their actions. But I can tell you
this, there will be no Soviet bloc in this country. If Ukraine has
a friend, it's going to be Austria. But the Austrians won't let you
stay, Kovalenko. You understand? They'll find a way to wheedle
Germany into taking you, under the guise of punishment. 'Your
problem, not ours. You did this.' So, no, I don't think you'll be
repatriated—any of you—but you will need to find an alternative."

Ivan nodded. "I'd like to help you find Antonia."

Viktor looked surprised. "I'd have it no other way. Listen, we
could go up to Berlin. That labor camp is nearby. Maybe we can
find some clues there?"

"Am I allowed to travel?"

"With me, yes, but Ivan, we'd be brushing up against the
Soviet zone. It's risky."

Ivan did not hesitate. "I promised I'd look for her, no matter
what."

"I see," Viktor said quietly. "Then of course you will take the
risks necessary."

Ivan looked back over the valley. Against his breast, the sketch
was safely stored in the metal tube. *Yes, there is a decision she has
to make.*

A few days later, Viktor returned triumphant. He had two
tickets for a train to Berlin and an invitation to meet some of
the Organization's leaders.

"The old guard is still there, but Melnyk is moving to Munich.
Something about a group of our people looking to get something
started. We're going to just miss him. And I have this." Viktor
pressed a list into Ivan's hands. "It's the labor camps around the
area. But, Ivan, they're not releasing any records yet. All we can

do is put in a request, but it will be months before we get any information."

Ivan took the list from Viktor and rubbed his chin. None of the names meant anything to him. But meeting with the old leaders and commanders was indeed a good way to start.

They went to say goodbye to the rest of the group, but Nadia was nowhere to be found. It was only when he was leaving that he heard her calling his name. Her face was glistening from exertion and he caught her in his arms.

"What's happened, Nadia? Why are you crying?"

But she was laughing, waving a sheet of paper, a familiar sight. And for a moment, Ivan thought he wouldn't have to go anywhere because she'd found Antonia, her name had finally appeared on the lists, but Nadia wiped her face and the document had someone else's name entirely.

"It's my brother," she said. "My brother is in Augsburg, and he's gotten a hold of our great uncle and his family in the United States. I'm going to Augsburg to be with him. We're going to apply for a green card to America."

She hugged him again, and he held her. Losing Nadia now was too final. For as long as she was around, Ivan felt he still had a little bit of Pavlo with him. And he wanted to see the baby. With only two months to go, Ivan had been looking forward to welcoming Pavlo's son or daughter into the world. She looked up at him, gently pulling away.

"I'll write to you," she said. "I'll let you know where we are. Maybe you will manage to..." She knew. She knew what was written on his heart.

Ivan pressed her to him again and kissed the top of her head. "He loved you so much, Nadia. I know it was not a long time but..."

"It was enough." She put a hand to her heart. "It was a lifetime of love that Half Cossack gave me. And he loved you so, so much. He truly did."

They embraced and kissed each other's cheeks over and over. Viktor was looking at his watch. "Ivan, the train."

Tenderly, Ivan kissed Nadia's cheeks one last time. "Good luck and good health, Nadia."

He watched her go for a moment, no idea where any of them would be in the near future. Despite having Viktor at his side, Ivan's loneliness felt absolute.

The train between Leipzig and Berlin had been canceled and Viktor found a bus the next day that would take them onwards to Berlin. The toll of the Allied bombings was staggering. Amid the rubble lay the clues to beautiful architecture and monuments. Ivan could not imagine these cities ever recovering. The trip was agonizing as the bus stopped in nearly every town. Ivan slept on and off, his thoughts about Antonia muddled. What if she was still in love with Viktor? What if it had only been the basic instinct to survive, to seek comfort during the war, that had thrown her into his arms?

The bus backfired, and Ivan let out an exclamation, as did many of the other passengers. He looked behind him and saw a sea of faces as shell-shocked as his own.

Later, while Viktor buried his head in a magazine, Ivan was gazing out the window just as a road sign appeared.

He snatched Viktor by the shoulder. "Look. Where's that list?"

But Viktor was too late to look, the sign already behind them. He handed Ivan the list just as the bus exited the highway.

Ivan scanned the names. "Look. Here. Wilhelmshagen. That's where we are."

Viktor frowned and peered past Ivan out the window. "It's too pretty here. Look at those lakes. Did they really…?"

The bus pulled up to the side of a park. Ivan saw a large clock tower on one end of the square. "Let's get off here."

Viktor did not have to be asked twice, though he did look reluctant. "We won't find anything, Ivan. I mean, we can go to the camp, but they won't let us see anything."

Whatever it was that spurred him on, Ivan knew that Antonia had been here, but how was he to explain that to the pragmatic Austrian?

Before they disembarked, Viktor asked the driver whether there were buses or trains from here directly to Berlin.

"You're practically in Berlin," the driver said. "There's regular public transport."

"Well?" Viktor asked Ivan, once the bus had pulled away. "Now what?"

Ivan stood beneath a beech tree and scanned the area. "I don't know. We ask where the camp was."

Viktor scoffed behind him but did ask the first woman he saw. She shook her head and walked away. He tried a man, but the man refused to even acknowledge that Viktor was speaking to him. Ivan stepped in front of a woman with a pram, but she immediately became hysterical and he had no choice but to get out of her way.

Pointing to a café, Viktor clapped his arm. "Let's go get a coffee over there."

Later, when Ivan returned from the washrooms, Viktor pointed out the waitress. "She said there were a lot of Eastern Europeans at a facility nearby. There have been some inquiries from people looking for relatives, for family. But, like I warned you, the bureaucrats are a long way from releasing records."

Ivan drank his tea, noticing the shifting eyes of the locals. The air was suspicious, unwelcoming. He placed some change on the table and rose, Viktor hurrying after him, but the next bus was not due for quite some time, and storm clouds were building in the distance, thunder already rumbling from the west.

"We'll have to take shelter at the pavilion over there if it begins to rain," Viktor said.

But Ivan did not want to stand around. "Let's walk."

They passed a bank, a doctor's office, and several shops closed up for the afternoon. On the other side of the square, Viktor was drawn to a stack of old books in a shop window. Ivan glanced at the rest of the displayed items: trinkets, mismatched china, vases, and old watches.

"Those are real leather and they look in good condition," Viktor said, eyeing the books.

Ivan huffed a little when Viktor pushed open the door and reached for the volumes behind the window. He picked one up and flipped through the pages as Ivan peered over his shoulder. Poems.

"*Kann ich behilflich sein?*" A man in a rumpled suit appeared from the back room.

Ivan pointed to the book and the man narrowed his eyes, assessing Ivan's height, looks, perhaps even worth.

"Do you want to buy this?" Ivan asked Viktor.

"For Antonia," the professor said. But when he checked the price, he told the man he was not prepared to pay so much.

The man impatiently beckoned them to the counter, and Ivan followed, Viktor already haggling and offering his first bid. He placed the book on the glass display, but Ivan turned his attention to a small rack with chains and necklaces dangling from hooks. A microcosm of lost things to lost people. Cheap glass beads, a faux pearl necklace, a silver necklace with one missing stone.

It was the gold chain, the gold locket, that made Ivan tense.

"Viktor," he said softly. He reached for it.

Viktor hadn't heard or was paying him no mind, too engrossed in his haggling with the shopkeeper.

"Viktor," Ivan said again, louder this time. He dangled the locket over his palm. Opened the clasp.

Empty inside.

"Where is the painting," Ivan demanded.

Viktor and the shopkeeper both stopped talking.

Ivan held the chain and locket up. Viktor's eyes widened. "Ask him," Ivan said, "where the painting is."

"*Russen?*"

"*Nein,*" Viktor said, finally tearing his eyes away from the necklace and pressing the hostile shopkeeper for information about the painting.

The man finally gave up arguing with Viktor and jerked a thumb over his shoulder, indicating the back room. He shuffled off.

Viktor touched the locket, murmuring, "He says a woman came in here with two small boys and sold it to him. Said she fell on hard times."

Ivan straightened, and pushed the locket to Viktor. "This is yours."

Before Viktor could respond, the shopkeeper returned carrying an old wooden box. He withdrew the miniature painting of Antonia.

"He says," Viktor translated, "he figured the locket was worth more if there was nothing in it."

Ivan scowled and delicately lifted the painting from the shopkeeper's hands. "This is the most valuable thing about it."

"How long ago was this?" Viktor asked the man.

"*Februar? März?*" February. March.

"How much do you want for it?" Viktor asked, without looking at Ivan.

"*Hundert zwanzig Mark.*"

One hundred and twenty marks! Ivan's neck grew hot. He knew damned well that couldn't have been anywhere near what Antonia had received for it.

The haggling began again but Ivan snatched up the locket in his hand and pointed at the shopkeeper. "Do you know where the labor camp was? Do you know? Do you know where the camps were?"

Viktor, stunned again, turned slowly back to the shopkeeper and started translating but the shopkeeper, his face flushed pink, waved his hands, and claimed he knew nothing about a camp.

Ivan reached into his coat pocket, withdrew twenty Reichsmark and placed the bills on the counter. The shopkeeper looked stunned. "Take it."

Viktor pulled out his billfold, but Ivan grabbed his hand and glowered at the shopkeeper.

"Take it."

Viktor's words were soothing, but the shopkeeper checked with Ivan again.

"For information?" the shopkeeper said.

Viktor nodded. Dangled another twenty marks.

"The woman in the painting. That was her. She looked in dire straits. The boys, too."

"Where did she go?"

The German shrugged.

"How much did you give her for this?" Viktor asked.

"She wanted sixty marks."

"How much did you give her?" Ivan repeated.

The man deflated. "I don't know. Maybe twenty."

Viktor put away his wallet.

"Then it's a fair deal," Ivan said.

He took the locket, took Viktor's hand and placed it in his palm, clasping his fingers shut over it. "It belongs to you."

As they left, the shopkeeper shouted, "*Nehmen Sie nicht das Buch?*" Aren't you taking the book?

Both men were quiet on the trip to Berlin. It was the forger who offered them a place to sleep but it took the men another week to find anyone who remembered seeing Antonia, or had had contact with her. Nobody could remember what name she had been given. It was also proving difficult to track down the artists on the list, especially since both Viktor and Ivan couldn't risk entering the Soviet zones. Their parameters were limited, the phone lines were unreliable, and no one they looked for could be found.

The trail went cold. Ivan returned to their host's home at the end of another long day of dead ends. He and Viktor were both dejected.

"Look what came in," Viktor said as they sat down at the kitchen table. "And look what it's called."

Eyes alight, he slid a newspaper over to Ivan. *Our New Voice.* The men looked at one another for a moment and Viktor said, "Vasiliev said—"

But Ivan was ahead of him. He snatched up the paper, and nearly laughed aloud to see that every article had a byline. He leafed through it, scanning the pages. How many articles of hers had he read? How many times had her words, her melody, shot straight to his heart? Viktor was peering at the pages as well.

"There," Viktor suddenly said. "That's her. That has to be her."

Ivan read the first paragraph, then the next. It was a plea to the Americans, the British, the French—all the Allied forces except Russia—to recognize that the Soviet Union would become a serious enemy to the free world. That yes, the Allies had won the war with the help of the Soviet Union, but the fact that Ukrainians in the DP camps were committing suicide rather than be handed over to the Russians showed that Stalin was to be feared as much as Hitler, if not more.

If you do not want to witness again the horrors you have begun uncovering under Nazi occupation, you must not turn your eyes away from the Hammer and Sickle. On the contrary, be vigilant. Stalin will do everything possible to draw a curtain over this unwanted union, and behind that curtain will be his personal laboratory. He will charm you, fool you, lie to you, just as an abusive husband does

to the outside world. But it is what he exacts behind closed
doors that you must fear. And he will make certain his wife
never steps out of the house, assuring she will never be able
to reveal the truth.

That was his Antonia.

Their host suddenly walked in and Viktor and Ivan both looked up at the same time. The man stared at them.

"Is this it?" Viktor asked, taking the paper over to him.

"Zieleńska," the man murmured. He repeated the name and then looked up, a hint of a smile. "Yes. That's it. That's the name I gave her. University of Krakow."

On the bus to Munich, Viktor unpacked the locket and tried to give it to Ivan. "You should give it to her. When we find her."

"It was yours," Ivan insisted. "She gave that to you."

Viktor eyed him and Ivan turned his head away to look out the window. It was just a thing. It did not belong to him. She had given him so much more, and if she and the Mazurs had all survived, if she were alive—even if she felt differently about him now—the time he'd had with her, the love they'd shared, however brief, was all he would need to hold on to. And knowing he'd kept his promise to find her.

The taxi driver offered to take them up the road to the Neubeuern castle, but Ivan and Viktor looked at one another and told him he could drop them off in the middle of the town. Above the neatly kept Bavarian houses rose a large craggy hill with a beautiful castle perched on top. This place was untouched. It was immaculate, the buildings whole, every walkway swept clean, every window adorned with boxes of geraniums. Even the cobblestones looked freshly laid. They had to walk past the row of medieval structures to find the path up to the castle, which wound round the hill like the garland on a wedding cake. To their left, the steep forested slopes, to the right, rolling meadows and the Bavarian Alps beyond. Finally, as they neared the top, the castle came into view. First a lovely circular courtyard with a fountain. Several children were playing with a patched-up leather ball. Ivan peered, looking for Konstantin or Nestor, but did not see them. An arch in the center of the castle led them to a garden in the back with views of the town and the hills beyond, and a medieval tower at the top of a precipice.

People were lounging in the garden and on the terrace. A man was playing the guitar and several women were singing along, but he did not recognize the language.

"I can think of worse places to put tired refugees," Viktor said with wonder. "This place is an oasis compared to the one in Salzburg."

Ivan had to agree. On the surface, it was stunning.

A woman dressed in a nurse's uniform approached them. "May I help you, gentlemen?"

Viktor pulled off his hat. "Please, we're looking for Antonia Kozak."

"Zieleńska," Ivan interrupted. Viktor nodded.

"There are so many of us here," the woman said apologetically. "I can't tell you who is who. But you should check in at the registrar's office. We're not happy about strangers walking the grounds. We've had some run-ins with the locals…"

Ivan frowned.

"Anyway, it's the building on the far left, where the children go to school."

Viktor thanked her, but as they turned in the direction of the registrar's office they saw a woman walking slowly toward them, as if in a trance.

Ivan halted. "Lena?"

She opened her mouth in a perfect "O" and stared at him. She started running to him but when Viktor moved from behind him, her eyes darted to Viktor, back to Ivan and then to Viktor again, recognition blooming on her face for a second time.

When Lena stumbled, Ivan caught her just in time.

CHAPTER 29

Late Summer 1945

Castle Neubeuern, Germany

ich laufe
du läufst
er/sie/es lauft
wir laufen
ihr lauft
sie / Sie laufen

As Antonia finished writing the last line, twenty-seven children filed into the classroom, ranging from ten to about fourteen. She dusted the chalk off her hands and checked for stragglers in the courtyard. It was empty apart from an old leather ball. The sun was warming the cobblestones so that they shimmered. The poplar was just beginning to turn from green to gold, and seven geese flew in formation to the south.

Antonia clapped. "All right, take your seats. Take your seats now. I know it's a beautiful day." She repeated it in the other languages, examining the faces of the children, all old enough to bear the scars and traumas of war. She glanced at the chalkboard and determined she could not bear to conjugate German verbs today.

She turned her back on the phrases she'd so carefully tried to make legible in her awful hand. The students were waiting, anticipating what she would do next. She ought to be teaching them English if she wanted to spoon-feed any hope here. German was hard. Life had been harder. And she wished fervently that she could make it easier for them.

"Open your notebooks," she said, the idea still forming in her head. "I want you to draw a picture of a world you *want* to live in."

There were some frowns, but a couple of the students seemed eager to tackle the task. Yet others had not quite understood what she wanted from them. She continued, the idea still not complete, but she felt a stirring excitement as it began to develop in her mind. "Yes, and when you are finished, I will have you pass your drawing to the next student. That student…"

She pushed herself away from the desk and picked up a notebook from Janosz, one of the Polish boys, who had already begun drawing. He looked up at her as if expecting to be admonished, so she smiled at him and winked.

"For example, Janosz will hand his drawing to Martin, and Martin will write what he sees in Janosz's picture, using only German verbs and nouns—no sentences. All right, Martin?" Not letting go of the notebook, she made an exaggerated jump from Martin to Isabella behind him. "Then Isabella will use Martin's words and Janosz's drawing to write a poem. Yes," Antonia decided. "That is what we will do."

She returned to Janosz and ruffled his hair. By the time she'd finished delivering her instructions, the students were beginning to work with eagerness. Antonia leaned on her desk for a moment before moving from student to student, delighted to see that the drawings were taking shape.

At the front of the room again, she gazed at them, these young souls, these survivors. She should have had them conjugate the word "to live" instead of "to run." Inspired, she went to the chalkboard and wiped away the verb *laufen* and rewrote the conjugations. It was a poem in itself.

Ich lebe
du lebst
er/sie/es lebt
ihr lebt
sie / Sie leben
wir leben

Wir leben. We live. Followed by the Ukrainian, the Russian, the Polish, the Latvian, the Lithuanian, the Czech and the Slovak. She looked back upon her students to see if she had missed anyone. A soft knock at the door sent a pang of guilt through her. The director would probably wonder why the students were drawing rather than learning German grammar.

"Come in."

But it was Lena who ducked her head in. "Antonia."

It was how she said it that made Antonia straighten, that caused her chest to constrict. *No. No more bad news. No.* But when Lena's mouth broke into a sly smile and she tugged at her earlobe, Antonia's heart tripped and stumbled in her breast. Her sister stepped aside and revealed the corridor. Antonia fell against the desk so hard that all twenty-seven faces looked up in alarm.

In the hallway, two men. One tall, reddish-blond, his mustache gone. And the second man. Not Pavlo... smaller. Darker.

Antonia looked out at the sea of twenty-seven young faces to excuse herself, but the only words that formed were, *We live. We live. We live.*

She took Viktor's deformed hand in hers, looking over the garden wall and onto the Bavarian town and valley. The sun was beginning to set behind the medieval tower, the lawn and flowers of the garden mottled amid the smears of shade and sun.

"This is not how I wanted to show you my country," Viktor said. She looked at him. "The area, I mean. Salzburg's just a stone's throw away from here, compared to Lviv."

Antonia turned to him, her question written in her expression. He had to tell her now. She had to know.

Viktor's eyes closed briefly as he drew in a breath. "Kiril Vasiliev took me out into that courtyard." His voice was shaking and he pinched his nose before continuing. "There was nobody else there except the guards. He threw me up against the wall and threatened to have me shot right there. I was to give everyone up. The entire Organization, all the names. He knew. He knew that if the invasion was already on, it wouldn't take much for the rest of us to join forces with the Germans and take up arms against the Soviets."

She waited as Viktor collected himself. His hand shook, cold against her skin. Or maybe she was the one who was shaking.

"He… he made me watch. He made me watch as they brought out your students, my students, the couriers… I witnessed their murders. I was certain he would bring you at any moment. And I did not know what I would do then. I was sure that would have broken me."

Antonia's lips trembled and he released his shaking hand from hers to wipe his face. He placed his glasses on top of the stone wall, but he would not meet her gaze.

"He took me to a cell after that. They stripped me and, when I still did not talk, they began torturing me. That's when I figured that you must have already been killed."

"I don't know why. To this day, I don't know why Vasiliev did not order my execution," she said. She looked at the nubs that used to be whole fingers. "That's how he got his hands on the locket."

Viktor nodded. "The day before Lviv fell, Kiril Vasiliev made a last-ditch effort, tried to bring me to Kyiv with him, but we were captured. The Germans executed him and the driver and the two guards with us. Being Austrian was the only thing that saved me, but the Gestapo sent me to Sachsenhausen. In return for everything I knew about the Soviet secret police, they did not have me killed." Viktor's breath hitched. "I was prepared to sell my soul by then. Just to live. I was such… I was such a coward."

Antonia shook her head, took his hand back in hers and he squeezed it gently.

"I couldn't find any of you," he said, gently withdrawing to a nearby bench. "I tried to write from Sachsenhausen, tried to get word. But… Well. You know the rest."

The One and a Half Cossacks had gone into hiding. She'd gone to Dolyna with Oksana.

Antonia felt heavy, as if she had not slept in years. Her tongue was pressed to the roof of her mouth. Her jaw was locked. She looked out over the rooftops of Neubeuern below and the rolling fields beyond, the mountain peaks to the south. Viktor stood behind her. There were so many words in Antonia's mind. So many sentences and phrases strung together. None of the languages she knew were able to help her now. Not a single one. Other than, "No."

Then Viktor moved to her, reached into his trousers pocket and Antonia gasped as he dangled the locket for a moment before pressing it into her hand. She undid the latch. Inside, a portrait of a younger woman. Her portrait.

Viktor chuckled. "Ivan was the one who insisted on getting off at Wilhelmshagen. As if he knew he would find you. Or something of you. I wanted him to give this to you."

Antonia closed the locket on herself and closed the distance between them. "It's yours."

"No, Antonia. You should find that person again, reconcile yourself with her, and then give her back to Roman to paint."

"It won't be the same."

Viktor sighed and shook his head. "How could it be the same? None of us are the same. Nothing is. Ever."

Antonia looked over her shoulder, aching. Ivan was somewhere in the castle, giving them the time, the space, but she felt an overwhelming urgency. Time was precious. The minutes, the seconds, were speeding by. But she had to do this. She had to hear Viktor out, come to terms with the fact that he was still alive.

"Walk with me."

He joined her, his arm linked in hers, and they strolled out of the garden and followed the road that wound past the back hills and rolling fields. The green meadows were still bright, the sun stretching its last rays across the landscape. The road circled back toward town, but Antonia led Viktor onto a trail. They walked through a patch of woods before reaching a clearing. Viktor suddenly bent down, his arm slipping from hers. When he rose again, he had a few stems of white forget-me-nots in his hand.

"Antonia…"

Now the words were coming. Words that mattered. "I loved you. Viktor, I loved you so much."

Viktor put a finger to her lips, his eyes steady on hers. He pressed the bouquet into her hand, and fresh tears flowed once more. Again, she checked the urge to look over her shoulder and stared at the flowers.

"You are one of the bravest people I know," Viktor said, his good hand clamped over hers. "One of the most courageous, determined, and smartest people I know. You inspired me…" Viktor drew in a deep breath. "But I also know that you always say what you mean. You loved me, you say."

She started to apologize but again he put a finger to her lips.

"The use of the past tense, Antonia, it's enough." He encircled her waist, kissed her cheek—the left, the right, the left—then sighed into the nape of her neck.

Antonia's middle shuddered from the sobs she was trying to hold back. She caressed his head and hugged him tightly. "I'm so glad that you are alive. So, so very grateful that you, Viktor Gruber, are still in this world."

He kissed her mouth, lingering only a second before turning her back up the trail and escorting her to the castle.

Ivan had likely noticed that they had left, because when Antonia returned, Lena was near the fountain out front and rose from the steps when she and Viktor approached. Her sister checked their faces, then said, "He's waiting out back for you. In the garden."

Before Antonia could go, Viktor touched her arm. "When is your operation scheduled?"

"Thursday. In two days."

"We just managed to catch up with you," he said.

Antonia nodded.

"Can we accompany you to Munich? To the hospital?"

Antonia glanced at her sister. "Lena was going to come with me."

"All right."

"Will you be here when I return?" she asked.

Viktor shuffled a little, his eyes darting to the passage that led to the garden. "I'm going to return to Salzburg. There's a group still waiting for me to help them. I promised Ivan I would try to prevent their repatriation to Ukraine."

"You should give me their names," Antonia said. "We have a system in place and I can see to it that they are included. Will you join us in Munich? Help put out *Our New Voice*?"

"Antonia, see to your health first," Viktor said gently. "When you're good, when you are rested and healthy, we can talk. But of course, it would be an honor and a pleasure to do what I can. From Salzburg."

He swallowed and she understood. He wanted the distance. Needed it.

She left Viktor in the courtyard with Lena and followed the covered passageway to the back. It was just before dinner, when the residents took a few moments to enjoy the last warmth of the sun before heading to the dining room. Children were playing with a ball and stick. There were plenty of people around talking, a group of her students were laughing together near the tower. She spotted Ivan standing near the birdbath, surrounded by roses and hydrangeas. As soon as she stepped onto the gravel, he slowly turned and faced her.

Every muscle tensed, she wanted to run to him, throw herself into his arms, but she controlled the impulse and just took him in from where she stood. He appeared to be doing the same. There were things that were different, and out of place. For instance, that straw Fedora he was twisting in his hands. The missing mustache. The short hair. Pavlo not at his side. Pavlo should be here. But when Ivan smiled—that smile he'd always reserved only for her—Antonia realized that most things were right where they were supposed to be.

He strode over to her now, that tall Cossack, striding with an expression that rippled with emotion once more. And she hurried, the urgency spurring her on. The moment he raised his arms to her, she fell into them, her face buried into his chest. Her hands pressed into the small of his back, followed them up his spine as high as she could reach.

"You're real. You're real," she whispered. "You're really here."

In the school corridor, the initial reunion had been hazy, the moment muddied by tears and laughter, shock and grief, relief and jubilation. And so many unsaid things. But here, in the sanctuary of the garden, with the church bells ringing the end of vespers below, Antonia inhaled the Cossack, kept her face pressed into his chest and tightened her hold just as he tightened his.

"Don't let me go," she whispered. "Don't ever let me go again."

By morning, wrapped in blankets on the bench outside, their dinner plates still stacked by the birdbath, Antonia's sense of urgency had begun to dissipate, but only a little. Lena, dressed, her hair braided and wrapped on top of her head, stepped out with Roman into the garden. The sun was inching its way up the chapel's steeple.

"Did you even sleep?" Lena chirped, a little too brightly.

Ivan shook his head and Antonia slipped out from under his arm and the sanctuary of the blanket to embrace her sister.

"We want to get married. Today."

Lena looked surprised but her eyes lit up. "Today? How do you plan to do that? You need to get a license from the—"

"I could care less what the authorities want," Antonia interrupted. "We want to marry in the eyes of God. We have a priest here, and the chapel. Ivan and I will take care of the civil ceremony and paperwork after my surgery. We can do it in Munich."

Ivan joined them now and Roman shook the Cossack's hand. "I think it's a fine idea. It's about time we had something to celebrate! Then let's get to planning a wedding."

Antonia grabbed Ivan's hand and he kissed hers.

"I'll be back," he said. "It's bad luck to see the bride beforehand."

For a moment, she regretted it, but Lena was already chattering away about who could do what by that afternoon. "Paulina makes beautiful arrangements. We could cut some of these roses and hydrangeas. We'll get the ladies from Polissia to collect something for a nice gown."

"Don't be silly, Lena," Antonia said. "I'd get married naked if I had to."

Lena stared at her in shock but a second later, they both burst out laughing, certain the images in their heads were the same. But Antonia was serious. She did not want a special dress, and nothing more than a small bouquet of white hydrangea from the garden. There would be no party, no festivities, simply the ceremony, and Lena and Roman were to be the witnesses.

When the priest was finally talked into performing the ceremony late that afternoon, Antonia gave Nestor and Konstantin the solemn job of weaving two rings out of wire. But when she ran into Viktor at breakfast, they approached one another awkwardly.

"You don't have to if you don't want to, and I'd understand…" Antonia started. She shook herself and tried again. "Viktor, Ivan and I are getting married. Today. And it would be our great honor if you would attend."

Viktor looked down, his ears turning pink, and Antonia was certain she'd made a mistake, but when he looked back up, he was smiling. "Ivan's already asked. And I've said yes, but only if you wanted me there."

Antonia embraced him and kissed his cheek, repeating what she'd said the day before. "I'm so very, very glad that you are still with us, Viktor Gruber."

The priest performed the entire mass with them, and Antonia clutched Ivan's hand beneath the embroidered sash that bound them in their union. Lena and Roman held the crowns of ivy and flowers over their heads as they made the procession around the altar three times. The boys handed them their rings, and Konstantin had even bound a knot on the top of hers.

As they spoke their vows, Antonia gazed into Ivan's face, flooded with such love, such relief, and such determination, that she realized she was reaching upwards on the tips of her toes. The priest then declared Ivan could kiss the bride.

Ivan took her into a gentle embrace, and she stroked his cheek before they kissed. Lena sighed so deeply next to her that Antonia burst out chuckling, the tears unchecked now. She reached up again and kissed Ivan, then Roman and the boys, and even Viktor applauded.

The priest looked miffed. "Well, I suppose declaring you man and wife now is a little superfluous. Enjoy your celebrations."

"It's going to be a calm night," Antonia said. "Just us."

However, when they stepped out of the church, the rest of the camp was waiting. A group, dressed in a hodge-podge of traditional costumes, approached the couple with bread and salt, and shots of *horilka*. Antonia laughed with Ivan at the surprise.

Ivan bent to whisper to her. "I suppose it will be another sleepless night."

The camp at Neubeuern castle had all pitched in to throw a party. Tables had been assembled and set up outside, musicians played, even some of the townsfolk had come up to join them, but when a car drove into the courtyard, Antonia set down her glass and walked toward a retreating figure.

"Viktor!"

He turned around, looking guilty. "I have to get back, Antonia. There's much work to be done in Gnigl."

Ivan joined them. "When will we see you again?"

Viktor looked grave. "As soon as we can. From what Antonia has told me about the Organization, I think both of you should apply for American visas. I'll do all I can to help."

Antonia looked at the castle behind her. "Come to Munich, Viktor. It will be like—" She was going to say *like old times*. But it wouldn't be.

"We could really use you," Ivan said, placing his hands on her shoulders.

Viktor smiled. He leaned into Antonia and pecked her cheek. "I promise, I will. As soon as I can. Good luck with your surgery. You'll hear from me soon. And congratulations to both of you."

He got into the back of the taxi and waved one last time.

Ivan pulled Antonia into him and wrapped his arms around her. He felt so solid behind her. "Tomorrow, I'm going with you to Munich," he said.

"Of course. It's just a routine operation."

"I'm not letting you out of my sight again." He placed a careful hand onto her throat and removed the scarf from around her neck as he turned her to him. His eyes lingered on her face before examining the growth, now grotesquely large. He bent down and kissed it. "I love you."

She laughed. "Me or the growth?"

"I don't really have a wedding gift for you except—"

"Come now, Ivan. You know I don't either."

"This."

He reached into the breast pocket of his too-small suit coat and withdrew a metal tube. A cigar holder. Inside, a tightly rolled-up sheet, heavy and familiar. Sketchpad paper. Antonia frowned, and cautiously unrolled it.

She gasped, immediately recognizing the sketch. The Cossack and the Hutsulka. "How…?" In the upper right-hand corner, she read,

With her.

I am.

The person.

I am meant to be.

She looked up, unsuccessfully trying to blink away the tears. "How did you get your hands on this?"

"It was in the house when I returned to Ulič. And that there?" He pointed to the text. "That is the poem I began formulating when you were in my arms that night."

She nodded and reached for his hands, kissed them and held them against her face.

"You never asked me about that poem." Ivan chuckled. "But I have never forgotten it."

"I did not ask," Antonia said and raised herself to kiss his cheeks tenderly. "Because you never hid your sentiments from me."

"Not another moment," Ivan said. "We don't waste another moment. Ever."

Antonia fought to keep her emotions down. That sense of urgency was still there, a tension so taut, her whole body was vibrating. "I promise, Ivan, when I come out of that surgery, we will never spend another moment apart."

She held the sketch to her heart.

"Together with the portrait in the locket, Roman will now have two new paintings to make from the homeland," Ivan said.

The homeland. Antonia looked up at her husband. *He* was her country. *He* was her home. He always had been.

EPILOGUE

March 1954

Bambrick, New Jersey, United States

Despite the enormous size, St. Stephen's Ukrainian Catholic Church had standing room only and Ivan lingered in the back as Father Gregory and the deacon finished giving Communion. Nestor and Konstantin had taken positions against Ivan's legs, Konstantin on the left, Nestor on the right, both gently rocking and bouncing off his upper thighs until he put a hand on each of their shoulders and they stilled. Solemn and shy, they glanced up at him. Both were so much taller than when he'd last seen them.

Everything, Ivan mused, was bigger in America. Not just the buildings. Or the beds and plates of food. But the churches.

The congregation sat back down as the priest took to the pulpit again.

"I want to remind you that you are invited to the Ukrainian Community Center afterwards for a very special event. Roman Mazur and his wife Lena are visiting from St. Paul, Minnesota and his collection of paintings from the old country are now hanging in our gallery for the next few weeks."

Father Gregory then raised an arm and indicated where Ivan and the Mazurs were standing. In that quaint Ukrainian-American accent, the priest continued, "He and his family are here for the opening. Let's make sure they receive a warm welcome. As usual, we'll be serving our Sunday lunch followed by a program."

Before he gave the final benediction, the choir in the loft above Ivan's head sang the last hymn. Ivan made the sign of the cross and the congregation began filing out of their pews, some familiar faces already encircling Roman, shaking hands, clapping him on the arm.

Ivan turned to Lena with a cautious smile. "It's astounding," he said, "the community, the—"

"*Dyad'ko!*" Uncle! A young boy was tearing up the aisle between the pews. An older man whirled around and caught him by the collar, then placed a hand on his shoulder.

Ivan stared at the boy. The curly brown hair, the bright blue eyes, the dimples and mischievous grin. A woman was hurrying behind them, reaching out to the child.

"Pavlo, I told you to wait for me."

Ivan was dreaming, he was certain of it. But no. The dark hair, those large brown eyes, the size of a sprite. He stepped into the aisle.

"Nadia?"

Her mouth dropped, and she stammered before she could get his name out. She ducked her head and when she uncovered her face, her dark eyes were shining. The boy, now sobered, hovered near the man.

"Pavlo." She moved the boy to stand before her. "This is a very, very special person. This was your father's best friend." She looked up at Ivan, the first tears rolling down her face. "He was your father's brother, really."

Little Pavlo looked up at his mother, frowning. "Another *Dyad'ko?*"

She smiled and straightened. Ivan opened his arms to her and took her into his embrace, the boy still appearing wary. People who passed by were staring, some with inquiring grins.

"I didn't realize you were in New Jersey," Ivan said when they pulled apart. "Actually, I had no idea where you were. I tried to reach you in Augsburg, but they told me you'd already gone. I didn't know you had—" He indicated the boy, tried to give him a reassuring smile.

Nadia stroked Little Pavlo's hair into place. "He came just as planned. But my brother and I found relatives in Ulm soon after I arrived in Augsburg. They had already begun securing a sponsorship through our uncle." She tugged the older man over and made introductions, and Ivan drifted with the three of them to the exit with the rest of the parishioners.

"What about you?" she asked. "When did you arrive?"

"I got to New York late last week. Still a little disoriented," Ivan said. America had hit him like a sledgehammer between the eyes. He'd never seen anything like it. The skyscrapers, the cars, the traffic, the people, the full shops and restaurants. He was reeling, and as much as said so.

"Here," Nadia laughed and crooked her arm, "hang on."

"Come, I want to introduce you to the Mazurs. They met me in New York. They timed the exhibit here with my arrival."

From the top of the church stairs leading to the street, he scanned the heads of the people, looking for his group. He could pick out the more recent newcomers from the settled generations of Ukrainians by the latter's quaint Americanized accents. Ivan spotted Roman and Lena following the church leaders to the community center next door.

"It looks as if they're about to go inside," he said, pointing them out.

"Do you want to go to them?" she asked. She sounded a little disappointed. The boy was following his uncle, but threw a look over his shoulder at Ivan.

It appeared that the congregation would linger in the sunshine for a while. Ivan looked over the grounds. It was a warm spring day, and a blackbird was singing somewhere nearby, showing off its range of melodies.

"What are all these buildings here?" he asked.

Nadia looked proud, her cheeks turning a soft shade of rose. "We have an entire system set up for the children. They go to American school all week, but on Saturdays we have a Ukrainian school from kindergarten through matriculation. Our community center has a gallery—but you know that already—and then there's a hall where we hold banquets, Christmas programs, folk dancing, the usual."

"The usual," Ivan declared. "I'd say there's nothing usual about it at all."

"But it is. Here, in New York, in Chicago, Denver…"

"The Mazurs said the local diaspora is also growing where they are."

"Real Ukrainian communities, rebuilding right here in the United States," Nadia said. She paused and he sensed the questions building up in her, but Pavlo was back.

"*Dyad'ko* wants to know if he should save a table for everyone?"

Nadia raised herself on her toes, and waved to her uncle. "Will you join us?" she asked Ivan. "I'll tell him to save us a seat for… How many people?"

"Just me," Ivan said.

Nadia's eyebrows knitted together but she raised three fingers into the air.

"Why don't you show me the grounds," Ivan said to both of them.

Pavlo ran ahead toward the one-storied school.

As they followed, Nadia said very quietly, "You never found Antonia?"

"I did," Ivan said. "I not only found her. We married."

"But that's wonderful," Nadia declared. "Then where is she? I would love to meet her!"

Ivan gazed up at the sky, tightened his hold on Nadia, a reassuring squeeze more for himself than for her. He did not want her to apologize.

"Antonia passed away. In forty-six."

Nadia pulled up short. "Ivan," she breathed. "I'm so sorry."

"She... she had complications shortly after thyroid surgery. A terrible infection and there was no penicillin. We thought we were going to lose her then. But she pulled through. She pulled through long enough to see the Organization back on its feet in Munich, and when they declared her president of the international congress, she..." He rubbed a hand over his head and cleared his throat. No apologies. No sadness. He'd promised Antonia that. "She fell ill right afterwards. The doctors say complications to her health, compounded by everything her body had gone through."

"But," Nadia breathed, "that's awful, Ivan."

"Her death was. But finding her, being married to her, that was the best thing that ever happened to me." He gazed at her and her face softened with sympathy.

"We both loved intensely and lost them early," she said.

Little Pavlo was holding the school door open for them and he stepped inside. While Nadia gave a tour of the classrooms and the rooms that the scouting organization used, Ivan told her how Viktor was compiling Antonia's work, had founded another newspaper, and established a worldwide network dedicated to freeing Soviet Ukraine from the outside.

"There are sometimes reports on the news," Nadia said. "And quite a few of our people here are involved, too."

Educating and informing. That had been Antonia's motto.

They walked back toward the community center, and Little Pavlo got absorbed into a group of children his age.

Spotting Lena and the boys with the people outside, Ivan said, "Anyway, the Mazurs got green cards via sponsors from a church in St. Paul. Once Lena and Roman got settled, they helped find someone to sponsor me."

Nadia smiled broadly and tugged him to her. "I'm glad that you are here. What about the others?"

"Terlytsia works as an editor for Radio Free America in Munich. Lys and Kulka, I just found out, are also in Minnesota."

Her eyebrows rose and she laughed. "Is Kulka making cognac?"

He chuckled. "Something like that. What about you? How are you doing here"—he waved a hand over the congregation of Ukrainians—"in the promised land?"

Nadia sighed, her smile wavering a little. "Good. We're good. I'm a caregiver, and working on a nursing degree. It's not always easy. It's taking me longer than I had hoped, but I'll get there."

Ivan beamed. "That's very good. And you are here with your…?"

She looked amused. "My brother. Our cousin and his family took us in at first. But my brother is a carpenter and he's been renovating houses in and around New Jersey. He got lucky. The whole family pitched in and invested in a really old house, but we remodeled it together and sold it for a profit."

Ivan saw Lena turn then, searching. He waved and she gestured that she was going inside.

"And?" Nadia asked. "Are you here in Bambrick to stay?"

He scratched his neck. "I'm to work on an apple orchard south of the Twin Cities." He tried to pronounce it and Nadia chuckled.

"Sounds like it might be Lake Pepin."

"But the Mazurs say it's hours away from them."

"You look disappointed," Nadia said.

Ivan glanced around and shrugged. He would miss this, knowing that it existed now.

They filed into the gallery behind the crowd and Nadia called Pavlo in. There was a table with Lena's two new books. Ivan was pleased to see that the stack was already dwindling. Music played softly through the speakers. Someone had recorded Lena on the violin.

As they entered the first display in the gallery, Ivan read the placards next to Roman's paintings. *Hutsuls in the Field. Carpathian Shepherd. Hungarian Officer. American Officer. Partisans in Slovakian Woods. Potato Farmer in Bavaria. Watzmann. Schloss Neubeuern.* There were still-lifes, too: bowls filled with apricots, flowers in a vase with a Ukrainian design, a posy of forget-me-nots and a cup of tea. Ivan recognized the Mazurs' china from Lviv. Roman's exhibit was a memorial not only to his own journey but an echo of all their journeys from east to west. From flight to freedom. From darkness to light.

He followed Nadia as she examined each one, Pavlo's hand in hers. She pointed out the different paintings, of the bathers in the Chiemsee, a church Ivan read was called St. Bartholomew on the Königssee. Another painting captured two women, one with cinnamon brown hair, on the shores of that same lake. The one that looked like Antonia was in the water, laying out a wreath. The other one was Lena, kneeling in the grass, a crown of flowers on her head, her hands folded in prayer.

"That's Kupala," Nadia said.

"Antonia told me," Ivan said, "they made the wreath for Pavlo, when they found out that he had been killed."

Nadia smiled sadly, and squeezed his hand before looking at the painting again. "That's beautiful."

They came around the next wall and Ivan put a hand to his heart. He sensed Nadia's inquiring look but could not tear his gaze away.

"That's her," Nadia said. "That's Antonia, isn't it?"

It was the portrait from the locket, a little different in composition to what he could remember, yes, but it was her. Another larger piece hung next to it. It was an oil painting of *The Cossack and the*

Hutsulka, based on the sketch, but there was a lot more activity in this painting. A lot more people. It was slightly chaotic. Konstantin was still there, flying by, his hat halfway in the air. But Antonia had a horse, and was about to mount it. Ivan was on the other side of a road, on his mare. The air was still charged between them—Ivan's intent gaze, Antonia's shy surrender and determination evident in the way she gripped the reins. Despite the flurry of activity, despite the road, there was movement to one another.

When he stepped back, he saw that there were two more framed paintings hanging next to it. He once again pressed his hand to his heart. Two pen and ink drawings. Two more Hutsulkas and Cossacks. One with Antonia standing next to his horse with hers behind her, the reins now loose, as if she had finally reached him. In the second one, they were riding side by side, and she was leaning in for a kiss. Both wore wedding bands, simple ones, like twisted wire.

His eyes burned and he shut them tight. He had promised not to mourn her, but to celebrate her. He had kept his promise to find her and now he would keep this one, too. With effort, he tore himself away from the images. Nadia had discreetly stepped away.

Little Pavlo came running around the corner—those curls, those blue eyes, the dimples, so like his father's—and Ivan watched Nadia bend down so that he could whisper in her ear. Laughing softly, Nadia held back her curtain of dark hair and whispered something back. She kissed Pavlo's head and he took his mother's hand.

"What is it?" Nadia asked Ivan. She was still grinning as she straightened. "Are you all right?"

Ivan looked around him, at the congregating Ukrainians in this hall. There were so many of them. Moving freely about.

Ivan studied the boy and the woman. He'd made another promise, hadn't he? The day of Pavlo's wedding. *If anything should happen to me...*

Nadia led Little Pavlo to him. "He wants to know whether you're a real Cossack, like his father."

Ivan laughed softly. "Your father and I? We were both Cossacks."

"Mama says," Pavlo said, "that I'm half of one."

"You're a whole one, Pavlo. Don't ever doubt that. A whole one."

Pavlo looked to his mother as if to confirm.

Ivan gazed down at Nadia. "There's something I haven't told you, yet."

She waited.

He hesitated, and lowered his voice. "I've been invited to interview with some… It's in Washington, D.C. It's an agency."

She held his gaze. She seemed to understand that he could not be more specific.

"Washington, D.C. isn't so far from here," she said.

"No?"

"Not at all."

"But Minnesota."

"That is."

"The Mazurs went through all the trouble to make arrangements—"

"To get you here. Not to force you to be a farmhand. Ivan, you and Pavlo, you were warriors. You fought for our freedom. And now you are. You are free." She put a hand on his arm. "Here, in America, you are a free man. You can decide to explore your options in Washington, D.C., or Minnesota, or you could stay. Here." She looked intently at him. "But it takes some getting used to."

"What does?"

"Freedom. And once you do? You don't ever want to let go of it. You will build your entire future on making sure you hang on to it. And if I know you, you will build your future on making sure others will be able to enjoy it."

When Little Pavlo craned his neck again, looking from one to the other, Ivan crouched down. He glanced again at the crowd of people behind the boy. A whole community. A whole community of Ukrainians right here. And Nadia said there were more of them. Everywhere. And many more trapped in the Soviet Union, depending on people like him to help end the brutality, the oppression.

"Your father was called the Half Cossack." He turned to the boy. "But he was one of the most whole and best people I have ever known, Pavlo. He died fighting so that you, your mother, and even I, would have a place to call home. A place where we can be the best people we can be. And free. Would you like me to tell you about your father during lunch?"

Little Pavlo nodded.

Ivan glanced up at Nadia. Her eyes were bright. They danced like Pavlo's used to.

"Good," he said. "Because a very wise woman once told me, that in order to forge your future, you have to understand where you came from."

A LETTER FROM CHRYSTYNA

Dear reader,

I want to say a huge thank you for choosing to read *The Woman at the Gates*. If you did enjoy it, and want to keep up to date with all my latest releases, just sign up at the following link. Your email address will never be shared and you can unsubscribe at any time.

www.bookouture.com/chrystyna-lucyk-berger

If you loved *The Woman at the Gates* I would be very grateful if you could write a review. I'd love to hear what you think, and it makes such a difference helping new readers to discover one of my books for the first time. Your feedback also helps me to develop as an author.

Please feel free to reach out and engage with me. You'll be immediately involved in my projects and be kept up to date on new releases, beta reading opportunities, advanced review copies, plus my historical and cultural background blog relating to my research, my travels, my experiences. You can get in touch on my Facebook page, through Twitter, Goodreads or my website.

Thank you so much and I look forward to hearing from you,
Chrystyna Lucyk-Berger

inktreks

@ckalyna

@ckalyna

ckalyna

BookBub chrystyna-lucyk-berger

www.inktreks.com

AUTHOR'S NOTE

The Woman at the Gates has been a cathartic project for me. It is based on true stories, inspired by real events and real people, and it is also wholly mashed up into this very fictional account.

But wait! How much of this is based on real events?

I'll get to that. First the background: What seems like a hundred years and several lifetimes ago, I interviewed my extended family for almost a year. I recorded everything on cassette tapes; that should tell you how long ago it was. I was fresh out of college, had landed my first job as an editor of a small-town newspaper, and I wanted to write a book because I promised my dying grandmother that I would "tell her story," thinking I was going to start translating her work. And this is where I'm going to digress for a second. My maternal grandmother, Olena Remenets'ka-Lucyk was an author, a playwright, poet, musician, and a composer. Yes, she is represented here as Lena Mazur. And she wrote historical fiction, but it took me writing this book to realize it. She wrote about Cossacks, and Hetmans and the history of Ukraine in the form of plays, novels and short stories. But it took me writing these passages in the first chapters to make that connection; that I had not only followed her footsteps as an author, but in genre as well!

And that is why I have written this novel. Because most of us spend our lives with our family and relatives, some living with us under the same roof (as my maternal grandmother had), and we still do not know them. It takes inquiring after and recording their stories, and then doing the historical research to connect the dots before we look up and exclaim, "Whoa! Wait? What? You survived that?"

But let's get back on track here.

You want to know what is true in this story, right? And where did I mess with historical facts? I'm going to do a broad sweep here on these pages and then encourage you to visit my blog for the details. First, how this novel came to fruition.

Shortly after I won an award for a collection of my short stories based on those family interviews, I pitched another book to Bookouture (*The Girl from the Mountains*).

They invited me to pitch a second one as well. *The Woman at the Gates* began as a simple two-sentence pitch. The conversation with my editor went something like this:

Editor: Have you ever thought about writing another book on Ukraine in WW2?

Me: (*Please no, please, please, please no.*) My father once said that my great-aunt was a spy? She helped people escape out of Soviet Ukraine? And she was in love with an Austrian who was killed? She never married and died tragically right after the war because there was no penicillin?

Editor: Yup. That's the one we want.

Me: (*dang nab it!*)

You have to understand that this family story—that project where I recorded my family's history—has been following me across oceans for over twenty-five years. Those few sentences were not a lot to go on. And I also knew I had an awfully mucky story to wade through.

I made the decision to mash my entire family up—maternal and paternal—and throw it all into one pot. *Red Hot Borscht.* That was my working title.

So, let's begin with the cast of characters:

Antonia Kozak is inspired by my father's stories about Antonina Remenets'ka. She was a spy, and while working in Ivano-Frankivsk, she befriended the Nazi administration, stole lists of people who were to be deported to the camps and got those people to safety. Earlier in her life, she was in love with an Austrian (a fictionalized Viktor Gruber here), who did die on the border while trying to get Ukrainian intelligentsia out of Soviet Ukraine. She was absolutely heartbroken and swore she would never marry. She died in Munich, in 1946, after a routine surgery to remove her goiter left her with an infection. Her character here, however, is strongly meshed with my maternal grandfather's. He was an academic, spoke many languages and wrote political articles, arguing the case for freeing the Soviet Ukraine.

My great uncle on my mother's side, who is ninety-four as I write this, spent several sessions Skyping with me to confirm some of my older research. "Chrystyna," he said, "I'm telling you, if you want to write historical books about the war, you need to look at what happened right afterwards, too. Oh! I can tell you stories!" Maybe next time, Uncle Pete. (My great uncle, by the way, is the inspiration for my recurring character, Kulka. No, this is not the first time he has appeared in my books, and yes, he was a sharpshooter at the age of thirteen, shot chickens for the cooks, was wounded in Austria near the end of the war, and reunited with his family at the DP camp in Gnigl, outside of Salzburg. Oh, and he did make that "cognac" in General Patton's kitchen out of formaldehyde. Served it up at my grandmother's wedding after testing it out on American soldiers. My husband and I had a strange concoction at his house not too long ago. He's a real hoot, I tell you.)

My grandfather, Stepan Lucyk (the inspiration for Roman Mazur) was a *Chiemsee Künstler*. He traveled with some of his remaining canvases from Ukraine, earned his passage to Bavaria by painting officers and partisans, and did get commissioned by the officers at the American base. He was very well connected to other artists across Europe and had studied painting in Paris. That network helped him and his family to escape Wilhelmshagen.

Our family cherishes his remaining works of art. Recently, I found some of his older paintings from the 1920s at an online auction house in Russia, with one still life of a vase of flowers, and a teacup. The owners were located in the Crimea. I'd like to think that was my grandmother's and grandfather's china set he painted.

The *Hutsulka and Cossack* is based on one of his paintings that hangs in my cousin's house. When I was getting married, I asked my father, Yurij Rafael Lucyk (my inspiration for Konstantin), who was also an artist, to redraw the figures for my wedding invitations in ink. The black-and-white drawings I wrote about in the epilogue are based on my father's. My uncle, Roman Lucyk, inspired Nestor, and their stories as boys at the Habsburg lodge in the Carpathians are depicted here, including the murder of my father's kindergarten teacher by the UPA (Ukrainian Partisan Army). If I'm not mistaken, her name really was Oksana. She had been brutally murdered and dragged behind a horse before they dumped her into the well.

And that brings me to the whole political history. You can read all about that in my blog. I cover it in detail in *Souvenirs from Kiev* as well.

Ivan's story really drives a whole mixed bag of events that took place in the province of Vohlyn', outside the Ukrainian city of Lutsk. The Ukrainian Self-Defense Legion here is based on the memoirs of my great uncle (mother's side) and the real (anglicized) name was the Ukrainian Legion of Self-Defense (anyone who knows Monty Python's *The Life of Brian* is probably grinning here). My great uncle was at the negotiating table with Commander Piz and Major Asmuth. Again, in Lutsk, not in Lviv, and not in Truskavets, but that would have complicated things for this novel.

Those memoirs inspired the Ukrainian commanders here, some real, and my now-deceased uncle is depicted here as Lys. However, he was not always scowling and he wasn't all that small, either. Ivan's character is also very much inspired by Sak. I'm going to leave it at that, because anyone living in Chicago who haunts the Ukie neighborhood knows darned well who that is. (Sak, you were always a romantic hero to me, no matter how gruff and tough you tried to come off.) And the duo, the One and a Half Cossacks, and their dynamics and antics are wholly inspired by two of my favorite men in the universe. They know who they are.

My grandmother, who is going to be ninety-eight when this book releases, is my other go-to source. She is not represented by any single one of my characters here, but her story is within these pages nonetheless. Anyone who has spent any time talking to her will recognize the peppered-in anecdotes.

So, what about the events? Here's my short answer. Likely everything that seems implausible—like the escape from Wilhelmshagen—is based on true stories. But these details will be revealed in the blog, together with "bonus material."

Ivan's story and the activities of the Ukrainian Self-Defense Legion and Organization of Ukrainian Nationalists has been pared down in this novel for the sole purpose of making this episode of Ukraine's political history digestible and understandable. We even shaved three chapters from Ivan's story, depicting how the Germans suckered the Ukrainians into fighting for them in those last battles before capitulation.

But trying to pull apart the threads of fact and fiction will be like trying to unravel all the ingredients from my pot of borscht. Impossible. But I'm going to try. I'm going try to explain to the historians of Ukrainian Studies (yes, it is a discipline; at Harvard, for example) about the decisions I took in naming, renaming, and perhaps even desecrating certain aspects of the history here. Please trust me: I have reasons for my decisions. I wasn't being lazy.

And for those who have picked this up for the story, I will be presenting all the juicy tidbits to satisfy your curiosity about what was true, and what was totally made up, and why.

I look forward to meeting you as you continue to journey through Antonia's and Ivan's worlds. Just pop on over to www. intreks.com/guide-ukraine.

GLOSSARY

Please note: Any foreign language phrases used, especially in dialogue, were directly translated within the text or were followed by an explanation.

Christbaum	Christmas tree
gost'	a guy, usually an affectionate reference
hetman	Ukrainian or Polish military commander
horilka	fermented spirit
Knödel	dumplings made of breadcrumbs
kokhanyi	beloved (term of endearment)
Kupala	Ivana Kupala is a pagan tradition at around midsummer where young women twist wreaths and float them in water. The men then retrieve the wreath and pair up with the owner of it. They must spring over a bonfire together holding hands, if the relationship is to last.
kvass	a Slavic and Baltic fermented drink traditionally made of rye bread
madiary	Hungarians
mamalyga	a style of cornmeal porridge
nalysnyky	crepes filled with savory or sweet filling
nashi	literally "ours" but the expression means "our people"
Nimaky	Germans

Nova radist' stala	"A New Star Has Risen"—a Ukrainian Christmas carol
Ostarbeiter	People who migrated to Germany from Eastern Europe to seek work
pan/pani	Mr./Mrs.
pyrohy	Ukrainian dumplings, like the Italian mezzelune
pysanky	hand-painted Easter eggs using the batik method
rushnyk	an embroidered shroud or, literally meaning "towel," which were draped over the frames of icons or photos of deceased family members
shanovna	a title of honor, literally "respected"
sharovary	the billowy trousers Ukrainian men wear, especially folk dancers
ublyadky	a slur, pl.
Untermenschen	the derogatory Nazi term for "subhuman"
vinok (sing.) vinky (pl.)	wreath, for the head usually
vybliadky	a slur, pl.

ACKNOWLEDGMENTS

I would not have been able to do any of this without the unconditional support of my husband, Manfred Berger, and my mother, Lesya Pundyk-Lucyk. Petro Karkoc and Svitlana Karkoc gave me precious time to catch up and confirm information. Olga Nohra, Sam Nohra, Stefan Lucyk, and author Anne Clare for your early reads and feedback. To Ursula Hechenberger-Schwärzler for your consistent support, and all my friends and family that I have had to put on hold "to get things done," your encouragement and confidence is what keeps me going.

Thank you to Julia Lucyk, for your assistance with the research. You would seriously have a future in this. To Cara Chimirri, thank you for opening the door and for making me confront my history again. I have learned so much and, hopefully, have set things right since my first attempt. And the team at Bookouture for your amazing abilities and support!

Looking to the heavens, thank you, Tato and Babcia, for your divine intervention in this incredibly emotional and cathartic process. *Вічная пам'ять!*

Made in United States
North Haven, CT
14 April 2024

51290040R00232